SPARE
BRIDES

By Adele Parks

Adele
PARKS

SPARE
BRIDES

headline
review

First published in Great Britain in 2014
by HEADLINE REVIEW
An imprint of HEADLINE PUBLISHING GROUP

3

Cataloguing in Publication Data is available from the British Library

ISBN 978 1 4722 0538 4 (Hardback)
ISBN 978 1 4722 0539 1 (Trade paperback)

Typeset in Bembo 12.25/14.5 pt by
Palimpsest Book Production Limited, Falkirk, Stirlingshire

Printed and bound in Great Britain by Clays Ltd, St Ives plc

Headline's policy is to use papers that are natural, renewable and recyclable
products and made from wood grown in sustainable forests. The logging and
manufacturing processes are expected to conform to the environmental
regulations of the country of origin.

HEADLINE PUBLISHING GROUP
An Hachette UK Company
338 Euston Road
London NW1 3BH

www.headline.co.uk
www.hachette.co.uk

To Alex Mahon

WINTER

1

LADY CHATFIELD – WIFE of Lord Chatfield, daughter-in-law to the Earl of Clarendale, daughter of Sir Harold Hemingford, Lydia to her friends – allowed her silk robe to drop to her feet. She enjoyed the feel of the fabric shimmying down her body, like breath. Now naked, she stood in her dressing room and wondered, as she often did at six thirty in the evening, what her maid, Dickenson, had picked out for her to wear this evening. She tried to guess, through a process of elimination, as her dress was probably in the maid's care now. A stain might be being dabbed into oblivion, lace might be being steamed so it would stand proud like a fence, or a hem might be being subjected to a last-minute stitch or two so that the correct amount of calf was on show. Dickenson was thorough; her most-often-used phrase was 'just to be sure'. She treated Lydia's garments like newborns: pampered, worshipped.

Lydia inhaled the dust and silence of the old house – resting after the bustle of tea, reprieved as there was to be no formal dinner here this evening – and scanned the padded silk hangers. She spotted her tangerine organdie and silk frock, the one with crystal beading shaped like teardrops, plus the teal moire taffeta silk that she liked to wear with a jaunty sash belt; in addition, she carefully counted numerous gowns in chiffon: saffron, scarlet, cobalt and emerald, all decorated with tulle or organza and delicate pearl beading. None of these colourful dresses would do. She examined the white and cream gowns. What was missing?

It was all a little frustrating really. If she'd had the energy, she might have been quite cross about the entire debacle, but she rarely allowed herself to become properly vexed nowadays; she considered doing so such poor taste. Taking everything into account, she had little to moan about. Yet she had expected a new gown from Callot Soeurs fashion house. She'd ordered an oyster silk treasure with lashings of diamanté beads spilling from the neckline down her breasts and shoulder blades. With painful clarity she'd been able to visualise the effect she would have made on entrance to the Duchess of Pembrokeshire's New Year's Eve ball. The dress had a darling plush fox-fur trim around the hem and cuffs and she'd planned to wear it with her purple velvet shoes, the ones with the elegant heel and glass beading. Purple with oyster and fur was the sort of combination that was bound to make the papers. The dress ought to have arrived before Christmas. It hadn't. It was difficult to complain; no one actually expected really decent service any more, not since the war. And the French – well, the French especially were horribly unreliable, a law unto themselves. That was why the English – beaten down by rules and queues – found them so fascinating and irresistible.

Lydia sighed. Her breath and mood clouded the cold air. Where was the housemaid? She ought to have poked the fire in the bedroom; a girl could freeze to death in her dressing room if the servants were slow. Lydia bit down on her irritation. It was misdirected and unfair. Still, it was hard that she didn't have anything new for tonight; she was sure that every other woman in the British Empire would have a clear idea what to wear as she watched 1920 melt away, as she sighed a relieved welcome at 1921. One year further on. One step further away. Making the whole ghastly business more past, less present.

She wished Dickenson would get a move on too. The goose bumps that were erupting all over her body looked ugly. She robustly rubbed her hands up and down her arms. Ought she to pop on her own drawers and brassiere? She didn't mind doing so; dressing herself was actually what she preferred, but Dickenson invariably made such a fuss if Lydia did take the initiative, grumbling, 'Is Lady

Chatfield trying to do me out of a job?' Silly really, since they both knew that Dickenson's duties extended far beyond those tradition- ally associated with a lady's maid, and that, in truth, she was stretched, often frazzled. As Lydia wondered whether she ought to reach for her silk dressing robe again, Dickenson burst into the room.

'You'll catch your death, standing around that way,' she cried. Then, almost as an afterthought, 'Sorry I'm late, my lady.'

'It's fine.' Lydia's eyes did not rest on Dickenson even for an instant. She didn't need them to. She knew what her maid looked like. She was petite, meticulous and she put Lydia in mind of a bird, because when she moved, she darted. She was always dressed in a black frock with a plain white collar, as was proper and required. From October to March she wore a dreary knitted black shawl that would have been better suited to a woman thirty years older. She pulled it close around her shoulders and held it there with an amber brooch that, if Lydia recalled correctly, had been willed to her by her aunt. Her eyes were so dark it was impossible to see her pupils; there was rumour of her having Continental blood, but no one ever probed. Her nose was long and narrow and her mouth was slightly sombre, even woeful. She didn't often laugh. She appeared old. She was not.

Lydia's gaze stayed trained on her own reflection, which anyone would have to admit was altogether more pleasing, more modern. It took a moment to adjust to; she was still getting used to her short bobbed hair. Like every fashionable woman she wanted to wear her hair cropped at the ear, as she favoured close-fitting cloche hats. Over fifteen inches had been lopped just before Christmas. She felt light and exhilarated, although Lawrence hadn't been overjoyed; on more than one occasion he'd wrapped a scarf around her neck whilst they sat by the fire or at the dinner table, making jokes about her feeling a draught. She smiled, indulging him, although she didn't find the joke especially funny; hadn't done so even the first time he made it. She suited the modern style. Her glossy black blunt-cut fringe framed her startling blue eyes and added a hint of danger and drama to her pale skin. When she'd worn her hair long she'd looked like a medieval queen – passive, protected; now, there was an edge to her, something thoroughly modern, and equally mesmerising. Her high cheekbones, creamy, pearlesque skin and full, almost fat lips were all the more notable now her hair was chopped. If only her nose was a little thinner. Sleeping for four years with a peg nipping the end had failed to do the job her governess had promised it would.

'I got held up, my lady. I was with the new cook.'

'How is she settling?'

'She's competent.' Dickenson drew her lips a fraction closer together. Lydia understood at once, but chose not to comment. She found running a house wearisome and would always prefer not to waste her time and breath on the domestic matters that she knew were ultimately her domain. Her maid, however, could not imagine a subject more fascinating or worthy and, unaware of her mistress's deep-seated indifference, pursued the subject with fervour. 'She's not at all happy with—'

'The workload,' Lydia guessed. 'No one is.'

'I chipped in. Helped with the . . .' Dickenson broke off and glanced at her red fingers, swollen so that they looked like raw sausages. Lydia followed her gaze, but had no idea that the experienced hands that would soon be running through her glossy locks, fixing a diamanté comb above her left ear, had just moments ago been scrubbing garden vegetables. She couldn't imagine such a thing because she'd never consciously given any thought as to how vegetables – or meat or bread for that matter – were prepared to grace her table. Lydia was aware that the house was functioning on a skeleton staff. She knew the problems, and the solution too, but patience was required. No one could ever say so – it was practically criminal, certainly disrespectful, to even think it – but the fact was they were all waiting for her father-in-law, the old earl, to die.

'We all have to do our bit. Things aren't what they were. They can't be,' she commented as she put her arms through the straps of a brassiere that Dickenson was holding for her. Dickenson ran around her mistress then touched the smooth, pale skin in between her shoulder blades, silently indicating that she needed to bend forward to lower her breasts into the supporting cups. Lydia obliged, then straightened and stood still as Dickenson continued to dance around her, hastening to fasten the small hooks and eyes and adjust the lace shoulder straps so they sat flat and comfortable. Lydia allowed the maid to drop a silk chemise over her head, the material fluttering around her like insect wings, then waited as Dickenson laid a napkin on the plum velvet stool in front of the dressing table. Lydia sat down carefully. She wished she was allowed to sit on the soft velvet – she liked the malleable, slightly crunchy feel of it beneath her – but Dickenson said it was unhygienic and caused unnecessary cleaning work, and insisted on the starchy napkin. 'Yes, we must all do our bit,' Lydia repeated.

If the maid was tempted to comment that Lydia did not seem to be doing anything at all, let alone her bit, she was wise and disciplined enough not to do so. Janice Dickenson had started her career as a kitchen maid in Lady Chatfield's family home. In those days Lydia called Janice Janice and Janice called Lydia Miss Lydia. It would surprise Lydia to realise that Janice was only thirty-one, just three years older than Lydia herself. The maid had joined the household at the age of twelve, when Lydia still inhabited the narrow corridors that led to a stuffy schoolroom but no other world at all; she had assumed that a girl with a job and an income, no matter how modest, must be properly grown up, maybe even ancient, an assumption Janice's mother as well as the staff and the entire family at Hemingford Manor also made.

The two girls had been friends, or at least friendly, then. On more than one occasion Lydia's governess had caught Lydia running in the street or spied her in the village without a bonnet, misdemeanours that resulted in Lydia being lectured on decorum and sent to bed without supper. On these unfortunate evenings Janice would sneak up to the nursery room with fruit, bread and cheese. This was at the housekeeper's instruction – Janice would never have risked taking food from the pantry of her own volition – although Lydia never knew as much and considered Janice an ally in her austere, unrepentantly strict home. Someone who could be relied upon if need be. Someone who might cover and console.

Lydia had married the Honourable Lawrence Chatfield eight years ago. She was a young, pre-war bride, awash with optimism and first love, a recognised society beauty. They were all so proud of her, so pleased for her, scoldings about undemure, hatless behaviour long forgotten. Marrying the third son of an earl was fitting, appropriate to her own rank and beauty. Lydia, naturally nervous at the thought of moving so far away from her family home, remembered Janice, who she had imbued with feelings of sympathy and sentimentality. She had plucked the girl, who was by then an under house parlour maid, from oblivion and asked whether she might like to be a lady's maid. Janice was not fuelled with unreasonable ambition, but she was fed up of plunging her hands into icy water every morning, cleaning fireplaces and front steps, polishing the shoes and boots of everyone in the household and washing endless pots smeared with goose fat and gravy (that particular task grated the most because, by rights, it should no longer have been her responsibility; there was a new kitchen maid employed for such menial work). She'd accepted Lydia's offer of advancement immediately.

No one had thought that the Honourable Lawrence Chatfield would ever climb to become the heir apparent, that Lydia might one day become a countess, but within two years of their marriage both of Lawrence's older brothers were dead. The middle son, a member of the British Expeditionary Force, died at the Battle of Mons, just weeks after war was declared. There were calls for the eldest son to enlist immediately, to justify and honour his brother's death presumably. No doubt he would have done, but before he could respond to Kitchener's pointing finger, he fell off his horse and broke his neck whilst chasing a fox with some pals and a pack of hounds. The consequences of these terrible losses were that Lawrence became the earl's only chance and Lydia's name appeared on a great many more invitation lists.

Janice too metamorphosed; she became Dickenson and, as such, she visited the finest houses in Britain, twice saw the King through a window and, now that peace was restored, had travelled with her mistress to Cannes, in France, and Lake Garda, in Italy. Whilst by Janice's standards Lady Chatfield's house, Dartford Hall, here in Hampshire, was very impressive – and certainly enough work to manage – she'd now seen enough to know that there was better out there, far better. Houses with a confusion of staircases and countless gilded rooms, coats of arms, turrets and chimneys aplenty, manicured lawns and hectares of hunting grounds. No one had hoped for as much for Lady Chatfield, but now it was acknowledged to be not only possible, or probable but a certainty. When the current Earl of Clarendale finally did die, Lydia would be raised to new echelons. His house, in West Sussex, sat in a six-hundred-acre deer park; it had more rooms than Janice could hope to count, and a full staff was guaranteed. There would be no need for her to chip in with the kitchen staff and scrub vegetables. The old duffer wasn't in hail health; he'd had a bad bout of bronchitis before Christmas, his third attack in eighteen months. Many said he was just hanging on to see a grandchild.

Dickenson knelt before Lydia, carefully drawing delicate silk stockings over her feet and smoothing them high up her legs to the top of her thighs. Lydia rose, allowing the maid to fit the long stays of pink coutil round her hips and clip suspenders to the stockings, then Janice carefully spread a pair of peach satin drawers in a ring on the floor, and Lydia stepped into them. Dickenson bent to pull them up, her ear inches away from Lydia's mound of pubic hair. Neither woman ever considered the intimacy of this process excessive. Janice did the dressing. Lady Chatfield was dressed. It was what it was, as it had always been.

'What will I wear tonight, Dickenson?'

'A man arrived from France just half an hour ago, my lady.'

'The dress!' Lydia clapped her hands with excitement.

'Yes, my lady. It's being steamed this very moment.'

'A delivery on New Year's Eve! Gosh, aren't the French wonderful?' Lydia was glad she hadn't voiced her earlier opinion about their friends on the Continent. It didn't do to appear too changie-mindie; this was one of the many reasons Lydia rarely spoke up. 'So tenacious,' she added.

Janice sighed and conceded, 'They certainly value the gown, my lady. I'll say that.'

2

SARAH GORDON AND her sister Beatrice Polwarth waited patiently in the drawing room for their sister-in-law, Cecily, to join them. They sat with straight backs and did nothing; they did not fill their hands and time with embroidery, or a book, or even a glass of sherry. Instead, Sarah silently noted that the silverware was gleaming, but the hearth rug was becoming rather worn, especially in the left-hand corner where people walked through the room; it probably needed turning. Beatrice listened to the fire cracking and popping in the hearth; she appreciated its woody scent as well as its almost too ferocious heat. Bea was rarely warm enough.

The sisters were never certain, until the moment of her appearance, whether Cecily's arrival could be guaranteed. Their brother, Samuel, was extremely unlikely to join them tonight. He rarely went out, and never to a ball; if he did venture forth, it would be to attend afternoon tea at the home of a close friend, something he'd accomplished twice in three years. No one blamed him, but it would be wonderful if Cecily joined them this evening; jolly. Samuel and the children were already in bed; they'd all be asleep before half past eight. Surely Cecily wouldn't choose to spend the last day of the year alone in her bedroom. She couldn't want that, could she? Everyone was aware that she needed some respite, although no one would ever say as much out loud, least of all Samuel's devoted sisters. The sad fact was that Cecily's life was as truncated as her husband's body. Her ability to have fun – even her sense of entitlement to fun – had been blown away with

Samuel's limbs on 9 October 1917; flesh and hope splattered across Flanders and buried deep in the mud there.

The word Passchendaele haunted the house. It could be heard in the tick-tock of the clocks, in the tip-tap of the servants' footsteps on the wooden floorboards. Passch-en-daele, Passch-en-daele, Passch-en-daele. It could be heard in the swoosh of the water pouring from the jug as Samuel's bath was filled; a heartbreaking weekly exercise that Beatrice in particular hated. Naturally, the manservants assisted willingly enough, and they had trained themselves not to recoil at the sight of their master's half body, but Beatrice could never bear to think of her brother naked and exposed so. Passchendaele was whispered by the wind as it whipped down the chimneys and crept into every room and could be heard in the thud of the gamekeeper's axe when he chopped firewood, and in the horses' hooves on the cobbles of the courtyard.

It was never heard on anyone's lips.

A carriage clock ticked out the oh-too-slow minutes. Seconds were fused as the hand relentlessly progressed and gobbled up time.

'Do you think Cecily will join us this evening?' Beatrice asked her older sister. The question was so frequently addressed that she knew the reply by rote, but at twenty-six years old, she still felt compelled to fill silences. She had not, as yet, met any that were comfortable and was only acquainted with the awkward variety.

'I do hope so,' Sarah replied, as Beatrice knew she would, as she must.

'I do too.' Beatrice fingered her beaded bag. It really needed a stitch or two. She could ask the housemaid but she didn't like to be a bother. She ought to have done it herself; she certainly had enough time. Guiltily, she arranged her fingers to cover the shabbiness.

'Although she may be exhausted. Her work is very tiring,' added Sarah, always the first to offer up an excuse for Cecily.

'Will my dress do?' Beatrice's change of subject was not motivated by vanity or selfishness; it was the result of a perpetual feeling of inadequacy that Sarah understood and instantly forgave.

'It's very pretty, darling. Quite suitable.'

Beatrice wanted to be convinced but wasn't. Something new would have been lovely. Out of the question, but lovely.

'Silk georgette wears surprisingly well and lace will forever be a firm favourite,' Sarah added, smiling.

'At least I can be sure that I won't encounter anyone in the same gown,' murmured Beatrice, looking forlornly at her lap.

It was odd that she minded. Given everything. After all, she was lucky to have been invited at all this evening: a duchess's party was bound to be deliriously exciting and beyond lavish, and her name being on the most fashionable invitation lists certainly wasn't a given; she was neither rich enough nor pretty enough to guarantee that that would be the case. She was only invited to so many delicious parties because, before the war, her brother had been close chums with all the great and the good: he'd played tennis and golf with the sons of Earl Lanestone-Holder, Lords Renwick, Elphinstone and Gainsborough and the like. He'd joined the Duke of Marlborough for the Glorious Twelfth, and danced with Ladies Lytton, Allesbury, Chatfield and countless other pretty debs; so many that Beatrice struggled to recall all their names. The ones left standing had pulled together, as was proper. Lydia in particular was fastidious about the issue: she always made sure Sarah and Beatrice were invited to every party she agreed to attend and, as a significant beauty and hostess, wife of the heir to an earldom, there weren't any parties that Lydia was not invited to, and only a very few that she failed to grace. Beatrice had never pursued the thought too thoroughly, but the truth was, she was invited to parties because her brother was a cripple and her brother-in-law was dead. Everyone felt sorry.

Tonight the theme was White Winter, which meant that all the women were required to dress in white or shades of. It simply hadn't been practical for Beatrice to consider buying a new white frock. If they were to stretch to a new gown at all, they would have to pick a sensible colour, one that she would get more wear out of: navy or green, something dark that wouldn't show every mark and would flatter her too full figure. Unfortunately, big-boned Beatrice never benefited from cast-offs. Sarah was older by five years but shorter by four inches. She had inherited their mother's grace, good skin and elegant bone structure. Bea had been left with their father's heaviness. Tonight she had had no alternative other than to wear one of her old debutante dresses. They'd had it altered substantially; they'd had to: when she'd first come out into society, dresses were still dragging along the floor, and shoulders were strictly covered. There was a photograph of Beatrice in this very gown's first incarnation; she'd worn it to the Queen Charlotte Ball. Uncomfortable in starch and bones, she stood in an old-fashioned ornate silver frame just two yards from where she sat now. She would not let her head turn in that direction; she'd never liked the photograph, and wished they'd take it down. Her season had been so horribly short.

Beatrice was terribly grateful to Lydia for her consideration and inclusion; if only she had more to spend on clothes. Still, a small bubble of excitement fizzed deep in her belly. Tonight would be thrilling; everyone had been talking about it for ever. Or at least for a fortnight. At the Duchess of Pembrokeshire's last party there had been fireworks and a champagne fountain, they'd eaten caviar and the band had been brought in all the way from Chicago, Illinois!

'Who do you think will be there?' she asked.

'Everyone you've ever known,' replied Sarah with a big smile.

Beatrice thought that at least half the people she'd ever known were dead, but she bit her tongue and did not say as much. Such a comment would sour the party atmosphere and mark her out as the old maid that she quite certainly did not want to be. She'd promised herself never to talk about expense or her health, even if someone enquired. Both topics were ageing and no one was really interested.

'Should I ring down and ask if Cecily has given any word to her maid?' she asked with barely concealed impatient excitement. 'We might be waiting for her and she might have no intention of showing up.'

'Yes, do.'

Beatrice got up, strode towards the bell rope and tugged it. Then she stood by the fireplace, lingering in the warmth of the flames.

If Cecily was coming, Beatrice wished she'd get a move on. She didn't want to be insensitive to the demands placed upon her sister-in-law, who had three children and an invalid husband to care for, but she had made such an effort with her hairdo, teasing her wiry, fiery locks into smooth finger curls, and she did not want to miss a single moment of the ball.

3

'HAPPY NEW YEAR'S Eve, darlings.' Ava Pondson-Callow, only child of Sir Peter and Lady Pondson-Callow, burst into the centre of the gathering and announced grandly, 'I'm here. Let the festivities begin.'

From anyone else this would be shocking, vain. From Ava it was simply an assertion of fact. Now that she had arrived, the party could at last begin in full. The grand ballroom had been carefully prepared and was beyond sumptuous – large and high-ceilinged, it was decked with an abundance of holly and ivy; candles in solid silver candelabras almost obscured the coats of arms that stained the windows. Lavish handfuls of white and silver beads were scattered over every surface imaginable and hundreds lay clustered in the corners of the room; the beads had caused two or three ladies to almost topple from their high heels, but no one could deny the effect was stupendous. Yet it only seemed to truly sparkle now that Ava had stepped on to the flagstoned floor.

It seemed that every attendant at the ball paused as Ava glided through the crowds; they craned their necks to see what she was wearing, stood on tiptoes to find out who she had arrived with, and practically pushed one another aside to discover how she'd styled her hair. The women lusted after her look; the men lusted after her full stop. Ava was simply mesmerising; she always had been and always would be. She was the one woman in London who had managed to remain glamorous throughout the Great War and beyond. Somehow, all the other women seemed to be stained with grime and grief, as though they'd fought alongside their husbands, fathers, brothers and sons in the dirty trenches. Not Ava. She'd looked exquisite even when she'd worn black for two of her cousins, and when she'd said goodbye to more than a handful of wonderful chaps whom she'd once danced with.

Ava was fast, but rich enough for it not to matter a jot. She was thoroughly modern. She wore lipstick, rouge *and* mascara; she smoked in public, drank cocktails, and it was rumoured that she had danced with a black man when she visited America last summer. At the very least she'd danced with him.

Whilst the women in the room felt eclipsed by her entrance, the men all seemed to twinkle a little brighter. They straightened their ties and backs, they broadened their beams and shoulders; they searched their minds for funny anecdotes and wondered how they could improve her comfort. Would she like a fresh drink, perhaps? Was she too cold, a little more coal on the fire? Or was it too hot in here? Ought they to open a window? They all instinctively raised their game because Ava had arrived. Lydia adored her, Sarah was amused by her and Beatrice sat in jealous awe of her.

Ava was carrying three small packages, each carefully wrapped in brown paper and adorned with silver antique lace. The neat folds in the paper suggested that they'd been wrapped professionally by a girl trained in a shop. Ava knew that Lydia at least would recognise the ribbon; it was currently the favourite of an expensive jeweller in Bond Street. The other two were mystifyingly ignorant about such things. She held the three parcels as though she was delivering gold, frankincense and myrrh to Jesus Himself, with poise, grace and a smidgen of self-importance. Her maid trailed behind her, carrying a distinctly more cumbersome pile of packages.

'I thought we agreed no gifts,' commented Lydia lightly, as she leaned in to kiss her friend on the air that whispered near her cheek. Even though she outwardly chastised, she was beaming, and Ava could tell she was delighted that she'd chosen to break the embargo, although Sarah and Beatrice shared an odd little glance. They were so dull. Ava frequently wondered why Lydia wasted her time on such old-fashioned, steady types. Ava herself did so because

16

she believed that they lent her an air of respectability which, whilst not absolutely paramount, created a charming paradox that confused people and there was nothing Ava liked more than being a mystery.

'We agreed to buy nothing, and really these are absolutely nothing, just trinkets. In fact Lady Cooper hosted a party last month and *all* her guests were given one of these as a favour.'

'But Lady Cooper is American,' spluttered Beatrice.

'By which Beatrice means very generous,' added Lydia quickly.

Ava knew that Beatrice had meant new and rather vulgar; she'd obviously momentarily forgotten that Ava's mother was also American. Lydia was trying to cover her gaffe, but there was no need. Ava didn't care. She was glad that Beatrice had for once forgotten about her ancestry; it meant Ava was doing a good job. She really shouldn't care what a young, lumpy naïf like Beatrice thought anyway; yet despite her unmitigated success in society, Ava was, in the deepest part of her soul, ever conscious of her American mother and the fact that her father's title was new, not inherited.

'These are beautiful,' Sarah offered, turning the gold lighter over in her gloved hand. 'Lady Cooper really bought gold lighters for the *ladies*?' she probed, obviously unsure whether to be excited or scandalised.

'No. In fact she bought lighters for the chaps and compacts for the ladies, but I thought that was predictable.' Ava sighed. It was a very articulate sigh; it told the world that predictable was a crime in her book.

'Very generous of you. Thank you,' murmured Beatrice, carefully placing the gold lighter back into its box.

'If you don't like it, pass it on,' snapped Ava as she drew on the end of her cigarette holder. Beatrice looked a little shamefaced and Ava knew she'd read her correctly. No doubt Beatrice was wondering whether her brother would enjoy the lighter; unquestionably it was far more impressive than the bottle of port she'd no doubt given him for Christmas.

'Excuse me, m'lady, should I put these other gifts somewhere?' asked Ava's maid.

'Yes, do.' Ava sighed again, now blatantly bored with gift-giving.

She couldn't be bothered to tell her maid exactly where the packages ought to be stored. It didn't make any difference; the girl would know what to do. It was a terrible problem, boredom. Ava had been so excited earlier this afternoon. As she'd driven down from London – a cold and bumpy ride only made bearable by the fur blanket Dougie had wrapped around her knees and the nips of whisky Johnnie had supplied, both men behaving very flirtatiously, touching her knee and elbow more than necessary – all she'd been able to think of was giving the gifts, but now she wondered whether she'd done the right thing after all. Sarah looked uncomfortable and Beatrice looked furious. How was she supposed to know they'd been serious about not wanting to exchange gifts? She'd been sure that was simply something one said to be polite. Why hadn't they gone shopping? They couldn't be *that* busy, could they? It wasn't as though they'd spent hours on their party preparation; just look at Beatrice's dress.

'Who's here?' she asked, turning her attention to more important concerns.

'The usual,' replied Lydia.

'So, no one then.'

'Ava, really! Is that any way to see in the New Year?'

'You think this year will be different?'

'Of course.'

'Better?'

'Of course.'

Ava couldn't decide whether to pity Lydia's incessant optimism or admire it. The women fell silent and for a moment were content to simply watch the other guests. This was the fun part of the evening, when the air oozed anticipation and no one had done or said anything they might regret in the morning.

'Look, there's Doreen Harrison,' whispered Beatrice excitedly. After Ava, Doreen was considered the most beautiful woman in current society.

'Don't you mean Lady Doreen Henning?' corrected Sarah. Sir Oswald Henning's first wife had died of flu in 1919. Doreen was half Henning's age; there had been talk, when she was a debutante, that she would marry Henning's son, but he had fallen in France and so it wasn't to be. Everyone hoped the young bride would be pregnant by spring.

Doreen had exquisite bone structure, but there was something about that jutting jaw that made Lydia ache for the new bride. She held her chin a little too high, suggesting that it was all too much effort. Lydia shook her head thoughtfully. 'I always pity second wives; it can't be easy. The original Lady Henning was so admired.'

'Still, Doreen's dresses are beautiful and they all come from Paris,' pointed out Beatrice.

'Have you heard? She's having an affair,' commented Ava flatly. She was very well aware that she was delivering scandalous news, but she affected nonchalance, implying she could not be shocked or even moved.

'No!' chorused the other three satisfyingly.

'Yes.'

'With whom?'

'Her dance tutor.'

'No!'

'I promise you.'

'She's such an absolute jazzing flapper.' Beatrice was thrilled yet flustered by saying the strange words out loud. She'd read them only last week, in a censorious newspaper. The daring term – which conjured up images of frivolous, scantily clad, coltish young women who drank, smoked and made love without discretion or purpose – did nothing to alleviate the impression that Beatrice was simply far too naïve to have any relationship with the words. Her attempts to appear worldlier than she was were doomed. Ava smirked superciliously. She was a woman who would have no problem with the term 'jazzing flapper'; indeed, she had defined it a year ago, and now she thought the whole concept of being irresponsible and undisciplined a terrific bore. This year, or technically next year, she planned on being serious. Terribly serious. Except, that was, when it came to frocks.

'Good news, don't you think? Significantly improves the chances of Henning gaining an heir,' added Ava with a mischievous wink.

The other three women looked incredulous; largely their incredulity came from the fact that Ava dared to articulate what everyone else was thinking. 'Oh, look, there's Freddie. I must go and say hello.' She melted back into the throng, leaving the other three girls battling with feelings of regret and relief.

4

'I THOUGHT WE'D AGREED no gifts! My heart sank when she sash-
ayed in our direction, with her maid laden like a donkey.'

'Don't be cross with Ava,' Sarah urged her sister. 'She's trying to
be kind. Hers is simply a different world now.'

'Yes, I know. But we'd agreed. No Christmas gifts were to be
exchanged.'

Sarah placed her hand on top of Beatrice's. The gesture was
supposed to be at once a comfort and a warning; she hoped that
both sentiments might be conveyed through two sets of evening
gloves. She could hardly say, 'Beatrice, hold your tongue.'

'How about I go and find us some drinks?' offered Lydia, sensing
an atmosphere but not entirely understanding it. The sisters nodded
with stiff gratitude.

Ostensibly, the decision not to exchange gifts had been reached
because Beatrice had joked about having no clue as to what to
buy Ava – 'What does one give the gal who has everything?' – but
Sarah knew that the real reason was because nowadays the sisters
couldn't afford the sort of presents that the girls used to regularly
heap on one another. Samuel had done his bit, his best under the
circumstances, but things were tight. Sarah knew that he'd fixed
Beatrice's annual allowance at £125; that had to cover clothes,
laundry bills, travel, sundries and tips to other people's servants.
They were on many counts lucky. When their parents had died,
within a year of each other, Samuel had made it quite clear that
there was no expectation for Bea to leave the family home. Sarah

and the children had returned there after Arthur's death, but with Samuel so reduced, Seaton Manor always felt as though it belonged more to Cecily than it did to Beatrice or Sarah. Indeed, it *did*. And one day it would be their nephew's. What then? Would they still be welcome? It was a question neither Sarah nor Beatrice liked to dwell on. To prolong their welcome as far as possible, the sisters tried to contribute to the household expenses when they could; neither had employed a maid since 1914, and they paid the butcher's bill at Christmas and Easter. Sarah, as a war widow and mother of two, had been allotted a slightly more generous allowance; this, combined with Arthur's pension, meant that she had £525 per year to live on.

'Perhaps we should have realised that she would want to buy gifts,' Sarah whispered to her sister once Lydia was out of earshot. 'I bet Lydia has bought some too. Only she's more tactful than Ava. Hers will be stored somewhere around and only produced to reciprocate. We could have dipped into my savings.'

'Dipped into your son's Eton fund to buy frivolities for our indulged friends? I don't think so.' In public, Beatrice was usually placid and respectful of the concept of rarely saying what she thought. For her to be quite so unguarded, she must be smarting under the slap of embarrassment and frustration.

'Beatrice, remember we are rather better off than most.'

Beatrice scowled at her sister. There were few things as annoying as being faced with an irrefutable truth if it contradicted your argument or mood. 'Maybe, but *still*.' The emphasis she placed on the word said it all. Sarah understood. There were only so many hand-embroidered tray cloths one could present without people realising one was strapped. Economising during the war had been seen as patriotic, but now it had returned to being considered simply mean. 'And it was the way she presented the packages. With such a flourish of grace. Limbs tapering in all directions like ribbons on a maypole. It is so annoying! One always feels so chubby and gauche in her company.'

'Darling, you're neither,' Sarah said soothingly and untruthfully. Beatrice had not been blessed with good looks or good luck. In another decade her wiry hair, thick nose and heavy ankles might have been forgiven; some chap might have focused on her pretty smile or been convinced that her broad hips were promising, but now men could be so picky. Perfection and extreme youth beat promising childbearing hips every time.

'How is it possible that Ava is two years older than I am?' groaned Beatrice.

'What do you mean?'

'Look at her, she oozes youth and vitality.'

'She does rather. She suits the new fashions.'

Ava did not need compressors to reduce her breasts as Beatrice did. Her narrow hips and barely-there buttocks suggested the boyish athleticism that was all the rage. Beatrice had so many reasons to be jealous.

'Do you think my hem is perhaps still a little long? Ava was wearing her skirt practically on the knee.'

'I think yours suits you where it is.'

Beatrice understood her sister's attempt at tact, and sighed. Ava had slim ankles, shapely calves and neat knees; the sort of legs people wanted to see on display. 'Yes, Ava really is in a different world.'

'It is a rather fabulous place to inhabit, don't you think?' added Lydia, returning with three carefully balanced coupes of champagne, full to the brim.

Beatrice took a glass and an enormous slug. 'It's just hard to think she did so well out of the war when we did so . . .' She didn't bother to finish the sentence. *Badly* didn't cover it.

Lydia stared into her drink; she would not contribute anything more to the discussion. Sarah knew that Lydia firmly believed she'd done rather too well out of the war too. She had no brothers to lose, her father was too old to be called up, and Lawrence – well, Lawrence hadn't seen active service. He'd served, of course, behind a desk. The entire duration of the Great War, behind a desk. Every man aged between eighteen and fifty had been asked to stand up; boys significantly younger had rushed at it. Sarah had lost her husband; Beatrice her young beau. Their brother had lost his legs and an arm. It was so hard not to be bitter. Silently the three women had followed

23

the same thought pattern and had arrived at the same conclusion. They didn't know how to comfort one another; instead they watched the dancers and tried to recapture the party spirit.

As usual, there were more women than men at the party, and anyway the men's black evening suits rendered them almost invisible among the women's shiny, pretty frocks. Girls partnered one another, glad of the exercise and not prepared to start the new year with their backs to the wall. Lydia fought the urge to go and circulate. She couldn't leave Sarah and Beatrice standing without company. If she did move on, there was little chance they'd be singled out to be spoken to. As a wife she elevated their cluster; alone, the other two women would be surplus.

Lydia spotted Lawrence across the room at the very moment his eyes searched her out. He was quite tall and extremely distinguished-looking, eminently proper. His hair was thinning, but she didn't mind that. His sort did tend to go bald prematurely. Perhaps it was the fault of the wigs they'd worn in the Regency period, she joked to herself, refusing to acknowledge that the real reason she liked him balding was that he appeared older than he was. Too old to have been called up, perhaps. Not a draft-dodger. Not that he was. It was just that . . . Her thoughts were spiky and disloyal; they flashed like fireworks in the sky, startling. Smoke lingered. Thoughts lingered. Thoughts could not be controlled but, thank God, speech and actions could. No one knew her secret thoughts because she was careful not to articulate them.

She shot him a glance and he understood what she needed in an instant. It was rare for a man to have such a finely tuned sense of social nicety, but Lydia adored his perfect manners and was extremely grateful for his endless resource when it came to small talk. He approached the ladies, kissed their hands, asked after their health and their journey to the party. He told them they looked ravishing and then asked Sarah whether she'd like to dance with him. The widow always got the first offer. She rarely accepted, but Lawrence considered it his duty to remember Arthur every time he attended a dance.

'No, you should dance with your wife,' Sarah replied gently, but firmly. Lawrence was a sound dancer. He would not land heavily on her feet, as so many men did, but Sarah didn't like dancing. She never had, much. Obviously, she'd had to dance when it was her season, but she'd been so relieved when she fell in love with Arthur and Arthur fell in love with her, and she'd known she'd no longer be obliged to dance with every man who asked.

'Beatrice, you won't turn me down, will you?'

Beatrice knew she ought to. Like her sister, she should redirect the polite and generous man back towards his wife, her friend, but unlike her sister, Beatrice absolutely loved to dance, was quite mad for it, and really couldn't bear losing an opportunity to be in the arms of a man, if only for the briefest of moments.

'Go ahead,' Lydia smiled. 'Sarah and I are going to hunt out the champagne fountain and get refills.'

Beatrice and Lawrence were almost instantly swallowed by the dancing crowd. Lydia linked her arm through Sarah's and they started to walk out of the ballroom, into the room where the cocktails were being served.

'That was nice of you,' commented Sarah.

'Not at all. I can dance with Lawrence whenever I want to. If we danced every dance together we'd have nothing to talk about over breakfast.' Lydia reached for two fresh glasses of champagne from a passing servant. 'Did you have a lovely Christmas with the children?'

'Absolutely. My two, Samuel's three, plus the cousins on Cecily's side. I lost count of how many there were running feral. I think Beatrice had a wonderful time. She was certainly kept very busy. It was chaos.'

'How is Samuel?'

'Oh, you know my brother. Sammy never complains. Doesn't say much at all.'

'Quite.' Nobody did. It wasn't done. Still, such a cruelty: both legs and an arm. It was the arm that seemed most brutal; it meant crutches were out of the question. Sarah had heard it said, in such cases, that it was a comfort that the man had married and fathered before he'd gone to war, and she supposed it was, but she'd never been able to bring herself to utter those words to Cecily. Nothing seemed much of a comfort to Cecily.

'How about you? How was your Christmas?' she asked with genuine curiosity.

'Lovely.' Lydia hesitated, then added, 'A little quiet.' Sarah read between the lines and surmised it had been ghastly.

'Did you stay in Hampshire, at Dartford Hall?'

'No, we went to the in-laws at Clarendale. My parents joined us there.'

'You ought to get a shorter table for the dining room when you move into the earl's place,' suggested Sarah. 'I know the one they have now. It must be ridiculous for family affairs. Six adults around a table designed for twenty. I imagine it's difficult to be festive, impossible to pull a cracker.'

Lydia giggled and squeezed her friend's arm. Sarah had correctly imagined the sober scene: grandparents-in-waiting looking at their offspring, wondering when there would finally be news.

'You're terrible to talk about my father-in-law's demise in that way, but you're right. Next year I must invite friends for lunch, or at least tea.'

'Believe me, I'm not in any way looking forward to the old earl's death, but it will be convenient when you are in West Sussex too. Clarendale is just a twenty-minute ride from ours; we'll be neighbours!' smiled Sarah.

'Maybe next year there will be a child to coo over,' added Lydia, elaborating on the imagined pleasures.

'Wouldn't that be lovely?'

'Yes.' Lydia bit her lip and Sarah watched some of her beauty leak out and puddle at her feet. 'I'm seeing another doctor on Thursday.'

'Are you? Who?'

'Doctor Folstad. In Harley Street. Came here from Norway. Has a fabulous record.' Lydia didn't look at her friend as she said this, because there was such a terrible feeling of déjà vu around the conversation that she couldn't face it head on. There had been countless doctors with fabulous records.

'Wonderful.' Sarah rallied.

'Isn't it?'

'He might have the answers.'

'I'm very hopeful.'

'Good show.'

'Would you come with me?' Lydia now allowed herself a swift glance at her friend's face. 'You could stay in Eaton Square with us, or if you didn't want to be away from the children, I could have a car sent for you. Or I'll buy a train ticket if you prefer.'

'Certainly I'll come.'

'Thank you, Sarah. Thank you very much.'

'Chin up.'

'Absolutely.' Relieved that she'd made the request and secured some support, Lydia beamed and threw back her champagne. She put the empty glass on a side table and reached for a fresh one. Lydia was honest with herself. She was not one of those women who hankered to hold an infant; she did not coo into prams or sniff babies to drink up their scent. Any child of hers would naturally spend many hours in the nursery and be significantly more intimate with his or her nanny than with any other soul on earth, at least in the early years. If it was a boy, he would go away to school at eight. She did not see a child as an extension of herself, or her property, or even her right. Her desire for a baby wasn't raw and instinctual, but more to do with an insidious, illogical but essentially real worry that without one she was nothing. She was useless. Pointless. What was the point of a woman like her if it was not to bring an heir to the nursery? None at all. She loved and respected her husband in the appropriate way. He was a decent, well-mannered, intelligent man, but he had never set her on fire. She had never expected him to. It was a good match. It had turned out to be a glittering one in terms of prestige and wealth, titles, all that, but it was an appalling one if she did not produce a baby. A failure. What would they do? What would they talk about as they aged, if there weren't children and grandchildren? She did not want to be remembered as the woman who brought a three-hundred-year dynasty to a grinding halt.

5

LYDIA AND LAWRENCE stayed at the ball until one in the morning, a better show than Sarah and Beatrice, who had both left just after eleven, but pathetic in comparison to Ava, who would still be partying when the kitchen maids started to light the fires for the New Year's Day breakfast of bacon and eggs.

'Is Ava quite all right?' Lawrence asked. He stood by as the butler held his wife's mink wide, waiting for her to shrug her way into its softness.

'She's fabulous.' They headed to their car and sat still while another two manservants placed large tartan blankets over their legs. The temperature had dropped below zero and the drive home would take an hour. Lydia was beginning to wish she'd agreed to stay for the weekend after all. She had been tempted, because it was so convenient, only she wasn't keen on party aftermaths. The morning after always seemed so horribly real in comparison to the glamour of the night before; the men smelt and the women regretted. Everyone had a headache. It wasn't pretty.

'Who is taking care of her?'

Lydia smiled. 'I think she rather takes care of herself.'

'You know what I mean. Who is she with?' Lawrence wasn't reassured.

'A whole gang, as usual. Freddie, Johnnie and Doug.' There seemed to only ever be a handful of men at these parties, but however many or few attended, they were guaranteed to be found clustered around Ava.

'Are they sober?'

'Absolutely not. But they are game and they'd rather die than leave her side. I don't think we need to worry. She's not travelling home tonight. She's staying for the hunt on Monday.' Lydia was usually thrilled with her husband's caring attitude towards her friends, but she wished he'd just give the driver the nod; it was late and she was tired. No, more than that: she was bone-sore weary, the way she so often was in company nowadays. She didn't know how to explain her mood, even to herself, so she simply struggled to disguise it. Harder when it was deathly cold and her feet were blistering.

'I really don't know how they do it,' commented Lawrence.

'Do what?'

'Stay up so late.'

Lydia decided not to mention the cocaine; her husband wouldn't approve. The fact of the matter was that many had turned to alcohol or drugs since the Great War to numb pain or as a means of escape.

The combination of five glasses of champagne, the rattling windows and the rumbling of the wheels fought against the freezing air and won. Lydia was rapidly lulled to sleep, only waking as they pulled up at Dartford Hall. Grateful to have lost the icy hour inside the fusty car, she stumbled out into the pitch-black night. The butler and a footman had, as ever, been on the lookout, and as they spotted the car approach they came outside to assist, their breath and impatience just visible against the night's blackness. Lydia shivered for them; they were only wearing waistcoats and jackets, as coats would have been improper.

'Happy new year, Jenkins,' she murmured sleepily.

'Happy new year, my lady. Can I give Cook any instruction as to what time breakfast ought to be served tomorrow?'

'Midday. I'm so tired. I need a glass of water.'

'Dickenson is up, my lady. She'll attend to everything.'

'Excellent. Good night.' Lydia nodded to the footman but didn't wish him a happy new year; naturally she hoped he had one, but she couldn't remember his name. The young staff came and went like April showers nowadays; she rarely got the chance to know them.

Lawrence followed his wife up the mahogany staircase. Two steps below her, his eyes were in line with her elegant, slim back, exposed by the daring dress that plunged to the waist, showing off her shoulder blades and the delicate bumps of her spinal cord. Impulsively he swept in and kissed her thin white skin. 'You look beautiful tonight.'

She stopped to appreciate the compliment and the sensation of his warm lips on her back. His whiskers scratched and stirred something. A memory rather than an actuality. A memory of wanting him, rather than the definite feeling of wanting him. Sex had once been so delicious and hopeful; now it was simply familiar. She turned and saw that his face was shining with expectation. It was different for him, clearly. The difference hurt her too.

'Are you really so very tired, my darling? It is a new year after all.'

That was true. She was too woozy to believe it might be properly satisfying, but she'd drunk an amount that meant it would be the uninhibited sort of sex that was always fun. She'd get into it once he started; she almost always did. Besides, he was her husband; she was his wife. It was her duty by law and tradition. She shouldn't refuse him too often. Theirs was a rare marriage because it wasn't made convenient by infidelity. Too many refusals might edge him along that dreaded path. 'All right then, as long as you are quick,' she replied. It was as generous an answer as she could muster.

6

AVA THOUGHT THAT men had their uses – they were excellent at fetching her drinks and mink stoles when she needed them, buying meals and paying for clothes and all that – but she probably wouldn't go so far as to say she'd ever met a *really* useful one. She would not even award her father that distinction; Ava had found she was not the sort of girl who simply adored her father, hero-worshipped him, just because of the intrinsic intimacy of their relationship. In fact, she found that the closer she was to a man, the more harshly she judged him. She could not ignore the faults that other women seemed to glide past. She saw the flaws and fears of men; she smelt out their inefficiency or arrogance, their wildness or weakness. Not that Sir Peter Pondson-Callow suffered from any of these specifically; he was not wild or weak or inefficient, and his arrogance at his abilities was countered by a deep sense of needing to be approved of. He was, however, a coldly ambitious man, and his ambition, left unchecked, could bubble into something more insidious, like greed or even cruelty. Ava had no problem with his avarice. He had made a lot of money – a *lot* – and she had benefited from his business acumen and ruthlessness; it would be churlish to despise him for that – foolish. Yet still she couldn't quite adore him, couldn't believe he was ideal just because he was her father. Unfortunately, he was not one hundred per cent appropriate; he wasn't quite *quite*. Not quite dignified enough, not quite calm enough, a little too commercial in the drawing room and a little too friendly with shop girls, who he liked to impress by paying for everything with filthy wads of cash. Simply put, he was not a purebred, which annulled his chances of being properly useful to Ava, no matter how rich he might be.

Her father had married her mother for money, and her mother, a plain girl, had married Pondson-Callow for his looks. They appreciated one another in much the way a farmer and a loyal sheepdog might: they accepted that their alliance was mutually beneficial, a fair deal. Undoubtedly, her mother had backed the right horse; her father had done a marvellous job at turning her respectable dowry into a small fortune. Before Ava was born he'd been awarded a knighthood for his industry; his efforts during the war had further increased their wealth fortyfold. He was indisputably a success. Her father seemed content with his side of the transaction too. As far as Ava was aware, he'd never complained that there was only one live child; a girl at that. He had no doubt calculated that as his title wasn't one that could be passed on, and his daughter was ravishing, forever appearing in the society pages, he could be sanguine. A boy might have been lost in the carnage in any case. Besides, all his friends' wives were plain-looking now. They were at the age when everything sank south and beauty no longer counted; when they had counted, Lady Pondson-Callow had allowed Sir Peter to freely pursue pretty faces, shapely legs and full breasts outside their marriage and had never so much as raised an eyebrow.

Ava had been brought up to believe that affairs were the only genuine excitement the rich experienced during the Edwardian period. Restricted as they were by protracted and inflexible formality and an intricate, if hypocritical, code of etiquette and values, sexual intrigue added impetus to an otherwise leisurely but dull life. The aristocracy protected their high social positions by adhering to a phoney social code where husbands, and sometimes even wives, took lovers. The majority were willing to ignore extramarital affairs so long as an outward appearance of domestic bliss endured. It was an extremely functional, although entirely depressing, modus operandi. Ava understood that the rules had been manufactured to warrant that family life was not ruined by sexual feats and adventures. Public exposure, which led to unharnessed gossip, resulted in names being cut from guest lists; the indiscreet were summarily and promptly made socially extinct.

Ava had often thought that if ever she was to settle on a man, he would have to be a thoroughly admirable one. By this she did not mean admirable in that hopelessly sloppy way Sarah or Beatrice might define the term. She was not looking for a knight in shining armour who would flatter and fawn, arrive at her door laden with acres of land and the neurosis of inheriting a title he couldn't carry; for one thing, those sorts of men invariably had such weak chins. Ava's definition of an admirable man was one who would (needless to say) be obscenely rich, because even though she had her own enormous wealth, she didn't want to be one of those women who was known for buying a title; he would challenge her, amuse her, perhaps even attempt to control her (no doubt he'd fail, but it would be exciting to see him try). Finally he would be horribly good-looking, completely breathtaking, the sort of man whose fidelity couldn't be taken for granted. It was a meeting of equals that she longed for.

Ava had not met such a man. She doubted he even existed. If he once had, the chances were he was buried in mud in France, face down in an unmarked grave. She reasoned that as the man she wanted did not exist, she might as well have lots of fun with those who did.

She had a thing for ex-soldiers, which was convenient, because there was hardly any other sort of chap around, Kitchener's propaganda had been so thorough and successful. There was something about their raw hedonism, their fragility, the fact that they were angry or damaged, that she found fascinatingly attractive, but they weren't the sort that she'd want in her life in any sort of permanent way; that would become quite a drain.

They'd found their way to the library, a group who were unwilling to go to bed, the ones who were planning to roar through the twenties, hoping to drown out the echo of the artillery, although they said that the reason they were still up was that someone wanted to find a particular book of poetry to check up on the exact wording of a poem. There was a bet running between two posturing chaps: two pounds was at stake. The discussion had become rather heated. Ava wondered if they secretly missed the war and now just needed something to fight about, a theory that gained more weight once they were in the library and there was some fuss about the fire being low. Ought they to build it themselves or call a servant? The chaps who had been arguing about the quote forgot the poem and started to argue about the best way to build a fire. Ava draped herself on a chaise longue and gazed disinterestedly at the shelves of leather-bound volumes; through the haze of the champagne she'd consumed, the books struck her as self-important and remote. She couldn't summon the energy to get up and find a collection of Donne to prove that the one with the moustache was right and the other was mistaken, something she was absolutely sure of. Her feet were icy; she wished the men would stop squabbling and simply call a maid to build the fire. One of the girls found a gramophone and some records. They rolled up the rug and four or five of the most game souls started to dance again.

Soon the music lost its flamboyant buoyancy and slower tunes were selected. Bodies melted into one another. Hands began to stray but weren't curbed. The other girls were kissing fellows now, hungry, enthusiastic kisses. Ava watched, wondering from where they summoned up the unchecked desire. She'd never been so consumed by a man that she'd consider being indiscreet in public; desire was always on her terms and in private, and whilst she'd probably made love with many more men than any of the other women in the room, no one could be sure. Her reputation was enhanced by eager whispers and keyed-up conjecture, but not sullied by indisputable facts. Freddie sat on the floor by her feet. He caught her watching the couples and misinterpreted her look of incredulity as one of longing; he kissed her foot, opportunistically. She could feel the dampness of his lips even through her silk stocking. That was Freddie's flaw. Wet kisses, somehow an embodiment of his general demeanour, which was one of soppy overeagerness.

Dougie passed Freddie a small packet; he took it gratefully. He'd

34

been given opium as a painkiller, to help after he'd been shot in the calf. He'd become rather fond, but the doctors had made a fuss, said he was addicted and refused to give him any more. He'd gone half mad with pain. Then a charming chap from America had introduced them to cocaine, and what a gift. Ava didn't indulge herself. She'd tried it once, like most things, because she couldn't bear not knowing. Admittedly the high had been stupendous – she'd felt invincible, alert, supreme, masculine – but it hadn't lasted long and the downer was more ghastly than anything she'd ever had to endure. She'd vomited violently, which was undignified. Then she'd felt anxious, something she'd never experienced before; she was usually assured in her actions and presence. She'd been convinced a maid was looking at her oddly and had had her dismissed. Terribly embarrassing, once she was through it all; she occasionally wondered where that maid had ended up. So now she simply watched as the boys pushed cold needles into their arms, enjoying their expressions melt as they anticipated the sweet relief that was to follow. She stood up and blew kisses to everyone; she always left the room before they started weeping and wailing, swearing and swiping.

Ava had been put in the South Wing, the one with the reputation as the most comfortable and close to the hostess's private rooms. She knew it was a compliment; that or an elaborate exercise in gathering gossip. Either way she didn't care; she had a room with an en suite, and that was so important on these weekend jaunts to the countryside. So many of these enormous houses were hideously uncomfortable and old-fashioned. Ava absolutely preferred London, where everyone and everything was modern. When she arrived in her room, she was surprised to find Lord Harrington lying on her bed in his night clothes.

'Charlie, I'd rather expected to be greeted by my maid,' she said flatly.

'I sent her away.'

'And how did you explain your presence in my room?' Ava took off her earrings and put them in a small china pot on her dressing table, then stared at her lover with nonchalance.

'I'm next door. I told her I'd made a wrong turn.'

'I don't suppose she believed you.'

'She's a maid, I don't suppose it matters.'

It mattered to Ava, but not as much as it ought and not for the expected reasons. Obviously, unmarried women were somehow expected to remain virginal until their wedding night, but Ava thought that was outdated and hadn't paid any attention. It was simply this business about feeding rumour that bothered her. She didn't like to be known; it seemed so very similar to being owned.

'Besides, since the duchess has thoughtfully given us adjoining rooms, I imagine she suspects we're lovers, and if *she* suspects, then everyone else *knows*. She's famously very slow on the uptake.'

Ava scowled, not wanting this to be the case. 'Let's hope it's just coincidence then.' Suddenly she felt a basic and needful desire flood through her body; it overtook her concern about the gossip. She changed her tone. 'So since you've sent my maid away, how am I supposed to undress?' she asked with a small smile.

Harrington patted the bed. 'Come here, I can help you.'

Afterwards, he asked, 'Did you like that?'

'Yes. You're very good.'

'Your best?'

'One of them,' she conceded. Lord Harrington looked disappointed, but wisely chose to rally. Ava was not a woman who responded to self-pity; in fact she was very likely to be regretfully contemplating the ghastly sameness of all encounters such as these. He jumped out of bed and poked the fire, and then he threw the rubber condom in the grate and poked it again, hoping it would burn. It was not the sort of thing one wanted one's wife to find, but Ava always insisted on one, seemingly unaware or at least unconcerned that the only other women who did so were French whores. She wouldn't trust withdrawal; in an amusing perversion of the usual roles of the sexes, she insisted that men were out to trap her.

Lord Harrington reached for two cigarettes and lit them both, handing one to Ava. She sat up in bed, not bothering to modestly pull the covers up to hide her breasts. She didn't think about it, but if she had, her actions would have been equally bold, because she secretly enjoyed the frisson of shocking. Clearly the lord liked it too, because he leapt back into bed with the energy of a child on Christmas morning. He swooped down to kiss her breast, and as he gently tugged on her nipple he mumbled, 'Darling, you are perfect, will you marry me?'

Ava took a long drag on her cigarette. 'That's terribly sweet of you, Charlie, but aren't you already married?'

'Well, yes, presently, but I'd divorce her. For you, my love, I would divorce her.'

Ava stubbed out her cigarette and considered. 'But if you were single, you wouldn't have any attractions at all,' she replied with a yawn. 'Now, darling, do be quiet. I want to get some sleep.'

7

THE DOCTOR'S SURGERY was almost identical to the half a dozen or so other doctors' surgeries Lydia had visited over the past seven years: austere, silent and tinged with the smell of chloroform, a smell that always made her feel anxious and nauseous by turn. The dark mahogany floors, shelves, wall panels and doors in the small waiting room shone with polish and elbow grease, but their shine didn't please or comfort Lydia in the least; she fought the feeling that she was trapped in a coffin. She couldn't stay seated for more than five minutes in a row, but leapt up from her chair and strode around the room. She fingered the brass bell on reception, touched the handles on the drawers of the impressive display cabinet housing an eagle that a taxidermist had captured mid pounce and flicked through the magazines set on the table until Sarah reminded her, 'Not everyone wears gloves nowadays.' Even though Lydia did wear gloves, for warmth and form, she instantly drew back, sat down and rested her hands on her lap.

There was no good news.

Dr Folstad was tall and slim, fitter than most men his age. His moustache, white and thick, drew Lydia's eye as it danced with his lip, probably made all the more fascinating by the contrast with his head, which was entirely bald and shone so audaciously that Lydia believed it quite possible that he had it polished along with the wall cladding and shelves. However, for all his reputation as an experimental, forward-thinking doctor, he had nothing new to offer Lydia, who had hoped for a miracle at best, innovation at least. Whilst he looked very different from all the other doctors she'd met, he sounded the same. He took her temperature, asked about her menstruation, made her lie down on her back as he put his hands on her belly. Just as all the other doctors had.

'Have you ever used contraception?'

'No.' Lydia was mystified. She was here to learn how to get pregnant. Not once in her eight years of marriage had she ever used contraception. Why would she?

'There are women who do, early on in their marriages, and it damages them in the long term.'

'Oh.' Lydia had heard this before. When she'd repeated it to Ava, Ava had laughed riotously and talked about the guff that men spouted in an attempt to terrify women. She'd commented that it was criminal, and then added that she only wished contraception had such long-term effects, as it would save her a lot of time and effort. Lydia had been too stunned and shy to ask exactly what Ava had meant by this.

Lydia had received several pieces of dubious advice during her desperate pursuit to conceive a baby, and had sat through many chastising lectures too. One doctor advised her to drink a pint of Guinness every day, as he was adamant that she lacked iron. For a year she'd waded through the thick, creamy beer every morning at breakfast, even though she wasn't keen on the burned, sharp, almost lactic flavour, and it often caused her to have a headache for the remainder of the morning. She only gave up the habit when another doctor advised her that the drink was making her less feminine and thus reducing her chances of conceiving. She'd been told that wearing high-heeled shoes had thrown her uterus into displacement; for several months she was unfashionable, bordering on the dowdy, and had only returned to heels when Ava had once again sprinkled her wisdom by commenting, 'Good God, woman, you're a fright. Lawrence isn't going to want to make love to you if you insist on dressing like a farm labourer. Then you'll never get pregnant.' Lydia thought she might have a point: heels were so much more flattering for the ankles and calves.

She nervously fingered the lace hem of her skirt, which sat a smidgen below her knee. She wondered whether she might get ticked off for that too. She'd once been told that short skirts were responsible for her infertility. Admittedly, that choice piece of idiocy hadn't come from a doctor; it was a great-aunt of Lawrence's who'd insisted that draughts 'up there' led to problems.

'Do you exercise?' Dr Folstad asked gruffly.

'I dance,' Lydia admitted carefully.

'Dancing. Hmm.' His tone was condemning.

'I ski in season, and play tennis and golf too in the spring and summer,' she added defensively, in case dancing was to be disapproved of on moral grounds, as well it might; one never knew what doctors despised.

'For sure. As all you young ladies do.'

Patronised and alarmed, Lydia asked, 'Is it wrong?'

'Not necessarily. Some doctors say excessive exercise in women is a problem. Others say it isn't.'

'What do *you* say?' asked Sarah. Her concern over the enormous fee this doctor was charging had shocked her out of her normal reserve.

Dr Folstad leaned forward and turned on the desk lamp. It had been a dull day. The sky, originally the colour of the hem of a wedding dress, had now darkened to something more akin to a groom's topcoat. It had drizzled non-stop since Boxing Day. The inclement weather was hard to ignore; it had a devastating effect on the perkiness of hats and hearts. The light from the lamp helped ease the gloom marginally, but Sarah wished someone would offer them a cup of tea; she was sure Lydia would benefit. Irritation at the lack of hospitality emboldened her further. 'Do you have a view?'

The doctor held Sarah's gaze, not offended, rather amused by her challenge. 'I think moderate exercise is to be recommended, as is the moderate consumption of alcohol. Drink milk but make sure it's pasteurised. Eat plenty of eggs and leafy greens.' Lydia nodded enthusiastically at every syllable that dropped from his mouth, as though he was spitting pearls. 'Try not to get too stressed, Mrs Chatfield. Stress is an enemy in all health issues.'

'Lady.'

'Sorry?'

'Lady Chatfield.' Lydia blushed, immediately wishing she hadn't corrected him. What did it matter if this foreigner failed to address her properly? Few Englishmen truly understood how to address whom, whom to address how.

'Lady Chatfield,' he repeated carefully; was he laughing? 'And you could try some new positions during sexual intercourse.'

Lydia sensed Sarah shudder at her side. It was good of Sarah to attend this appointment, as sex and all the associated, wasn't a subject she'd ever felt comfortable discussing, even before she became a widow. Before, she had found it embarrassing; now, no doubt, it was both embarrassing and painful. Lydia had married a year after Sarah, and she remembered trying to talk to her friend about what to expect on her honeymoon. Sarah had told her to pack Hartmann's Hygienic Towelettes and lots of spare pairs of knickers, and not to worry if she didn't immediately get the hang of it. Still, blushes aside, if positions could help, then Lydia had to know more.

'Any you'd recommend especially?' she asked, taking care to keep her eyes trained on the green leather desk.

'I have a leaflet. Produced in Oslo but written in English.' He didn't need to be any more specific; both the women already understood that the leaflet would no doubt be considered obscene in British terms. Whilst having children was deemed patriotic, any discussion as to how this might come about was still judged as perverse. Folstad stood up and rooted in a cabinet drawer; while he had his back to them the women shared a quick glance. They were unsure whether to be excited for Lydia, hopeful or panicked. Lydia wanted to giggle. Nervous.

'Here we are.' He handed her a very thin five inch by three inch sheet of paper. It was the same thin texture as her confirmation Bible and she wondered whether this was significant; she read so much into everything nowadays. The print was tiny and difficult to read. There were no pictures.

Blushing again, Lydia folded the piece of paper in half and then into quarters, and carefully stowed it in a buttoned pocket inside her bag. 'Do you think it might be worthwhile my husband coming to visit you?' she asked tentatively.

'I can't imagine there's any point in that,' replied Dr Folstad. 'What possible help would it be? No doubt your husband is a busy man, and invariably the problem lies with the woman, you know.'

'I see.'

'Vitamins are essential. And cod liver oil. Do be sure that the receptionist has your correct address. I send bills out on a Tuesday. Any questions?' The doctor's moustache stayed still for a moment.

'No, I don't think so.'

Just one. *Why? Why not?* But she knew he couldn't answer that.

8

O<small>UT ON THE</small> pavement it was miserably cold. The streets were teeming with people rushing to find shelter from the drizzle that had started while they were visiting the doctor; umbrellas popped up like shiny black mushrooms, but neither Lydia nor Sarah had one with them. The bitter January air scratched the women's faces; helplessly they watched as a gust picked up a brown paper bag and carried it bouncing along the street. A small child gambolled after it, laughing; a nanny ran after the child, scolding. Lydia and Sarah wondered what to say to one another. The doctor's hopelessness and blame sat heavily on the pavement with them, more solid and real than the longed-for Silver Cross baby carriage with a plump heir inside. Lydia rallied first. She was more familiar with this situation than Sarah; she'd been found culpable often enough.

'Well, I'm stranded somewhere between painful outrage and a genuine interest in the leaflet,' she commented, forcing a bright smile to her face. She threaded her arm through her friend's.

'Should we find a tea house? Warm us up?' Sarah suggested. *Warm us up* was new-speak for *cheer us up*. No one admitted to needing to be cheered – it seemed unpatriotic – but everyone felt it. Gloomy Januarys were the worst.

'Yes, tea.' It would solve little, but both women needed to believe in this, the great British myth that everything would at least be better after a hot cuppa. 'Let's go to Maison Lyons at Marble Arch. It's so very glam. Look, there's a cab.'

As hoped, the familiar white and gold façade did something to lift the spirits of the two friends. Lydia pushed open the door and both women tumbled into the welcome glare of the large, bustling food hall. They excitedly drank in the intoxicating sight of the fancies on offer. Fat pink joints of ham hung temptingly from hooks, alluring jewelled cakes, light pastries and delicate hand-made chocolates were displayed in glass counters, crates of exotic, colourful fruits that had been shipped to London from all over the Empire were stacked around them, as well as slabs of smelly ripe cheeses and displays of impressive wines and champagnes. The women breathed in the luxury and allowed themselves to let drop a small amount of the tension that perpetually gripped them both.

'Do you have much delivered from here?' Sarah asked conversationally.

'Yes, when we're in Eaton Square, it's so convenient. They deliver twice a day, you know.'

'How marvellous.'

'I come here to have my hair done occasionally too,' confessed Lydia. 'There's a salon in the basement.'

'Do you? Why? I thought Dickenson had clever fingers and some flair that way.'

'Yes, but sometimes it is fun to . . . oh, I don't know . . . mix with other gals, I suppose. You know, the ones that aren't like us.' From the look on Sarah's face, it was clear she had no idea what Lydia was on about; what possible attraction could there be in rubbing shoulders? 'I like the smell of hot hair,' Lydia added lamely.

The five-storey building offered a different restaurant on every floor, all of them huge and bustling. The establishment sometimes stayed open twenty-four hours a day, and various fashionable orchestras played on each floor almost continually. Lydia wondered whether the number of patrons that came through the doors indicated that she and Sarah were not alone in needing somewhere cheerful to take sanctuary; did all of Britain feel the same, or were the other tea-drinkers feeling fabulous? Certainly many looked blissful as they jumped up from their seats and danced to the sinewy jazz notes that jerked and jostled their way past the clinking of cups and saucers, and through the ribbons of cigarette smoke.

The women settled on the second floor because they didn't want to eat more than a cake. They were led to their seats, and as they threaded through the chairs and chatter, the waitress said she'd fetch the trolley so that they could see today's pastries.

She noticed his uniform first.

It was habit. For years she had noticed every uniform on the streets. At first there were just a few, worn by the overzealous or the desperate. Then there had been many, too many, the streets turned khaki as swathes and swathes of young men marched through, towards the stations and ports. Then there were too few again. The uniforms that did come home were shabby, tucked up to hide a lost bough, or trailing a sleeve, a ghost of a limb.

Now uniforms were few and far between again. Worn mostly by poor, damned men, begging for food or casual work, hoping to kick-start some common decency or at least guilt. But this one was worn by a man with ramrod posture, a man with an air of resilience and triumph. His strength and masculinity oozed out and engulfed the entire room; Lydia noticed that Sarah was watching him too. Every woman in the room was. Some were doing so carefully, from under their lashes or out of the corner of their eyes; others were brasher, and practically allowed their jaws to openly hit the table. Lydia stared. She was incapable of not doing so, even though somewhere, on some level, she realised it was unacceptable.

It was habit too to wait, to see if they could stand, if both arms were in place, if when they turned they might be scarred, burned beyond recognition. But this man turned and he was perfection. It was his absolute perfection that struck her. During the Great War they'd said they were fighting for the women and children, for the farms and the fields. Lydia had never quite believed this, even though she knew she ought. It was hard to swallow when so many women had been left broken-hearted, when so many children had lost a father. Now, suddenly, she understood why they had fought. They had fought for this man. Not men like him; this man alone, in all his perfection.

'Are you all right, Lydia? Do you know him?' Sarah asked.

'Know who?'

'The man you are staring at.'

'No, certainly not.'

'Gosh, what a shame. He's divine. Beatrice would love an introduction.' Sarah sat down, smiled at the waitress and began to look around the room, sizing up the other customers' plates, trying to decide which cake seemed the most appetising.

Lydia had forgotten how to sit down. She'd simply forgotten, as she realised that her breasts were aching, actually aching with longing. She glanced at the man again and felt nothing other than a terrible confusion as she understood that what she was experiencing was extreme desire. In the instant she understood as much, she was ashamed to admit that she had never felt anything similar with Lawrence. Flustered, she dropped like a sandbag into her chair. She made an effort to behave as she should, as she usually did. She tugged on the fingers of her gloves and took them off, set them aside. She picked up the menu and tried to focus, but the words swam in front of her, morphing and misbehaving. Sarah commented that she might have a teacake or perhaps a macaroon, for a change. 'I wonder what the Russian pastries are like, exactly.'

Lydia found it impossible to do anything other than smile weakly; although she had tried the Russian pastries only last week and had found them overly sweet and a little heavy, she simply couldn't impart this wisdom. She began to play with the tablecloth, all the while strangely aware that he was in the room. Then she blurted, 'Should we look at the leaflet?' Somehow, illogically, the two things seemed related. The perfect man and the exotic sexual positions.

'Not here, Lydia.' Sarah coloured.

'I need a cigarette.' Lydia offered one to Sarah, who refused; although practically everyone smoked in public, Sarah and Bea were still resistant. Lydia inhaled deeply and tried to think about the menu.

'Excuse me, is this yours?'

The perfection was talking to her. He was right by her side, just behind the cigarette. His nostrils flared as he took in her smoke. She felt queer that her breath was now inside him. Moved. Up close, he was more beautiful than she had believed possible. His skin was fine and hung on his sharp cheekbones; his dark hair was long and flopped over his right eye, as was fashionable, but even so, it could not hide his eyes. Green. Enormous. Sad. He held out her glove. Red, it lay like a gash in his hand.

'Yes, it must have fallen off the table,' she mumbled.

'Well, luckily I was passing, so I could avert any real disaster.' His tone was humorous; his enunciation was not quite middle class. He was trying to hide an accent; she couldn't yet tell which one. She was frozen; he shook the glove a fraction, as if reminding her that he was offering it. She took it from him and their fingers touched; the jolt dashed through her body, then found a harbour below her stomach. She fought the mad urge to stand up and kiss him.

'I like your eye make-up.'

'Sorry?'

'That smoky, smudgy look you've mastered. It's very attractive.'

'Oh.'

'Well, good day, ladies.' He nodded his head a fraction.

'Goodbye,' Lydia replied.

Both women watched the soldier leave the café; it was impossible to turn away.

'Wasn't he forward?' commented Sarah.

'Absolutely.'

'Handsome enough to be forgiven, though,' she added, with a playful smile.

'Indeed.' Lydia summoned a giggle. It was a little higher than her usual pitch, but she was determined to turn the event into a harmless, flirtatious moment. She couldn't allow that it was more.

'Gosh, Beatrice will be devastated to have missed that excitement,' added Sarah. 'I wonder who he is.'

'I have no idea.'

'Officer rank.'

'Really?'

'Yes, a staff sergeant major. Didn't you notice the insignia? A non-commissioned officer, but an officer all the same.'

'Oh.'

'Well someone must know him.'

'I suppose.'

Sarah then confided, 'Not that Beatrice would stand a chance. Not really. I'm certain a man like that has his pick of beauties and fortunes. And Beatrice . . .' Sarah sighed, not cruel enough to finish the sentence. It was unnecessary anyhow: Lydia understood.

Lydia breathed in deeply. She tried to adjust her world, straighten it, because it was tilted, just a fraction, and she felt dazed and confused as a consequence. How strange he'd made her feel. Yes, he'd have his pick of women, and she was married. Happily so. She stretched and strained to regain a sense of reality.

'Let's take Bea a cake. She'll like that.'

Sarah beamed, always impressed by her friend's thoughtfulness. 'What a lovely idea. Shall we take the macaroon?'

'Yes. That's perfect.'

Perfect.

9

IT HAD BEEN a long day. Endless and drab. The trees were beaten by the wind. The sky was tin grey. Her nieces and nephews had not provided the respite that Beatrice had hoped they might. They had not shattered the monotony with delighted squeals or warm, enthusiastic cuddles. Instead they had squabbled and behaved badly. The two older boys had refused to permit little Jimmy to join them riding; her nieces had been prepared to allow him to tag along, but he'd been ungracious about it and lashed out, insisting he didn't want to be with the girls. He'd flung his wooden pull-along duck, which had caught Molly's kneecap, causing her to howl. Bea suspected the reaction was disproportionate to the actual injury, but her tears had been loud and fearful enough to bring Nanny running from the nursery. Nanny had thrown Beatrice a furious glare, effectively communicating her condemnation of Beatrice's inadequate mothering skills.

Why would she be any good at controlling the children? At mothering? She was not a mother. She probably never would be. Not a mother, not a wife. The thought was not a new one, but every time Bea encountered it, anguish and disappointment engulfed her like a wave.

As she wiped little Jimmy's nose and tears – because having caused his sister to cry, he too was now crying, although it wasn't clear whether he was bawling with frustration or shame – she wondered what Sarah and Lydia would be doing right that moment in London. She knew there was an appointment, but Sarah had

49

not been prepared to share any details; she was eternally discreet. A shard of irritation spiked inside Bea's gut. Why hadn't Lydia invited her to accompany them? She could jolly well do with a jaunt into London. It would be such fun. Her soul was weary with the view from the house. The relentless browns and greens of the fields held no charm for her. The bare, spindly trees with their gnarled branches pointing like pensioners' fingers into the melancholy sky were too familiar. She did not like to see the half-moon prints of her boot heels in the mud, tattooing her endless toing and froing into the earth. She felt tracked and trapped. Everything was despairingly well-known. She imagined her sister and her friend cosy in a café. Smoke and warmth oozing, so it was impossible to see clearly. The waitresses would be neat and efficient, able to call to mind the entire menu. Beatrice thought it must be jolly to be a waitress; to have a place to go, something to do, a uniform to wear. Not that she could ever consider it. Obviously not. Out of the question. What would people say?

Samuel had slept badly last night. She'd heard him cry out in his sleep, and then she'd heard Cecily run down the corridor, her slippers slapping on the floorboards indicating that she hadn't taken the time to put them on properly in her haste to dash to her husband's side. Beatrice knew better than to get up and offer help. Cecily always refused, and Samuel was frantic on these occasions, behaving as though he didn't recognise his little sister. Instead she'd put her pillow over her head and tried to drown out his screams, tried not to think of their root cause. As a consequence, today Cecily and Samuel had slept late, or whether they slept or not, they'd stayed in their rooms, unprepared to face the day; she and Nanny were trying to muddle through. It was always the same: on the rare occasions that Sarah was away from the house, Samuel was invariably more fretful. Did Sarah have some sort of calming influence? Beatrice knew that if this was the case, she should by no means resent it, and yet she did. It must be lovely to be needed in that way. In any way. Last summer Beatrice had spent a whole week in Hove with their aunt and uncle, but her brother had not called out once. She knew, because it was the first thing she'd asked on her return.

Bea, Jimmy, the girls and Nanny all trailed back into the house, sulky and silent except for Jimmy's helpless, tearful gasps that hadn't quite subsided. The weighty wooden door banged behind them; the stillness of the house oppressed her. She felt the heavy air squeeze her lungs, hamper her breathing. Suddenly she couldn't bear it. She knew she was not capable of smiling and chatting with her nieces and nephew. Momentarily she was out of resources and she needed to be alone. In her small room she could be who she was. Only there did she find any peace. Since the older nephews were now with the stable boy, Nanny could take the girls and Jimmy up to the nursery. They really weren't Bea's responsibility. Not absolutely. No one was.

Beatrice stumbled up the stairs and closed the door behind her. She leaned up against it and gulped the cold air of her room. There was no fire burning. She hadn't expected one. The maid would not think to heat her room at two in the afternoon. For once she didn't care about the chill. She felt apart, adrift, drowsy. She rejected the chair and did not pick up her novel; instead she climbed into bed and pulled the covers up over her head, hiding like a child. Depression seeped into every fibre and sinew of her body. She was deeply ashamed of what she was. A woman alone in the world without a man, so desperately available, so clearly superfluous. She felt coldly redundant and discarded; she felt it in the fabric of her tweed skirts, she smelt it in the air of her clean and functional bedroom, which would never be stained with the musky scent of lovemaking. She heard her lack of value in every word of her polite and regular conversations with her married friends as she asked after their husbands and their children, because of course she was duty-bound to enquire, to be relentlessly cheerful. But she was not cheerful. She was an aberration to the law of nature and the expectations of society. Not that one must allow self-pity; after all, she wasn't alone. There were a million women like her. But the vast number did little to soothe; instead, the volume of disappointed and broken hearts seemed threatening, almost horrifying. She imagined them, these lonely women, piled up in a huge heap; a scrapheap. It would tower.

It was not enough. This loaned life, in which she borrowed clothes, homes and children – it was not enough. But what more was there? Where was her life?

10

LYDIA MUCH PREFERRED the London house, sitting gracefully on the south side of Eaton Square, to Dartford Hall, which spread out over a sizeable chunk of Hampshire. She delighted in people and shops and therefore adored having vast quantities of both on her doorstep, although she told everyone that her overwhelming attraction to London was that she couldn't live without the galleries and theatres. It was fair to say she was fond of both, but largely her appreciation was for the splendid audiences that one found at such places, rather than the art itself; she liked to be shoulder to shoulder with others who were equally fashionable, excitable and impressionable. Besides, there was something about the symmetry, modernity and compact stoutness of the London home that appealed to her in a way that the sprawling, draughty country manor did not, and as she was not the one who had to worry about carrying coal up and down the four flights of stairs, she could see nothing inconvenient about it at all.

Technically, Eaton Square did not belong to Lydia and Lawrence yet. The property belonged to Lydia's in-laws, but the earl had generously offered the young people free rein, and Lydia had taken up the offer with enthusiasm. In the London home she tried to stamp a more informal approach on all proceedings. She had an open-house policy and warmly welcomed guests with a cocktail whenever they chose to drop by. She refused to adhere to enforced visiting hours, or rituals such as consuming copious amounts of strong tea and cucumber or pâté sandwiches just because it was four in the afternoon. She operated with a skeleton staff, completely happy not only to mix her own cocktails, but also to arrange the flowers for the drawing room; in London she did not expect the silver to be polished more than once a week. She had even tried to sit next to Lawrence at the dining table, rather than hold their positions at opposite ends, but Lawrence had said he found it disconcerting and preferred to look at her face on, rather than have to turn to his side.

Although usually a generous hostess, Lydia was relieved that Sarah had caught the train back to Seaton Manor and that no one had popped by, out of the blue, this evening. She had turned down three invitations to soirées, so nor were they expected anywhere. She had reasoned that if Dr Folstad had anything marvellous to convey, they might spend the night celebrating together, and if – as she had expected and dreaded the case would be – he had little or nothing new to say, she would not be able to muster a public face and instead would need to be cosseted by Lawrence and their home. Naturally, she still dressed for dinner. Lawrence expected such things, and the servants would be disturbed if she sat down to dinner in a day dress, but if she closed her eyes now she probably wouldn't be able to say if she was wearing teal or midnight blue. It didn't matter. She wasn't sure what was on the menu, although the housekeeper had checked it with her this morning; no doubt it would be delicious, but that didn't matter either. Less and less did.

The under butler served dinner and then melted into the wallpaper. His discretion was exemplary, and Lydia, considering herself to be quite alone with her husband, brought Lawrence up to date.

'So, in short, this doctor had nothing new to offer,' she finished with a heavy sigh.

'Did you expect him to have?' Lawrence heartily pushed the tines of his fork into his mouth and hungrily swallowed the bloody roast beef. Lydia, by contrast, had spent the duration of the meal unenthusiastically chasing her food around her plate.

'I'd hoped.'

Lawrence shot her a look which was a complicated mix of sympathy and frustration. Obviously he hoped for an heir too, very much so – hoped and prayed – but they had been married for eight years now. Eight years. One had to be realistic. Practical. Lydia wasn't getting any younger; he didn't really imagine their chance of producing an heir was at all robust now. It was unfortunate. Very much so but it was as it was, and there was no point in wasting energy wishing it was otherwise. He dearly wanted her to spend less time worrying and move towards accepting it. Once she did so, they could sort things out differently. They could travel abroad more often, perhaps spend more time with their numerous godchildren; they could even consider taking in a ward. People did accept such things and considerably worse. It wasn't very British to be maudlin or obtuse. It was so much better to be sanguine.

'What will we do?' she asked, dropping her knife and folk with a clatter and clasping her hands on her lap.

'We'll do without, I suppose,' he replied calmly. He regretted that he sounded brusquer than he wanted to appear – than he was, in fact – but he found it uncomfortable to talk about emotions or sex, and here she was hoping for a conversation about both, at the dinner table. It was awkward. Yes, he was sympathetic, and he fully understood that it was much harder for a woman to bear these things. Quite naturally she must blame herself; regret that she was in some way lacking and couldn't fulfil her role and duty, yet he wasn't a tyrant: he'd never once censored or charged her. She couldn't complain on that count.

'But I can't do without,' she murmured.

There had been a time when every word that dropped from Lydia's lips had enthralled Lawrence Chatfield. They had only met seven or eight times before they married, and so novelty had no doubt bound him as part of the attraction, but there was more than that. She was a beautiful creature: innocent as her sort of girl was expected to be, but not giddy or tiresome, rather quietly assured of her own ability to captivate; she was always just the right side of flirtatiously encouraging. He thought her self-possession came from being the youngest of four children. She had watched her three older sisters make solid marriages and therefore she was confident that with her beauty and charm she would do equally well. If not better.

He'd been besotted by her.

The jut of her chin gripped him; her small white hands, whether at play or rest, fascinated him, and he could have stared into her eyes for hours in a row. Every thought, observation or piece of small talk that she let drip from her plump red lips he drank up, like a man marooned on a desert island. Now, sometimes, he thought she sounded whiny. Occasionally, when he returned after a particularly tricky day at the Home Office, she would drone on about clothes, or company, or cocktail parties, and he would shut out the noise the way one shut out the buzz of an insect at a picnic. Needless to say, he loved her. Dearly. She was still a beautiful woman, and he was very proud of her. Considering they had nearly a decade as a couple chalked up, there was enormous genuine affection between them, but he couldn't sincerely say he remained besotted; that would be ridiculous. Such notions were erased with marriage. Indeed, in a good marriage, where intimacy flourished, fanatical obsession must flounder. And since he was no longer besotted, he simply couldn't find the energy to treat her with kid gloves all the time.

'Darling, you might just have to. Can you pass the salt?' He leaned forward, towards his wife, suddenly aware of the under butler. Some people thought the servants were deaf and blind, but Lawrence knew better; he was well aware that anything he said would be reported in the downstairs quarters within the hour. 'I believe Cook has been a little light with the seasoning, don't you?' He stage-whispered his criticism; despite his efforts to shield the staff, there was six foot of table separating him from his wife. Lydia picked up her fork again but didn't comment. He continued to rally; he thought it best to move the conversation on. 'I'm sure there's a party, isn't there? At the weekend?' There was always a party. 'Something to look forward to?'

'Not this weekend. I've already turned down everything we were invited to.'

'Why?'

'I don't know. I was rather . . .' She couldn't finish the sentence. *Sick of it all* sounded too harsh. Lawrence looked confused, concerned. 'Tired,' she offered. Lawrence saw her as a delicate thing, although she was not in the least. She was slim and short, but she thought of herself as strong. 'Ava has invited us to her father's place in Herefordshire the weekend after this,' she admitted grudgingly.

'Well, there you go. That's something.'

'Yes, it's something.' But not enough, and nowhere near anything. Lydia listened to her husband's cutlery scraping against the fine bone china and tried to block out the sound of him chewing the beef and enthusiastically licking his lips. Generally he was a discreet eater, famous for his manners and decorum, but today every bite seemed amplified and dreadful. She scrambled around in her mind for something to talk about. She could tell Lawrence Sarah's news, although there was nothing substantial, just chatter about the children and hats; he wouldn't be interested. She could mention that Sarah had caught the five o'clock train back to the country and couldn't be persuaded to either make use of their driver or stay the night, but he might be irritated and believe that Lydia hadn't tried hard enough to persuade her; he was very protective of Sarah and all their widowed friends. 'I met a handsome man today,' she blurted.

Lawrence glanced at her. 'Someone for Ava?'

'No, I don't think so.'

'Beatrice?'

'No.'

'Oh. For who, then?'

'Not for anyone.' Lydia could not imagine the perfect man with anyone in reality. He was a vision. Separate. Difficult to categorise. Ava was physically his equivalent, but Ava was never really interested in finding anyone permanent. And if she was? Well. The thought of the perfect man and Ava together sent a spear of panic through Lydia's body. It wouldn't work. She was comforted by the thought that if Ava ever deigned to marry, she would marry up. A duke or an earl at the very least.

'Then why mention him?'

Why indeed? Lydia was regretting that she had. But he was there. In her mind. She'd found an inexplicable need to take him out of her head and make him more substantial, more real, by mentioning him in the oak-panelled dining room. Anything, anything to block out the sound of mastication, she told herself.

57

'He was striking.'

'Where did you meet him?'

'In Lyons.'

'The coffee house?'

'Yes.'

'Who introduced you?'

'No one. He approached me.' Lydia felt compelled to add, 'Us. Sarah was with me.'

'You can't talk to total strangers in coffee houses, Lydia. It's not proper.' Lawrence laughed indulgently. He could not imagine a world where his wife might be genuinely attracted to another man. She was not that sort. Oh yes, as a girl she had been jolly, some might say flirtatious, but as a wife she'd always been entirely decent and correct. He was well aware that not every wife in their set was as faithful and single-minded, but they were both repelled by the untidiness of adultery. Besides, there was not a hint of the flirtatious about her now. Not since this whole baby business. She wasn't the jolly type either.

'Do you think we are being punished?' Lydia rushed the idea on to the table with a scared breath.

'Punished? What an extraordinary thing to say. Why would we be punished?' Lawrence replied in a considerably more hearty voice than the one he'd used when commenting on Cook's seasoning.

Lydia's response stuck in her throat like a splinter from a chicken bone. She could not swallow the words but it was agony to cough them up. She'd played with this thought late at night as she lay awake, lonely in a huge house full of people; alone because they could all find sleep and yet it eluded her. She'd let the thought become a theory as she sat in countless austere doctors' waiting rooms, suffocating under the gloom of bad news delivered between the panelled walls, and then she'd let the theory become the only possible explanation when each month she bled rather than bred. 'I think that perhaps God is punishing us for not doing . . .' She faltered. Could she say 'your'? No, she could not. 'For not doing our duty.'

'What do you mean?' It was clear to Lydia that Lawrence

understood her perfectly, because in an instant his ruddy complexion vanished and he became ashen. He glanced at the under butler, who kept his gaze locked on his shoes, despite the fact that he was trained to keep his eyes ahead, his chin up at all times. 'What can you mean?' Lawrence repeated, dazed. Then he waved his hand to silence her, because he realised there was a very real danger that she might tell him exactly what she meant.

He'd done his duty! He'd served. Not on the front line, perhaps. His was a strategic position. It was important work.

'There won't be anyone to pass Dartford Hall on to, or Clarendale or the title, anyway,' Lydia pointed out. The *anyway* was the give-away. The insult. The abuse. Was she saying he might as well have died at the Front because his line was going to end with them? Was that all he meant to her?

She feared she might cry. She hoped not. Lawrence had never been the sort of man who melted at the sight of a woman's tears; he always became discomforted and inept when there was any show of sentiment.

'It will all go to my cousin William, as you well know, Lydia,' he snapped.

'Yes, and he was at the Front for several months and was deco-rated,' added Lydia thoughtlessly.

'Your point?'

She did not hesitate. 'I suppose there's some justice in that, at least.'

Lawrence glowered at his wife. He silently counted to five, then ten. 'Lydia, you are not thinking clearly. You are in danger of being hysterical. I think today has been a strain. I suggest you have an early night.' His staccato sentences betrayed the fact that he was finding it an effort to maintain his composure.

Lydia met her husband's eyes and took a deep breath. 'You are probably right, Lawrence. I shall go to bed at once.' She pushed back her chair; he stood up too, through habit.

'I'll have Dickenson sent up to you.'

'How thoughtful. Good night.'

'Good night, Lydia.'

11

S ARAH WAS AMBIVALENT about Ava's invitation to visit her father's estate. Her initial response was to feel flattered to have been invited at all. Ava wasn't reliably polite the way the rest of their set were; she had no scruples about snubbing those she considered tedious, whereas others would invite the right families through good form or habit. Sarah knew that Ava believed that she and Bea were dull, and so she was never absolutely sure they'd be invited to her luncheons and soirées, let alone included on a weekend party; even Lydia's influence was not guaranteed over the headstrong Ava. However, swiftly following the feelings of relief at being included, Sarah was plunged into a dilemma as to whether or not she wanted to accept.

Sarah had little genuine personal interest in such parties nowadays; she'd actually prefer to stay at home with her children and her brother. She had no ambition to marry again, to indulge in social climbing or even to master a new hobby, which was the acknowledged *raison d'être* for these get-togethers. She accepted that a variation in company could be entertaining, but she was also adult enough to know that, equally, it could be disturbing; she'd been to numerous weekend parties where she was patronised, scandalised or simply irritated by complete strangers in whose company she was forced to dwell for forty-eight hours or more.

Sarah was thirty-one but felt older. She had ceased to be young the moment Arthur signed up to defend King and Country. The weight of fear and dread had engulfed her for ten months, leaving her skittish and unreasonable. She found it impossible to care about the things other young women did, such as going to the cinema or learning the latest dance craze; all she cared about was him coming home. Safely. When he didn't return, the fear and dread was replaced by the more cumbersome weight of grief and responsibility, which sapped all her energy and any remaining vitality. After the telegram, the world was simply never as colourful again. Besides the everyday changes that his death brought – financial insecurity, the terror of bringing up two children without a father and the social demotion of being a widow rather than a wife – her world turned grey because she missed him. She missed him so much. When she first read the telegram her heart heaved. It felt as though it had jumped right out of her body and escaped. She was sure it was severed from her because she felt nothing but shock. Horror. But then it returned. She knew it had come back because it hurt so much. There was an actual excruciating pain in her chest for days, weeks. She felt that someone was squeezing the life out of her by clasping her heart tightly. The grip was agony. She would die too. She'd loved him so! He had been a handsome, honest, funny man. He'd made her feel safe and valued. She missed his conversation, his jokes, his arms, the smell of his pipe. She missed the weight of him in bed at night.

Initially everyone respected her right to shun company, but after two or three months, well-meaning visitors returned and told her she had to buck up and carry on, 'At least for the sake of the children'. There was too much general grief to allow anyone the luxury of personal wallowing. Eminently sensible Sarah knew this advice was wise and fair, although it didn't make it any more palatable. She did buck up: she forced herself to style her hair in the mornings (although she still kept it long and wore it in a bun, clasped at the back of her neck, as she'd worn it when Arthur went to war; she didn't bother to keep up with fashions), she took the children on outings, escorted her sister to tea dances and, when Samuel came back injured, she spent a lot of her time helping Cecily with all her responsibilities. Sarah lived a perfectly useful life. She found pleasure in small things, such as knitting pullovers for the children; the repetitive click-clack of the needles soothed her through the dark evenings. She liked to take long walks in the country with the children; if there was a wind, they'd fly kites; if the air was still, they'd play with a ball. She went to church regularly and tried not to ask why too often. The one thing she could not return to was gardening. She no longer enjoyed the feel of mud beneath her fingers; the earthy smells distressed her, the wriggling worms revolted her, and once, the stench of rotting foliage made her physically vomit. She made jam and visited elderly neighbours, she read poetry. Undoubtedly she was old before her time.

Sarah's apathy towards outings such as this weekend party at Sir Peter Pondson-Callow's country estate was because she firmly believed that she had already had her fill of life. She did not hope or expect to meet an equal to Arthur; everyone else was simply less. It was hard to eternally deal with less. She was prepared to creep into middle age, inaudibly and carefully. She did not want to cause anyone too much trouble and she very much hoped she could be useful to those around her. Being useful was a poor relation to being loved, yet it was some sort of solace for the broken-hearted.

However, Beatrice's case was quite dissimilar. Beatrice was twenty-six. She had never been kissed. It was easy to forget her relative youth because her density somehow negated any thoughts of girlishness; her surprising height and solid breadth was equated with maturity at best, masculinity at worst. Beatrice's comely body stayed under wraps; woollen stockings and flannel petticoats had not fallen from her repertoire. It was miserable that she was still totally unaware how it felt to have someone's lips crush down on hers, or to experience the exquisite and erotic strangeness of another tongue inside her mouth. The thought sent shards of regret through Sarah's body. She longed for her sister, at least once, to feel what Sarah had felt in Arthur's arms. She was a realistic woman and did not think that finding a husband, or even a regular lover, was a foregone conclusion for Beatrice; far from it. Bea's age, weight and financial situation all conspired against her now there was such a scarcity of men; in all probability she was destined to be an old maid. Sarah, though, was a determined and hopeful woman and refused to deal in probability; she could not yet quite give up on the *possibility* that there might be a man out there who would do just perfectly for her sister. A man who would appreciate her quiet, shy manner and warm, open heart. Perhaps an older man. A widower who was looking for a wife to help with an established family; the sort of man who might not be averse to adding another baby to the nursery. Or maybe she would find a wounded soldier. There were so many men who had naturally lost their confidence and *joie de vivre* when they lost an arm or leg in France. Beatrice might turn out to be a patient nurse; if those chaps would only give her a chance, she might yet find some warmth and companionship. Sarah knew that widowers and veterans were not likely to be found in their own drawing room, or at least the ones that did visit had already been considered and found unwilling or unsuitable, so it was essential that Beatrice kept circulating. Bea had once commented that she felt like one of those ballerinas in a musical box – the ones that spun on and on in a desperate effort to entertain – but Sarah had told her that nothing was to be gained by becoming fanciful. Bea had to continue to meet new people. They must not give up. Sarah, as her big sister, felt compelled to attend the weekend party, because whilst she was not quite a chaperone, she was at least emotional backing.

Sarah realised that Beatrice's excitement at accepting the invitation was no doubt also marred by a level of despair about whether her wardrobe, figure and conversation were adequate for such an occasion, not to mention her concern over how much to tip the servants on a country estate. She knew that Beatrice tried not to indulge in self-doubt, but, like every woman, she was more aware than anyone of her own personal disadvantages and drawbacks. Sarah often privately thought it a huge pity that Beatrice had never managed to go up to Oxford. When their father had been alive there had been talk that such a thing was a possibility; although they couldn't risk educating her before she joined the marriage market, it had been a recognised alternative if her season didn't prove fruitful. But their father had died when Beatrice was seventeen and the family fortune, such as it was, passed to Samuel. No one could have expected him to put a younger sister through university; he had his own family to provide for. All the same, Sarah was certain that Bea might have done well there. She was by no means slow. Her current conversation was only limited by lack of experiences; reading the newspapers regularly wasn't enough. Still, there was no point in dwelling.

Sarah's assumption that Bea was riddled with weight and fashion insecurities proved to be correct. In a desperate attempt to quickly reduce herself, Beatrice had eaten nothing other than grapefruit for three days now. Yet an honest look in the mirror forced her to admit that nonetheless she still had wobbly flesh on her arms and belly, her thighs remained puckered and her bottom continued to sag. In addition, she admitted to terrible acidic cramps in her stomach, and her nephews' vulgar comments made it impossible to ignore her embarrassing wind.

'What were you thinking?' Sarah asked.

'I thought perhaps if I lost weight I might be able to squeeze into something of Cecily's.'

'The skirts would be daringly short, wouldn't they?' commented Sarah. Bea towered several inches above any other woman they knew.

In the end, Bea borrowed a sequinned evening cap and an adorable bag, decorated with fine wool petit point. Such joy and gaiety in the brilliant design of two mythological birds! The bag was lined with aqua silk and inside there were two pockets that held a matching change purse and silk-backed mirror. The bag closed with a jewelled *cloisonné* clasp and had a linked chain handle. Beatrice commented that she hoped it was dazzling enough to draw attention from her old and endlessly altered dresses. She fingered the bag repeatedly, as though she was playing with a lover's hair. Sarah found it hard to believe that she too used to feel such ecstatic entrancement about bags, dresses, dances and shoes. She had persuaded her sister to be bold and splash out on a pair of new evening shoes. 'Shoddy shoes are a complete giveaway.' Inspired by Lydia's terrific fresh hairstyle, Bea had also chosen to take the plunge and have her own chopped. The effect was modern, but not flattering. Her wiry, fiery locks sprung up off her head, and it was almost impossible to get a cloche to sit straight on the springy coils.

Sarah's other concern on Bea's behalf was that Ava might not be a perfect hostess. She didn't doubt there would be hot-water bottles in plush covers, writing paper, stamps and port aplenty; she simply feared that in her own home Ava would see no reason to curb her caustic tongue. All of Ava's friends were so ornamental, with the notable exception of Bea. Bea would need to gird her heart against the possibility of countless sly digs and jokes at her expense. Sarah couldn't understand why a woman such as Ava, who had it all – beauty, brains, extreme wealth – would be so cruel as to constantly highlight all that Beatrice lacked. It was pitiless.

Despite her reservations, Sarah was relieved that the weekend got off to a good start. They were a party of thirteen the first night, eight women and five men, including Ava's parents. The bias in numbers towards the women was notable, but not, Sarah thought, insurmountable. The evening was cheerful and natural; they'd rolled up the rugs, and whilst Sarah had made her excuses before midnight, some, including Bea, had danced until three. By Saturday afternoon Sarah began to relax as she discovered that, rather than degenerating into home manners and being rude or transparent in her impatience with Bea, Ava had upped her game and become considerably more charming and delightful. Sarah suspected that Ava had seen the advantages of surrounding her father with plain or disinterested girls; pretty ones brought with them the shadowy threat of dangerous scandals. Ava had identified a use for Bea and Sarah: they were from a steady, old family and they lent respectability to the Pondson-Callows' home, something that Sarah knew Ava felt it lacked; they cushioned rumour. Whatever the motivation for her charm, Sarah was grateful for it. Ava was prepared to more than fulfil her responsibility as a hostess; besides serving lavish treats that both sisters enjoyed particularly, she had invited three single chaps to stay, none of whom Beatrice had met before. Bea would have to be made of stone not to be excited.

Lydia, Ava, Beatrice and Sarah sat together in the drawing room. Sarah thought it one of the most beautiful rooms she'd ever been in. In many ways it resembled a number of other country manor drawing rooms she'd visited. Sir Peter and Lady Pondson-Callow had bought this place just a year after the war, but they'd worked swiftly to give the impression it had been in their family for generations. Like many of Britain's country houses, it had been commandeered during the war and used as a convalescent home; noble and patriotic, no doubt, but disastrous for the state of the grounds and the interior. Then the family who owned it had been hit by towering death duties and had had neither the will nor the means to restore it to its former glory. Rumour had it that Sir Peter had picked it up for a song. Now there were Romneys and Raeburns aplenty hung on the walls, but the portraits were of strangers, not ancestors. On the whole it was conventional and correct, yet it was somehow *more* than similar rooms in other people's country houses: more resplendent, more inviting. Some might be snobby and point out that the 'moreness' betrayed Sir Peter and Lady Pondson-Callow's newness, but Sarah was generous. She didn't resent their propensity to be ostentatious; she simply wallowed in the lavishness on offer. The hearth rug was a little thicker than usual, there were perhaps one too many Fabergé cigarette boxes, and the Cartier mantelpiece clock was a little larger than necessary, but the resplendent flower arrangements and generous number of small silver dishes offering up chocolates suggested a genuine desire to welcome. The plump silk cushions, the oyster shot-silk drapes and golden gilded chairs showcased the family's extreme taste.

Ava's father was engaged in taking Lady Jennings and one of the highly valued single young men, Harry Fine, on a tour around the house. Two other ladies and Ava's mother had retired to their rooms to sleep off the excesses of the previous night. The remaining men were in the games room playing billiards. Here in the drawing room the four friends could enjoy each other's company without being disturbed. There was an enormous fire thriving in the hearth, and even though lunch had barely been cleared, the maids had brought in plates of almonds and segmented pineapple. The women lay about languidly, idly chattering and nibbling; everyone was glad that they had taken a walk this morning and were not expected to brave the bleak, chilly January afternoon. Quite naturally, as they were alone and shrouded by their long-standing intimacy, they talked about the other guests, specifically the single men.

The previous night Sarah had established that Mr Lytton published books. He managed to do so because he was the godson of a peer who, following the Great War, no longer had a son to nurture or support and had therefore taken an interest in Lytton. He introduced him to the right sort of people and, whilst to date there had been little in the way of monetary favours granted, there was always the hope that the peer might settle a private income on him any day now. Sarah had been surprised that Ava had bothered with a working man until she ascertained that Mr Lytton knew a great many bohemian artists and writers, which meant he was always first to offer a mischievous anecdote, and this passed as brilliant conversation. He'd made Ava laugh at least four times last night; a loud and raucous laugh. So few people were able to claim the same thing; no doubt that was how he'd earned his place. He'd arrived on Friday afternoon by train and walked the three miles from the station rather than taking a cab or calling the house to request a car, and had continued to behave strangely since. He'd pronounced himself a vegetarian, had refused to retire with the gentlemen after dinner, saying he preferred women and gossip to men and whisky, and had not brought tweeds with him, but set off on the walk this morning in a dark suit and white shirt, a get-up more suitable for the office than a ramble. Ava, with her sharp eye for quality, must have quickly appraised the suit and, although she could not have failed to notice that it was off-the-peg rather than Savile Row, all she said on the subject was, 'I do like your tie, Mr Lytton. How would you describe that colour? Saffron?'

'Mustard,' he'd replied unapologetically.

'Mustard. Exactly. So interesting.' It was one of Ava's peculiarities that, whilst she could be harsh and brutally condemning if she was not on one's side, if she took to one, one could do no wrong. She liked her guests to be somewhat quirky; it eased the ever-present threat of tedium that she struggled with. Besides, as Lawrence had bowed out of the weekend visit, Ava desperately needed men to make up the numbers at dinner and so she could not afford to be rude. Lytton was the sort who would have no conscience about going home and leaving them in the lurch if offended. He had been placed next to Beatrice at dinner last night, which Sarah had thought helpful. He spoke with a heavy Scottish accent and, although it made him difficult to understand, especially after he'd had too much wine, the fact that he was largely incomprehensible was forgivable because all the women agreed he sounded manly, almost exotic.

'I would go so far as to pronounce him sexy,' commented Ava, now they were alone picking over the bones of the activity of the night before. 'I think he might be good in bed.' The other women inwardly gasped but didn't interrupt. 'It goes without saying that one would have to wear a blindfold; his face reminds me of a soundly slapped bottom. Still, I don't mind a blindfold in the bedroom,' she added slyly. 'Maybe I could use his *interesting* tie.'

'Ava!' Sarah and Bea cried in unison. It was impossible not to be shocked.

'Ava, you're a horror,' murmured Lydia, flashing an indulgent grin that she wasn't quite able to suppress.

'What do *you* make of Mr Lytton, Beatrice?' Ava asked.

'He's uncompromising, original,' Beatrice said with a shy smile. Sarah could see from Bea's flushed cheeks that her sister was thrilled to be part of this discussion about men. No doubt she felt flattered that Ava was hinting that her guests were viable suitors, as though she was the sort of girl who might catch a chap. It made her daring and giggly.

'Yes, isn't he,' agreed Ava.

'But I don't think he found me at all so.'

Ava sighed in a way that must have punctured Bea's euphoria. If she had been hoping for some token disagreement, none came; there was something about the sigh that suddenly and certainly discounted Bea from having romantic aspirations – however tentative – towards Mr Lytton. Sarah could almost see the cogs of Ava's mind turn as she recalculated and decided that she'd been ambitious in considering

Lytton for Beatrice. Maybe she'd thought that his lack of birth and height, his pale skin with its sprinkling of freckles and small snub nose might all add up to mean that he was accessible. Perhaps she had reasoned that as a bohemian he might not demand aesthetic perfection in a wife, but since Sarah had noticed that his hungry, alert eyes had drilled into Ava and Lydia at dinner last night, but glazed over when Bea enquired what type of books he published, Ava could not have missed the same. Mr Lytton's aspirations were higher than Beatrice Polwarth. The two of them were not even. He was allowed to be ordinary-looking, even unattractive, strapped for cash and inappropriately dressed because he was a he.

'Harry Fine is very affable. Attractive too,' commented Lydia, moving the conversation on.

'I think Harry Fine is already completely in love with Lady Jennings, don't you?' commented Bea excitedly. She was generous enough to celebrate other women's good fortune.

'Yes. Completely in love. After all, she is an heiress to an absolute fortune,' added Ava.

'I think he's sincere,' insisted Sarah.

Ava raised an eyebrow sceptically. 'He sincerely needs the money, that much is true. Terrible gambling debts, I hear.'

'In that case, you're very wise to let him fly, Bea,' added Lydia, kindly implying that Bea might have stood a chance in influencing the man's decision.

'Anyway, I think Harry is a little dull, to be frank,' added Sarah.

'But Mr Oaksley is interesting.' Once again Bea smiled shyly. 'Would you say handsome?'

'Yes,' said Sarah and Lydia.

'Well, he was lucky. There's hardly any scarring on his face, although I can't vouch for the body,' added Ava. Sarah was relieved that she couldn't. Really, no man was safe from the woman. 'Thinking about it, Arnie Oaksley is your best bet,' finished Ava enthusiastically. 'Terrible thing, losing one's sight. Awful, but certainly he's the best bet for Bea.'

'Because he's blind?' Sarah could not keep the indignation out of her voice.

'Because he plays the piano and likes to go for country walks. They are *simpatico*,' replied Ava, the very picture of innocence. 'I do think it is rum of the chaps to expect him to play a billiards game. I hope there isn't a wager. It can't be a fair match.' She beamed mischievously.

Sarah shuffled uncomfortably; she'd exposed her insecurities and Bea's deficiencies by thinking the worst of Ava, and she was now not sure if thinking the worst was justified or not. Ava had a subtle way of making one feel conspicuous and wrong.

'I can't imagine he's noticed me,' Bea said coyly.

Again, if she'd hoped that the other women would protest and insist that he couldn't have failed to have fallen for her, lock, stock and barrel, then she was disappointed. Instead she was greeted with the honesty of old friends and family.

'Well, it's your responsibility to get noticed in that particular way. You need to show him that romance is a possibility. That you are open to it,' declared Lydia.

Bea blushed, but was determined. 'Any clue as to how I should do that exactly? Should I run into the billiards room and throw myself on the table yelling, "Take me, take me"?'

The other women laughed, but not cruelly. 'Well at least go and ask if he wants to take a stroll before tea,' suggested Sarah.

'You could walk round the gardens,' added Lydia.

'Bit bloody miserable at this time of the year,' pointed out Ava, who never had to inconvenience herself by going out into the cold in order to seduce a man.

'But the season means you'll need to cling to one another for body heat,' encouraged Lydia.

After a little more cajoling, Beatrice agreed to go and find Mr Oaksley. Sarah accompanied her to the games room, because no one could expect her to make that sort of entrance solo.

12

LEFT ALONE, AVA and Lydia fell silent. They were tight friends, and generally had more than enough to say to one another, but Lydia had been distracted since she'd arrived and was not as chatty as usual. Most of the guests assumed she was feeling the lack of her husband; Ava wasn't so sure. After some moments listening to the fire crack and pop, Ava stood, yawned, stretched like a cat and ambled to the gramophone.

'I have Marion Harris's latest tune. Would you like to hear it?'

'Is it as sad as all her others?'

'Yes.'

'Then no, thank you.'

'You're not a fan of the blues, are you?' asked Ava, as she pulled long and hard on her cigarette, held in an ostentatious opera-length silver holder. Ava had caught on to the musical movement when she visited the States last year, and was following its increased popularity with avid interest.

'It's not for people like us, is it?'

'Isn't it?'

'I don't understand that relentless misery.'

'Don't you?'

'No. How could I? How could you?'

Ava shrugged and asked, 'Some jazz, then?'

Lydia wasn't sure if she understood jazz music any more than she understood blues. She found the big swinging bands unpredictable, almost risky, but the tunes did at least perk her up rather than drag her down. 'If you like.'

'I do rather. Music is a stimulating jab into exhausted, careworn souls. I find that jazz stirs our uncertain and stumbling morale.' Ava wound up the gramophone and carefully placed the weighty disc on the turntable. She eased the needle into position as though she was lowering a sleeping baby into a crib. She was fascinating to watch, as she did everything with such deliberate precision and elegance. The perky trombones and sensuous saxophones blared into the room; she danced alone on the Persian rug for a minute or two. Whereas others might self-consciously shuffle, Ava gave herself entirely to the moves. She never cared if she was alone, observed by adoring crowds of hundreds or scrutinised by just one person; she was always herself, it was the secret to her success. She lifted her legs and wiggled her hips to the rapid, assertive rhythms.

'What do you make of Beatrice's new crop?'

'Unfortunate.'

'Yes, I imagine the effect she hoped to achieve was glorious; the effect she did achieve is monstrous. Still, there's something endearing about her misguided attempts to be glamorous. If I were her, I'd settle into being plain. I'd embrace it. Become an archaeologist; go on a dig in Egypt.'

'Oh, Ava, you couldn't imagine what it must be like to be Bea. For one thing, how would she fund a dig in Egypt? She can't afford that.'

'Really?' Ava looked surprised, as though it was the first time she'd considered Bea's financial situation.

'Really.'

Lydia thought she might jump up and learn the new step when Ava commented, 'Sarah told me you met a dashing officer in a café last week.' She managed to disparage the place of introduction, just as Lawrence had, by a slight inflection in her voice and the fact that she made her eyes widen a fraction, suggesting disbelief.

Lydia stood and walked to the fire; rather than join in the dancing, she feigned warming her hands in order to buy a few moments to gather her thoughts. She'd been expecting and dreading that Ava

72

might want to talk about her meeting the beautiful officer. She'd known that Sarah would have mentioned the incident; they were all starved of news, and besides, he was notable. She had thought of him often since they met. Frequently. Constantly. It was oddly important to her that the first time she spoke of him to Ava she got it right.

Eventually she said, 'I'm not sure dashing is the right adjective to describe him.'

'Really?'

'Dashing is so clichéd. So used. It suggests a frantic energy and fashionable charm that wasn't true of him. There was nothing practised or urbane about him.'

Ava stood still, although the band played on. She studied her friend carefully. Lydia still had her back to the room; now she was showing undue interest in the ornamental Chinese mudman that Charlie Harrington had given Ava at Christmas. The elder sage was holding a peach, the symbol of immortality; Charlie had bought it thinking the Chinese salesman had said the fruit was a symbol of immorality, therefore the perfect gift for Ava. An amusing enough joke, Ava thought, though she decided not to share it right now, but to continue pursuing the more interesting topic of the mystery officer. She perched on the edge of a chair, looked past her friend and into the mirror that hung above the mantel and asked, 'Then how would you describe him?'

'He was . . .' Lydia scrabbled around her mind, desperate to find a word other than 'perfect' that might describe the man. She wanted to explain that he had struck her as the embodiment of all that was magnificent and masculine, forceful and beautiful. How could she explain that she'd instantly, perplexingly, been frightened and delighted by him? She'd thought of him since. At night. When she bathed. When she dressed.

Or undressed.

The fact that she found him unforgettable horrified her. In the end, she said what was most true and least exposing. 'He was different.'

'How different? Good different or bad different?'

'Oh, most definitely good different.'

'I see. What's his name?'

'I don't know.'

'Pity. You could have invited him here to dinner.'

'How many are we tonight?' Lydia took this opportunity to turn back to face her friend and to redirect the conversation. She couldn't do the former without the shield of the latter.

'We're thirty-nine, but, as ever, the balance is wrong. Far too many women.'

'I'm so sorry that Lawrence has stood you up.'

'Why didn't he come?'

'Officially, he has a paper to finish for the PM for Monday. Truthfully, we're cross with one another. I mean, he does have a paper, but he could have done it here. You know. He has done so on many an occasion.'

'I see. Do you want to talk about it?'

Lydia shook her head mournfully. Ava was relieved; she believed they'd said all there was to say about the baby business. 'Well, we shall manage. There are twenty-two women and seventeen men. It could be worse. But really, Lydia, when will you learn? If you meet a suave sort, you must get a card. Was he interesting?'

'We hardly spoke, but yes, I think so.'

'Interesting and pretty: what a shame you let him slip. I could do with someone new to look at. Besides, he might do for Beatrice.'

Lydia watched Ava's hard, flat body shake a little with merriment. She couldn't stand it, but her indignation was not on Bea's behalf. She couldn't tolerate the idea of Ava laughing about the officer, or setting him up with anyone. As disloyal and diabolical as the thought was, she felt he was degraded by being linked with Bea. She could not endure it.

'No, not Beatrice,' she spat. She turned again to watch the flames in the fire soaring and diving; she must not expose her indignation.

'No?'

'No. He's not her type.'

'Darling, that can't be possible. You know Beatrice considers grandpapas and the wounded. If you find this chap handsome and amusing, then *surely* Beatrice will.'

'I don't think so.'

'Then who were you thinking of? He has to go to someone. He's a spare man. It's your duty to introduce him to some gal.'

'I'm not sure,' Lydia stuttered.

Ava had the answer she wanted. She instinctually understood everything about such things. Lydia did not want to share him. She did not want to give him up. 'So how are we going to find him? This mystery man of yours? If he's so divine, surely someone ought to know him. I ought to have slept with him.'

Lydia tried not to look hurt. 'You're awful.'

'I must find him, mustn't I?' Ava stood up and nonchalantly walked towards her friend. They gazed at one another's reflection in the mirror. Eye to eye, they both understood the moment; it was the one where Lydia could let it go. Or she could push on. She chose to push.

'Yes, do find him. But . . .'

'But what?'

'But don't sleep with him, Ava. Don't take him.'

'You said he was divine.'

'He is.'

'Then why wouldn't I?'

Lydia turned and grasped her friend's hand. It was silky smooth and small like a child's. She would not look at Ava, but she knew that Ava had already seen all there was to see. 'Gosh, it's silly, but I find I've developed rather a thing for him myself.'

'A thing? How is that possible? You're Lydia, you don't do *things*. You leave that sort of mess to the rest of us.'

'I'm not going to do anything at all. I have no intention . . . Only I can't quite bring myself to think about *you* doing it.'

'I see.'

Both women fell silent. Lydia abandoned all show of dignity and pushed on, desperate for a pledge, 'So you'll leave him be?'

'I will.'

She sighed, relieved. She firmly believed that if Ava wanted a man, she could have him, and Ava would want the perfect man if she saw him; how could she not? Lydia had had to put the barrier in the way. Her request was irrational, revealing and ignoble, but she could not stop herself. For the first time in her life, she felt the vines of jealousy creep through her body. Ava was single and free to pursue; Lydia was not. She shook her head, confused. 'We may never find him, and he may be married, of course, in which case this entire conversation is irrelevant,' she blustered, trying to erase the tension that choked the room.

'Why would you think that? Half my lovers have been married. They are the very best sort. So discreet and practised and grateful.'

'You say the most terrible things.'

Ava smiled unhurriedly. 'Yes, darling, I do. That's what separates me from the pack. Everybody else simply thinks them.'

13

LYDIA, SARAH AND Beatrice stood together in the crowded drawing room, waiting with varied levels of patience and animation as the extra guests arrived for dinner. Ava, as the hostess, had to circulate. She moved through the throng, greeting and delighting. Her many attributes sharpened in front of their eyes. Her beauty ripened, her conversation sparkled, and without exerting any real effort she became everyone's focal point. She saturated the space around her with an aura of rare magnificence; to many she seemed more exquisitely regal than even Her Highness Princess Mary. Ava progressed at an unhurried pace, the dignity of which contrasted with the frenetic energy that surrounded her, as her guests eagerly tried to catch and hold her attention. Artfully, she appeared to scarcely see those clamouring for her notice, which encouraged their desperation. Then, when they seemed to be on the brink of collapsing with frustration and despair that she'd never turn their way, she would bestow a smile that singled them out in time and space, convincing each and every person that he or she was her particular and absolute favourite. As she passed by her best friends, she whispered into Bea's ear, 'Have you seen Lady Anna Renwick is wearing teal evening gloves?'

'Not white?' asked Bea.

'No.'

'Or black?'

'Are you deaf? I said teal.'

'Well I never.'

'No, darling, *you* would never,' commented Ava, and melted back into the crowd, leaving Beatrice unsure about her view on teal glove wearing.

'Teal gloves, how exciting,' commented Bea, avoiding making a gaffe by committing herself one way or the other to the effect and appropriateness of the fashion; exciting could be a good or a bad thing.

Lydia sighed at her life; a life where coloured evening gloves defined excitement. She had forced herself to be polite to the three or four people who'd approached her in the last half-hour, even though she had found them predictable in their conversations and concerns. The women had complimented her on her dress – gold velvet decorated with a substantial amount of intricate jet beading; she'd agreed it was divine. The men had asked after Lawrence, commenting that it was a shame he couldn't join the party and sharing their opinions that he was, perhaps, rather *too* conscientious, because everyone knew what all work and no play led to. A dull boy. Lydia nodded and shook her head when appropriate; she smiled gently, but did not let loose her full beam. She found she was not required to actually say much, because these old duffers were quite content carrying on the conversation without her active participation. She too wished Lawrence was here with her. She was used to having him by her side. He padded her out. The evening afforded her a brief insight into the lives of Sarah and Beatrice. Not Ava's life, because whilst Ava was technically single, she never required or requested any padding. She was substantial enough.

Lawrence and Lydia very infrequently quarrelled; if a difference arose, they chose instead to be cool and silent with one another until their anger subsided. After their rare disagreements Lawrence often congratulated her on her good sense and conduct. He was naturally peaceable and, whilst Lydia was considerably more fiery by instinct, she had learned to curb any hint of ardent fury or zeal. Girls of her sort were taught by their mothers that angry, emotional scenes were unattractive and led to premature wrinkles; happy faces all round were infinitely preferable, significantly more flattering. But this recent tension was darker and deeper than anything that had gone before in their marriage. The things that had been said at last week's dinner polluted and stained the atmosphere in their smart London home. She had shared with him her greatest dread, not out of malice, but because she didn't know who else to voice it to. She had held the cruel thought tight to her for years now; it had bubbled like a cancerous growth in her head, malignant and stubborn. On Thursday it had erupted, her private menace spilling out across the napkins and glassware. She wasn't sure why, but she hadn't been able to curb her desperation a moment longer. Not a moment. So there was no chance of her remaining silent for a lifetime. She'd hoped her husband would reassure her, explain things to her; maybe he would show her a way of looking at things in a different light. She wanted her pervasive horror to be contradicted, blocked, eradicated.

Instead he'd called her hysterical and sent her to bed like a naughty child.

She did not believe she was hysterical, misguided or even superstitious; she saw things clearly. There was a moment when the men of their generation had been required to stand up and define themselves as men. Lawrence had hidden behind a desk, and now they were being punished for his cowardice. It was what she believed and it was therefore real. Loss could not be avoided. It would seek you out. Why should they think they could be any different from anyone else? They had no right. Lydia blinked repeatedly. She was surprised to find tears welling in her eyes. It would not do. She must find a way to bury the thought again. She could not think of her husband this way. It would destroy them.

'Look, isn't that the Duchess of Feversham?' asked Beatrice, breathless with excitement and the ethereal whisper of potential scandal.

'Yes, it is,' replied Lydia, who was considerably more composed. She surveyed the indulged, coddled people with indifference. She was accustomed. She had grown up with them and was aware of all that they had to offer and all that they lacked. The Duchess of Feversham was a soured woman who existed within a loveless marriage; both she and her husband regularly took younger lovers.

Lydia was not judgemental; she just found their set-up depressing. However, the war had limited Beatrice's exposure to society, and she was still considerably more romantic about the aristocrats she hailed from. Lydia considered that the war had changed the playing field so significantly that it was unlikely that Bea would ever become as weary as Lydia found she was tonight. Bea would not have the resources to fund a continued association with this society, or even a role within it. Lydia found this particular train of thought upsetting and so shied away from it. She preferred to pretend that Sarah and Beatrice had the same money and opportunities as she possessed. It was better not to think about the truth of things. Although the idea that she was forever thinking it was better not to think did not bear examination either. She roused herself. Chummily, cheerfully she commented, 'You've seen her out many times before; why the fuss, Bea?'

'Yes, at parties, where we might have been in the same room along with three hundred others, but tonight we're only forty. It's almost intimate.'

'Actually we're thirty-nine,' corrected Lydia, thinking of Lawrence.

'No, we are forty. Ava told me that the Duchess of Feversham has brought along an extra man,' chipped in Sarah.

'Oh. Who?' asked Beatrice breathlessly. It was hard for Lydia to maintain the pretence that they were even when Bea insisted on being so green, so artless, so easily impressed and urgent.

'I have no idea.'

'Her latest lover, no doubt,' offered Lydia.

'I only know that he catapulted through the ranks during the war. Terribly brave. Went in as a commoner, came out practically one of us,' said Sarah.

'Well, Ava's mother will be pleased. Whoever he is, he'll even up the seating plan, although it is all rather last-minute,' commented Bea.

'She will.'

'Ava has dined at the duchess's house several times,' mused Beatrice.

'Yes, she has.'

'I wonder which house exactly. You do know they have half a dozen.'

'Yes.' They all knew this, had always known it, but Bea never tired of repeating the fact. Probably because her own assets were depreciating, she had become obsessively interested in those who had money to burn. It wasn't greed or even jealousy; her fascination was similar to that of a palaeontologist studying dinosaur bones: she simply wanted to know all there was to know about this strange and alien species. Lydia decided to throw her a nugget. 'The Duchess pays up to a thousand guineas a night in fees for the entertainers at her parties, you know.'

Bea gasped. 'What do they do for that?'

'Quite literally anything, I imagine.'

'They say she has had all her underwear embroidered with coronets,' chipped in Sarah.

'And she's just bought a second Rolls-Royce,' added Lydia.

'No?'

'This time in purple. It has the coronet on it too.'

'Well!'

It wasn't clear if Bea was impressed with the ostentation or horrified by it, but her face stretched and contorted like melted rubber. Suddenly Lydia felt enormous affection for her friend. It must be lovely to be so *bothered*. Lydia found she was rarely bothered about anything nowadays. 'I think we should go in to dinner. I heard the gong,' she said calmly.

'Who is taking you in?' Bea looked concerned again. As one of the least important guests at the table, she couldn't hope that Lady Pondson-Callow would have allocated her a spare man. Lydia, as a married woman, was more entitled to an escort. Bea quickly started to calculate who might be taking whom. Would there be anyone left for her?

'Shall we all three go in together?' suggested Lydia, linking her arms through the sisters'.

'Dare we?' Bea giggled.

'Oh, with you two flanking me, I feel equal to it,' smiled Lydia.

She had not expected to see him ever again, but as she had

81

fallen asleep imagining him for nine days, when she did turn and see him at her side, he felt strangely familiar. Lofty, magnificent, audacious. So familiar she dispensed with formality and talked to him as though they were picking up a conversation they'd started in the drawing room, just five minutes ago.

'I didn't know you knew Miss Pondson-Callow.'

'I don't. I came with the Duchess of Feversham. Miss Pondson-Callow called her this afternoon and asked for a spare man. That's who I am; a spare man.' Lydia felt sick at the thought that he'd arrived with the notorious duchess.

'What a surprise,' she mumbled.

'Life is full of them.'

'We met in the café on Marble Arch. Maison Lyons, a week last Thursday.' She added the detail because she was terrified that he might not remember the incident, so brief and insignificant in reality; so large and all-consuming in her mind. The moment she offered the circumstances she felt silly, exposed.

But he did remember her. 'I don't think we actually met.'

'True, there was no formal introduction.'

The eyes again. Too knowing, too deep, too vivid to allow her a modest pretence of disregard. It was obvious he knew the effect he had on women. He'd probably known since he was a boy holding on to his mama's apron. Sitting next to him now, she had the chance to notice more details. He had a lean, ravenous face, draped with a clear, almost translucent skin. He was sinewy, taut, well-defined, strong. Lydia didn't doubt that it was the war that had shaved off all that was unnecessary about him.

He picked up a wide, shallow glass of champagne and sipped at the lip while holding her gaze. 'I'm Edgar Trent. And you are Mrs . . . ?'

'Lady Chatfield.'

'But I should call you . . . ?'

'You *should* call me Lady Chatfield, but I think you are going to call me Lydia.'

'I think I am going to call you Lid.'

'Nobody calls me Lid.'

'I didn't imagine they would.'

'It isn't any sort of name. It's simply a reduction.'

'Yes. It's plain and confident. You'll grow into it.'

With this he turned away from her and started to talk to the lady seated on his right, as was the proper etiquette. Lydia felt a spike of indignation that he was implying she wasn't yet straight-forward or confident, and at the same time she was doused in a vibrant sense of excitement as she realised he was flirting with her. Pulling her out. Wrapping her in the golden light of his notice. She looked up and saw that Sarah was sitting opposite her. She was beaming and mouthed, 'Isn't that . . . ?' Lydia nodded. 'How strange, what a coincidence,' Sarah mouthed again. Lydia turned to look up the table, where her eyes met Ava's. Ava winked at her. It was a knowing gesture, too knowing. Uncomfortable, Lydia quickly looked away.

She tried to talk to the old chap sitting to her left as they drank their soup, as she was expected to. He was a friend of Ava's father and the usual type of gentleman that Lydia found around her own parents' table. He had a portly body, a creased face and a triangular clump of hair in the centre of his head. He was affable and polite, but Lydia identified something in his manner that she recognised with increasing frequency nowadays in men her father's age – he was apologetic.

The last generation were distinctly divided.

Some arrogantly demanded that the world return to what they had known before: a world where everyone knew their place and stayed in it. The old men who thought that way, with their red faces, deep tones and bulbous noses, droned on pompously. They seemed irritable and impotent. The other half were intimidated by the generation that had fought in the Great War. These old men had nothing similar to compare it with; the Boer War was dwarfed by comparison. They could not relate and yet they'd let it happen. They were ashamed that they were alive when so many of their sons were dead. These sorts were confused and dismayed by the losses too, but not the loss of order; specifically the loss of life. They felt they'd let down their sons. Which indeed they had. This chap was the latter sort. The more bearable. He talked about his pheasant shoots, his dogs, the difficulty in finding a skilled man to repair the hundred miles of dry-stone walling that surrounded his estate, but what he had to say was not said with the entitlement of old; his tone was more one of humble gratitude. He was aware that he was privileged, but he seemed to understand that his biggest privilege was that his son had been too old to fight, his grandsons too young. He talked of his large family with affection and recognition that they were an accomplishment. Not because they would inherit his land and titles, but because they rode, danced and sang, squabbled, drank and gambled. They were alive.

Normally Lydia would have found this man a jovial enough dinner companion. As a woman who considered herself way beyond common flirtation or dalliance, her preferred companions were the old, interesting fellows; the ones who appreciated her conversation and her beauty but placed her far away from suspicion. Tonight, time stretched endlessly, reminding her of the tedious journeys she'd made as a child in the rumbling brougham. *When will we get there?* she'd nagged. Although the carriages had been considered the ultimate in comfort, Lydia had loathed the stale, cramped journeys and only managed them by focusing on the moment she'd be allowed to tumble out and run free, stretching her legs. She felt the same sense of confinement now. She held her body rigid and unyielding, pointing, like a magnet points north, towards the old man, because she dreaded that if she turned her head – even a fraction – and allowed herself a glimpse of Edgar Trent, she would not be able to drag her eyes away from him again. Ever again.

She would not allow herself to look at him throughout the course, yet her being was with him entirely. She was conscious of him – tantalisingly close to her, right next to her – in the purest and most exquisite sense of being conscious of a thing. She sensed his movements as though the rippling of his shoulder muscles, the bend of his elbow, the turn of his head caused a tsunami in the air between them. On three, maybe four occasions, she experienced the warmth of his actual touch as his jacketed arm nudged against her bare one. His contact felt firm and deliberate; she did not

believe it was accidental. She could smell him. Early on in the
evening he smelt of Pears soap, no nonsense. Later, she imagined,
he would smell of cigarettes and red wine, a lot of nonsense. Whilst
listening to her companion talk about dry-stone walling, her ears
strained to pick up Edgar Trent's tones. His laugh, which came
often and loud, rattled through her body. It caught in her chest.
It settled between her legs. She was quickly drunk, although she
was unsure if it was the champagne or him that had caused the
intoxication. After a millennium, the crockery was cleared, the fish
was served and it was the appropriate moment to rotate once again
and speak with him.

The wait had been too much, too long. It had been cruel and
had destroyed any chance she had of remaining aloof or appropriate.
She turned to him, helpless.

'So, Lid, say something that will impress me.'

'I'm sorry?'

'Oh, that doesn't impress me at all. Try again.' He picked up his
glass and glugged back the entire contents as though he was in a
hurry.

'I don't understand.'

'I think you do. Isn't this what is expected at events such as
these? You say something audacious. I say something flattering. We
begin a flirtation. A flirtation at the very least, or perhaps a love
affair at most.'

'I don't . . . I don't . . .' She wanted to say she didn't understand,
but she did.

'Sorry, have I ruined everything by jumping the gun? Should I
have played along more subtly?'

Recovering, Lydia said, 'You're being very rude, Sergeant Major
Trent.'

'Am I? I don't mean to be. I'm delighted that your friend has
sat us next to one another. I can't think of anyone I'd rather flirt
with.' He brushed his eyes over the other guests as though
confirming his selection. He swiftly licked his firm, cushioned lips
and added, 'Flirt at the least.'

'I don't think that's why we were seated together. No one even knew you were coming until today. You are only making up the numbers because my husband has to work and couldn't be here.'

'But you wouldn't have been seated next to your husband,' Edgar Trent pointed out.

Lydia faltered. 'No, I don't suppose I would have.'

'The seating plan has been tampered with. We've been set up.'

As Lydia accepted the thought, she turned her head once again towards Ava, who was staring right back at her. Ava raised her glass; Lydia felt the truth of the gesture like a poke.

'Our hostess clearly hopes that we'll flirt to a shocking, shameful, unprecedented level.' He flicked his eyes around the table for a second time. 'Consider, this place is full of those distinguished by birth but not much else, the academic erudite who talk about theology and economics but not much else and eminent businessmen who value money but not much else. She needs to be entertained.'

'I don't think Ava would do that, set us up, as you say, simply for entertainment.' But even as Lydia heard the words tip out of her mouth, she knew that it was just the sort of thing Ava would do. She also became aware that simply by having this conversation she was flirting with him. Very much so. It wasn't a suitable conversation; it was open to misinterpretation. She ought to cut it dead. She really ought. 'Besides, you arrived with the Duchess of Feversham. Surely she's the lady you need to be flirting with.' She flashed him a look that deftly communicated her knowledge that he must be more than flirting with the duchess. 'I'm no use to you at all.'

'I did arrive with the Duchess of Feversham, but I'm her cover. Matthew Northbrook is her lover. Those in the know are aware of that.' Ava was in the know. 'You see, people think of me as a ladies' man.'

'Do they just?'

'They do, and so I'm a likely suspect as the duchess's lover, but blameless if anyone does any digging about, therefore a brilliant foil.'

'I see.'

'Quite clever, don't you think?'

'I suppose. But then those sorts have to be.'

'What sorts?'

86

Lydia paused, then added, 'The adulterous sort. I imagine it takes quite some planning.' She'd picked her words carefully. She wanted him to know she was not that sort. She was not an adulterer. Never had been. Never wanted to be.

Edgar paused; they both reached for their glasses, both found them empty. Lydia inclined her head a fraction, enough for the under butler to be by their side in an instant. He offered the wine but Edgar waved it away and asked for a cocktail. It wasn't done to drink cocktails with dinner. Lydia had a feeling Edgar knew as much and didn't care.

'So are you a ladies' man?' she asked, once their drinks had been delivered. She'd chosen to reject the wine as well and join him in drinking cocktails, just to be polite. Or was it impolite? She wasn't sure. 'Is it a fair assessment?'

'It is.' His words had a physical impact. It was as though he had leaned over and licked her mind and – shockingly – her upper thighs too. Because she felt him. She felt him in an absolute sense. 'It's a common and general turn of phrase but essentially accurate. What do they think of you?' he asked.

'They think of me as happily married.'

'Do they now?'

'They do.'

'And *are* you happily married? Is that a fair assessment?' Lydia paused for a beat longer than she should have. 'I see.' And he had. He'd seen a green light, because Lydia was breathless and slow.

'Well of course,' she muttered finally, but she sounded unconvincing, unconvinced. Why? She *was* happily married. Not today, obviously. There were issues, but generally speaking she was happy.

He paused, stared at her for the longest time. Long enough to make her oddly ashamed; she looked away.

'I bet when you were a debutante you were an accomplished flirt.' Lydia had been. Some might even remember her as a bit of a tease, certainly an enormous giggle. 'I bet you drove men mad,' he added with some amusement.

'Oh, yes, they fell for me like apples fall off a tree,' she replied with a deft mix of irony and honesty.

'Landing hard, getting bruised. I know how it happened for you.'

'Do you?'

'Yes. Your husband. Solid sort. He came along and said he wouldn't stand for any of your nonsense, as he liked to call it. He said you had to pack it all in and marry him. It was coming to the end of your season and you were rather relieved. You found it a little tedious being forever sparkling, didn't you? I bet you did. I don't imagine he was the first proposal; he might have been the fifth or sixth. But he was the first one you could take seriously. The other boys had all worshipped you a little too ardently, a little too quickly, and you insisted their heat was insincere.'

Lydia nodded, fascinated by the accuracy of his account. 'Mostly they were rather silly,' she admitted.

'Quite. But he saw potential in you. He thought you could be better. Better behaved. Under the correct guidance. He saw himself as just that. You believed the same to be true. Am I right?'

He was. No one had ever taken the time to understand the exact reasoning behind Lydia's acceptance of Lawrence's proposal. They were simply pleased she had accepted him. After she had discouraged a number of chaps whom everyone considered totally appropriate, her parents had concerns she might turn out to be wilful. When she said yes to the Earl of Clarendale's son, they had been so relieved. He was eminently eligible; if they'd wanted to be Victorian about the business, and had found her a match at birth, they could not have chosen better themselves.

People talked of marriages of convenience and marriages that were love matches, as if the entire business was an either/or situation. In Lydia's view things were rarely so clear cut. She had found Lawrence attractive, suitable, pleasant-tempered and moral; added together, she'd thought she was being offered a good deal. What she felt for him was a lot like love, as near to love as she'd ever known, and so she gave it that label. She had been keen to get on with it. The business of being married. She wanted to be more than a girl waiting for invitations; she wanted to be a woman dispensing them. Sure enough the parties and dancing were delicious to begin with, when the spring months first heated up and exploded into summer, but the entire business of what to wear, whom to talk to and wondering whether anyone might say a fresh word ever again meant things had become tedious and exhausting by the time the leaves on the trees were turning golden brown. Lawrence probably hadn't given too much thought as to why Lydia had accepted his proposal after only four meetings. If he had thought about it, no doubt he'd have reasoned that she had settled down because he was masterful and insistent. He had no idea that she wanted to be off the merry-go-round, and that the timing of his attentions had been fortunate.

Yet this man, this Edgar Trent – with whom she had swapped only a handful of sentences – seemed to know her soul. How could that be? No, it could not be. She would not allow herself to be fanciful. It was much more likely that her story was a predictable one. This was not a flattering thought, but it was more rational. No doubt there were countless other women out there with the same story. This man had probably met, seduced and 'understood' plenty of these other women in order for him to be so sure of her predictable story. The thought offended her but forced her on to be more frank.

'Actually, he did not use the word *better*. He said I could be *more*.'

'So ever since you've striven to be just that. You're the perfect wife, mother and hostess. Am I right?'

Lydia sipped her cocktail. 'Don't mock me.'

'I'm not mocking you, Lid. I understand.' Edgar Trent suddenly dropped his gaze and stared at his plate. 'We both know that sometimes being more leaves you feeling as if you are less.'

All around them jewels glittered, satin lapels shone; the servants approached and retreated as they served food, poured wine, removed dishes. Lydia became aware that a footman was standing by her shoulder waiting to retrieve her plate. She had not touched the salmon, but all the other guests were sitting, plates cleared, waiting for the roast course. Only her food and Edgar's remained uneaten. She felt that every eye in the room bored into her. Swiftly she brought together her knife and fork. 'You can take it.'

She turned back to the old chap whom she knew she must talk

to throughout the roast, but she willed away each laborious moment. The words he offered up drifted past her like dandelion seeds on the wind and she could do nothing to capture them and continue the conversation. All the while she strained to hear what Edgar was saying to his companion. It was agony. Now, if he laughed, she felt anxious; could the woman be more entertaining than Lydia? But if he fell quiet, she resented any intimacy they might be forging. She felt he was being wrenched from her and was desperate until the salad was served and she was able to turn to him once again.

She did not flirt with him in the traditional sense. She felt that the skills that had been so perfectly honed before she married – but had been quenched and quashed for years now – could have sprung back into life if she'd wanted, and this time she would have been a thousand times more alluring than she'd ever been before. As a woman, not a girl, she had the ability to be polished – frank, elusive, candid and coy by turn – but she could not bring herself to flirt with him like that. She would not pick imaginary lint off his dinner jacket, she would not squeeze his arm and then appear surprised and delighted by his dense muscles, she would not laugh at his jokes even before she heard the punchline. She needed to give him something different. Something more.

He was a seductive and challenging blast of ambiguities. He liked her. That much was transparent. There were moments when he was animated and amused, when he roared with laughter at something she had said, and moments when he let his gaze linger on her mouth for a moment longer than was comfortable. A moment longer than was acceptable. But this man stayed apart. This man was not for conquering. Even if she had been single and in a position to entice. There was something about him that suggested he would never fall under anyone's spell. Charm was not a valid currency for him. He was separate, unreachable. Even when he placed his hand on her knee, an inappropriate, but welcome gesture, he was apart.

14

E DGAR TRENT ACCEPTED a cigar and, because he wasn't familiar
with anyone in particular, stood with a group of similarly
aged men who were talking about the grouse-shooting last week
and wondering whether it would be too cold for a drive in the
morning; if not, they might take one. They were all – him included
– at that pleasant stage of inebriation when the world is warm,
fluid and accepting; the sharp bits have been blunted, if not
smoothed away, and yet the hangover is too far over the horizon
to be a concern.

Edgar felt exhilarated the way he always did at this point in the
evening. He had, as usual, identified the most attractive women in
the vicinity. It was a primitive, unquashable routine. Wherever he
was, whether he was at a party, or in a public house, at work or
walking in town, he spotted them, noted them; if there was time
he hunted them. It was a compulsive pattern. Sometimes, if he
needed to be expedient, he did not bother with chasing the most
attractive women; they often required wooing and charming, and
it could eat time. Sometimes he simply identified the most cheerfully willing. Tonight he felt he had time; he felt it would take time.

Ava Pondson–Callow had initially caught his eye. How could
she not? Ava oozed confidence and experience. No one could ever
pin an actual scandal on her, but somehow she wore her knowledge
like her magnificent and numerous diamonds, boldly for all to see.
He'd observed her this evening, before dinner, walking the drawing
room, flashing her sharp and clever eyes at men and women alike;

eyes that pulsed between chilly indifference and warm invitation. Intriguing. Edgar Trent thought she was the sort of woman who might be compared to Helen who launched a thousand ships, or Godiva who rode naked to lower taxes: an exceptional and complex woman. A single woman. She ought to have been his goal tonight. But he found she was not.

Lid was different from Ava. As beautiful, but not as sure. She was dark and petite, where Ava was blonde and elegantly lofty. Ava exuded intrinsic self-reliance. Lydia had an air of discontent about her that she largely concealed behind her fabulous dress, but he wondered what it was that provoked her restlessness and where it would take her; she didn't seem to know. It was her uncertainty that absorbed him. Theoretically she was not available, not at all. But he had touched her knee twice; the first time she'd shivered but moved away, the second time she'd let his hand linger. He'd felt the firmness of her leg under the thin silk dress.

He knew the power he had over women. It used to matter a lot to him. Since the war, it mattered less. Everything was less since the war. He knew how to get women to fall in love with him. He knew how to get women to fuck him, even when they didn't really want to, even when they really *shouldn't* want to. It passed the time. Time that should be so precious was in fact an aching gap, and so he sometimes filled it with fucking.

Would he have Lady Lydia Chatfield? Should he pluck her or pass by? There were other woman here tonight he could have. There were always women aplenty. Lydia was delightful, posh, poised. These three things ought to add up to a safe bet, but there was a hint of something else that caused him to pause for thought. Vulnerability. Vulnerability was a menace. It made women messy and unreliable. He did not need or want that. He should pass her by.

And yet. As he pulled on his cigar, drawing the delicious smoke and tobacco into his lungs and then out into the over-grand smoking room, he recalled the sudden gleam of her pale arms at dinner and her delicate, almost pearlescent skin draped around her collarbones. He found that details came back to him in a way that was more interesting than irksome. She had neat, tiny ears, shell-like, and she tucked her hair behind them whenever she was nervous; her lobes were pink and fleshy. He wondered what it would feel like to take her lobe in his mouth. Her eyes shone like fathomless lagoons. And she was amusing. Her conversation challenged. He noted her laugh.

He would not pass. He would play.

Having made this decision, Edgar was bitterly disappointed, on returning to the drawing room, to be informed that Lady Chatfield had retired to bed, complaining of a headache. He looked around at the bevy of sparkling beauties that remained, but felt suddenly and overwhelmingly bored. It was as though someone had turned out the lights.

15

AVA, AS HOSTESS, felt she had the right to visit Lydia's room even before Lydia was dressed. She arrived with her maid, who was carrying an enormous breakfast tray, the post and the papers, and who had instructions to build a hearty fire in the hearth, as it was dwindling.

'Budge over, darling. I'm chilly.'

Lydia groaned but obediently threw back the satin bedclothes so that Ava could slip between the sheets. The mattress barely moved as Ava was so light, but she made her presence known when she put her icy feet on Lydia's warm legs.

Lydia jumped. 'Your feet are cold.'

'I know. That's why I put them on you, to warm them up.'

'You should have invited Lord Harrington this weekend. He'd have kept you warm,' said Lydia. She was teasing and scolding at once. She didn't approve of Ava's liaisons with married men, but she accepted them as an intrinsic part of her friend's lifestyle.

'Charlie is becoming horribly clingy. I deliberately withheld an invitation. I can't have him slobbering over me in front of Mummy and Daddy. So you'll have to put up with my cold feet.'

When they were debutantes, they'd often shared a bed early in the morning, as it was an expedient way to swap the previous evening's gossip and secrets. Obviously, since Lydia had married, it wasn't appropriate for Ava to rush into her bedroom, dive into her bed and chatter. Both women missed the intimacy intrinsic in time spent together before hair and teeth were brushed.

'How are you so impossibly glamorous at this time of the day?' asked Lydia as she turned and eyed Ava's delicate cotton baby doll, which peeked out from behind her heavily embroidered peacock-coloured dressing gown.

'Single girls don't let themselves go the way married women do, you know.'

'Charming.'

Ava laughed. 'I'm teasing. You look very beautiful too, darling. You haven't become a slattern since you married. Thank God. Not like Ella Deramore – did you see her last night? Such a shame, she was last year's hit at the deb balls, but she's piled on the pounds. No one would guess she's several years our junior. I'd say ten pounds in six months' marriage.'

'She may be pregnant.'

'I hope so, for her sake. If you *have* to be one or the other, fertile is always preferable to fat. Either way, if she carries on at this rate, by the time they reach their silver anniversary she'll have to be hoisted into bed like Henry the Eighth. I thought her dress was going to rip at the seams.' Aware and appreciative of her own superior metabolism, Ava sat up in bed and drew the breakfast tray towards her. 'Hungry?'

Lydia sat up too and eyed the tray: fresh grapefruit, sardines on toast, soft-boiled eggs, and porridge made with cream and adorned with honey, nuts and slices of apple. It looked delicious, but she wasn't hungry.

'No, strangely, I'm not.'

'You ought to be, you barely touched dinner last night. Cook is suicidal.'

'It was delicious.'

'I know, but I can hardly explain to Cook that you didn't eat it because you were involved in an intensive flirtation, can I?' Lydia glanced swiftly at Ava, wondering how she always knew everything. 'But then you ran away. How very Cinderella of you. Did you leave a glass slipper? Are you hoping Sergeant Major Trent will search the kingdom for you?' Ava was tucking into the sardines and giving the impression of teasing indifference, but

Lydia knew her well enough to realise she wanted all the details.

'He's the chap I met in Lyons, actually.'

'Really?'

'You knew.'

'No. Not at first. I had no idea who the duchess would bring as her cover, but now I understand it all perfectly.'

'What do you mean by that?'

'You know very well what I mean. You said you had a thing for him, and you certainly do. That much was clear to everyone at dinner.'

'Was it?' Lydia asked, horrified. She wasn't used to attracting scandal and didn't want to become so.

'Quite certainly, but take comfort from the fact that no one cares about your little intrigue; most of us have our own to concentrate on.'

'There is no intrigue.'

'Isn't there?'

'No.'

'But you want there to be.'

'I don't. That's why I went to bed early. It's all becoming rather intense and . . .'

'Exciting?'

'I was going to say wrong. I'm glad I'm going home today, and so will he be. We'll never see one another again.'

'Ah, well, about that.' Ava got out of bed and drew back the curtains. Snow was falling swiftly and had settled overnight. 'Three or four inches. Stations closed. The roads are impossible. You won't be going anywhere, darling. No one will.'

Lydia felt a sharp spike of exhilaration. She would have run. She had planned to do so but fate had intervened and she couldn't quite bring herself to regret it. She got out of bed and stood with Ava. The women slipped their arms around one another's waists and stood, backs to the room, watching the world transform. The window framed them like a work of art. Outside, the snowflakes were falling swiftly; there was a white blanket as far as the eye could see, clean and glittering, stretching across the courtyard, the formal gardens and the fields. A couple of gardeners were already sweeping the paths. Lydia sighed at this. She knew other servants would be up on the roof shovelling the snow away too. She wished they could have left it alone a little longer. She delighted in clean, untouched snow the way an artist might delight in a clean, untouched canvas; it held promise and possibility. She resented the black trail they were leaving behind their heavy wooden brooms. Swish, swish: the brooms moved back and forth, the gardeners shuffling after them. The pliable powdery snow flew readily to mounds at the side, revealing the grey gravel of the path. The women watched as the men worked on, the path seeming to stretch endlessly. Lydia had a strange sense that they might keep clearing past Ava's father's borders, past the neighbouring farms, until the land ended and they arrived at the sea. She almost wished they would. More, she wished *she* could. Her life suddenly seemed to be one of tedious order, irrational rules and restrictions. Some limits were imposed by society; often times she reached for the brakes herself. If only she dared to just keep going and going and going until she had gone as far as she could and there was nowhere left to voyage.

'Tell me, Ava, what do you know of him? Tell me everything.'

16

Edgar felt trapped by the snow and also exhilarated by it. He was often confused by the two contradicting emotions: that of feeling trapped and that of relishing the challenge of disentangling himself. He didn't understand it but knew it was to do with what had happened in France. The mud had trapped him; he'd trudged through it, sunk into it. Then he'd crawled through it, slept in it; the mud and the blood. It had rotted his boots, seeped into his skin, into his mouth, up his nose, but somehow he had not drowned in it. When he'd had to, he'd burrowed deeper into the mud, urinated, puked and bled into it, but he had not been smothered by it. He had been promoted and decorated, he had been a success. A success because he hadn't been buried in the land; he had clambered, fought and clawed his way out of it. Edgar thought it was a miracle or luck that he hadn't died in the war; his point of view wavered depending on his mood.

When he opened the curtains and saw that the snow had seized the land overnight, he felt an overwhelming need to trample through it. Spoil its perfection, stamp his presence upon it. He realised that he would not be able to catch a train or cadge a lift out of the house that day, and he felt imprisoned. It was not that he objected to staying at the smart country house for longer than he'd anticipated; he objected to not having a choice. He had to show the elements that he was no one's prisoner. He could not bear to remain indoors a moment longer than absolutely necessary. He had to forge ahead.

He pulled on the thickest pair of trousers and the only jumper he had packed and rushed downstairs. A manservant provided him with Wellington boots, but Edgar didn't want to ask for a route. He needed to explore and conquer unaided; this urge in him had saved his life thus far. He was frustrated that he came upon fastened windows and locked doors; the servants clearly had not had a chance to open up the entire house yet – curtains were still drawn, blinds remained pulled shut. Edgar impatiently dashed from door to door and tugged on locks. He suspected that the only door that would be open before eight in the morning was the servants' back door to the yard and stables, but he could not use the servants' door. His disinclination was nothing to do with a sense of snobbery; he had no problem with passing through the colder corridors or the functional kitchen, but the guests were supposed to be as indolent as the master and mistress of the house, and his appearance in the kitchen would cause concern that he hadn't slept comfortably or that he had been inconvenienced because the main doors were locked. There would be a fuss. Possibly someone would be scolded.

At last, in a smaller drawing room, he found a window he could budge without damaging the shutter or lock. He clambered out like a burglar, not giving any thought to how eccentric his ways might seem to his hosts. With no twinge of reluctance at ruining the thick carpet of snow – quite the opposite – he set off towards a pocket of trees about a mile away. He walked with haste, enthusiastically kicking the powdery snow. The chilly air and the vigorous pace made his cheeks tingle. He liked it. He liked to feel things – good or bad, physical or emotional; it proved he was still alive. He needed the proof, because sometimes he doubted it.

He marched on and on. He glanced back at the huge, creamy brick house, which now looked like something in a fairy tale, decorated with lace and icing sugar. The snow had stopped falling for the moment. Daylight had conquered the black night but the blinds were still down on all but one or two of the windows; the other guests were still asleep. He couldn't help but feel superior. Edgar didn't admire those who slept soundly. He knew that the only people who could do so were those who hadn't lived. Some men had died asleep in the trenches. He didn't blame them; he pitied them. Theirs had not been peaceful or even slothful sleep; wounds or exhaustion had brought about a lack of consciousness, yet shrapnel still fell and limbs could still be torn off. It didn't seem fair. Sleep wasn't the sanctuary people believed it to be. He was never peaceful now, but he found some sort of relief when he was alert. Then, at least, he could see what was coming. Whatever it was. He could be ready.

Lydia was coming.

He could see her tramping through the garden towards him; she was following his footsteps. He recognised her even at a distance, although she was little more than a dark silhouette against the whiteness. As she moved closer, he noted that she was dressed in tight trousers and a bulky, expensive-looking fur hat and coat; it was a modern look. She gripped the coat tightly to her skinny body. She wasn't wearing gloves, which he thought was odd. He waited for her to catch up. There was no question that he'd do otherwise.

'Good morning, Lady Chatfield.' She looked startled and a smidgen disheartened; he was glad his formality had unnerved her. She'd disappointed him last night. He felt her flight like a blot on the familiarity they were forging. He felt the need to spit back.

'I saw you from my bedroom window. Out here all alone. I thought you might want some company.'

She must have hurried to catch him up; her cheeks were pink and attractive. Her eyes were still smudged with last night's make-up. He realised that she wasn't wearing gloves because she had dashed out of the house in an effort to reach him. It was risky and impetuous. He began to like her again.

'It's too beautiful a morning to waste,' he commented and, to underline the point, he set off again, trudging in the direction of the trees. Lydia had to dash to match his long strides; after a hundred yards he noticed as much and slowed down his pace. He peeled off his gloves and wordlessly handed them to her.

'But what about you?'

'I'll keep my hands in my pockets; if you do that, your coat gapes open.' It was true her fur coat had no clasp. 'Why are women's clothes so impractical?'

'So we look gorgeous.'

Lydia slipped her hands into his gloves. They were far too big, but she didn't care. Wearing them was about more than whether she was snug or they were friendly; she felt his gesture was bigger than that. It was a question of tenure and possession. The issue was not who owned the gloves but who owned whom. By handing them to her, he was taking ownership somehow; ownership of the situation. Of her. By silently, obediently, slipping them on, she was acquiescing. She did not turn and glance behind her to consider whether anyone was marking their progress from a window in the house, she did not worry about what the servants must have thought as she'd demanded they hurry to open the main doors, and she did not dwell on Ava's shocked but amused face as she fled the bedroom and chased after him. She did not care about any of it. Last night she had run away from him. This morning when she'd spotted him trudging through the draped landscape she'd known she had no choice: she had to run towards him. The truth was, he'd detonated a flurry of conflicting sentiments. She was utterly and irretrievably drawn to him, yet she ought not to be. Shrapnel sliced into her conscience, shame flooded her veins, yet sparkling slivers of rich, colourful possibility exploded in her heart.

'Why did you vanish last night?' He looked irritated. Frustrated. She couldn't bear to have upset him.

'I had a headache.'

'Really?' he snarled. The lie seemed to hurt him. Insulted, he looked at her and his gaze teetered on the verge of being a glare. It levelled her, sliced her, made love to her. Lydia was appalled and anxious and yet unable to turn away. Did he feel it too? He must. She did not demean them with the pretence of masking chatter. She wanted him like a hungry animal; small talk might smother them. She caved in.

'No, not really. You know I am married.'

'Yes.' His face didn't move a fraction. He gave nothing away, but she was glad that at least he didn't feel the need to add anything tiresome like, 'He's a lucky chap,' just to make it clear that he was interested in her.

'I thought perhaps, last night, we were stepping over a line. The champagne cocktails, I suppose.'

'Do you really think it was the champagne?' He stopped walking.

'No,' she admitted, with a sigh.

'Nor do I.' He set off again. They were almost at the thicket of trees. Lydia wanted to be in the woods with him. She told herself she wasn't hiding, but she knew already that they were, and always would be. She dashed after him.

'I *had* to leave.' Did he understand her position? Her duty?

'Yet today you sought me out.'

'Yes.'

'What am I to deduce from that?'

'That I am weak.'

'Or maybe brave.' He stopped, now under the trees, and turned to her again. She shrugged. She didn't feel brave; she felt dazed and helpless, yet exhilarated and alive. His face was just inches from hers. She leaned a fraction closer but he moved away and dug into his pocket.

'I've a flask here. Do you fancy some whisky? You look blue with the cold.' He took a swig and then handed it to her. He ought to have offered it to her first, yet she already sensed he probably didn't give too much value to what ought to be done. She put her lips where his had been a moment before and let the hot, golden liquid pour through her. He dug out a packet of cigarettes and offered her one in exchange for the flask. The air was still, yet he cupped his hands around hers as he lit her up.

They stood together in the profound silence that the snow brought. A silence thickened and complicated by desire.

'I like the snow,' she commented at last.

'Tobogganing, snowmen and all that,' he guessed dismissively.

'No, not just the frivolities. It seems magical. For a time it seems that the world is wiped clean and we're being offered a fresh start.'

'It isn't that at all, though, is it? It's a case of everything being covered up. Underneath these frail inches of snow there still lies the solid earth, the reality. The dank, crawling soil or the hard, inert concrete. Nothing is new; the old is simply hidden from view for a while.'

'It is at least a respite, then. If not renewal.'

He shrugged. She wasn't sure if he didn't agree or didn't care. He was complicated. Everyone was nowadays. The snow couldn't have been much fun in the trenches. The war had robbed the world's youth of their simplicity as well as their sanguineness.

'You were in uniform the day we met.'

'Yes.'

'You're still in the army?'

'Correct.'

'Are you waiting for a decommission?'

'Not especially.' He shrugged.

'What did you do before the war?'

'This and that.'

Lydia accepted the answer without a second thought. Few of the young men she knew were actively employed doing anything especially organised, beyond having fun. And Edgar Trent would have been very young before the fighting started; he might not have established a career. She suspected he was younger than she was, but she was determined not to ask.

'Someone said you were frightfully brave.'

He flicked his eyes at her and let them linger. He smiled, amused. 'So, you've been talking to someone about me.'

She blushed. Caught. 'Well, in passing. To everyone, to no one in particular,' she said evasively and untruthfully. She had grilled Ava for every detail but not dared breathe a word of him to anyone else. She feared she'd be too transparent.

'So you've been talking to someone, everyone and no one in particular about me?'

'Quite so.' Lydia smiled, then pushed on. 'I heard you were swiftly promoted.' Ava had referred to him as a professional survivor, fighting through countless shows, wounded twice. Down but not out. Picking up out of each battle another 'pip' and a new decoration, time after time.

'Yes. I joined as a private. I'm a sergeant major now.'

'Incredible. How must you have felt?'

'Tired.'

'Such bravery,' she murmured.

She felt dazzled by his magnificence. They were all brave, absolutely, but so many had failed to return, or had come back ruined. There were those that had never even . . . She blocked the thought. It wouldn't do to start to draw comparisons between Edgar and Lawrence. Lawrence would be trounced, and no woman wanted to think that about the man she'd married.

'That's what they said. It's not how it felt. You start to live with such intense fear that you forget to recognise it. People think it's bravery. It's numbness. I was not brave so much as desperate. Desperate to stay alive. I did what I had to do. They made me a hero.'

'How marvellous.' She regretted the fact that she sounded gushing, but she was enthralled by the strength he exuded.

'They made me a hero and left me fit for nothing.' He threw away his cigarette; the red tip glowed against the snow, and then died. 'If I accept a decommission, I'd struggle to make a living. I can't go back to where I came from but I don't fit in around here.' He glanced about.

Lydia tried not to show her surprise. Men found work through their friends and their fathers, didn't they? The very idea that a man might struggle to find a position was alien to her. Briefly she wondered, what was this man worth? What family did he hail from? The two questions had always been intrinsically linked in her mind; one equalled another. Now she wasn't so sure. He looked majestic and priceless, but the clues he was giving suggested he was a working man, from no family at all.

'I shall remain a soldier until they tell me they no longer want me. In the meantime, I'm accepting all the training and education they offer me. Haven't you noticed how it works? The labourers' kids leave some dump of a school at fourteen, to start the same manual jobs their mams and dads did. The middle-class kids go to grammar schools and then find some clerical position, and the posh schools make professionals of all their boys. No one sees education as a way of changing things, getting out of the lane you were born into, but it should be. Then the war came along, and men like me. Education hasn't changed things much yet, but experience has. I've got a chance now. So it's not so bad, the army. At least now that the war is over.'

'And there will never be another one,' Lydia stated emphatically. He glanced at her through the blue light and the snow that fell from the tree branches, then threw his head back and let out a sarcastic bark that was supposed to approximate a laugh. 'That's what they promised us, didn't they? The war to end all wars?' she added defensively.

'Yes, they did.'

'Are you cynical?'

'I'm thoughtful.'

She heard the criticism. '*I* think.'

'Do you?'

'Yes.'

'When?'

'Excuse me?'

'When exactly did you think last? Of course this war is not the war to end all wars; how could that be? How could war stop a war? Don't be ridiculous. Think about it, Lid.'

Lydia felt stupid and infantile. She hated the fact he could make her feel like a child when she knew already that everything depended on her being a woman to him.

'Yet you haven't applied for a decommission. Surely if you expect more wars, then you ought to get the hell out of the army.' Suddenly she was afraid. Her core froze at the illogical thought that he'd be taken from her. He wasn't hers to lose. They weren't at war and, even if they were, he was a good soldier; he'd survived the last one. Yet she was ambushed by fear. Nothing made sense. She didn't understand him today. Last night he'd been relaxed, charismatic and bubbling with *joie de vivre*. Today he was harsh and elusive. She was surprised to find both versions of him equally compelling.

'As I said, what else would I do? I hacked my way to this officer rank. Cut, slashed, shot and stole.' He stared at her with the intensity she had come to expect from him, challenging her to be shocked or sick; she stared back at him, unflinching. He seemed relieved, let out a sigh. His breath clouded the air between them. She wanted to gulp it down, the air that had been inside him; she wanted it inside her. 'In a way, I had a successful war. Not as successful as your friend Ava, whose daddy made the boots for the troops, but still, if you stand very close, you can smell my success.' He leaned towards her as though he really thought she might breathe in his scent. She closed her eyes for a moment and sucked him up. 'It lingers, doesn't it? Obviously it does or else I wouldn't be invited to a place like this.' He casually gestured behind him, towards the enormous manor house; his gesture swept up the gardens, forests and hunting grounds. 'I wouldn't get the chance to meet a woman like you.' He abruptly drew away from her, her body tilted towards the gap he left. She almost slipped.

'I imagine you're very highly decorated.'

'Oh yes, I have medals. Lots of them. I don't know if I deserve them, but I do know that I deserve the champagne parties, the dancing and the pretty, loose girls.'

Lydia blushed; she wasn't sure if it was because he might have counted her among the pretty, loose girls, and therefore she ought to be offended, or simply because those girls existed and she was indignant and envious: what if he did *not* count her among them?

'I'm not saying another war is imminent, I'm just saying that I doubt we're done with atrocity. Anyway, I have no intention of fighting again. I'm looking for a cushy desk job. I think I deserve it.'

Lydia blanched at the phrase, one that she ran through her head with terrible regularity. He seemed to understand the one thing she was trying to hold away from him.

'What did your husband do during the war?'

She looked away. 'He served with the Home Office. A civil servant.'

'I see.'

'Yes, you probably do.'

'You must have been relieved: no danger from bullets or gas in Whitehall.'

'I think we should be getting back.'

'Do you?'

Lydia bit her lip. *Yes, of course. No, not at all.* 'Well at least we ought to keep walking; we'll catch our deaths standing around like this.'

So they set off. They weaved in and out of the trees, further into the forest and away from the house, leaving a trail of footsteps behind them that showed they walked in step and ever closer.

17

AVA DID NOT resent the snow or the added inconvenience of forty guests staying a day or two longer than initially expected. She relished the idea of a lot of company, and always appreciated anything out of the ordinary; snow provided a diversion. Her mother did not share her love of distraction and became exhaustingly flustered. Lady Pondson-Callow consulted with the housekeeper, who consulted with Cook, who lost her temper with the kitchen maids before it was agreed that they had plenty for lunch and dinner today, even breakfast tomorrow might be possible, but after that who could say? Lady Pondson-Callow could say; she ferociously imparted to the staff the paramount importance of free-flowing hospitality, and instructed that extra girls be called in from the village because several batches of bread, pies and puddings would need to be baked immediately.

'Mummy, our cellar is second to none in the country. Believe me, no one is going to care what we eat,' commented Ava with a yawn, but she didn't waste any more time trying to pacify her mother's nervousness at the demands of being a hostess for a prolonged period of time. It was boring. Ava's mother had never got over the fact that she was American and always, in Ava's opinion, tried a little too hard. Something Ava thought unforgivably stupid because it was so obviously counterproductive; the right sort of people gave the constant impression that they hardly ever tried at all. Ava knew that traditionally daughters were supposed to share their mother's concerns, and when a genuine common interest was absent then they were supposed to fake it. She thought it was beyond tedious how often women were meant to fake something or other to save someone or other's feelings, and refused to ever do it on principle. She knew she did not play the part of the unmarried-daughter-at-home particularly well; she had no interest in such a passive, inert role and wondered how any woman could abide it. She disliked the fact that whenever she gave an order to the servants, they would imply that they had to defer to her mother before carrying out the instruction. 'Just bring the damn coal,' was a frequent cry of the twenty-eight year old. She did not like having to say where she was going when she left a room, and she thought the questions of whether she took a bath in the afternoon, slept all morning or ate off a tray in the library were entirely ones that she could decide for herself.

However, weekend parties at her family home were not without their compensations. Her father was at times an old stick, but always wonderfully generous, so her friends were guaranteed to be well fed and entertained; she was able to ride her horse vigorously for miles and miles, and the countless rooms inevitably yielded up a diverting intrigue which she could talk and think about for at least a week. It was largely for this reason that she was unperturbed about the fact that her guests would not be able to leave today. She could see that at least three ill-advised romances were bubbling up under her nose. That sort of thing took the edge off the boredom that usually lingered in the air like last night's cigar smoke.

Ava generally spent most of her time in London, where it was considerably trickier to be weary and people tried hard not to be dull. She lived in an enormous bachelor-girl flat in Chelsea and had done so since 1915, when she'd insisted on moving up to town to join the war effort. She had not wanted to be a VAD; nursing was ghastly. Factory work was out of the question; she considered manual work mind-numbing and so had found an administrative position at the Foreign Office. Largely her duties were secretarial, although after briefly meeting her, the PM once commented that no doubt she did a fine, if unquantifiable, job of keeping up the spirits of all the chaps she worked for. He joked that they ought to send her out to the Front to remind the boys what they were fighting for. Ava had replied that she wouldn't mind a jot, she'd like to see the war at closer range, but no one had taken her seriously.

In London she preferred to believe and give the impression that she was completely independent. Indeed she did not have to consult with anyone as to how her staff ought to be managed, what time she should rise or return and whether attending a suffragette meeting really was a good idea. However, her father settled all her bills including the rent, utilities, staffing costs and groceries and, on top of that, he'd bought her a car and gave her a generous allowance for clothes, so her independence was as illusory as it was convenient. Ava no longer worked in the Foreign Office, because whilst she had been efficient, bright and committed, none of her skills could mitigate the fact that she was a woman. After the war she was obliged to give up the job that she had found surprisingly stimulating, so that a returning soldier might find employment. She and thousands of other women were told to return to concerns considered more fitting to their sex. It wasn't law but it was seen as unpatriotic to do otherwise. Her boss – a portly, ineffectual chap who had bungled and worried his way through the war, unknowingly depending almost entirely upon Ava's efficiency to save him and his department from certain embarrassment, if not disaster – had advised her that she ought to find a good chap to settle down with. 'Even with these awfully scant pickings, *you'll* have no trouble,' he'd said jovially, allowing his eyes to meander the length and breadth of her body.

'That's really not my plan at all,' she'd replied.

'Really?' The Old Harrovian had not been able to hide his surprise. 'I thought that was what all you young ladies wanted. What *are* your plans, then?'

'I'm afraid I don't know,' Ava had admitted with a defeated sigh.

'I see. Well, in that case I shall look forward to receiving the invitation to your nuptials.'

Ava had bristled as she'd stepped out into the street, carrying nothing other than a desk journal, empty from the following week of any appointments other than social ones. It wasn't the old duffer she was annoyed with – his attitude was all too familiar for a man of his class and age; she was furious with herself. She ought to have had a better answer, but what was she to do? When the war broke out, for most it was an unmatched, unimaginable catastrophe, for some a frustrating disruption to their personal plans; for Ava it was the first taste of freedom.

Ava's problem, if it could be called such, was that everything in life had come too easily to her. She wasn't used to being challenged and she had never felt the stinging slap of failure. Without either, it was practically impossible to clear one's mind sufficiently to decide how it ought to be used; it was so easy to become fogged with boredom.

Her upbringing had been charmed and peaceful. The affection of her mother and father was guaranteed, as she was their only child. Universal admiration was guaranteed, because not only was she spectacularly good-looking but she combined this blessing with an attitude that suggested she really didn't care what the world thought of her looks, or anything else come to that. Such commitment to indifference guaranteed the intensification of the universal adoration. She was astonishingly bright and found studying a breeze. Her parents were modern enough to employ the most prestigious tutors available; ones that parents normally only invested in if they had sons to educate. Besides fluently mastering French and German, Ava could read and write Latin and Greek; natural curiosity had led her to excel in her studies of the sciences and geography, she had a thorough understanding of ancient and modern history and English literature, and – because her father liked to talk business in the evenings – she was coached in mathematics, economics and commerce as well. Reading music presented no problem to her, and she played both the harp and the piano with extreme competence. Her long, strong limbs meant that she was a natural athlete and, as such, she played a decent game of tennis or golf when called upon. She could swim, ski and dance with energy and flair.

No one was more aware than Ava of the irony that with all of these talents she was the one amongst her friends who was the most easily bored and the most frequently restless. She had never gone up to Oxford, although many of her tutors had mooted the possibility. Her mother had thrown up objections – she was afraid a formal education would ruin Ava's chances of a really good marriage – and Ava had felt no longing to attend an institution that, whilst professing to be the epicentre of brilliant minds and allowing women to attend lectures and take exams, would not permit its female students to matriculate. It was only last year that the university had finally agreed to allow women to graduate with mortar and gown, but even then Ava had not been tempted. She knew that what others revered as a place steeped in time-honoured tradition she would simply loathe as claustrophobic and limitingly sexist. The ideas of curfews, monitoring of the company of the opposite sex and deferring to the word of a chaperone were unthinkable. When the war first came along, Ava hadn't realistically expected to be in the thick of it, but she certainly didn't want to be a Rapunzel locked away in an ivory tower. She had been hopeful that because the country was desperate for a workforce, perhaps a girl like her might be acknowledged, one day respected. And for a brief period of time she had indeed felt the electrifying buzz of being useful.

Her love affairs provided a certain amount of distraction. The only fear that Ava had was that in the end that was all they were. A distraction. Not that she believed a fruitful love affair was her goal – she did not – but there was no dignity in frittering away time either, and after a while, the men became interchangeable. Her mother complained that Ava was anti-marriage; she was not. She simply had never met a man who was her equal and who recognised her as his. Men adored her, worshipped her and lusted after her. They thought she was beautiful, sexy, witty. They wanted to own her. They did not understand her. She doubted they valued her, at least not for the right reasons. She saw nothing to gain by committing to a man who would want to subdue and control her. She had never seen a marriage that led to more freedom for the woman. She existed in a perpetual state of rebellion, although sometimes she almost forgot exactly what she was rebelling against, exactly what her cause was.

Ava had always been interested in Lydia's more simplistic view of the world, her less demanding expectations. Lydia had only ever articulated one ambition: to marry well. She had never expressed any sense that there might be more to life than finding a decent, reasonable man to earn for her. Lawrence was distinguished rather than handsome, intelligently thorough rather than a genius, but add to these attributes his family, and he was in Lydia's mind quite indisputably ideal. At least he had been. His sensibleness about the lack of heir might for many confirm that opinion, but apparently it was not so for Lydia. She had not confided as much to Ava, but she had hinted that his deficiency of passion about the lack of a baby infuriated her. His cold self-preservation during the Great War repelled her.

Ava watched Lydia run across the clean sheet of snow in the direction of the dangerously attractive officer. He was certainly wonderful to look at. If it wasn't for the promise Lydia had extracted, Ava might have been tempted herself. He was very much her type for a dalliance. Angry, damaged, beautiful. She wondered whether he could be trained, enslaved to anything other than fury; she felt a pinch of regret that she'd never find out. Ava adored her friend, but doubted that Lydia's girlish, flirty ways would be weapon enough to slay or soothe this ferocious man's will, but then that probably wasn't Lydia's aim. What could her aim be? Did she even know? Lydia had always been so faithful and dutiful, it seemed oddly out of character for her to be dashing across the snow, towards trouble, with such determination.

Ava turned from the impending calamity and slipped back between the sheets, sucking up the remnants of warmth that her friend's body had left. She reached for the newspaper and decided to turn her mind to bigger concerns. Unemployment was on the up again: two million. Seventeen per cent of the workforce. It was unbelievable. And what was this? Some brave woman was planning to lecture about constructive birth control. Marie Stopes. Ava made a note of her name; she'd make an interesting dinner guest. Lady Pondson-Callow would be distraught.

18

BEATRICE FELT VIVID with excitement. Her fingers trembled a little as she fastened her corset, and she hadn't been able to eat a full breakfast, something that had only ever happened once before and that was when she'd had laryngitis. She saw the extra time the snow-in had provided as a blessing. An actual gift from God.

Last night she and Arnie Oaksley had chatted fluently throughout dinner, *and* he'd sat with her after he returned from the smoking room; they'd both agreed that the habit of the chaps going off to smoke and the women going off to gossip was horribly dated, that nowadays all the best hostesses gave up the segregation and allowed the sexes to mingle when the effects of the delicious food and the copious amounts of alcohol were at their highest. They had stayed together until after eleven. The situation was . . . Bea hesitated as she searched for the most accurate word; in the end she settled on *promising*. The situation was promising. A delightful, hopeful word.

Arnie Oaksley was about five foot eight or nine; Beatrice generally wore two-inch heels, so if she threw her shoulders back, she was a fraction taller than him. It didn't matter. Not to her and, for once, not to him either. He was a neat man, slight and inexcessive. His ears were smaller than most men's but his chin was impressively angular, which compensated. He had a thin moustache that was struggling to take up residency above his lip, suggesting it was a relatively new addition; perhaps to mask the small scarring that remained around his mouth. Beatrice wondered who had made the decision to allow a moustache to grow. Did he have a manservant to help him to shave and trim; could he have suggested it? She wondered what colour his eyes had been. She couldn't remember whether she'd ever met him before the war. It was possible; during her debutante days she'd briefly met so many young men. She planned to check her old dance cards when she returned home, cards she'd sentimentally kept, tied together with a length of cream lace, suggesting a level of romance in her life that simply did not exist. Irrationally, she hoped they might have danced together back then, an irrelevant fact since evidently he'd been too slight and she too plain for either one to have remembered the other. Yet if they *had* danced, she'd be able to make something of that. She might force a memory; try to decide if his eyes had been light or dark. She'd certainly be able to make something out of the fact that they had known one another before. People longed for that in particular, relationships that had endured; they desperately sought them where they really were not.

Arnie Oaksley had been very interesting company last night. He'd talked about breeding Labradors, and had told her about a piano concert he'd been to recently; he'd been impressed by the pianist, a talented young woman named Myra Hess. Admittedly no one could have described him as especially jovial. Sadly, there was no hint of flirtation; their differing sexes (and certainly as to how that difference might be of interest to one another) were not acknowledged. He treated her as a neutered tomcat might treat a pampered pedigree kitten, with polite diffidence but no sense of playfulness – that was perhaps a little too much to hope for – but he had been sincere, thoughtful and sensible, qualities Beatrice could be wildly excited about. He did not wallow – the decent ones tried not to; in fact his lack of sight was not mentioned except as a backdrop to his few not especially funny jokes and one awkward incident.

'Dominoes rather than cards for me tonight. I lost a fortune yesterday, just couldn't read the blighters. With dominoes I can at least feel the bumps,' he said with a forced laugh. Beatrice thought perhaps he'd used the same line before. She agreed quickly and, rather than becoming bored or embarrassed by the lengthy pauses in between each of his turns, she admired the way he painstakingly ran his fingers over the dominoes. He played well, snapping the bricks into order, making only one mistake, which was matching a seven against a five. Beatrice refrained from saying anything, something she regretted when the game could not be completed.

'Have I made a mistake?' he asked. 'There ought to be another seven. Are you holding on to it?'

'No.'

'Then I must have laid something incorrectly.' He started to efficiently finger the bricks that snaked in a line in front of him, keen to find the error. Beatrice was stunned. He must have put some effort into developing extra capacity to remember such things; she hadn't thought he'd notice. The corner of his mouth twitched with exasperation and Beatrice felt increasingly flustered.

'Gosh, yes, there.' She took his hand and placed it on the offending domino. She was too anxious to fully appreciate the fact that she was touching him for the first time. 'I've obviously drunk more than I should. I hadn't realised you'd mislaid. Just didn't see it,' she gabbled. Then she clasped her mouth shut, mortified at the choice of her words.

'Don't.' He did not specify whether he meant 'Don't say anything else, as it is embarrassing us both' or 'Don't cheat for me in the first place.' She didn't get the sense that he meant 'Don't worry that you've just inadvertently referred to sight.' His irritation sliced the air like a blade.

'How can you know what's been laid with such accuracy?' she mumbled, trying to re-establish some of the evening's atmosphere of pleasure.

'I picture them in my head. Don't underestimate me.'

So that was the 'don't' he was referring to.

Very soon after that, he said he was going to bed. Beatrice was left to deal with the shame of patronising a man she was trying to flirt with.

She was determined that she would not make the same mistake

116

today. This morning at breakfast, Sarah had advised her to treat him as she treated any other man she might be interested in, but that was more easily said than done; she had so little experience with men that she was, naturally, nervous and clumsy. She had hoped that his blindness might be an advantage to her, an unspeakable thought but the truth all the same. He might get to know her before he judged her. She reasoned that it was not possible that he'd care what she looked like and, besides, he might need her as much as – if not more than – she needed him. However, his blindness could not be an advantage to her if she handled him incorrectly; if she hurt or offended him.

'A gang are out playing in the snow; are you interested?' she asked him, when she eventually tracked him down in the second drawing room. He was sitting stone still on the sofa. Even though it was only morning, the room felt stuffy, fetid. It was Arnie's isolated immobility that made him appear an invalid, rather than the black bandage he wore across his ravaged eye sockets. She wanted to see him run in the snow.

'Snowballs aren't my thing,' he said with a shrug. 'Ready, aim, fire.' He made his fingers into a gun and waved his hand around madly. Bea couldn't work out whether he was trying to be funny or whether he was vexed with her.

'No, I can't imagine they are, but I think the plan is to build a snowman.'

Arnie paused. She assumed he was pondering whether he could get involved in that activity; she'd already considered as much and decided he could. 'How does it look out there?' he asked.

'It's beautiful,' she sighed. 'Clean and peaceful. It's laid rather well. It is inches deep.'

'Still falling?'

'On and off, but no, not this exact moment.' He looked hungry for more, and she feared her answers were lacking. They didn't convey the splendid surprise that snow always was. She tried harder. 'I always think snow is rather bold and yet egalitarian.'

'How so?'

'Well, it transforms everything into one. Stone, brick, path, grass, field, roof all become one thing: whiteness. It unapologetically transforms everything that's ordinary and known into something delicious and pure. It's a child's world when it looks this way. Almost comic. Roofs and treetops become marshmallow mounds, everything serious is temporarily obliterated by soft, fluffy pillows; the churches and school halls, the gutters and banks – they all disappear briefly. I always think of snow as impish and implausible.'

'What does it look like right now?'

'For the first time today there's a hint of blue sky, and it's enough to allow a bright streak of winter sunshine to slither down from the heavens.'

'Will it melt?'

'Not yet, but there are scattered diamonds all over the fields; glinting and winking magically, mischievously.' She turned to him and shot out an honest thought. 'You must miss it.'

'Yes, I do.'

Beatrice rushed to the window and opened it, allowing a cold but appealing blast of fresh air to ambush the over-hot drawing room. The laughter and squeals of the other young guests, playing at a distance, seized the room. He raised his head a fraction, like an animal sniffing the air. Bravely Beatrice advanced towards him and tugged at the sleeve of his jacket. 'Come on, everyone is having so much fun.'

The building of the snowman was a success. Beatrice did wish she had a pretty sealskin cloche hat, just like Ava, but she didn't care quite as much as she might have done before. Nor did she panic when the snow began to fall in damp eddies and flurries, causing her hair to frizz tightly around her head. For once it didn't matter how she looked. Arnie called to her two or three times, as he and the other chaps gamely rolled the huge ball that was to make the snowman's body. Everyone was tottering and groping their way through the snow; Arnie didn't stand out. Bea helped the women roll the head and sought out the branches for its arms with a cheerful girl named Lucy, and whilst she had no idea where either Sarah or Lydia was – her usual social props – she felt very much a part of everything.

Afterwards, when the air started to turn chilly and stark, everyone dashed to the dining room, where they were served soup and venison pie. It was a casual lunch, but there was still a seating plan. Lady Pondson-Callow had decided the youngsters were bubbling to the point where they might just erupt, something her daughter was waiting for but she dreaded, and so she dispersed the younger guests across the tables, mixing their playful ways with more staid manners. Bea was disappointed to find herself sitting on a table with the Duchess of Feversham, the very woman who the night before she'd been so thrilled to talk about and could not have imagined talking to. Now, she just wanted to stay close by Arnie's side. She endured the endless rise and plunge of soup spoons, the clink of silver on china, the discreet slurps and the polite enquiries after her health, but all the time she wondered who was he talking to and whether they'd help him find the salt on the lavishly decorated, rather too crowded, table.

Lady Pondson-Callow's plan worked. After lunch the atmosphere altered considerably as the youngsters – having endured Edwardian manners and conversations, which always induced resentment and boredom – felt swiftly deflated and suddenly cross with the snow; it had been a jolly diversion this morning, but now the cold, soggy afternoon was swiftly losing its light and it simply seemed inconvenient. People wanted to go home and get on with their own business, but if they had to stay then they expected diversion. No one could ride or hunt or walk; it was agreed that summer was more fun. The more slothful retired to bed, vowing only to rise for dinner and music. Lady Pondson-Callow had insisted that the gramophone must not be brought into action nor the rugs rolled up until at least tea time; she was determined that standards were to be maintained, even in inclement weather. The more serious-minded settled into the afternoon with books borrowed from Ava's father's impressive library, and many of the men took themselves off into the billiards room, where they planned to drink and smoke the afternoon away.

Beatrice was pleased that Arnie didn't take that option but instead chose to sit with the remaining women and one or two of the older men and listen to those who were able to play the piano. Bea was one of the first to be persuaded. She knew she was a good musician – she practised diligently and had a good ear – but she was also polite enough to realise that after three songs she should give up her chair and allow others to showcase their skills. She sat down next to Arnie without considering that she ought to appear less keen.

'Bravo, you play well.' His words sat on her shoulders like a rich theatre cape; luxuriant and transforming.

At four o'clock the snow started to fall again. It came down determined and dense, settling silently layer upon layer, crushing any hopes that the guests might be able to depart early the following morning.

'I don't think anyone is going anywhere for at least another twenty-four hours,' commented Harry Fine.

'You are all most welcome,' stated Sir Peter, and the speed with which he was filling up sherry and port glasses underlined his sincerity. His wife looked more concerned; she wanted to question both the judgement and the propriety of pouring drinks all after-noon. But in the end, all she did was ring for tea.

'I can't think why anyone would want to leave,' commented Arnie as he bit into a generously buttered crumpet. The tea and the implied compliment warmed Beatrice in her gut. A smudge of butter glistened on his moustache. She had an urge to dab it away with her napkin. With her lips. She was having the most romantic weekend of her life.

19

LYDIA KNEW SHE was behaving shockingly, with no discretion or consideration, but she was helpless. He was superb. It was frighteningly uncertain, yet unequivocally clear. They stayed out all morning and did not return to the house even for lunch. Lady Pondson-Callow's carefully calligraphed name plates advertised their absence. They were both missed and instantly linked. Eyebrows shot up to hairlines, communicating everything.

The Duchess of Feversham, a notorious scandalmonger, always desperate to divert the spotlight from her own misdemeanours, was unable to resist drawing attention to Lydia's non-appearance. 'Won't she be very hungry?' she asked mischievously.

Mr Lytton sniggered. 'Perhaps she's getting her fill elsewhere.' None of it was new; the crude guffaws and spiteful insinuations were commonplace. People had long since become bored of Lydia's goodness; it reflected badly on them. The hint of a flirtation was naturally going to be greeted with extreme joy.

Lydia knew there would be talk, but she didn't care. Let them talk.

They walked for miles. Through the forest of gnarled trees, colourless and spiky. Lydia's fur coat became heavy with the weight of melted snowflakes. In the distant fields the animals searched for warmth; the sheep in one field huddled together, the horses in the other hugged the wall. First and most ferociously Lydia's nose began to sting with the shock of the extreme cold, then her ears and lips stung too. Her feet became numb in the thick white carpet, but she didn't care. She didn't complain. She was afraid that if she hinted at any discomfort, she'd not only sound spoilt but he might insist they returned to the house, out of consideration. She couldn't go back there. Outside, alone amongst the silent flurries, they existed. They were something. She believed they understood one another and were connected; although nothing overt had been said, she felt it. He *must* have thought of her over the last nine days. It was impossible to imagine that something as momentous could flow just one way. It would be as wild as suggesting a river could be turned around, dragged from the sea, pushed back through plains and forests, up mountainsides. It was unnatural. She couldn't believe that of the world.

Yet she also felt that somehow they would not be able to hold on to their precious connection under other people's gazes and comments. Whatever this was, it was too new, too rare to be exposed. It would be threatened. Perhaps ruined. They needed to be alone to solidify. They were so different from one another. He was slippery, a practised womaniser; a war hero to boot. She was no more reliable. Married and terrified.

'What are you thinking about?' he asked. His voice cut through the clear, cold day. They'd walked in silence for about a mile.

'Us.' She cursed herself for her indiscretion. It was a ridiculous, ill-considered answer. It showed her hand.

'There's an "us", is there?' He seemed amused. She didn't nod but glanced at him and he held her gaze. 'Are there children, Lid?'

This was more than a polite, conventional enquiry. He wanted to know where she stood, what he was dealing with. He was assessing the complications and the potential disruption and distractions; she understood as much. She shook her head and looked away. 'No, no children. We've tried. We want them. I can't have any.'

'I'm sorry.'

'Yes, it's sad.'

He put his hand on her shoulder and squeezed it. Her skin blistered under his touch. The gesture was tender and yet rallying at the same time. She wondered how many soldiers he'd comforted with the same action.

'It is very sad. You see, I rather think that without a baby, I don't amount to much at all.'

'What can you mean?'

'It's my job. I'm supposed to provide an heir.' She didn't know what made her confess this. She'd never stated the facts quite so baldly to anyone, not to Sarah or Ava. But then she didn't have to; they understood how it worked in her world. Edgar might not.

'You seem quite substantial enough to me as you are.'

His words soothed, a dock leaf applied to a nettle sting.

Last night they had flirted relentlessly. Today, things were different between them: initially austere and stark, she now sensed a softening. What they had was certainly more formal, and yet it seemed more sincere; these were not two things that necessarily went hand in hand. Lydia pondered as to why there was a change between them. Was it a deepening or a distancing? She felt icy panic at the thought of distance. Perhaps the change of mood could be put down to nothing more than the lack of intoxicating champagne, or maybe it was the fact that they were outside, surrounded by nature's frosting rather than tiaras and cigar smoke. She considered the fact that he was aware that last night the intensity of their flirtation had filled her with guilt and fear and made her flee. He did not want her to flee again? The possibility that he wanted her near him thrilled her. Assured her. Whatever the reason for the shift between them, he saw to it that she felt safe rather than threatened. Excited rather than afraid.

They followed usual conventions, inasmuch as they scurried around for people they had in common. They found names they both recognised and then exchanged stories about the company they kept. They swapped views on films they'd seen at the cinema, plays they'd watched at the theatre and art that hung in London's galleries. They found that they had both enjoyed a recent exhibition of Federico Barocci's work and a Cubist exhibition showing the work of Picasso and Georges Braque. He saw more value in the Dada non-artists than she did. She knew little about them, but what she did know enabled her to dismiss their work as inferior to Leonardo da Vinci, who the Dada movement mocked. He seemed indifferent to whether she agreed or disagreed with his opinions, whereas she longed for their thoughts to fall into line.

He told her how he had been picked up by her set; whose house he had dined at, whose deer and pheasant he had shot. Every time he mentioned a woman's name, she wondered what the exact nature of the relationship was. She frantically assessed the probability of the woman succumbing to his charms. She considered the woman's beauty, history and marital harmony; she agonised over whether he might have . . . would have wanted to . . . After all, he was a self-confessed ladies' man. What did that mean, exactly? Oh God, she knew what it meant. Thoughts of who he'd had assaulted her tranquillity. Was he linked to anyone now? How did those sorts of things begin?

And end?

Certainly, she knew that people had affairs – she was not an idiot – but as it had never been a route she'd wanted to pursue herself, she'd never thought about the detail. Now she wondered who made the first move, and how. Did the woman have to give some sort of signal? How did one know if a move had been made? It would be too awful if there was some sort of code and she failed to see the hint. She wanted him. Quite simply that. He had long, dark lashes that curled like a woman's ought to. Lydia had heard women admire such lashes before, but personally she'd never thought much of them on a man. She'd thought they were effete. They seemed so greedy and unnecessary, but since the war she thought that men were entitled to everything. To jobs, to long eyelashes, to her body. The thought made her gasp. She wasn't sure where it had come from. Where it was going.

It was so very different from the flirtations she'd had before she married, because then the rules were quite clearly understood by everyone. Nice girls, like Lydia, might smile and pout but they were never allowed to be alone with a chap. Back then, the gentlemen hadn't expected anything from her beyond the promise of the last dance, and she had never harboured any ideas about the sexual possibilities – delightful or erroneous – that a liaison might offer. Lydia's sort had hardly known anything about all that.

It was only once a girl married that things became clear. And now everything was muddy again, because what she felt for him wasn't girlish excitement. Her years of experience as a married woman meant that her ambition for him had gone long past securing a waltz. She ached for him; low, low between her legs, and in her breasts. She wanted to taste him. Put her lips and tongue on his skin. A snowflake settled on his right eyebrow and she wanted to kiss it into oblivion.

Edgar appeared cautious. She watched for a signal, a sign that he knew how she felt and that he felt the same, but none came. She wanted to believe they had both accepted the inevitability that they would be together and it was simply a case of them each working out how it would be accomplished, but she couldn't be sure. It was possible he was thinking about something totally different, some*one* totally different. The thought was horrifying. She wanted to throw off her clothes, there in the snowy forest, naked and ready for him, but it was a ludicrous thought. She'd catch pneumonia.

'Where are we going?' she asked.

'I think we'll pick up the path to the village soon.'

They did, and she was grateful. In the village they'd have a chance of finding food and warmth. They passed the church; the snow on the path leading to it had been churned by more determined worshippers than those to be found at Ava's house party, although the gates were shut now, service over, hymn books closed. They passed the war memorial and paused out of habitual respect, then Edgar said, 'Come on, don't linger. I imagine you are hungry, aren't you? You must have skipped breakfast and it's almost midday.'

The post office was the only place that was open; Lydia wondered whether Lawrence might have tried to send a cable to Ava's, whether he was expecting news from her. She shoved the thought from her head. She couldn't think about Lawrence right now. He was not of this world. This unrecognisably white world, devoid of familiar landmarks or routes. She was free and separate in it.

'Let's go to the pub,' Edgar suggested.

Lydia was taken aback. She'd never been in a pub before. She didn't know anyone who had, other than the servants. 'It's shuttered,' she pointed out, stalling.

'We'll get them to shift. Everyone needs the trade.' He banged on the door and was proved right: after a few moments, a rotund and pink-faced landlord opened up. Lydia followed Edgar over the threshold, feeling daring and dangerous.

The pub had been standing for over three hundred years; the walls were wonky and the ceiling low. Edgar had to stoop or else he would have banged his head on the cracked and compacted oak beams, worn and tired with the weight of the roof. The landlord said that Lydia could sit in the snug and he'd bring them soup.

'The fire is in the bar,' pointed out Edgar quietly. 'We'll be in there.'

The landlord wasn't pleased, but he didn't say anything more, and he served them both cider when Edgar asked for it. There was something about Edgar that would not be argued with.

The bar smelt of damp dogs and earth. Two large mongrels monopolised the best spot in front of the big fire that was housed in a dirty brick chimneypiece. They were curled around the legs of a small round wooden table; two high-backed chairs, boasting worn leather cushions, waited for Lydia and Edgar to complete the country tableau. They sat down and watched the flames leap. One of the dogs whimpered in its sleep; the other sniffed Lydia's legs. On the table there was a pewter candlestick, with just an inch-long stub of candle protruding. The landlord was not prepared to give them the benefit of warmth or light, but Edgar lit it. The right side of Lydia's body felt numb with the cold, whilst the left side, closest to the fire, was scorched. She tingled all over. She kept on her coat but slipped off his gloves and balanced them on the ends of the handles of the fire irons, in order to dry them out. Her wedding ring spun loose on her cold finger. Neither of them seemed in much of a hurry to talk now. The silence between them was peculiarly rousing. They both knew that if they said any more, it had to be significant. It had to stir and move.

The cider arrived in thick stoneware pots with off-white strap handles. Both the lip and the handle were chipped. It was very different from the crystal flutes, tulips and coupes that Lydia was used to drinking out of. Edgar watched her, gauging her reaction to the basic provisions.

'Good health,' she offered.

'Cheers,' he replied. They banged the pots together. The yeasty smell made Lydia feel drunk even before she tried the cider. She was thirsty from the walk, so she glugged rather than sipped.

'I should have asked for tea,' she commented. The dryness hit the back of her throat, bubbles bounced on her tongue. The poor man's champagne. The soup came: salty leek and potato, served with coarse brown peasant bread. There were no place mats or napkins. The landlord breathed on the spoons and wiped them on his shirt before he handed them to Lydia and Edgar: a dare, a challenge, a protest that Lydia hadn't obediently sat in the spot designated for women. She took the spoon, trying not to give any indication that she felt a bit queasy; Edgar seemed not to notice the landlord's gesture or, if he did, he did not dignify the gripe with an acknowledgement. The soup was hot; it burned Lydia's throat. She stopped drinking it but instead bent over it so she could get the benefit of its warmth. Edgar broke his bread and threw it into his soup as though he was feeding ducks. He dragged the spoon towards him and then put the entire bowl of the spoon in his mouth. Instead of despising his uncultured manners, Lydia was excited by the thought of his appetites; she'd always been taught to tip the bowl away from her and take slow, unsatisfactory sips. Her habit was inadequate in relation to her hunger.

Lydia simultaneously wilted and yet flourished in the proximity of his glorious confidence. He was just as valid and marvellous as she'd imagined when they first met in the café; more so. The way he held his head, the shape of his jaw, the bulk of his thighs fascinated her. She wanted to touch him. To reach out, and stroke and pet him. More. She wanted more.

Suddenly, a heinous possibility flung itself into Lydia's head and she wondered how she could have failed to think of it until now.

'Are you married?' she blurted. It was an indiscreet question. The tone she used made it impossible to pretend it was a polite enquiry; it was desperate. She was begging. She was not sure what she was begging for, exactly. If he was married, maybe she would find it in her to step away. Maybe. She could stop this adventure before it became a scandal, or a disaster. But if he was married, she might die. Stop breathing. It was a ridiculous thought. Indulgent and exaggerated, and yet she felt it was so. She did not want this man to have one woman he placed above all others. Even if it was a woman he might betray or possibly despise. She did not want that woman to already exist, because she wanted to be that woman. A woman above all others.

Even a woman he might betray or despise.

She would take whatever was on offer. She was helpless. Hopeless.

He shook his head, and she breathed again.

'I'm glad.'

'Why, Lid? What does it matter to you?' He cocked his head to one side.

'You know why,' she muttered. Exposed.

'So what's your husband like? Who is he?'

'He's a lord; when his father dies, he'll be an earl. The Earl of Clarendale.'

'I see.'

Lydia was appalled at herself for offering this up as an explanation as to who Lawrence was. There must be more to him than that, but what more need there be? She thought Edgar would think she had been an avaricious, ambitious deb, and so to disabuse him she added, 'He wasn't the heir apparent when I married him. That wasn't why I picked him.' Edgar didn't ask why she had picked him, but she offered lamely, 'He has lovely manners.'

'That must be helpful.'

'It is.' She felt awkward. It was a stupid comment. Lawrence was sensible, dignified and confident too, but somehow none of that seemed enough. Edgar was magnificent, brave, beautiful. The reality of Lawrence temporarily evaded Lydia. She was doing him a disservice. Besides the fact that she was falling in love with another man, she was doing him a disservice because she couldn't recall the essence of him. The point of him. 'Of course, if I can't produce a baby, the title that's been in the family for hundreds of years will be futile.'

'I'm sure everyone would be devastated.' Edgar drained his pint and looked irritated. He signalled for a refill. Lydia had only drunk half of hers, which was just as well, because he didn't offer her a second. It was strong stuff; her eyelids already felt heavy and her thoughts were woozy. Fuzzy. She was embarrassed that she hadn't explained the situation clearly. It was not just concern over a baby or a title. It was not about a marriage and whether it thrived or even survived. Her fertility seemed to have much greater meaning. Frustrated, she stared out of the window. A lattice of lead framed the small, thick panes of glass, making a mosaic of light that distorted and obscured the reality of the outside world. Despite the awkwardness of trying to explain her soul and core, she felt cocooned; they were in their own world.

'They kept him out.'

'Who?'

'His family. They'd already lost two sons. One in the war, another to a riding accident. His father knows people.'

'How fortunate for him.'

'Yes. I suppose.'

Edgar took another huge swig of his cider and then swiftly turned his head towards the fire, away from her, his black hair swishing over his left eye. His gestures were already becoming familiar to her. He was different, a thing of beauty; she almost gasped. She needed him to turn back to her. Desperately she blurted, 'I think we're being punished. Lawrence and I. Do you think that's possible?'

'I don't believe in God.'

This didn't answer the question as to whether he believed they ought to be punished. 'He must seem like an awful coward to you,' she sighed. Lost.

'Ah, fuck it, at least he survived.' Lydia had never heard anyone say that word before; at least, she'd occasionally heard it on the street, but no one had ever directed it at her. Edgar saying it was strangely ugly and deeply arousing. Suddenly a look came over him that she didn't know or understand. He seemed charged up, furious. He dragged his chair closer under the table, towards her; the wood squeaked a protest as it heaved along the floor. 'At least he didn't fall foul of the propaganda machine. He had the sense, or the connections, or the sheer arrogant self-interest to resist that crap. Perhaps there's more to him than you are telling me.'

'I don't understand.'

'You think war is glamorous, don't you? The medals, the words they bandy about, like "bravery" and "duty". You think war is sensational.'

'No, not at all. I've seen what it does. Some of my best friends—'

He didn't let her finish, but barked out a derisive laugh. 'What, some of your best friends are black, or queer, or dead?'

She didn't know why he was mocking her. She didn't know what she'd done wrong. The conversation had escaped. It was now an unwieldy spillage staining their short but vitally important history. She wanted to howl. She'd been trying to tell him something important. She thought he'd understand.

'Shall I tell you the filthy secret about war? The dirtiest tool they use?' He was leaning very close to her now. She could see every muscle in his face; they jumped, as though someone was pulling strings connected to the tissue. The movements were random, jerky. 'It's not the guns, the tanks, the gas. They are not the dirtiest weapons. It's sex.'

'Sex?'

'Not surprisingly, they didn't say that.'

'The decency brigade would have been outraged.' She tried to lighten the atmosphere with a joke; he played along and offered up a brief, polite smile, but then leaned back in his chair, away from her. His eyes glazed. He was losing interest. She was losing him.

'Quite.'

Lydia felt miserably wrong for attempting the joke. She should have accepted the heavy sense of oppressive truth and pain that stained the atmosphere. He'd been trying to talk to her. 'What do you mean?' she asked.

'They called it love. But it's sex. Do you love your wife, your girl, your country? Will you kill for her? That's what the politicians offered. Threatened. If we didn't fight, we didn't love our women. We were unmanned. We didn't know the meaning of the word then, although we soon learned. Your husband . . . Well, it seems to me he had the balls to ignore them. He had the last laugh.'

'No. It wasn't like that. I don't see it that way.' Lydia stumbled on her words because he was going too fast for her. She wanted to think his reasoning was faulty, but she could see the sense, and besides, it was the first time anyone had offered her something robust as a defence for Lawrence's actions. He'd had the guts to see through it all? Could that be the case? But how could Edgar admire Lawrence for that? He was a decorated soldier. A brave man.

'So I feel entitled,' added Edgar.

'Entitled?'

'I should and will take it all. Everything they promised me.' Lydia was not sure what 'all' he was referring to, until he added, 'I'll have every girl that will spread her legs, because they promised me that.'

'You're vile.' She recoiled, shocked, but also, she couldn't deny it, deeply, deeply aroused.

'I'm honest. I'm entitled to Lady Feversham, Lady Cooper and Lady Jennings.'

'No, no you are not,' she insisted.

'Why?'

'Because of me.' She banged her hand on the table and the spoons rattled in the soup bowls. The landlord stopped drying pots and stared at them. Edgar didn't notice; his eyes were trained on her. She felt the heat of a blush flare up from her heart; it crept over her neck and jaw. It was not embarrassment; it was anger and fear.

'You?'

'Yes, yes. I can't bear it. The thought of it,' she admitted.

'But what have you to do with me, Lady Chatfield? You are another man's wife.'

Lydia stretched across the table and kissed him passionately. She felt his lips resist for a fraction of a second; then they accepted her. The kiss was the sort that made her shiver. She felt it through her entire body. It was firm and dark, strong and intoxicating. Then it was over. He broke apart and firmly pushed her away. His blunt bristles scratched her lip. She sank back in a puddle of shame. He'd pushed her away. He didn't want her. He'd said that he would take at will and he'd implied indiscrimination, but he didn't want her. She had thought he did. She could not understand it. She could not bear it.

Edgar drank his soup in silence and, even though she had not finished, he left the table and went to stand at the bar, where he started up a conversation with the landlord. Lydia noticed that the skinny young girl who was polishing the glassware was lingering over her work longer than was feasibly necessary. She kept turning Edgar's way and flashing broad smiles. Even though Edgar had his back to Lydia, she could sense that he returned the smiles. She felt sick and faint.

She hoped that when they walked back to Ava's, they would have an opportunity to retrieve some of the earlier intimacy. She felt the need to apologise or at least explain, although she wasn't sure how that apology might begin or what it was for exactly. Would she need to apologise for meeting him after she'd married? For marrying a rich and titled man? For marrying a man who didn't fight? For kissing him?

She didn't get the chance. The villagers thought the very suggestion of them walking home was dangerously eccentric. Horses were brought for their use, and two young boys led them through the snow, robbing them of privacy and the prospect of any more discussion. Lydia tried to object, to insist they could manage, but Edgar swiftly tightened the horse's saddle and simply said, 'Hush. This is better.'

She didn't know if he meant it was better simply because they'd be home quicker and drier; if so, she was ripped by the hurt that he had opted for such a practical physical response to their situation. Or might he have meant that if they were chaperoned, it was better for appearances? For her reputation? Possibly. If this was the case, her heart hardened a fraction as she resented his acquiescing to tiresome convention. Another thought struck her, and it was the worst of all. He might think riding was the better option for the very reason that she loathed the suggestion: because it obliterated any chance of them talking. Or her trying to kiss him again. The humiliation throbbed through her body. The pain filled her lungs as though she was a drowning woman too far from the coast. She'd lost him. Already. Before he was ever even hers. The thought was horrifying.

Edgar rode in front of Lydia, his horse cutting a path for hers. She ached with uncertainty as she followed him. What was he thinking? What did he mean '*better*'? The only thing she was certain of now was that she was neither courageous nor determined enough to do anything other than follow him. Follow wherever he led. He would set the pace. He would call the shots. She was putty in his hands.

The afternoon light seeped away and by the time they reached the Pondson-Callows', a thick dark indigo sky dominated. The snow had begun to fall again. This time it was direct and dense. Never-ending. They would not be able to leave in the morning. Lydia was grateful: it might offer another opportunity. She was mortified too: if he refused to speak or acknowledge her tomorrow, she didn't know how she would get through the day. The thought of any day without him seemed like no sort of day at all.

Without a gasp of wind, the diffused flakes settled into something that suggested solidity. But it was a lie. The snow wouldn't stay for ever. The deep layers simply offered a trick; a belief that they had all the time in the world. Lydia would be a fool to believe that. No one could believe such a thing any more. Everyone had to live for the moment, didn't they?

20

SARAH HAD ASKED Dickenson to let her know the moment Lydia returned. She sensed a crisis and knew that Lydia needed her particular care and attention. Somehow Lydia was the sort of woman that other people felt they ought to protect, although Sarah could never work out why this might be the case. Many might argue that Lydia was the most fortunate of the four women; she was the one who had everything, or at least everything other than babies. Thinking about her own children's warmth, the soothing weight of them as they climbed on her knee or slipped a sticky hand into hers, Sarah accepted that it was indeed a lack, but so many women of their generation would not feel the comfort of a heavy baby in their womb or arms. Beatrice didn't have babies, or even a man with whom she could possibly hope to make them. At least Lydia could be consoled by a wealthy husband, a secure and constant income, living parents and (although it pained Sarah to be shallow, she knew that the world was, so she added it to her mental tally) a beautiful face. It was a mystery as to why Lydia extracted a sense from others that they ought to provide a shield, yet she did. Perhaps it was the beautiful face. She had a small head, but large lips and eyes, and despite her penchant for heavy eye make-up, she often looked like a child. On this occasion it was clear that the person she needed protecting from was herself. Both maid and friend bustled into her room with an air of panic and concern.

'Look at you, you are in a state,' Sarah declared the moment she saw her shivering, bedraggled friend.

'Am I?' Lydia shrugged, her expression evasive, secretive; whatever was on her mind, it was clear that she was unconcerned about her wet hair and clothes.

Dickenson swooped and gently started to ease her mistress out of the damp garments. 'Why, you are wearing jodhpurs!' she gasped, unwilling to find a tone that would hide her disapproval.

'They were the first thing to hand, and anyway, it turned out useful. I came home on horseback.' Lydia stepped out of her clothes. The soggy garments fell to the floor like hunted deer.

'I'll draw a hot bath,' muttered Dickenson.

Lydia seemed hardly to notice her near nakedness. She wandered to the window and stared out into the blackness. Only in the grounds closest to the house could anything be seen at all. There was a couple standing in the courtyard: Lady Feversham and Matthew Northbrook. Mr Northbrook was smoking; Lady Feversham picked up a handful of snow and shoved it down the neck of his jacket. He chased her around the snowman Beatrice and Arnie Oaksley had helped to build earlier.

'I say, look at that enormous snowman. Marvellous.' Lydia's tone sounded forced; Sarah didn't believe for a moment she cared about the snowman. 'Did you help build it, Sarah?'

'No, but Beatrice did.'

'Such fun.'

'Yes, you've missed quite a day.'

'I can imagine. Snowball fights, hot chocolate . . . Was there sledging?' Lydia giggled breathlessly, but Sarah thought there was a false ring to the animation and charm. Lydia seemed keen to keep up this pointless chatter indefinitely; as she and Sarah had been friends since the moment Lydia was born, Sarah recognised her tactic as diversion.

'Where were you all day?'

'Out.' Lydia beamed. It was a tense but determined smile and she stared unblinkingly at her friend. Sarah nodded and bit back any more questions; she was probably better off not being burdened by too many details.

'Lawrence is here.'

'Lawrence?' For a moment it seemed to Sarah that Lydia couldn't place her husband. The second she did, she looked stricken.

'He can't be.'

'Well, he is. Apparently he had a change of heart yesterday, and decided to come along after all, but then there was a problem with the car's engine – the cold, I suppose. Once it started snowing, he and the chauffeur had no choice other than to bunk down at a pub. They stayed in that little village we passed through on the way here.'

'West Claxinton?'

'Yes, that's the one.'

'Oh, my God.' Lydia sat down heavily on the chair in front of the dressing table.

'The car's still done for. So he walked here this morning. Through the snow. He's been asking for you.'

'Where did you tell him I was?'

'We didn't know where you were, so we couldn't say for sure. I guessed you'd probably gone with the housemaids to the hospital to see the patients had enough milk and such, since not all the deliveries can be made because of the snow.'

Lydia nodded; both women knew nothing was less likely. Sarah had panicked and suggested to Lawrence the one thing that might induce her out of a warm house on a snowy, freezing-cold day. It was not a particularly authentic-sounding alibi for Lydia; still, Lawrence had accepted it. Lydia was so pale, Sarah imagined she could almost see right through her to the heavily patterned wallpaper on the other side of the room. She looked as if she might faint, as women used to in their grandmothers' day.

'How would I have explained it?' Lydia mumbled.

Sarah wasn't sure exactly what Lydia had to explain. How deep was this mess? She hoped it had been nipped in the bud, this flirtation. She was pleased that Lawrence had decided to join them after all; she hadn't accepted the excuse about him having too much work, not for a moment. His arrival was the very thing Lydia needed: an open demonstration of his love and commitment. It was obvious they were struggling with the issue of an heir, naturally, but they'd be foolish to allow it to fester. 'Ava has been keeping him company.'

'I must get a note to Edgar.'

'A note to *Edgar*?' How could she think of him? Sarah stared pertinently at Lawrence's bags. Lydia's eyes slid to the leather luggage lined up along the left-hand side of the bed. Smart, masculine, heavy. She looked to Sarah as though she wanted to howl at its intrusion.

'Darling, can I come in? Are you decent?' Lawrence opened the door but he did not venture into the room. It was not the prospect of his wife's nudity that bothered him; it was seeing her in a state of undress while other women surrounded her. It was always awkward. He found women and their almost cloying intimacy a little too much. He liked the way chaps operated, with firm boundaries.

'No time for notes,' hissed Sarah. She was both furious and disappointed with her friend, yet she was loyal, and she swallowed up the awkward moment. 'Lawrence, my dear, there you are. We were wondering where you'd got to. Lydia will be so much happier now. She's missed you.' She kissed Lawrence on the cheek and held him in a friendly embrace just long enough to allow Lydia to gather her senses, but not so long as to make Lawrence aware that she needed to do so. 'I shall leave you two alone now. See you at dinner. I understand that drinks are at seven. We're to be seated by eight.' The door closed behind her.

'Lydia.'

'Lawrence.' Lydia did not run into Lawrence's arms as he'd hoped. Instead she remained in her seat, in front of the dressing table. He couldn't see her eyes because Dickenson was now robustly towel-drying her hair and obscuring her expression.

'You're shivering.' He looked around for her robe.

'So, you finished your dreadfully important work?'

'Work? Oh, yes.' Lawrence wasn't sure who the pretence was for, Dickenson or each other. Either way, he appreciated it. Things were deuced awkward between him and Lydia. This damned baby business. This Lydia was the one he felt comfortable with; the one who spent her day doing charitable deeds, the one who would retreat into decent manners when required. With a little bit of care on both sides, they might very well be able to bury the nastiness of last week. They could make a good show at forgetting it. Her behaviour had been unacceptable. She had been, by anyone's estimation, hysterical. Obviously her hormones were not all they should be. If they were, there would be a baby, no doubt, and she wouldn't have need, let alone inclination, to indulge in all this silly talk about punishments. What rot.

'Well that must be a big relief to you.' She had not yet said she was pleased to see him. Naturally he assumed she must be; every woman liked her husband by her side at this sort of do. Besides, with the snow, they might be here for days. She couldn't possibly want them to be apart for so long; although it was quite clear that she was still out of sorts. Nose out of joint good and proper. She was making him work for it. Well he'd be damned if he'd apologise. Certainly not in front of Dickenson. The servants loved that sort of thing, and it didn't do. A man mustn't look weak. Gossip started. Best he ignored her girlish sulking and pretended everything was in splendid fettle. He wasn't going to waste another moment on this nonsense.

'What a journey I've had. Damned motor. We broke down about seven miles away. Had to walk, in the snow, to the local village. We were lucky to find board.'

'You should have telephoned.'

'Oh, I know Pondson-Callow would have sent out the carriage, but it was snowing quite heavily by then. Not safe for horses.' Lawrence brushed aside his inconvenience. He didn't like to appear helpless; it was important that everyone saw him as a strong and energetic man. It had been tricky during the war, no doubt about it. If only the civil servants had been given uniforms, there wouldn't have been quite so much pointing and questioning in the street. Those horrible women who were always handing out white feathers used to infuriate him. What did they know? Privately, although he'd never admit it, he'd sometimes, fleetingly, wished he didn't always look quite so healthy, quite so vigorous. He'd heard of chaps who had started to carry a stick or developed incessant coughs, just to make things easier in public; chaps like him, ones that served, but served in an office. Essential workers — bankers, doctors, dentists — were in the same position. He was damned if he'd become one of the apologetic ones. What he did was vital. Well, important. Certainly valid. So he went the other way. He'd taken care to walk to his full height, to project his voice loudly and confidently, to keep in shape. It was no good being ashamed of where he was. What he was. That way ruin lay. That was why he was so damned cross with Lydia for saying such a ridiculous thing about her infertility. How could it be his punishment? He hadn't done anything wrong.

This morning he'd insisted on walking here straight after church; he'd carried his own luggage. He hadn't imagined in a month of Sundays that Lydia would have made such an early start; frankly, he was rather surprised that she'd chosen to spend her Sunday doing good deeds. Impressed, certainly, but he'd expected to find her still in bed, probably with a hangover. He'd thought she'd have a spot of kedgeree and then be the first to demand a snowball fight. It was wrong of him to be disappointed that she'd been out all day. Hospital visiting was the right sort of thing, obviously; admirable. Although he hoped to God her absence today wasn't something to do with their fight; he feared she was in danger of catching religion. People were going, rather extremely, down one path or the other nowadays, either declaring that they were agnostic or converting to Catholicism. He did hope she wasn't going to become one of those overly worthy or religious women; they made dull wives.

'Would you like to wear your blue silk georgette, my lady? I have it laid out.' Dickenson reached for the dress Lawrence most liked to see his wife in. He'd bought it for her on their last anniversary. Whilst undoubtedly a modern cut, it was pale and feminine, embroidered with daisies and cornflowers, which reminded Lawrence of more innocent days, when they were both unquestionably youthful and all about beginnings. The skirt was an abundance of minute pleats, and there was an overlay of something or other — lace? Something light and shy, at any rate. It was an extremely pretty dress. Dickenson held it with reverence.

'No. That dress isn't right at all. I need a party dress.'

'But it's not a party, my lady. It's dinner.'

'It will turn into a party, if I know Ava Pondson-Callow. One that lasts until the early hours. She's bored of being cooped up.'

'Actually, I spent most of the day with Ava; she was in rather good spirits.'

Lydia ignored Lawrence and continued to address her maid. 'What one wears has a dual purpose, and every woman worth her salt is inherently aware of both, Dickenson.'

'I thought the idea was to look nice, my lady.'

'It has to flatter, of course, but beyond that it has to demonstrate one's sense of status and style. It is an illustration of a woman's understanding of the significance of the event she is attending. If she gets it wrong, then she is telling the whole world that she's clueless. We don't want the world thinking I'm clueless, do we?'

Uncomfortable, Dickenson shook her head. The pretty blue silk georgette lay lifeless in her arms. 'Which do you want?'

'The silver tulle and lamé number. I want to shine tonight. Bring my pewter mesh evening bag too, the one with the enamelled mounts embellished with leather and pearl. You did pack it, didn't you?' She sounded tetchier than usual, more demanding and desperate. Lawrence thought she'd probably been out too long in the cold. 'And my grey leather shoes, the ones with the lattice openwork and steel bead decoration. I want to shimmer tonight. Positively glitter.'

It was all too much for Lawrence. The feminine activity and industry required to look gorgeous was not something he liked to witness, preferring instead to think of the process as somewhat magical. 'Well, I suppose you need to be getting on.'

'Yes.'

'Would it be easier if I found another room to dress in?'

'Yes, darling, it would.'

Lawrence didn't read too much into the fact that the first and only time his wife had thrown an endearment towards him was when he offered to leave her alone.

21

LADY PONDSON-CALLOW had accepted that she had to make a good job of a bad situation. If she was to deal with forty house guests for the second night in a row, she was determined to do so spectacularly. She had the housekeeper write out the name of each person staying on a separate card, and then had spent much of the day placing and replacing them to her satisfaction. Starting with her own card at one end and her husband's at the other, she had put them in the order in which they were to sit at the table. It had often been said by various hostesses that this practice was a little like playing solitaire, because the trick was in the sequencing; Lady Pondson-Callow thought it was rather more like playing God. Tradition had it that she ought to place the lady of greatest honour to her husband's right, the second in importance on his left. Then on either side of herself she ought to seat the two most important gentlemen. The remaining guests were to be fitted in between. An effort was to be made to ensure that people were seated by those they found congenial or, if the mood struck her, those they found controversial. Either arrangement made for a diverting dinner.

Lady Pondson-Callow had scrupulously followed these rules at last night's formal dinner. She'd found herself wedged between Lord Feversham and Sir Oswald Henning. So many dull old men to entertain. Tonight she was determined to sit next to the elusive Sergeant Major Trent. Everyone wanted to know more about him. If his conversation was anywhere near as stunning as his looks, she was in for a treat and, if it wasn't, well, she still wouldn't complain. Sir Peter had been equally disgruntled with last night's seating plan. Traditionally the guest of honour was the oldest lady present, and so he'd had to make do with a couple of old, dreary dowagers. Lady Pondson-Callow understood her husband well enough to know the importance of providing him with a harmless distraction; if she didn't, there was always the danger he'd go and search out some entertainment of his own, which could rarely be contained so well. She was desperate to shake things up a little tonight, but she had a horror of doing anything that might be considered *nouveau*. She wondered whether there was a new bride among her guests; no one could object to a fresh honeymooner taking precedence over older people. Oh yes! There was Doreen. Despite the fact that she was already rumoured to be sleeping with her dance tutor, she was less than a year married, technically still a new bride. Peter would be so much happier leading her into dinner, which left Lady Pondson-Callow free to sit with the dashing officer. The effect of this decision was to cascade right down to the likes of Beatrice and Mr Oaksley.

The seating arrangement was generally a secret between the hostess and her staff until the moment gentlemen filed into the drawing room for pre-dinner cocktails. At that point each gentleman collected, from a silver tray, a diminutive envelope addressed just to him, inside which there was a card with the name of the lady he was to take down to dinner. Having shaken up the seating plan to the point of controversy, Lady Pondson-Callow didn't want to be bothered with the disagreeable grumbles that were likely to ensue, so she instructed the butler to display the entire arrangement on a board in the hallway at tea time.

'How very modern, my lady,' commented the butler.

'I'm well aware of that, Farrell, and, as you can imagine, with my distrust of the modern, I have not reached the decision lightly, but on balance it's better this way, rather than having the shrimp ruined by awkward, protesting silences. Best everyone gets used to where they are sitting sooner rather than later.'

Beatrice was bitterly disappointed to discover that she was not to be seated near Mr Oaksley at dinner. She hadn't expected that her personal desires might have reached the lofty heights of Lady Pondson-Callow's consciousness, but she had hoped. Taking all her frustration and converting it into courage, she went to Ava's room to beg her to intervene; if things were swapped around, she and Arnie could continue their intimacy uninterrupted.

Beatrice found Ava admiring herself in a full-length gilt mirror; she was wearing her underwear and a rose velvet evening coat lined with peach satin.

'How do you like my new look?' Ava asked brightly. She turned the full effect of her widest beam on Beatrice. The beam cut through the cigarette smoke and the chaos of the room. Bea cast her gaze about, because the coat didn't have a clasp and Ava's underwear was sheer; she could see her deep magenta nipples and her mound of pubic hair quite clearly. It was disconcerting. There were huge piles of discarded dresses, undergarments and stockings everywhere. Records, fallen from their sleeves, littered the floor around the gramophone, and jewellery, lipsticks and shoes were scattered like confetti on every surface imaginable. Ava's maid was carefully sorting through a pile of garments that had been casually tossed on to the bed. She was returning exquisite dresses – copper, magenta, cobalt – to padded silk hangers at about the same rate as Ava pulled something from her wardrobe and dropped it again. The room was awash with gleaming sequins and silks, which reflected in polished metal clutch bags and modern aluminium and mirrored furniture. Everything shone.

'Gosh, you have such beautiful things.'

Ava allowed the slouchy, beaded velvet evening coat to fall to the floor and reached for another frock. Bea scooped up the coat, which embodied the flapper's party-until-dawn attitude. Like its owner, it personified opulence combined with mischievousness. The sensual silky velvet, the luxurious ruche collar and the elaborate embroidery on the hem and the sleeves all whispered prosperity and prominence. She stroked it longingly.

'You know I'd let you borrow anything, only . . .'

'None of it fits.' Bea wasn't ever sure if Ava's generous offers were genuine, or simply a subtle way to draw attention to her weight problem.

'Cheer up, Beatrice. You know you're terribly lucky with the current fashions. The garçon look hides—'

'A multitude of sins. Yes, I do know. You are always telling me.'

'Simple, straight and waistless is not only liberating, it's—'

'Forgiving. Yes, I think you have mentioned that.'

'For those who need it. Come here.'

Beatrice walked towards Ava with trepidation. Ava brazenly and efficiently ran her hands down Bea's ribs, waist and hips. 'For God's sake, Beatrice, you have to ditch the whalebone corsets. Men won't dance with you if they can't feel you. Buy an elastic girdle. How many times do I have to tell you?'

Beatrice flushed. Her pudgy, ringless hands hung limp and pink by her sides. Ava abruptly turned to examine her reflection. 'Help me, what should I wear?'

Bea was astounded that her opinion was being sought, and on such a subject by such a one. But the illusion that she was useful as anything other than a messenger was smashed when Ava continued, 'Did you see anyone on your way over here?'

'Yes, Kitty Hatfield.'

'Was she dressed?'

'She's wearing silk satin, in blush.'

'Details!'

'It has small girlish pink beads clustered like cherry blossom falling down from a recently shaken branch.' Beatrice had thought the dress was divine.

'Girlish, you say? She's thirty-five, she ought to know better.'

'She can carry it off. You know she can.'

'But for how long?' Ava dragged on her cigarette and muttered, 'I suppose her lack of a family helps.'

'What do you mean?'

'Well, because she's not tied down with a husband and brats, everyone thinks of her as young. It seems to keep her young.'

'On the outside, at least,' mumbled Beatrice, who thought that nothing could compensate for a lack of a family, not even a decade taken from your age.

'Darling, let's not kid ourselves that there's anything more. Did you see anyone else?'

'I saw Doreen Harrison . . . I mean Lady Henning. She was in velvet.'

'Velvet is so heavy,' sighed Ava disapprovingly.

'I'm rather a fan,' gushed Bea.

'I don't doubt *you* are. It hides everything that needs to be hidden,' added Ava, 'but Doreen could wear chiffon.'

Bea chose to ignore Ava's jibes; her day with Mr Oaksley had made her somewhat immune.

'Everyone is talking about Lady Feversham. Apparently she's wearing silk dupion with sequins, diamanté pastes, crystal beading, a lace overlay and a taffeta bow.'

'So it's true that Lady Feversham really doesn't know the word "no".'

Bea couldn't help giggling. Steeling herself, she asked, 'I was wondering whether there was any flexibility in the seating plan?'

Ava looked at Bea in the mirror from under her eyelashes; she was applying a daring scarlet lipstick that Beatrice wasn't sure would be considered appropriate even at a nightclub. 'I see, you want to sit with Mr Oaksley again, do you?' she asked in a teasing tone. 'I'd love to help, but I wouldn't dare fiddle, darling. My mother has been perfecting the seating arrangement all day. Lydia and Lawrence's domestics have twice thrown a spanner in the works this weekend. One moment he's not coming, the next he's here. It's all hellishly inconvenient.' Bea had been too immersed in her own budding romance to give any thought to the Chatfields. One knew they were a marvellous couple. They'd sort themselves out. 'I simply daren't cross my mama,' added Ava. Both women knew this was not true; Ava often actively worked to infuriate her mother's plans.

Ava suddenly grabbed another dress and hoisted it on, shooing away her maid, who tried to help. It was a rose-coloured silk with purple velvet straps and pleats. There was a sinuous, serpentine pattern of embroidered beads and gold thread along the hem. All three women looked at her reflection. She was tremendous. Bea felt confused and queasy as she had two simultaneous thoughts. One was what a great, great pity it was that Mr Oaksley would never see such beauty again, and the other was what a relief.

Bea was somewhat mollified when Ava added, 'I can see that you two have been getting along famously all afternoon. It's always best to leave them wanting more. A little break from one another's company will only sharpen things.'

'You could see we were getting on well?' Bea asked with an excited, just suppressed smile in her voice.

'Yes.'

'You think he likes me?'

'He definitely doesn't dislike you, but one doesn't want to run out of charm,' added Ava, effectively puncturing the balloon of confidence she had just inflated. Her maid stood offering the choice of two pairs of shoes; Ava pointed to the ones with tortoiseshell buckles. 'You can use dinner to think of some more amusing anecdotes to fling his way tonight.'

Beatrice followed Ava's advice, however sardonically it was given; it was advice about men, from Ava, and therefore invaluable. Throughout dinner she concentrated on the conversation and company so that she had something fresh to relay to Mr Oaksley. She was delighted to note that whilst the vast majority of the men went to smoke, he bravely broke convention and followed the women as they filed through to the larger drawing room. Harry Fine led Mr Oaksley to Beatrice's side; clearly by request. Bea thought she might burst with delight. He sat down next to her and smiled.

'Where were we?' he asked.

Emboldened by champagne, like a bud unfurling under the attention, Beatrice chatted animatedly; her usual shyness had now vanished completely. She was able to relay one or two anecdotes from dinner and she asked him about the company he'd sat with.

'How did you find them?'

'Dull,' he replied. Did he mean by comparison to her? He must. Beatrice felt the compliment flip her innards; it was as though he'd just called her beautiful. She wanted to thank him but knew she must not; instead she offered, 'Still, the food was delicious.'

'By George, yes. I'm not complaining. We're all being very well looked after.' He leaned closer to her and whispered, 'They seem to have money to burn.'

'Yes, they are rather lucky, I suppose.'

'You suppose? How can being so wealthy be anything other than lucky?'

'Well . . .' Bea hesitated; she didn't like to gossip. Ava had a sharp tongue on her but she was a friend. Arnie seemed to understand without her having to say more.

'Ah, you mean because of the way they made their money?'

'Yes.'

'I heard they've amassed an absolute fortune since nineteen fourteen, putting boots on our boys' feet.'

'Quite.'

'The whiff of war profiteers, edging their way into society by paying for the privilege, clings to them, does it?'

Bea winced and then forced herself to nod. Then she remembered gestures were lost on him. 'You know how people can be about new money,' she whispered apologetically. In truth, she was one of those people; she preferred old money, but since she had no money at all, either new or old, no one much cared what she thought about anything anyway, except perhaps Arnie.

'Still, they do throw good parties, and old money doesn't stretch to that.'

'No, I suppose there's hardly any old money left, just old names, and even then not so many of those,' sighed Bea.

'I think doing well out of the war seems rather more sensible than doing badly,' commented Mr Oaksley. Bea didn't know his tones of voice well enough. Was he bitter or philosophical?

'It's not a matter of sense, though, is it? It doesn't seem right.'

'Why can't anyone understand, nothing about it was right!' Mr Oaksley snapped. Suddenly he looked pale and tired. His breathing was sharp and shallow. Beatrice wanted to mumble an apology, but just as the words were forming, she saw him take a deep breath; as though a switch was being flicked, she watched as he made a conscious effort to shun the gloomy direction their conversation had taken. Brightening, he asked, 'Have you known Ava Pondson-Callow long?'

'My mother and Lady Chatfield's mother were debs together, so we go back yonks. Lydia came out at the same time as Ava, they became tight and Lydia made the introductions.'

'I think I remember reading about Lady Chatfield's season.'

'No doubt. It was very successful. Both she and Ava were gorgeous. Never out of the papers. So much fun. You should have seen them.' It was just a turn of phrase, but Bea felt self-conscious and rushed to correct things. 'Well, you say you did. Back then, you could.' She stumbled. 'Oh, sorry.'

He didn't acknowledge her gaffe. 'Did you get a season?'

Bea was thrilled that he might think she had turned eighteen during the war and therefore had to forfeit a traditional debutante season. Most people assumed she was four or five years older than she was, never younger. They looked at her rather than listened to her.

'Yes, I did, although I was not the same success as Lydia and Ava or even my sister. Not by a long way.'

'Really, why was that?'

Beatrice regretted admitting as much. She could hardly say, 'Because I'm so ugly and the world is so shallow.' She chose a more tactful route. 'I was rather a provincial debutante. My clothes were London, but I was not. They wore me rather than the other way round, I think.'

'You don't sound as though you enjoyed it.'

'It's hard to remember clearly. Everything is viewed with a filter now, isn't it?'

'You could say that.'

Again Beatrice became aware of the dark bandage and nothing else in the room. 'I'm sorry, that's an awful metaphor to draw.' She giggled nervously. It must be the champagne. Why was she being so careless? Arnie tapped her leg and smiled. The tap seemed to excuse her. The smile delighted her. Something rigid and compacted deep inside her began to melt; a warm, fluid feeling gushed around her stomach again. 'You know how it was before. Such an age of richness. It would be wrong to say I didn't enjoy it. I went to dances, paid calls, we were called upon and I played a good deal of bridge, tennis and golf. I had music lessons.'

'Such gaiety.'

'Well, yes, but no. For the men, perhaps, but we girls knew the dances for what they were. It was a race. It was all about who would be snapped up first.' Bea remembered sitting on hard chairs, her back to the wall, watching other couples spinning, other hands clasping, other skirts whirling. She'd longed to dance with the boisterous young men, the conversationally inept young men. The men who gained dignity through death. What a cost.

'Were you snapped up?'

No, she had been left over. 'There was someone. But the Somme . . .' She trailed off. No doubt Arnie assumed the situation was too painful to talk about. The Somme was recognised to have been an orgy of slaughter; fifty-seven and a half thousand British men fell on the first day. But they'd been told that no good came from poring over these things; besides, there was nothing to say that hadn't been said. Nothing to say that made anything any better.

'I'm sorry.'

Beatrice felt a flush of guilt squelch through her body, replacing the warm, exotic sensation she'd been enjoying. She often made much of the young man who fell in July 1916, along with almost sixty thousand others, but she knew it for what it was, not so much a grand passion as a brief matter of convenience. He was a chubby and plain chap, the younger brother of a friend of Lydia's. He had no one, she had no one; they weren't drawn together so much as shoved together by well-meaning matchmakers. They'd only walked out the once; they shared tea in Lyons on Tottenham Court Road. Bea had been chaperoned by her aunt. Luckily, the aunt was understanding and realistic – there was a war on, and besides, she was aware that Bea would never have an abundance of choice; she certainly didn't want to put unnecessary barriers in the way of any potential romantic progress. She'd sat at a nearby table and left the young people alone.

Throughout the tea they'd both displayed every symptom of dread and dismay, and it had not been clear which they dreaded most, the embryonic courtship or the imminent dismissal to the Front. He had been wearing his uniform, which made Bea feel proud. People had nodded and murmured their approval; it was before conscription, his bravery couldn't be doubted. Beatrice had been entirely caught up in the episode, and if he'd proposed over the egg and cress sandwiches, she no doubt would have said yes, although in truth she did not know him. Both horribly shy, they only swapped a handful of sentences in total. He'd asked her if she liked the pastry she'd picked. She'd told him she did, very much, and he offered to buy her another. He said he liked a girl who liked her food. She'd commented he should stock up on treats because they'd be harder to come across where he was going. He'd looked sad and she'd wished she hadn't said anything. He'd asked her to write. Hadn't he? She always told people he'd asked her to write but she wasn't *absolutely* sure this was the case. Maybe her aunt had recommended they swap addresses.

The letters weren't great epics as people imagined letters to and from the Front ought to have been. They didn't discuss life and death and the metaphysical. They did not talk about holding one another, having one another. She told him what she was sewing at home, whether she'd taken the dogs for a walk that day; he often wrote about the weather. He asked for her photo and she happily sent it, but she could not fight the feeling that he wanted her photo more for the fact that all the other men had photos of sweethearts, not so much that he wanted her face to be close to his heart. She sent him cigarettes. He thanked her effusively and asked whether it was too much to hope she might knit him some socks for Christmas. He never saw Christmas. Perhaps if there hadn't been a war, they could have married and existed in a state of polite plumpness. But he'd been blown to bits and so she would never know.

Bea had grieved for her lost chance. The biggest tragedy was the number of blighted possibilities.

'Of course the war was the most incomparable tragedy, we all understand that now, but for women like me, it initially seemed simply an irksome disruption to my personal plan.'

'Which was to marry?'

'Quite so. I'm ashamed that I didn't see how big it was. For you, the boys and men, certainly, but also for us. The women.'

Bea and Arnie sat listening to the cheerful strains of the gramophone. She could sense the ghosts of countless young men dancing in the rooms where they had once partied. The smoke from his cigarette make her eyes feel scratchy.

'You're staring at me,' said Arnie.

'Yes, I am.'

'People do that.'

'Do they?'

'Yes.'

'How do you know?'

'I sense it. I hate it.'

'You shouldn't, it's better than being invisible.' Bea sighed, giving away more than she'd intended.

'What do you look like, Beatrice?'

She wondered whether she could lie. If he ever held her (and she hoped, so dearly, that he would), then he would soon know about her curves that flowed into bulges; he must already have detected her unladylike height. However, she could omit to mention her small eyes, which looked like raisins, lost in the puffy dough of her fleshy face. He need not be aware of her heavy lids that always looked unintentionally slothful. But then she remembered the 'don't'.

'I'm quite plain.'

'Right.'

'I've had compliments on my smile.' Lydia had complimented her on her smile; no one else. Not really.

'Can I read you?' He held his hands up. Self-conscious, but animated, she put her fingers over his and guided him to her face. He pressed firmly from her cheekbones down to her chin; careful but deliberate pats, rather like a doctor examining her to see if her glands were swollen. She wondered how well trained his fingertips

151

were. It was possible that he would notice her too long nose that ended with an off-centre blob, suggesting that there had been extra flesh and the angels had simply screwed it up and slung it on. On a man the nose might indicate character; Beatrice considered it nothing short of a disability. Could he feel the slight slackening of her jowls? Would he notice that the gap between her nose and mouth was about half an inch longer than optimal? The firm patting gave way to more gentle strokes as his fingers spread across her cheeks and nudged up to her lobes. They swept down again, taking in the shape and length of her nose, then up and up around the arch of her eyebrows (which were a little heavy; Ava thought she ought to pluck). His fingers were icy against her flushed cheeks; they probed.

'I think I have a picture of you now.' Beatrice hoped not, but she was glad to have had his hands on her. She had never been touched in that way, or any like it.

'Why aren't you dancing, Beatrice?'

'Oh, I don't enjoy dancing very much,' she lied. She couldn't imagine how he'd dance; the floor was crowded, arms were flailing, he might get inadvertently punched.

'What do you do with your time?'

'I paint.'

'Oh.' The conversation faltered. Beatrice wished she'd said that she played tennis or golf, although would that have been any better? You had to see to do those too, surely.

'I play the piano too, as you heard.'

'Very expertly.'

'It's my biggest passion.' This was a lie. Beatrice's art was her first love, but she was certain she was not the first woman to lie to a man about her skills and hobbies in order to impress or please. 'Do you play?'

'Yes, I do. You know, from memory.' How would he learn new songs? By ear?

'I enjoy walking.' This at least was true.

'Yes, fresh air, the answer to everything.' There was no conviction behind his words.

Beatrice didn't know what was happening. Why the conversation about hobbies, which should have been a light and easy one, edging towards a greater familiarity and understanding of one another, seemed to be so difficult and tense. She sighed and grasped the thistle.

'Can you see anything?'

'No.' He sighed at the finality.

'What's it like?'

'It's not the blackness of closing your eyes. It's less safe than that. It's a deep, deep, dark void, a grey that is almost black. I sometimes think I might fall into it, through it. I only know I'm looking at the sun because I feel it on my skin.'

'Do you have family?'

'My father. My mother's dead and I'm glad about that. She died in nineteen twelve and I think that must be quite wonderful to never have known that we did this to each other.'

'How do you manage?'

'Slowly. Everything takes longer. I feel hopeless and vulnerable. It's hell, actually.'

He laughed, but it was a bitter laugh; how could it be anything other? He also sounded relieved that she was asking, that he could tell her how it was. No one else wanted to know. It astounded her that he'd used the word 'vulnerable'. She had never heard anyone – man or woman – admit as much. Bea thought she might squeal. Let out a totally inappropriate sound because she was so shocked and moved by his frankness. She bit back her reaction, took a deep breath and then tried to rally.

'You can still hear, feel and taste the world around you.'

'Yes.'

'That's something.'

'So I'm told. It wasn't gas. I took a bullet in the right eye socket, shrapnel ruined the left. The pain, and the noise that came with the pain . . . unbelievable. It was excruciating. I mean literally unbearable. I didn't understand those words until that moment. I vomited with the pain. I screamed and screamed and screamed. This howling and puke were coming out together. You know, I still hear and feel that pain.'

'It must be a very hard thing to forget.'

'I don't remember the pain. I feel it. Over and over again.'

'Oh.' Bea was floored. She didn't know what to say. How to comfort.

'I wanted to die. I knew I was going to die.'

'But you didn't.'

'They tell me it was a miracle that I survived.'

'There must be a reason.'

'Do you think so?'

'My brother lost his legs. His left just below the knee and the other just above it. I never can understand why they chose to cut him off that way. I suppose they wanted to keep as much of him as possible, but it doesn't help his balance. Not that he walks. I'm afraid he's in a chair.'

'No crutches?'

'He lost his left arm too.' She wasn't sure if she was trying to tell Arnie that she had experience with horrific injuries, or if she was trying to tell him that there were other, worse injuries. If they *were* worse. Who could judge? She could not imagine having to live without sight, but then nor could she imagine having to live without the ability to dress oneself, walk, bath unaided. It was a hideous choice. Not that these men had had a choice. None of the women who nursed them had either. She didn't often talk of Sammy. People found it difficult to know what to say. They stumbled into basic platitudes, at best, or shocked silences, admitting that words couldn't comfort. Perhaps nothing could. Perhaps that was why she had told Arnie about him, so that he'd be stunned into silence; or maybe she was hoping he'd understand and offer something fresh and meaningful.

'Who looks after him?'

'His wife and my sister.'

'Not you?'

'Not so much. The two of them have it sewn up.' Beatrice knew it was wrong of her to resent the fact that she wasn't even needed in the role of dutiful sister, but she did feel something a lot like resentment. She felt her first inadequate attempts at nursing him had

154

been held against her; she hadn't been given the chance to overcome her squeamishness, her fear. Cecily and Sarah seemed to have a tacit understanding that too much ought not to be asked of the little sister; she wasn't quite up to the job. 'I could do it.' The champagne swirled around her head and her thoughts made ambitious leaps; ones that sober she would never have considered articulating.

'What?'

'I could look after you.'

'Are you a nurse? Were you VAD?'

'No, but I don't imagine that sort of nursing is still required, is it? I mean . . .' She dared not hesitate or think about what she was saying, because if she did, she would never finish the sentence. She rushed on like a wave. 'I could look after you.' There, it was done. She had thrown the thought out for him to inspect and now she had repeated it; there was no chance of miscommunication or denial. It was what she had been thinking from the moment he'd agreed to walk around the garden on Saturday afternoon; possibly before that. Before she'd met him.

'Are you proposing to me, Miss Polwarth?'

'Yes, I think I am.'

'Am I what you want?'

'Yes.'

'And you know this after less than forty-eight hours?'

'After many years. I think we could be comfortable together.' She thought of the slackening in her stomach. 'I really do.'

Arnie Oaksley held his head very still, his equivalent to staring off into the distance, Bea suspected. He had fallen into his own thoughts. She also sat very still, her face aflame with excitement and shame. She had just proposed to a man. She had proposed. It was unbelievable, yet she stood by it. She thought it could work. They'd both benefit.

'Are you ever lonely?'

'All the time.' He sighed.

'I might help there.'

'You don't know me.'

'Well, then, we'd have plenty to talk about.'

155

He nodded, and then fell silent for a minute. 'Can I think about it?'

'Yes, you should. Please do.'

'I think I need to go to bed now.'

Their roles were the reverse of the standard. She had proposed and now he needed time to consider; he wanted to retire to his room, like a shy debutante. Beatrice felt empowered and yet terrified; she supposed this was how every young man – at least those without the benefit of title or extreme wealth – must feel. Hopeful. Terrified. She wanted to push him, ask him when *exactly* he might make up his mind, but she could not. She had used up all her courage and did not even dare reach out and touch his arm to steady him as he stood up. She watched him rise, wobble and step away from her; a servant swiftly moved to his aid. She was left in a quagmire of hope and regret and uncertainty.

The air shimmered with life and possibility.

22

LAWRENCE AND EDGAR, in the same room, was a cosmic cataclysm that left Lydia breathless. She was a jumble of inconsistent emotions. She was used to feeling proud of Lawrence, grateful for him, but when she thought of him here, now, a peculiar haze of embarrassment swept through her entire being. She harboured an uncharitable feeling that he didn't seem to measure up, that he wasn't quite all he could be, all that she wanted. She was ashamed to find that she was irritated by him, and frustrated with him. His laugh grated on her nerves; it sounded overly hearty and confident. She resented the way he walked into a room as though he owned it; what had he done – other than inherit vast wealth – to entitle him to behave with such confidence and composure? She hated herself for judging him, because she knew that after her behaviour today, society would think she was the one who needed to be censured, and that she'd be found lacking. Yet judge him and condemn him she did.

She wondered what Edgar must make of him. Perplexingly, she didn't want Edgar to find Lawrence lacking; she hoped he'd be impressed by his impeccable conduct and his thorough, traditional education at least, but she despaired that that would be the case. How could he be? It wasn't enough any more.

Whatever she thought about Lawrence paled into irrelevance the moment thoughts of Edgar seized her mind. She longed for him. She ached to talk to him. Or at least to stand close so she could listen to him. He was a light and she was irresistibly drawn;

like a helpless moth she would bash and beat her wings up against him until she dropped with exhaustion or went up in flames. Her consciousness was tattooed with the thought of their kiss. Over and over again she imagined the feel of his bristled cheek scraping against her smooth one as she moved towards him, as he pulled away; the soft dryness of his lips as they lingered. Then left.

It was a relief that she was not placed near either of them at dinner; she would not have been able to fake wifely duty towards Lawrence or a suitably polite public indifference towards Edgar, yet she resented every moment that she was not with him. The only way she had reconciled herself to the dead time before dinner was by thinking that she was dressing for him. Which of her countless dresses would dazzle him most? As she slowly rubbed luxurious cream on to her elbows, neck and thighs, she knew it was for him. Picking out her scant silky underwear was for him. Putting on her scarlet lipstick was for him. It was all for him.

It took everything she had to remain in control, to remain sensible to the reality and not to scream out to Edgar, to launch herself across the dinner table. She imagined tossing the candlesticks and flowers to the side, throwing the plates to the floor and letting them crash and smash. She wanted to crawl towards him through the debris, careless of the spillages and broken crockery; she wanted to make a noise and declare herself his. It was Lawrence's formal smiles that pinned her to her seat. It was nothing to do with a sense of duty or warmth; she was restrained by a nagging sensation of embarrassment. She did not feel embarrassed because she wanted Edgar; the embarrassment was that she was with Lawrence. Lydia knew that if she made a scene, Lawrence would be without option: he would have to extract her, own her, take her away. That was how these things worked. She didn't want to be publicly owned by Lawrence. Never again. So she had to put her thoughts and feelings in incubation.

Besides, Edgar had pulled away from her kiss.

The thought whipped her, but rather than accepting it as a closure to a brief and ill-defined dalliance – an impossible, impossible thought – Lydia remembered the beat before he'd moved off.

He'd kissed her back, she was almost sure. Desire made her almost sure.

After the meal was over, Lydia had to go with the ladies into the drawing room. The men stood up in unison as the women trailed out. She passed him, the tallest man by inches in the room, and she breathed in possibility. He stood with his back to her, hands clasped behind him. She swapped her clutch bag from her right to her left hand, so that she could brush her fingers against his without anyone noticing. Flesh against flesh, just for the briefest of moments; he flinched, her knees buckled.

'Oh, darling, do watch your step,' whispered Ava, who somehow was at her side. 'You might fall.'

Lydia hoped Edgar might send in a note with the butler; a suggestion as to where they might discreetly rendezvous. He did not.

She sat anxiously. It was impossible to make conversation with any of the guests; they were all insufferable. Tedious. His were the only words of value. His thoughts were the only ones she considered sharp or purposeful. Did he even know that Lawrence was her husband? He must by now. Someone would have said. Had they been introduced? Might they be at this very moment talking to one another, wrapped in cigar smoke and the bonhomie that came with downing whisky? The thought was unbearable; that Lawrence had access to Edgar's company when she did not was an aberration.

The men lingered over their spirits and cigars for longer than was acceptable. Her eyes bored into the clock, but she couldn't get the hands to speed up. She curtly rebuffed every enquiry into her health and her occupation today, painfully aware that the women who asked really only wanted something they could gossip about. When he finally entered the room, along with all the other men, Lydia noticed that he had a new swagger to him that she hadn't yet seen. He was drunk. Most of them were, but his inebriation somehow was wrapped in a shadow that hinted at menace or aggravation. She stood up because she couldn't risk him failing to spot her and settling elsewhere, but then hastily sat down again. She did not want to lose her spot; she wanted him to join her on the sofa.

He did not.

He strutted in the opposite direction and plonked himself down on another sofa, one that Lady Anna Renwick was occupying. As there were already three people sitting over there, he had no alternative but to sit very close to Lady Renwick. It was noticeable. Her arm was squeezed so tightly next to his that her breast was pushed almost out and over her neckline. It was obvious and sordid. Painful.

Lawrence, by contrast, did come to find her. 'I'm done in. I'm off to bed.'

'Right.'

'Are you coming too?'

'I find I have lots of energy.'

'Do you think you'll be very late?'

'Yes.'

'Then I shall ask Pondson-Callow for another room. I don't want to be disturbed.'

'Good idea.' He kissed her cheek; she had to force herself not to move away from his touch.

'Good night.'

'Good night.'

Lydia watched for the next hour as Edgar chattered to Lady Renwick, leaning in ever closer, almost impossibly so, whispering into her ear. Twice he touched her upper arm, the one dangerously close to her heaving breast. Lydia felt each of his caresses like a blow. They danced. Lydia and Edgar had not danced. It was such a conventional and acceptable part of a courtship, but the opportunity had not presented itself. Would it ever? Lady Renwick was drunk too, so their dancing was chaotic and clumsy. Limbs tangled where they shouldn't have. His arms snaked down her back, around her waist. She accidentally dug her elbow into his rib; they both thought this was hilarious and fell into one another's arms, laughing. Delighted. Their flirtation was drawing eyes and comments. It couldn't not; it was the brash and bold sort of flirtation that had no mystery or witty elegance to it. Lydia told herself it was inferior in every way to what she'd enjoyed with Edgar Trent last night and today.

Except they could dance in public.

Except he did not pull away from Lady Renwick's kisses. Lydia wanted to kill her. And him. And herself.

The music got louder. The room was exhaustingly hot and overcrowded. Despite the fact that it was still snowing outside, someone opened a window; smoke and morals drifted out.

Ava sat down next to Lydia; she lit a cigarette and passed it over, then lit another for herself and inhaled deeply. 'Having fun, darling?'

'Not at all.' Lydia tried to drag her eyes away from him, but failed spectacularly. Ava's gaze followed. 'What is Anna Renwick wearing?' Lydia snarled. It was an inadequate cover for her thoughts, but all she could muster.

'Good lord, it's a trouser suit.' Ava sounded somewhat envious, but she was clearly awed too. 'I ought to have thought of that first. Tell me I'm not losing my touch.' Lydia knew it killed Ava that a younger woman had stolen a march on her fashion antics, but she couldn't bring herself to care, as it was killing her that the same younger woman was stealing Edgar from under her nose. While Lydia could not find it in herself to be graceful, Ava's passion and respect for style meant she could. 'A deluxe evening version of a trouser suit, shimmering with sequins. How utterly marvellous. Look, it goes all the way up to between her legs.'

'Well, I suppose it must.'

'It's very daring, very revealing. I suppose she is making that her thing.'

'What? What's Anna Renwick's thing?'

'She's a dramatic and witty dresser.'

'Plus a bit of a slut.'

'They make a lovely couple.'

'Don't.' Lydia's hand trembled as she held her cigarette high, the stem of ash threatening to fall on her shimmering silver frock. The jealousy slit through her being, shredded her sense of propriety, left an open gash where her common sense had been.

'But, darling, it's simply a fact. He's beautiful and poor, she's . . .' Ava paused. Lady Renwick was not beautiful, but she was well put together, attractive. Lydia's mother would describe her as a woman who made the best of herself. 'She's handsome and rich. They are the very epitome of the modern-day romance.'

'Please, don't.' Tears bit nastily at the top of Lydia's nose.

Ava would not indulge her. 'Darling, what did you expect? He's a beauty and a beast. You are a respectably married woman. The whole flirtation was doomed before it began.'

'You normally encourage this sort of thing.'

'It's not right for you.'

Lydia blanched; a flicker of concern spilt across Ava's face. 'Please don't tell me you've already done the nasty. Today? Hell's teeth, you *are* a fast worker.'

'No, no, of course not,' Lydia snapped.

'Well, thank God. That's a relief.' Ava sipped her champagne. Her head almost fitted into the glass. She looked out from underneath her lashes. It was clear from Lydia's expression that she did not thank God. 'Anna Renwick is single, Lydia. Like your sergeant major. Be reasonable. There aren't enough chaps to go around; you can't expect to bag two. He ought to marry, then you can both do as you please.' Lydia loathed everything Ava was saying. She stared sulkily at the floor. 'Lydia, my angel, you must know that he was simply having fun with you. Don't look so serious. Surely you can't have imagined . . .' Ava either didn't know how to finish the sentence or didn't feel the need to finish it. 'Not you.'

'You don't know what you're talking about, Ava.'

'I always know what I'm talking about.'

'I refuse to accept your clumsy clichés. One single man plus a single woman does not add up, in this case.'

'But then when has two men and one woman ever been the correct maths?'

Lydia felt the air thicken, choking her. She glanced at Edgar again. He was practically wrapped around Anna Renwick. It was agony. She couldn't stand to watch him demean himself, slurring drunkenly over his words and another woman's body. She couldn't stay in this room. She rushed out, grateful that Ava's level of concern and judgement meant that she neither called after her nor followed her.

23

Edgar sensed her dash from the room. Although he had been trying to ignore her all night, her beauty and intensity was such that he couldn't quite discount her. She had crawled up under his skin. It was inconvenient. It was exhilarating. He extracted himself from some woman's hot embrace by promising, insincerely, that he would be back soon, and left the drawing room by another door.

A flash of silver around the corner in front of him. He trailed her. A boy with a net chasing a butterfly. She slipped into a room he had yet to explore. He followed. Inside, it took a moment for his eyes to adjust. The room was lit only by the blue moonlight flooding through the window; the drapes had not been drawn. A stately leather-topped desk revealed that it was Sir Peter's study; Edgar took in huge gulps of dust and the smell of old paper.

Hearing the door open, she turned and glared at him. She stood behind the desk, haughty. Her dress fell in cascades, like a waterfall. She moved in a flash; he didn't notice her lithe fingers scrambling desperately around the desk. She found a heavy glass paperweight, one that Lady Pondson-Callow had commissioned; it housed a small ammonite shell, something she'd picked up off the beach the day Sir Peter proposed to her, at Lyme Regis. The paperweight was a rare testament to Lady Pondson-Callow's sentimentality. Lydia hurled it at Edgar. He instinctively ducked, although her throw was inadequate and the paperweight did not land anywhere near the target, if he was such. It didn't even hit the wall and smash satisfyingly; it fell against the leather chaise longue in the middle of the room and then bounced on the floor. It may have left a dent on the wooden floorboards.

Lydia let loose a cry of frustration and humiliation. He moved swiftly across the room and grabbed both her wrists, in case she intended to attempt any more hooliganism. She struggled against his grip, but the protest was as token as it was futile; he was infinitely stronger than she was.

'Think what you are doing. You can't behave like this,' he told her sternly. She stared at him, fury and passion pouring like a gushing wound.

'Why are *you* behaving like this?' she demanded. 'That girl is a frothy nothing.'

Her jealousy was mesmerising, her imperious dismissal of the young debutante magnificent. 'You could have had me!' Her pathetic admission was heartbreaking.

Lydia quivered in the darkness. They were both breathing heavily. Desperate, Edgar looked away from her and towards the window; he spotted a fox, at a distance, autographing the freshly laid snow with its tail and paws. It was impossible to ignore what was between them. He'd been enthralled by her exquisite looks and seemingly impervious, haughty demeanour; still, he might have been able to let that go. Pass it by. But her angry, uncontainable jealousy was irresistible. It was not to be discussed or debated any more. They both knew what they would do, and how.

Not even caring enough to take the time to lock or barricade the door, not considering anything as pedestrian as being discovered, he let go of her wrists and clasped one hand behind her head. The silky feel of her hair caressed his fingers for just a moment as he pulled her face towards his and clamped his lips down on hers. His other hand slid over her body: her breasts, her waist, her arse. He felt the muscled hardness of her through her thin dress, he felt the small mounds and curves, he felt her nipples harden. She was not wearing any sort of corset or girdle, not even a bandeau brassiere. Her audacity caused his cock to shudder. This woman wanted him to know her body. She had counted on it.

She bent towards him, melted into him. He broke away, but only to pick her up and land her on the desk, a move he accomplished as though she weighed little more than a toy. She sat facing him, lips and legs slightly open. Invitingly. His fingers slipped up under her skirt, hers weaved into his hair and pulled him towards her again; their mouths banged heavily on one another, almost painful, totally delicious. With a swift, practised confidence that should have worried her, he undid his trousers, pushed her dress roughly up her thighs and pulled her knickers away. He was inside her. It was awkward for a moment; she tilted her hips, lay down on the desk, and then her hot flesh accepted him completely. He put his hands on her small but perfect tits and went at it. Lost himself in her. Deep in her.

24

SARAH WASN'T CERTAIN, at first, exactly what she was witnessing. Of course she knew that it was sex; she simply didn't know who was having sex, or how and why it had come about in a private study. She'd followed Lydia out of the drawing room because her friend had looked shocked and upset, possibly drunk. She'd been sure she had come this way but she'd checked in the library, the smaller drawing room and the dining room and she hadn't found her. Assuming she had gone to bed, Sarah was debating whether she ought to follow her and talk to her to see what was on her mind, or whether she should simply slope off to bed herself. It had been a long day. Snow was somehow draining in a way no other element seemed to be. The elements had a disproportionately large effect on Sarah's mood; inclement weather made her think of what Arthur and the men on the Front had endured for four winters – though not that many, if any, were out there for four; no one lasted that long. She would never have thought to enter Sir Peter's study; studies were personal and off limits, even to house guests during parties, but the door was ajar and she heard something. An animal? Could one of the lap dogs be trapped in the room?

His buttocks were beautiful. The sight of them and his wide, perfect, youthful thighs made Sarah gasp. She wanted to turn away, she knew she should, but she couldn't. His broad shoulders and imposing height meant that she instantly identified him; certainly she knew it was a clandestine thing, a secret, not hers to share, but still she lingered in the doorway. His naked lower body brought a whisper of a memory of Arthur's body. It had been such a very long time since she'd touched him, or even seen him, that the reality of him had completely disintegrated, and she found, agonisingly, that the memory of him was fading too. She couldn't remember exactly what his smile had been like, she'd forgotten the precise tone of his voice and the particular feel of his hands on her body. The raw maleness thrusting so close by painfully underlined the fact that her memory was inadequate, a let-down. She couldn't remember the essence of Arthur. She couldn't remember the tremendous, wonderful feeling of him inside her. She was so embroiled in the unrefined and unrestrained sexual act, it took her a moment to see or care who was under the officer.

Lydia.

She couldn't see the woman's face or upper body, but the skirt of her dress was splayed out over the desk, unmistakable; in the moonlight, Sarah saw and recognised the shimmering silver. She knew the shoes, too. The grey leather shoes, the ones with the lattice openwork and steel bead decoration, perched on the end of the shapely legs; legs that were wrapped around Edgar Trent's torso.

Sarah ran. As she fled, she considered that she ought to have closed the study door behind her. What if someone else was to discover them? But then she cast the thought aside; it wasn't her problem, it wasn't her mess. She dashed up the wide marble stairs and headed for the bedroom she was sharing with Beatrice. As widow and spinster, neither had the status that was required to secure a room of their own, and she hoped that Beatrice wouldn't yet have turned in; she wanted the bedroom to herself for a while. She was not normally a person who craved privacy, far from it, but suddenly it was a necessity. She needed solitude, space, seclusion.

No one had tended to the fire; what was left of it whimpered in the grate. The maids were beleaguered with the number of guests, and as neither Sarah nor Bea had their own lady's maid to prioritise their comfort, it was obvious they had been overlooked. Sarah hauled a log out of the wicker basket and threw it on to the ailing coals. The flames half-heartedly licked around the log, but it would take some time before it caught. Hunched over the dressing table, Sarah gasped in the chilly air, trying hard not to spew up her misery, which was likely to flood from her like a stinking bodily fluid. She felt empty. Her loneliness had a breadth and depth and height and weight that staggered her. It sometimes seemed fathomless.

Arthur had been dead for over four years, and every night she still sprinkled Colgate shaving powder on to her pillow because it smelt of him. Everyone agreed – many had said it – that four years should be long enough. And maybe it should be, especially when each hour often felt like a week, but time refused to be linear and logical for her. Sometimes she couldn't remember being anything other than a dreary and heartbroken surplus woman; her married life was a distant memory, almost another life. At other times, four years seemed to vanish in a frantic instant and she'd forget, yes, forget, that Arthur was dead. She'd see a man in the distance who walked as Arthur had walked, or wore his hat at a similar dashing angle and she'd believe – just for a moment – that Arthur had come back to her, believe he was alive. The four years would vanish then; time would reverse. It was madness, of course. But madness she couldn't resist.

The sex she'd just witnessed had been such an instant. Suddenly time crashed and collided, imploded. She now remembered what it felt like to be touched, to be taken. But this time it was different; her memory wasn't intrinsically linked to Arthur. She couldn't remember Arthur's touch. It was agony. Hateful.

About two years ago, she'd allowed a man to kiss her at a dance simply because he'd smelt like Arthur, of pipe smoke and deciduous forests in autumn. At least she'd thought he had, but this man had smoked a different brand of tobacco, and the smell of deciduous forests was manufactured, a cologne rather than the true aroma earned by striding through a wood. The man on the dance floor was a poor shadow, a ghoulish imitation. His teeth had clashed with hers and his mouth had not fitted correctly at all; it was slack and somewhat off-centre, whereas Arthur had had neat, warm lips. The terrible, shaming thing was that the man was married. Sarah had felt instantly horrified with herself; horrified that she'd kissed a married man, disgusted that she'd erased Arthur's last kiss. She did not want to become one of those women who settled for being a mistress, just because there weren't enough chaps to go around. It was dishonourable.

But then loneliness was relentless, and a poor opponent to honour.

She felt lonely now, in this cold spare room. She wished for and dreaded Bea's return. Bea would at least be company, a distraction, but how would Sarah be able to chatter about Beatrice's night now that she harboured this immense secret? Because a secret it must be. Sarah felt dirty and disappointed. She shouldn't have lingered, but then she shouldn't have had to see it in the first place. She assumed her disappointment was towards Lydia. How could she be so thoughtless, so selfish, so reckless? There was every chance that right now someone else was discovering them. Not someone who scurried away, aghast and ashamed; someone ruinous, who might expose them or blackmail them. Sarah knew that people had affairs. She wasn't an idiot or an innocent. But she had never imagined Lydia might count amongst that number; she would not have believed it if she hadn't seen it with her own eyes. The light in which she viewed her friend shifted slightly as though someone had placed a scarf over a table lamp. Poor Lawrence.

But, for all that, Sarah felt most disappointed with herself because – as she slipped out of her evening clothes, tugged on her heavy flannel nightgown and then settled between the cold sheets – she was forced to admit that her greatest concern wasn't Lydia. She felt the springs of the mattress poking her. She was surprised; she had imagined everything in the Pondson-Callow household would be brand new, but apparently even their wealth didn't stretch to indulge widows and spinsters. Her friend was no doubt hurtling towards a calamity, but Sarah didn't care right now. She was dealing with a deeper, more profound and alarming dissatisfaction. She was frustrated with herself because she'd thought she had it all sewn up. She'd believed she had a foolproof, failsafe, infallible plan. She wasn't over Arthur, she'd known that and, despite how often people told her she ought to be, she knew how it was for her. So she'd planned to keep her head down; her children, her invalid brother, her crocheting and church visits were to be enough. She'd wanted a quiet, careful and useful life. She had not allowed herself to consider anything more. To hope for abundance again seemed selfish and disloyal. So she was deeply disappointed to discover that she was not as oblivious and closed off as she'd hoped. Seeing the pale buttocks in the moonlit room, smelling the sex, a heavy scent on the air, folded in among the dust and woody logs, she realised she didn't want to creep towards middle age, inconsequential and contained. She didn't want to end like that.

It wasn't over for her. She wanted to live. She wanted more. But what more could there possibly be for a woman like her? She had capped her expectations because it was safest. She'd always thought wanting too much, having too much, led to heartache; loving Arthur had taught her that. Yet she'd found that her spirit had crept, like a determined moss, out of the cracks between the hard paving slabs of life, and was unwavering in its resolution to flourish. She wanted more. Still.

25

B Y TUESDAY AFTERNOON the snow had thawed sufficiently to allow a group of the young men to take themselves off to the station and catch a train to London. They did so because they were aware that it would be rude to burden their hosts for a moment longer than necessary with their presence. It was rumoured that the cook had already had a tantrum because she'd been reduced to serving a cheese and bread buffet lunch that day. An extra forty guests, even for a house as sumptuous and wealthy as this, was a strain. The laundry and wood chopping alone must be an inconvenience.

The party was over. It was time to say goodbye. Lydia was unsure whether she had the strength to do so. They had not found a way to be alone together since Sunday night, despite it being all and everything she wanted. Sarah had become inexplicably clingy and had practically refused to leave her side from dawn to dusk yesterday. Lydia had felt her friend's presence as constraining and primitive as a metal cage. She wanted to shake her, scream at her or run from her; instead she played the piano with her, embroidered with her and took a walk in the snow with her and Beatrice. She couldn't find a way to make a different choice.

Edgar too had been made unavailable. For the greatest part of yesterday he, along with all the other able-bodied men, had been recruited to help shovel the snow off the paths and driveways. The servants couldn't manage on their own; his refusal to help would have been impossible, beyond rude. Since Sunday Lydia had existed in a severe state of agitation. She found it difficult to follow other people's conversations; she couldn't eat, or sit still. When she tried to read music, the notes jumped about the page; when she went for a walk, she got lost and retraced the footpaths a few times, as though she was trapped in a maze. The table arrangement at meals had not been kind to them either; it seemed everything and everyone was conspiring to keep them apart. After that first evening, Lady Pondson-Callow was too aware of the value of both the handsome sergeant major and the beautiful socialite to allow them to be paired more than once. She separated them, shared out their company, lavishing treats on all her guests.

Lydia had longed for yesterday's dinner to finish and the socialising to begin; she was sure that then they would carve out a little space, an iridescent light where not only their consciousnesses could come together but their bodies too. However, by the time the evening came it was apparent that most people had become weary of the party and each other's company. No one suggested dancing, which afforded opportunity to flirt and chat, as it required too much energy. Instead the guests divided into groups of four and played bridge, where minimal conversation or effort was required. Lydia was given to Kitty Hatfield, Lord Feversham and Sir Peter. Edgar was seated with others. She felt his gaze on her all the time. It was heavy, like a damp blanket. It sat on her neck, her breast, her hips.

She had begun to think she'd almost imagined it. Lying on the desk in the study, him thrusting into her, having her, owning her. When he'd pulled out, wiped himself with a handkerchief, she hadn't moved. Still and wide open, she'd allowed the ecstasy to flow through her; moving, even an inch, would break the spell. She was satisfied and starving all at once. She wanted to do it again. Again and again.

'You should get back to the party. Your husband will be looking for you.'

'No, he won't be.' She'd sounded heartless which was odd, because she had never been as aware of her heart as she was in that moment.

He'd said, 'You are quite unaware of the effect you have.'

'I wish I did understand it more.' She wanted to hold on to it. What if this was to be their last time? The first and last, all at once. She would not be able to endure that. She had felt the blood move around her body. She had felt a current in her brain. It was like someone had turned on the electricity and now she could see and hear and feel everything so much more clearly, so much more deeply. He'd pulled her off the desk, kissed her forehead and walked out of the room.

The silence and separation since were leading her to believe the entire encounter hadn't really happened, yet she had a small bruise on her right buttock, the buttock that had scratched up against the corner of an open book on Sir Peter's desk as Edgar had pushed her backwards and forwards, over and over. She looked at the small purple bruise, the size of a strawberry, in the long gilt mirror in her room, and caressed it like a lover might.

Lydia had thought about scribbling a note, having Dickenson deliver it; she was almost certain that she could rely on her maid's discretion, and in these circumstances almost certain would have to be enough. But when it had come to it, she didn't know what to write. What to say. She'd sat at the desk in her bedroom, stroking the thick, creamy paper, repeatedly picking up her pen only to put it down again. She thought of a lady she'd heard of, who once had an affair discovered because her suspicious husband had found the words she'd written to her lover recorded on the blotting paper. Lydia could not imagine Lawrence being as distrustful, or as resourceful. It wasn't that that was stopping her. For a moment she tried to imagine what it would be like to be discovered. She could not decide whether it would be horrific or wonderful. She'd picked up the pen again but didn't know how to address him. *Darling? My love? Edgar?* What should she say? *Meet me? Take me? Take me away?* She'd given up.

So, despite longing for him, dreaming of him, feeling giddy or sick whenever she saw him, she had not touched him since Sunday night. They'd behaved towards one another with the utmost decorum and restraint. On only one occasion had they managed to exchange a handful of words.

This morning, after breakfast, Lydia had tried to slip into the library alone, but Sarah had clung to her like a limpet, insisting on joining her. Further, she'd been adamant that Bea come too. Beatrice had been mooning around after Mr Oaksley for the entire weekend; Sarah had commented that it was becoming a little obvious (she meant embarrassing) and she was resolute that Bea give him some space.

'But I barely spoke to him yesterday,' protested Bea.

'He knows where to find you,' pointed out Sarah.

Lydia found the exchange uncomfortable, as it could so easily have applied to her situation too. The sisters bickered all morning. Bea was frustrated and resentful, Sarah was unusually short-tempered and sarcastic; at one point she muttered that it was like escorting a bunch of children to a sweet shop. Lydia didn't quite get what she was on about but was irritated by the enforced company. Her irritation turned to something bordering on fury when Edgar finally entered the library; she recognised the moment for what it was: the one where he had come to find her, the one where they might have been alone but weren't. Their exchange, by necessity, was brief and impersonal. A sense of urgent desperation hung over it.

'Ladies.' He nodded towards them and then turned to the shelves. Lydia watched as he placed his finger on the spine of a book and then walked the length of the room. His trailing finger became mesmerising. She felt the sound of his shoes, clomping on the floorboards, reverberate through her body. Like a silly schoolgirl she jumped in.

'Sergeant Major Trent, how unexpected.'

'I do read, Lady Chatfield.'

'Well, absolutely.' She blushed. It was hard to judge what the others must make of his abruptness. They couldn't imagine it was a challenging, enticing exchange between lovers; it must sound caustic to them.

'I'm not a scholar. I didn't study these books and plays at school, so when I'm in this sort of house I always try to pick up some volume or other.' Lydia's eyes widened; although he wasn't looking at her, he seemed to understand how she might misinterpret what he'd said. 'I don't mean I steal them, although thank you for the vote of confidence, Lady Chatfield, and the impertinent assumption; I mean to read whilst I'm here.' She wanted to giggle; he was playing with her. 'I'm leaving today, so I'm just returning this volume to its rightful place.'

'What have you been reading?'

'Joyce's *Ulysses.*'

'How did you find it?'

'Unfathomable. What are you reading?'

She held up the slim volume of Rupert Brooke war poems. He sighed, almost bored with the predictability of her choice.

'You don't approve.'

'I've never read it. I was there. I don't need to be burdened with another man's account. Especially a dead man. Why would you want to get embroiled in all of that? You'd be better sticking with Edith Wharton's *The Age of Innocence.*'

And then he left the room.

She could not resist reading deeper meaning into every word he'd uttered. What had he meant? Was it anything more than a book recommendation? She thought it had to be. Over and over again she played the words through her head. He'd warned her to ignore the edition of poems that was generally agreed to be the zeitgeist of their generation's feeling on the war; instead he'd pointed her towards a masterful portrait of desire and betrayal among society people who 'dreaded scandal more than disease'. Lydia knew the book. She thought it ended tragically. Was he warning her off? Stepping away?

Now Lydia stood in the hallway with the bouncing dogs and the cumbersome bags; various chaps dashed about saying their final goodbyes and demanding the servants find them a hat, their gloves or a walking stick. Lydia and Edgar seemed solid against the frenetic activity but their solidness was drenched in sadness. She did not want it to end. Did he? Even the torture of being within proximity but unable to talk to one another was better than the thought of not being under the same roof. Lydia wondered when she'd see him again. The thought that she might not was crushing.

Constrained by convention, she kissed the cheeks of all the chaps she'd known before the snow-in, and shook hands with the newer acquaintances, although if pushed she would have struggled to recall any of their names; she'd only had room in her world for one man and had rudely neglected all of Ava's other guests. As she moved along the informal line towards him, the hairs on her arms pricked up. He held out his hand. She took it, shook it, could not let it go. They turned their bodies away from the others, carving out a space in the world where there could be just the two of them.

'How will I reach you?' he asked. The relief was overwhelming. Her knees shuddered.

'This is my card.' She'd had it ready, secreted up her sleeve, just in case he gave even the smallest indication that he might want her details. He discreetly took it from her and slipped it into his pocket. Then he shrugged himself into his jacket, refusing the help of the footman. Ava tutted; she thought him rude. Lydia thought he was independent. Forward.

She watched as the troop of men set off along the driveway. It was oddly reminiscent of when the women had watched their men go off to war. Lydia thought it particularly strange that, again, Lawrence was with the women and not the men; she sighed, irritated. She watched until Edgar's shape merged with the group and his outline could no longer be distinctly identified. She watched until they went through the gate and turned the corner and there was nothing and no one to watch.

'Come in, you'll get a cold,' said Sarah. But Lydia remained standing in the driveway, staring at the space that he'd left, feeling the emptiness swallow her. His absence more real than Lawrence's presence.

It was the maid's scream that she heard first, then the general calling, a number of voices. Male ones were in amongst the higher-pitched yelling. Lydia was drawn back to the house, where she was confronted by Ava, looking unusually shaken.

'What is it?'

'It's Mr Oaksley. He's only gone and hanged himself.'

SPRING

26

THE SUN SHONE, a buttery yellow, which encouraged tulips and chatter to bud. Finally. Lydia breathed in the spring's warmth and unfurled herself. After weeks of emotional hibernation, she stirred. He'd summoned her. She leaned out of the car window like a child joyfully riding a carousel pony, then, barely waiting for the automobile to stop, she swung open the door and leapt out, a mass of chiffon and expectancy. Giddily she waved at the chauffeur, her good mood overwhelming etiquette.

'What time shall I pick you up, my lady?' he called.

'Oh, don't bother, Stevenson. I shall catch a taxi back to Eaton Square, or maybe take an underground train.'

She ran up the museum steps, ignoring her driver's protests that she'd find all sorts on the tube. 'There are no first-class carriages like on a proper train,' he warned ominously.

She didn't stop to take in the beauty and splendour of the elaborate portico, and danced on the spot with impatience as she was forced to pause and stand by while the doorman slowly pulled open the heavy, elaborate wood-panelled door. He tipped his hat as she darted through the entrance.

She spotted him instantly. There he was. Tall and magnificent against the colossal marbled pillars. His broad back to her. Light-headed and volatile, she ran to him, her heels clip-clopping on the black and white tiled floor.

'Hello.'

He turned to her. She saw anxiety sitting in tight knots on his

179

face; when he saw her standing before him, his face opened up into a broad beam. She felt soothed. She wanted to kiss him. Was going to. Push her lips on to his. Feel him, again. For a moment she didn't care about propriety or being spotted, or even about how he might receive her kisses, but he held out his hand for her to shake, stopping her. 'Hello, Lid.' If she was disappointed by his careful greeting, she forgave him and lit up with delight when he added, 'I'm so very happy you came.'

It was simple, direct. It was how she felt. So very *happy*. She had not seen or heard from him for six weeks; it had felt like six years. She'd almost drowned in a sense of pointless desolation. At times she'd felt the slow minutes pull at her back and legs; she'd ached as though she was an old woman. At other times it felt as though time was scalding her; she was jittery and wild. She had continued, as she must, but she had functioned rather than lived. She had attended parties, laughed, drunk and danced; she'd worn silk, satin and chiffon in cobalt, magenta and emerald. The same woman, to all intents and purposes; not the same woman at all. Without knowing it, she'd become the draw of every eye in these past weeks. Everyone agreed that there was something about her. Something electric and different. The naïve couldn't comprehend; they wondered whether she was at last pregnant, which she was not. The more knowing exchanged interested glances above her head. They recognised that she was a woman on the cusp; it was simply to be decided whether she was on the cusp of a love affair or some other disaster. 'Perhaps bankruptcy or alcoholism,' Harry Fine offered sardonically. 'There's certainly an energy to her. Or at least a sense of desperation.'

At every party she'd craned her neck, beyond eager to catch a glimpse of him, but she'd never spotted him at any of the lunches, soirées, dinners or balls. Without him there was no point in her being there, being anywhere. She found the sudden craze for themed dressing infuriating, as it further hampered her search in crowded rooms.

'What is this fad with fancy dress?' she'd muttered sulkily at the last ball, where guests had been required to dress as fairy-tale characters.

'Wishful thinking,' Ava had replied with a yawn.

'What do you mean?'

'We'd all rather be someone else, darling. Wouldn't we?'

'Masks are rather super, I think,' Freddie had remarked, with his usual puppy-dog enthusiasm.

'Yes, useful if you have anything to hide.' Sarah had directed this comment at Lydia, but Lydia was too self-absorbed to notice even a warning.

'We all have something to hide,' Beatrice had observed sadly.

'Not me,' replied Ava.

'No, I suppose not. You are openly scandalous.'

But she had not found him. He did not turn up at anyone's country house, hunt or shoot. Lydia despaired. She reran every conversation they had had in her head a hundred times; she thought of the hairs on the back of his hands, the mole on the side of his neck. Every detail seared into her consciousness, everything else dull and bland. He had her address and telephone number. He knew where to find her. She did not know where to find him. She was paralysed; it had to be him who made a move. Then, at long last, he left his card. No formal note. No explanation. Just the words *V&A, 2 o'clock, 2nd March*. His handwriting was extremely neat and careful. It filled her with hope, as it showed he had deliberated.

There was not an instant when she thought she might resist.

And now here he was, just in front of her. She could touch him. She could not. He handed her a guidebook and asked her whether there was anything in particular she wanted to look at. She shrugged her shoulders, unable to care enough to make a choice. All she cared about was being near him.

'The medieval and renaissance halls, perhaps?' he suggested. 'That period is blood long ago shed, and therefore palatable.'

She nodded, overeager. They walked just a short distance; Lydia stared at the floor, because she feared that if she looked at him, he would see everything in her face, and she also feared that he would not. The huge black and white marble tiles were suddenly replaced by intricately laid mosaics of the same colour.

They stood side by side, in silent awe of the ancient reliefs and sculptures. Lydia had benefited from several lectures by various and renowned artists; she had knowledge and views to share but she couldn't summon up words. Eventually he said, 'You know, we largely have a man called John Charles Robinson to thank for this collection. He became curator in eighteen fifty-three. During his ten-year tenure he hunted out the rare, the old and the beautiful.'

Lydia wanted to make a joke that it was unusual indeed for a man to have that particular selection criteria; in her experience men only pursued two of the three, but somehow she could not be flip with him, not yet. She did not have the confidence. Instead, she slipped into the role of student and he the role of teacher; she hung on his every word like a squirrel grasping a swaying branch. 'Revolutions throughout Europe meant that many aristocratic families were impoverished and many religious institutions had been dissolved; artworks were flooding on to the market. Robinson amassed the world's greatest collection of Italian Renaissance sculp-ture outside Italy.'

'An opportunist,' she commented lightly.

'A man with a good eye and an ability to see the intrinsic value.' Edgar's voice cracked a little. Lydia felt embarrassed. Her cheeks burned. Why couldn't she hit the right note? Why was she being so awkward when she was generally so gracious? She wanted to be her best self with him; she feared she was coming off quite dull and silly. Edgar continued, 'He believed that good taste could, and should, be taught. He believed that the better arbiters of taste acquired it through a process of osmosis, since childhood, but that the masses needed a museum to provide a training.'

'He sounds a frightful snob.'

'I think he was a friend to the poorly educated. I've spent a lot of time here.' His difference spilt between them. They continued to browse, not saying much to one another; there was too much to say. Where to begin? The air between them was charged. She felt that if she stuck out her tongue, she would taste it. She would taste the want.

They stopped and took stock of Giambologna's statue of Samson slaying a Philistine. They were both irresistibly drawn to its ferocious manliness. Lydia could clearly see the Philistine's buttocks, and if she straightened her back, she got a peek at Samson's pubic hair too. She was glad the statue was mounted on a tall pedestal, high up, far out of reach of her touch, because if there had been a chance, she might have stretched and stroked it. Somehow she would not have been able to stop herself. All her self-control was being channelled into not touching Edgar; she felt weakened, exhausted. She blushed at the thought of her own immodesty and she blushed more when she realised he was watching her. Carefully. Reading her.

'Do you like this one?'

'It's very aggressive.'

'Yes.' His affirmation was also an explanation of its appeal.

She could not help herself; she reached forward and caressed the only part of the statue she could reach, the sole of the foot of the Philistine, which was exposed as he knelt begging for his life.

'And?'

'It's very passionate,' she admitted.

In the six weeks since they'd last seen one another, she'd lost weight, although there was none to lose, and she was verging on gaunt; he looked as healthy and robust as he had when she first laid eyes on him. Clearly, whatever had happened at the Pondson-Callows' had not put him off his food. She resented and admired his equanimity but most of all she feared it. Was it possible that it had all been one-way? That their union had been an incident to him? Nothing more? When she was a child, she'd had the misfortune to slip whilst walking near a river one frosty January morning; she'd fallen and was plunged into the icy whirling water. She remembered being shocked rather than afraid. She'd come up gasping, feeling astonished with life, jolted out of any sense of contentment or self-satisfaction. People had fussed and worried, there was talk of pneumonia, but even as she'd stepped out of her wet clothes and been placed in front of a huge fire in the nursery – her small feet dangling from beneath the enormous rough towel – Lydia had recognised the incident as affirming. She'd never felt that same exhilaration again.

Until he'd entered her.

It couldn't be a single incident. She wouldn't accept that. Her adultery was a catastrophe that had torn a hole in the fabric of her life. It was against everything she believed in. But all she knew was that if it didn't continue, that hole would get even bigger. There was no turning back, no patching up.

She continued to wander around the vast hall, her eyes slipping from one stunning effigy to the next, statues of gods and warriors. She stared at the broad shoulders, the taut pectorals, the muscular upper stomachs and the slight hint of a curve in the lower abdomens that slipped, melted, into slinky Vs like arrows, pointing, forcing her attention to their manliness. Were men ever that perfect? Any of them? She thought perhaps Edgar was. She had not seen much of him, that night in the study. It was dark and fast. She'd closed her eyes. She'd felt him and she knew enough from his height, breadth and forearms to hope for magnificence; her heart quickened at the thought of such erotic beauty so close to her but covered up, out of sight, out of reach. She felt spasms, low in her stomach, high above her thighs, in the area she didn't know how to name but believed in entirely. Her husband certainly did not have taut muscles or broad shoulders. He had a perfectly respectable build, an inch above average height maybe, but there was no strength in his calves or thighs, in his back or forearms. His stomach sagged slightly, like a lazy breeze. His strength came from inheriting an ancient title and hundreds of acres of land, and his confidence was the result of an ability to discern which claret would best complement which Continental cheese. A decision he made with the butler, who talked to the housekeeper, who conferred with Cook.

It didn't seem enough.

The statues became difficult to look at. There were so many bosoms and penises. Lydia could feel the sculptors' hands on the clay and marble almost as she had felt Edgar's hands on her body. A myriad of thoughts flung through her head. She thought of her bruised buttock, the way she'd acquired the blemish; she considered the leaflet the doctor had given her suggesting alternative sexual positions, and she began to feel breathless.

184

'I like it here. It keeps us civilised. It reminds me that we are small but that it will go on,' commented Edgar.

'What will?'

'Time.'

She had hoped he would say that they would go on. Lydia Chatfield, née Hemingford, and Edgar Trent as lovers. It was agony that he didn't refer to them as an item or a possibility. He didn't mention the study or the weekend at all. She didn't know where she stood or what he wanted. They were intimate strangers.

She sighed and looked around her. She had no idea how to start the conversation that she had to have. They wandered around the William Morris room and saw various treasures that had once belonged to Marie Antoinette. Lydia couldn't give them her attention. She was absorbed but her taut nervous energy was focused entirely on Edgar. His chiselled bone structure covered by paper-thin skin and his eyes the colour of dappled summer light falling through trees had a sinuous charm and compelling beauty that surpassed all the exhibit pieces.

There were a significant number of young women sketching, serious and focused, capturing what other artists had already created, and whilst Lydia understood the practice on an intellectual level – studying the great artist was an approved technique for learning oneself – she found something insidious in the occupation of these earnest young girls. They copied what the male artists had made. The work of the male artists would endure; the women's work seemed counterfeit or diluted by comparison.

'Oh, my God, that's Beatrice,' Lydia whispered, shocked. Beatrice was bent over her sketchpad, solemn and involved like the other women set on imitating. Lydia's first thought was to turn in the opposite direction to avoid an awkward introduction and the dredging up of a reasonable explanation as to why, exactly, she was in the V&A museum this bright spring afternoon with a strange gentleman.

A man, at least.

Lydia noted the curve of Beatrice's bent neck; it was familiar and startling. Vulnerable. Her short hair didn't suit her. She used to wear it braided at the back in a French plait; it had been unfashionable, but flattering. There was something about seeing her hunched into such a tight ball of concentration that reminded Lydia of the girl Beatrice had once been; the fun, hopeful girl who'd blended optimism with a penchant for serious study. It had been a long time since Lydia had thought of her that way. If people thought of her at all – just her, not her as an adjunct, sister to Sarah and Samuel, aunt to a bunch of boisterous children – they tended to think only that it was a pity. The issue as to how Lydia would explain her own presence was momentarily blurred as she considered why Beatrice was in the museum, here in London. The opportunity to dodge was taken from her as Edgar rushed forward, practically shouting, 'Isn't she a friend of yours? Over there, near the Shakespeare bust. She was at the house. Beatrice, you say? Beatrice!'

Beatrice heard her name and looked up. Both women were flustered. They allowed one another a moment. Beatrice closed her sketchpad, Lydia constructed an alibi. They kissed on the cheek. As Lydia withdrew from the embrace, she quickly went on the offensive.

'Beatrice, what a surprise. What are you doing in London?'

'Didn't Ava mention it? I'm staying with her for a few days, in Chelsea.'

'Ava? No.' Lydia politely hid her astonishment that Ava would extend her hospitality in Bea's direction. 'How lovely.'

'I come here to the museum so I'm not under her feet all day.' Bea shrugged; the gesture suggested that whilst Ava had opened her doors, she might not have opened her heart to Bea, and that the stay wasn't necessarily a delightful and totally relaxed one. 'It's very pleasant here.'

Lydia glanced around. 'Wouldn't you be better visiting a tea shop?' She didn't know why she'd said such a stupid and frivolous thing. She'd actually found the last hour in the museum one of the most thought-provoking and charged of her life, but still part of her would have preferred to stride through the streets with Edgar, visit busy restaurants and shops, if only she could. Given a choice, she wouldn't hide away. She wondered why Bea might choose to come somewhere so quiet.

'I like it here. I find it soothing. It's austere yet peaceful.'

'I see.' Lydia blushed. She was aware that Beatrice must be going through a hard time. That awful business with the chap she'd been flirting with at the Pondson-Callows' must have unsettled her. They hadn't seen a lot of one another since that weekend. Thinking about it now, Beatrice had only attended one or two of the subsequent parties. It wasn't like her.

Lydia wondered how she ought to introduce Edgar, but was saved the trouble when he assumed a familiarity with Beatrice and said, 'Let's have a look, then.'

'Oh, I'm . . . It's not finished.'

He ignored Bea's demurring and firmly took the pad from her grasp. 'These are damn good.'

'Do you think so?' Beatrice blushed with delight.

Lydia leaned over his shoulder to look at the drawing book. 'Goodness, Bea, you have a gift. I never knew.'

'Really? I've always enjoyed sketching. It's just a hobby.'

'You're extremely talented.'

The threesome huddled around the sketches and Lydia was forced to reappraise and reject her earlier assumption that these artistic women, huddled on the benches and floors of the museum, were imitating or parasitical. The sketchpad erupted. There it was, on the paper. Dark and light lines, strokes and delves. Sex. Beatrice had sketched sex. Sex and desire and – Lydia turned another page – misery. Bea was able to illustrate a depth that she never articulated.

Edgar coughed and Lydia suggested they ought to take tea.

'Will you join us?' She prayed that Beatrice would decline – she couldn't stand the idea of sharing her precious moments with Edgar – but, having just witnessed the tender rage and beauty in the sketches, she couldn't walk away from her friend. There was a loneliness on the paper that Lydia was unable to ignore.

Still, she was relieved when Bea replied, 'No, thank you. I want to finish this today.'

'If you're sure.'

'Yes, I am quite sure.'

Suddenly Lydia wanted to leave as quickly as she could. She realised that thus far Bea hadn't asked for an explanation as to why she was out with Sergeant Major Trent, and that was a blessing. She would need time to think of a viable excuse. The women kissed one another on the cheek once again, then Lydia turned to Edgar.

'So, tea?'

Edgar held out his hand for Beatrice to shake and said, 'I'm so terribly sorry to hear about your loss. I was only vaguely acquainted with Oaksley, but he seemed a very decent chap. He gave our country everything. My sympathies, Beatrice.'

Bea held on to Edgar's hand and nodded briefly. She didn't say anything. Lydia saw that she was fighting tears.

27

BEATRICE WAS STUNNED. The sergeant major was the first and only person who had mentioned Arnie to her; acknowledged that she might be feeling a loss. Grief. The world was so saturated with grief that people had become hardened to it. Bored of it. Arnie had died inconveniently late; three years ago, on a battlefield, his demise would certainly have solicited much more sympathy. Yes, Sarah, Ava and Lydia had said how awful the entire thing was and that she must be shocked, but they had not hinted at the core of it. They had not admitted that another door had slammed in her face. Perhaps the last door. She was now alone in a black corridor of despair.

One of the other female artists, sitting just two or three feet away, nodded at Bea; perhaps she'd overheard the condolences. Perhaps she had her own anguished story. Bea had met quite a few other girls here, girls about her age or a little older. Well, not met exactly. They tended not to introduce themselves to one another, but rather to work peacefully, silently, side by side. There was some solidarity in that. Some company. Bea thought she might need some new pals. Despite Ava's unexpected and undoubtedly generous offer to visit her in London, she didn't feel quite as shored up by her friendships as she used to. Not since Arnie. It made no sense. She had only known him for a weekend; most people would agree that she had no real right to feel so terrible, yet she did. Naturally, she couldn't expect a great deal of sympathy from Sarah, who had lost an actual husband rather than a brief encounter, but both Sarah and Lydia had been distracted and distant since the weekend at the Pondson-Callows' and no help to her at all. Bea guessed they might be sharing a secret, yet another one that she was not privy to. It was frustrating and demeaning. She felt locked out and discarded from their intimacy. Another expulsion.

Perhaps Ava was feeling the same. Perhaps that was why she'd casually thrown out the invitation to Beatrice. Bea really couldn't think of another reason. She'd always been aware that Ava tolerated her rather than sought her out. Why the sudden change? Still, she had not questioned Ava's motives too closely; she'd bitten off her hand, practically packed the suitcase before the telephone line cooled down. She was so sick of feeling like a spare part at Seaton Manor. Sammy retired to bed as soon as supper was over; his painkillers made him drowsy. Cecily was becoming increasingly reclusive. Both she and Sarah turned in as soon as the children and Sammy were tucked up. Bea frequently found herself alone in the drawing room, wondering what she could do with the evening stretching out in front of her. She knew there would be many more of them to come. 'I'd better get used to it,' she told herself, and then she wondered if talking to herself was a sign of madness. Certainly a sign of loneliness. She made plans. One night would be devoted to sketching, the next knitting, a third watering the plants or writing letters. She found it helpful to write lists and decide what to do day by day. She could usually amuse herself until nine o'clock. Then she lay on her bed and sniffed her pillow. It smelt of her hairspray. Never of anyone else. 'I'd better get used to that too,' she told herself.

London and Ava's invitation was some sort of escape. Even though, as it had turned out, they hadn't seen that much of one another. Ava was always at some meeting or other. Causes. Bea had thought that was all over, now that the suffragettes had got what they wanted, but Ava had tutted crossly when she had suggested as much and said that Bea ought to come along and see how things really were.

'Women in Britain can only vote if they are over thirty and

meet certain property qualifications. How can you think the job is done? Neither of us has the right yet.' Bea had noted the frustration flare through Ava's body; it made her rigid. She was normally such a serene woman, but this thought set her nerves on edge. 'Women living with their parents, those in service and the younger gals who worked tirelessly in the munitions factories and such are being ignored. It's not on.'

'You can't change the world,' Bea had sighed.

'Why not? I thought that was what it was all about. The Great War and everything.'

'I thought it was about trying to keep things the same.'

'Well in that case it was a bigger catastrophe than even I could possibly have imagined.'

Bea had shot Ava a look of rebuke, sensitive to Arthur's sacrifice, to Sammy's, to Arnie's.

'Sorry,' Ava said sulkily. 'I don't always engage my brain quite as swiftly as I allow my tongue to function.'

Still, Bea had declined; she wasn't yet ready for rowdy meetings. She needed cool, slow spaces. She needed to feel her smooth pencils and charcoal in her hands, the texture of the thick parchment of her sketchpad under her fingertips. The letter was secreted between the pages of her book; she kept it with her always.

Beatrice took comfort in the women she'd become acquainted with at the gallery. They were like her. Respectable, but not wealthy, sincere, a shade too grave, and many of them were plain. The gallery was chilly, but no colder than her bedroom at home; besides, when at closing time she struggled to her feet, her legs numb with crouching on the marble floor, she knew she was only a short tube ride away from the sumptuousness of Ava's apartment. Ava always saw to it that there was a fire burning and scones with butter and strawberry conserve waiting for her.

Bea was so enchanted with the idea that the sergeant major liked her work and so touched that he'd acknowledged her loss that it took her a full fifteen minutes before she considered what on earth Lydia was doing out with him. Was he a friend of

Lawrence's? Where was Lawrence? She didn't pursue the mystery for more than a few minutes. She wasn't of a suspicious nature, and even if she had been, Lydia's behaviour was always exemplary. Bea didn't doubt there must be a reasonable explanation for them being out together alone, if indeed they were alone.

Besides, she didn't really care enough about other people's lives to want to involve herself unnecessarily. That way danger lay. Look how it had ended with Arnie. Once again, perhaps for the hundredth time, Bea flipped through the pages and found the envelope. Her name, *Miss Beatrice Polwarth*, written in his hand on the front. It was a messy, childlike script. Each letter unnecessarily large. It must have been extremely difficult for a blind man to write with ink. Since receiving the letter, she'd closed her eyes and written her name over and over, in order to gauge what level of concentration was required, to understand how difficult a task writing the letter had been for him. Her script, normally so neat and precise, became a spidery scrawl. She'd had a glimpse of how tiring and demanding even the smallest task must have been for him. The thought had ripped at her heart. She berated herself for underestimating, for miscalculating. She sighed wearily; she was not sure she could make herself read the note again. But then she didn't really have to; she knew what it said by heart.

> *Dear Beatrice,*
> *What you feel is pity. If not pity for me, pity for yourself.*
> *Don't.*
> *Yours with respect,*
> *Arnold Oaksley*

The words tortured her conscience. Why had he written to her? Why not to his father? There hadn't been any other note, Sir Peter had reassured her on that point, quite vigorously. There had only been her at the end. Or had she brought about his end? Was it the case that he'd rather be dead than with her? The lofty arches of the museum began to swim in front of her. She needed some air. She might pack up early and walk back to Ava's tonight. She couldn't bear the idea of getting on the cramped and stuffy tube. She didn't want to be so close to so many people. She didn't want to have to walk past the soldiers with missing limbs who begged outside the tube station. She did not dare do it.

28

A VA NOTICED BEA'S peaky pallor she moment she came in the front door. She looked cold, even though the sun had finally squeezed through the clouds and was still warming the streets now at five o'clock. Ava couldn't understand how such an insulated person could feel the cold so vitally.

'I have cake and port,' she declared. She was feeling munificent. Today she had been with her new friend Marie Stopes and some other interested parties. They'd spent the afternoon trailing from door to door in the East End of London talking to women ravaged with poverty and numerous children about contraception. Marie had written a sixteen-page pamphlet called *Wise Parenthood: A Letter to Working Mothers on how to have healthy children and avoid weakening pregnancies.* Even though the pamphlet was distributed free of charge, it was rarely well received. The level of illiteracy and the sustained mistrust the poor felt for the meddling middle and upper classes meant that the women who most needed advice were reluctant to listen. Often these campaigning days were exhausting. The earnest and conscientious could not cut through the fumes of cockney tobacco and the air of exhausted indifference; jeers and catcalls drowned out Ava's salient points about birth control. However, today she had met and charmed a raucous, bibulous, but undoubtedly influential matriarch, who had insisted that her three daughters, two daughters-in-law and eleven granddaughters (two of whom were already obviously pregnant) listen to 'What the posh lady says about the shunning of getting one in.' It had been a great success. If just one unwanted pregnancy was avoided, then Ava had achieved something today. She felt celebratory.

Bea collapsed into a chair by the fire and threw down her hat. 'Thank you, cake and port is just what I need.' She ate greedily, as though she was alone.

Ava wasn't famed for having an especially sentimental bent, but she did see the pity in a girl eating alone; it prompted her to ask, 'So, how was your day?'

'Productive.'

'Can I see?'

Ava had asked the same thing every night for the past four days, but Bea had always baulked at the thought of exposing her work. Today, she was emboldened by Edgar Trent's comments; she dug around in her satchel and retrieved the sketchbook.

Ava carefully turned the pages and echoed Lydia and Edgar's enthusiasm. 'These are quite special, Bea. I'm surprised.'

Bea sighed. 'I do wish you could have stopped with the first sentence. Why do all your compliments have to come with a barb?'

Ava smiled. Recently Bea had started to say what she thought, and Ava liked it. Everyone assumed that her impatience with Bea came from the fact that Bea was so hopelessly frumpy; it did not. What Ava objected to was her passivity. Now that she was proving to be a little more spiky, Ava was finding her all the more palatable.

'I'm not trying to be barbed. It's just these sketches are so unexpected.'

'What were you expecting?'

'Oh, you know, wishy-washy landscapes in pastels.'

'I see.'

'These are . . .' Ava thought about it. 'Tender, yet angry.' She had not thought Beatrice was particularly familiar with either emotion. She looked up at her. 'Darling, what are you angry about?'

Bea glared. 'How can you ask?'

Ava thought this was unfair. She had a full and busy life. She met hundreds of people through her parties and soirées and hundreds more through her campaigning and charities; most of them were angry. One had to ask. She wasn't the sort of woman who had time to spare conjecturing and imagining what was on the mind of others. She felt much more comfortable with facts. She took a sip of port. Its velvety taste was too much for such a bright spring evening; she wondered what she should switch to. Gin was vulgar, sherry was ageing, champagne was frivolous and cocktails were lethal. That decided it. She rang for the maid and asked her to mix champagne cocktails.

Once they were furnished with drinks, Ava asked, 'Are you enjoying your break?'

Bea nodded tightly. Ava had invited Beatrice to London because Sarah had asked her to. No one ever said no to Sarah because everyone felt bad about Arthur dying and all that effort Sarah put into caring for her disabled brother. Sarah had suggested that Bea needed a change. Ava had, for once, bitten her tongue and not said what she was thinking – which was that Bea certainly didn't need a rest; what did the woman do all day?

She considered Bea's tight nod. It was obvious that the girl was churned up about something; her eyes bulged, she blinked rapidly. Was she about to cry? Ava hoped not. A good hostess couldn't ignore tears, but they were terribly dull.

In many ways Bea was proving to be an easy guest to accommodate: she ate anything, at any time, was quiet and grateful; as long as there were chocolates, hot water and a fire, she seemed to be in heaven. Ava could provide all of these without inconveniencing herself at all. A rare breeze of guilt blew across her; admittedly she hadn't done much to entertain Bea. They hadn't actually spent any time together alone, they had so very little in common. Manners dictated that she'd seen to it that her invitations to lunch parties and dinners were extended to Bea, but other than that she'd left Bea to her own devices. She could have, perhaps, taken her to the Birdcage in Piccadilly, a famous but very tame underground dancing club. It oozed nostalgia in a way that Ava found a little nauseating – the men wore white tie and tails, they all kept carnations in their buttonholes. Alcohol was not permitted. Obviously alcohol was illegal in a number of dancing establishments, but the Birdcage had rather a quaint view of rules: they abided by them.

Iced coffee and a brilliant soft pink drink were served with tea-time cakes and sandwiches. They played pre-war waltzes and one knew the evening was over when the band struck up the National Anthem. Ava sighed to herself, admitting it was quite likely to be Bea's idea of perfection. Ava herself only ever condescended to attend if the Prince of Wales asked her personally.

'Your sketches really are quite exhilarating, Bea.'

Ava's belief that one ought not to be too sympathetic and nice was given credence when Bea immediately burst into tears, something she'd always resisted doing despite enduring years of Ava's spiky comments. No doubt embarrassed by her lack of control, she quickly became hysterical. Some people were beautiful weepers; Bea was not. Her face looked like a world map, with purple blotches of shame drifting like continents. Snot, saliva and tears poured forth. Ava wondered whether she ought to offer her hand-kerchief, but she was worried that any further act of kindness might aggravate the situation. She was relieved when Bea retrieved one of her own from her bag.

'I'm so very lonely,' Bea gasped. Ava initially misheard her and thought she had said, 'I'm so very lovely'. She'd wanted to giggle because, well, frankly, the girl had a face only a grandmother could love; Ava often found mirth in the most inconvenient of places. When she finally understood, she sagged. It was a stark, barren confession.

'But, darling, how can you possibly be lonely? Since you arrived in London we've dined out nearly every evening and lunched twice.'

'I don't mean this week.'

'Well, absolutely, the countryside is dreary. If you must live in the sticks, then a certain amount of isolation and boredom has to be endured,' commented Ava, who thought anywhere without a London postcode was nowhere at all. 'But you are often invited to someone or other's for the weekend, and house parties are always heaving. One often struggles to find five moments of peaceful time. I can never keep up with reading the newspapers at the weekends.'

Bea shook her head, indicating that Ava didn't understand.

'Well, what do you mean, then?'

'I think I'm just beginning to understand that I'm never going to marry.'

Ava wondered how it had possibly taken Bea so long to reach this conclusion. She was twenty-six, plain, strapped for cash and inadequately educated. The country was down almost a million marrying-age men; how could she ever have thought her chances were good? Then Ava's quick mind made an unconscious connection. A vision flashed into her head, brutal and unwelcome. The men had tried to keep her away from Mr Oaksley's room. Her father had insistently yelled, 'Keep back, keep back!' and someone had intercepted her, dragged quite roughly at her arm in an effort to lead her away from the mess. But she'd seen him, or rather the shape of him, just for an instant. He'd already been cut down from the rafters and was lying on the polished floorboards. They'd tugged a cover off the bed and pulled it over his face, but she'd seen his legs, sticking out from under the makeshift shroud. They were at an awkward angle, like a fallen fawn; in all the confusion and panic, no one had yet thought to lay him straight. His shoes were shiny, glossy like a child's hair. Ava had wondered who polished them. Who took care of him. Before he took care of everything.

People had differing views on suicide. Some said it was selfish or sinful, others were dangerously close to understanding it too well; everyone agreed it was bitterly sorrowful.

'I proposed to Mr Oaksley, you know,' muttered Bea.

Ava had not known this. She paused for a moment and tried to think of how best to respond. Clearly gasping, 'After just two days of acquaintance?' was not that.

'Did he give an answer?'

Bea met Ava's eyes, her expression spitting out pain and exasperation. For possibly the first time in her life, Ava was conscious and regretful of saying a tactless thing.

'I think his reply was loud and clear,' Bea said flatly.

'No, Beatrice, you can't think that. You don't imagine his death was somehow your fault?'

'How else can I think of it? He clearly considered death a better alternative to living with me.'

'No, Bea. No.' Ava made her voice firm. She needed to be convincing.

'Or at best he thought he would be a burden to me and didn't want that, so you know . . .' Bea couldn't finish the sentence; a fresh tsunami of tears overwhelmed her.

Ava thought that, despite Bea believing the contrary, it was good luck that she had alighted on a maimed soldier thoughtful enough not to exploit a willing girl who so wanted to subsume her own needs; it was a narrow escape. She considered. Frankly, she thought that the timing of Arnie Oaksley's death, coming so soon after Beatrice's proposal, meant that the two things were probably somehow related, at least in the dead man's head, but she could not allow Bea to believe such a thing. Not for a moment. It had irritated Ava that in the past Bea had made so much of the death of her beau at the Front. The loss of the young man – any young man – to the dreadful war business was undoubtedly lamentable, but as their relationship had amounted to one chaperoned trip to a tea shop, Ava could not allow Bea the right to grieve. She'd been impatient with what she saw as excessive parading. Now she was beginning to reappraise; to burrow more deeply into the source of the grief. What did these losses really mean to Bea?

Bea's face was buried in her handkerchief. She was trying (and failing) to blow her nose delicately. It was a lost battle. There was nothing delicate about Bea; she was a robust woman, the sort that had shored up the corners of the Empire for generations. A respectable girl brought up to expect marriage and motherhood; without one, she could not hope for the other. Ava thought she would have made what was conventionally agreed to be a good wife. She'd have been supportive and loyal; instinctively she'd have known when to probe and when to turn a blind eye, and she'd have been a good mother, particularly to boys. She had that no-nonsense approach about her that meant she would not have been distressed by the experimental stages, such as worm-eating when they were infants or excessive drinking when they were adolescents. Bea had shared a nursery and schoolroom; she was of the bracket of women who were discouraged from having private or independent thoughts. She was bred for companionship. Her future had been smote on the French battlefields along with those of nearly a million British men, not to mention the further nine million men born on other shores.

It was futile to suggest that Beatrice ought to make more of herself. She was not that sort of girl; not a flimsy silk sort. She was a black cashmere stockings, liberty bodice, dark stockinette knickers, flannel petticoat, long-sleeved, high-necked, knitted woollen spencer sort of girl. Like many sheltered women, she'd been bred ignorant, romantic, idealistic, utterly unsophisticated.

Ava downed her cocktail and then left her chair to join Bea on the sofa. She wondered how close she ought to sit. They didn't do physical intimacy as a rule. Ava wasn't sure that either she or Bea would be comfortable if hugging was involved. She settled on putting her hand on Bea's arm. 'Listen to me, Bea darling. You had nothing to do with what happened. I'm quite sure that Mr Oaksley had planned his suicide for some time before that weekend. His situation was beastly.' She didn't dare risk saying the words she felt truly fitted the unfortunate man's situation. Unbearable. Intolerable. Insufferable. She felt any one of them would be too distressing for Bea.

'I could have helped him,' groaned Bea.

'Maybe, but some people don't want to be helped. I imagine he was very tired. He'd been brave for quite a few years. He's at peace now.' Ava was surprised to find herself settling into the accepted platitudes that so many millions had doled out for years now. She didn't believe the clichés about bravery or peace, but they were all they had so she coughed them up. 'Do you know what I think?'

'What?'

'If your proposal had any impact at all, it was probably a comfort.'

'Really?' Bea looked at her with shy desire.

No, not really. Ava did not believe that the man had gone to his death thinking how marvellous it was that a desperate, chubby girl was prepared to marry him, following just the briefest of associations, but she never had any qualms about lying for expediency, and she had lied for much less worthwhile reasons than this. 'Most definitely.'

Somewhat comforted, Bea put down her handkerchief and picked up her cocktail. For a moment they sat in a more serene silence, each pursuing their own line of thought as they allowed the chilly cocktails to take effect. Ava felt a rare but sincere moment of sympathy for Beatrice's predicament; she was infuriated by the enduring inequalities and tragedies that they all had to stomach. Bea was thinking about the last time she'd felt intrinsically linked to the fabric of life. The last time she was useful and needed. 'It wasn't as bad during the war; we were all so busy. I didn't notice the loneliness. There were the sewing guilds and the fund-raisers, parcels to send to the soldiers.'

'Do you remember those awful entertainment evenings for the wounded?'

'Lydia's singing!' Bea smiled, despite her gloom.

'It can't really have aided recovery, can it?' asked Ava, with a sly wink.

'Quite the reverse.' The women giggled. The tight air loosened around them. The dread of solitude slackened. Bea asked, 'Do you remember how we celebrated Armistice night?'

'Of course. At the Ritz.'

'We sang patriotic songs.'

'Cynthia Curzon wore nothing other than a Union Jack!'

'We thought all our troubles were at an end for ever.' Bea paused and swallowed. 'You see, I'm not sure what I shall do if I don't marry. It's all I've ever imagined. All I've been brought up to. What can I do, if I don't do that?'

'The terribly good thing about the war is that—'

Bea gasped. 'Ava, how can you even begin a sentence like that?'

'Darling, every cloud has a silver lining and all that. I was just going to say that it opened doors for us.'

'Us?'

'Women.'

201

'But they all died. The men. Our men.'

'Well, not *all* of them, but that's not my point. Think, no chaperones to scrutinise our every move. A valid excuse if one wants to avoid matrimony.'

'But why would one want that?'

'Because, darling Bea, being married doesn't necessarily mean you'll be happier.' Ava couldn't help a hint of condescension sneaking into her voice. She was, quite simply, the more worldly-wise of the two. 'I see countless cases that prove otherwise, every day.'

'Oh, but you mean poor people. Drinkers. Brutes.'

'Drinkers, brutes and unhappy marriages are not confined to one class. You know very well that the concept abounds among our sort too.'

'Oh, don't. It's all too sad.' It was clear that Beatrice wasn't quite ready to step out of her fairy-tale, make-believe world. Ava decided to accentuate the positive instead.

'There are plenty of things you can do with your time. You could go abroad.'

'I can't afford it.'

'I find there's always someone willing to pick up the bill.'

'I imagine *you* do.'

'No, not like that. Someone who needs a companion. Perhaps a middle-aged widow who wants to learn about the classical artists in Italy. These people advertise in *The Lady*, you know. You could sketch.'

'The object of travel to the Continent is to bring home a young man.'

'The object is to have *fun*. Lydia and I have gone abroad for the past two years and we've only ever thought about having fun.'

'Maybe it is just about fun if you are married or simply gorgeous.' Beatrice sounded accusing. 'But no, not at all for me. I can imagine the humiliation. It will be like going to a dance full of expectancy and hope only to return with a relentless sense of ineptitude when one fails to click with anyone, except it will be a hundred times worse because dances are on every doorstep but abroad is such a distance.'

'Would you think of golf lessons? Or joining the Women's League of Health and Beauty? I hear it's incredible fun and chummy, you know.'

'Hobbies.' Bea sighed, articulating that she didn't think hobbies were enough.

'Then you must get a career. You could teach, or join the civil service.'

'But those are consolation prizes.'

'I disagree.'

'I feel like a lesser being. An unmarried woman. How low can one go?'

'It is true that single women are underestimated and underrated, but just because others think little of our position doesn't mean we should fail to appreciate just how wonderful an opportunity is being presented here. Singleness isn't an illness or a state to be despised; it's an endless opportunity,' said Ava firmly. 'You know there are women accountants, engineers, doctors. You could go into law or banking.'

'No, I couldn't.'

'Why not?'

'Well, how would I begin? It's impossible. Quite hopeless. Those things are possible for women like you, maybe, I suppose. But . . .' She left it hanging. The air was awash with loneliness and self-imposed limitations. Ava saw a lack of confidence, thought and ambition. It wasn't Beatrice's fault; they'd all been encouraged to think small and narrow.

'Do you know what? I need to introduce you to some more people.'

'Like who?'

'Like my friends that I was out with today. Campaigners, suffragettes.' Ava saw the horror on Bea's face and couldn't resist adding, 'Do-gooders. Come on, there's no time like the present. I shall cancel dinner with Lady Cooper, because really, how many times can we chat about frocks, and the exceptional view from her box at the opera? I'll telephone my women instead. You need to meet fresh faces. Not fresh men. Fresh *faces*.' She jumped up and walked towards her telephone; she instructed the operator. 'Belgravia 214, please.'

The thought of a fresh face brought to mind a familiar one. 'I saw Lydia today,' commented Bea.

'Really? Where?'

'The V and A Museum.'

'Lydia? In a museum? How utterly astounding.'

'She was with that terribly handsome man.'

Ava put the phone down without speaking to Lady Cooper. She felt the earth shimmer a little. She felt askew and yet she was certain that she knew what was coming. 'Which one?'

'Sergeant Major Trent.'

'Are you sure?'

'Quite sure. They talked to me. He's a lovely person, isn't he? So polite and sincere.' Not for the first time Ava doubted Bea's ability to make sensible judgements about people; she really didn't have enough experience of the world. This suspicion was confirmed when Bea added, 'What do you think they were doing there together? Is there a particular exhibition that everyone is seeing? I didn't know that Sergeant Major Trent was a friend of Lawrence's.'

Ava wondered whether it was time to shove the baby bird out of the nest. It would not do for Beatrice to blithely drift through the world in a state of naïve wonderment and innocence.

'I don't think he is a friend of Lawrence's, Beatrice darling.'

Ava's hint settled like rain on a parched field. Bea gasped. 'No, not Lydia.'

'I'm afraid it looks that way.'

Ava never understood the girls who accepted the rules, who didn't baulk at them and strain at their ribbon chains. Lydia had been such a girl and Ava used to long for her to kick up her heels a little. Now that she had, it was terrifying, unsettling. It was another war; smaller, quieter. A domestic front but still real and destructive. Now Ava just wanted her friend to melt into the accepted, to blend. To fuse.

29

THEY FOUND A tea room near South Kensington tube station. It was steamy, smoky and crowded. Lydia could smell coats that had served throughout winter and bodies that didn't have frequent access to hot water. The teapot was chipped and cracked in two places; brown veins of tea stains showered over the lip. She wanted to send it back but couldn't bear to look fussy.

She was beginning to despair. He had not said one thing that might suggest she should hope. He had been polite and careful. He'd pointed out things of interest in the museum; they'd both been fond of Dante Gabriel Rossetti's painting *The Day Dream*. He had talked about the long winter and everyone's dire need for spring to blossom; wasn't it marvellous that the sun was finally out? He'd told her about a Noël Coward play he had seen recently. But he had not referenced the fact that they were lovers. He gave no indication that he too burned. It was perfectly possible that rather than meeting to cement their relationship, he was politely defining their new status as well-mannered, distant acquaintances. She had to find a way to introduce the subject of *them*; she had to be sure of where she stood. She took a sip of tea. It was strong and bitter, but she noticed that there was only one teaspoon in the bowl of sugar and none on her saucer; how would she stir if she added sugar? She'd have to drink it as it was. She scrambled around her brain to look for a way back into *that* weekend.

'It was very kind of you to pass on your condolences to Beatrice.'

'One of the servant boys ran to the station to tell us all the news.'

'Yes, I know. Some of the men came back to the house.' He had not been among the number; she'd been disappointed. 'To see what they could do.'

'Ghouls. What could they possibly do? How could they help?' Lydia knew he didn't really expect an answer. 'Was he her fiancé?'

'No.'

'I saw them together quite a bit. I thought there must be something special between them.'

'Not really. It was just that weekend, but I think she'd hoped . . .' Lydia trailed off, uncomfortable with the awareness that her situation was in some ways very similar to Beatrice's. A weekend was a short period of time if one measured it by the hands on the clock, yet it could be a lifetime.

'I expected to see the suicide in the papers, but I didn't find anything.'

'Sir Peter has enough influence to keep it out.'

Edgar nodded curtly. He looked amused and yet infuriated at the same time. Power – the use and abuse of it – always exasperated those who were toothless.

'Besides that awful thing, did you enjoy your stay at the Pondson-Callows', Sergeant Major Trent?' It was ridiculous to call him Sergeant Major Trent, but she felt she had to because they were in public, elbow to elbow with complete strangers; who knew who might be listening? This place looked just the sort of place servants gossiped, and besides, today he had not given her any reason to call him anything other.

'It was an education.' He stroked his upper lip, hiding his mouth, a gateway to expression and emotion. She wondered if it was a deliberate habit.

'What did you learn?' She dared not breathe until she heard his answer. Whatever he had to say had to be imbued with deep meaning; after all, secret metaphors, hints and codes were the tools of the adulterer.

'I learned that I don't belong there.' The world shifted; it spun a little faster, making her dizzy, and yet simultaneously slowed right down, dragging her under like an enormous wave. She heard a rebuff; she felt the sting of rejection. He was backing away.

'Well,' she gasped. She wondered how he could ever have thought he did belong, and in the same instant she wondered why he should not. It was complex.

'I admit there is an undoubted sense of beauty, but it was overwhelmed, in my opinion, by a sense of the ridiculous.'

'What do you mean?'

'No one was very real there. Well, except for Arnie Oaksley, I suppose.' He glanced at her. It was a challenge. *She* had been real. As she'd lain spread and open to him on the desk, she was more honest and valid than she had ever been, than she was being now when she addressed him as Sergeant Major Trent. Did he know? Did he need her to say so? She wasn't sure whether she dared. Would he believe her?

'Are people especially real elsewhere?' she asked instead.

'Maybe.' He shrugged.

'Where?'

'You know where.' He looked right at her. Stared this time. Green arrows darting to her soul. She understood.

'But we can't stay on the battlefields.'

He sighed and mumbled, 'I wish that was true. I find I can't get off them. Nor could that poor sod Oaksley, by the look of things.' He lowered his head. There was nothing to do but listen to other people's chatter and the sound of china cups clattering on to saucers. He reached into his pocket and pulled out a packet of cigarettes; he lit two and handed her one. She'd noticed that he smoked each cigarette as though it was his last. A habit, perhaps. Something he'd developed in the trenches. She knew he was trying to appear relaxed, and that he was nothing of the sort. It took some moments before he pulled himself back on track, before he remembered that it was considered rather off to sit in a busy cafe and talk about the war. 'It wasn't a bad place to spend a weekend,' he admitted finally. 'It had a certain charm.'

If he was hoping to pacify her, his comment had the opposite effect. Lydia felt jabbed with irritation. He was not answering her real question about that weekend, or if he was, then his judgement that she had 'a certain charm' was not flattering. Not enough.

Haughtily she answered, 'Many consider Ava's home among the most beautiful in England.'

'I'd prefer it if the Pondson-Callows weren't trying so damned hard to pretend they were something else. Isn't it enough to be clever and phenomenally wealthy? Not to mention beautiful. Do they have to pretend to have history too?'

'You think Ava is beautiful?'

'I have eyes, Lid.'

Lydia fought a curious agonising pang. It was ridiculous. It was a fact that Ava was beautiful; it wasn't news to her. Of course every man noticed. But she feared it was more. She was losing him, he'd moved on. Already. Although he wasn't hers to lose. What had she expected? What had she hoped for? Nothing could come of this. And yet . . .

Angrily she snapped, 'Is it that you just don't like my sort?'

'I met a number of brave and impressive aristocratic men in battle. They weren't all lofty or indolent.'

'Well then.'

'And I met a fair few nasty bastards too. They weren't all heroes.'

'I see.'

'Do you? I wonder.' Edgar looked exasperated. She didn't know what she'd done wrong, but she felt she had made a gaffe. The whole afternoon had had that air to it. They were missing one another or knocking up against one another; they weren't merging into one as they had before. 'I know that you see that wood must be chopped and carried, along with coal scuttles, breakfast trays and hot-water bottles, but do you see the people who actually do these things? Or is it lost in the code that life must simply be made as pleasant as possible for the wealthy, irrespective of the cost.'

'You sound like a Bolshevik.'

'That's nonsense. I am no such thing. I'm an Englishman and I'm proud to be such. But we could do better.'

So he was angry with her. Why? Because she was rich? Because she was other? Lydia saw a glimmer of hope. He was not done with her. Anger showed that he was, at least, still involved. He thought that she had views and hopes and beliefs; he wanted to hear them. He wanted to tell her his. Lawrence simply thought she was beautiful although rather useless, like an elaborate, expensive ornament.

'Why are you so angry with me? What have I done wrong?' She wanted to reach across and lace her fingers through his. She couldn't stretch across the no-man's-land of the wobbly café table.

Instead of answering her question he asked one of his own.

'Why are you here?'

'You invited me.'

'Yes, I did, didn't I?' Edgar pushed his hair out of his eyes. It was a straightforward gesture; Lydia shivered as though he'd just trailed his fingers up her thigh. He sighed, heavily. 'That Oaksley fellow, I hardly spoke to him.'

'The party was huge; it's impossible to chat with everyone at that type of gathering.'

'I ignored him, or as good as. Everyone did, except for your friend.' He took another drag on his cigarette, his hand quivering slightly. 'After the war, your sort wanted everything to return to exactly as it had been. That's what those weekends are about: you think if you party hard enough, you'll turn back time. But my type – the working man, and woman – we saw that could never be the case. We wanted change. We still do.' Lydia realised he wasn't angry with her; he was furious and unforgiving of himself. 'I forgot as much that weekend. I shouldn't have ignored him.'

'You can't save everyone,' she said carefully.

'I'm well aware of that,' he sneered. 'Do you know something, Lid? Holding on to my anger is the best thing I can do. If I suppress it, it might dissipate into despair. I might just admit to how bloody futile it all was. How bloody useless it all is now.'

Suddenly he flopped, as though his skeleton had been sucked out of his body. He looked weary, lost. Lydia reached out and touched him lightly with her neatly manicured finger.

'I do understand. You think I don't, but I do.'

'How?'

'After you. After us. I felt the same. I wanted change. I want change, now.'

30

Edgar's anger engulfed the room, the street, the world, and then it became so enormous that it collapsed in on itself. He felt foolish for not being able to forget and move on. After all, he was one of the lucky ones. He'd got through. He didn't have any life-ruining injuries. He should just get on with things. Others did, didn't they? He wasn't sure. Other people's lives always looked rosy from the outside, but if you got close – and he had no wish to do so – the lives of strangers were just as likely to be blighted with cankerous doubt. Generally Edgar tried very hard to disguise his anger. He had some tricks. He held his cigarette with considered nonchalance, or linked his hands behind his head, making a pillow, slouching in a parody of relaxation. He laughed loudly, he drank quickly, he ate heartily and fucked greedily. He was covetous, avaricious. He ached with hunger. A hunger for lost time, but he knew he couldn't ever satiate that particular craving. He wanted to make up for lost time. They all did.

It wasn't possible.

He cloaked his anger but for some reason he couldn't hide the truth of his self from her.

He wondered why.

She was very attractive, but there were always lots of attractive women lined up around the walls of dance floors, serving at tables or in shops, waiting to be noticed. She was wealthier than most of the women he'd had, but then every woman at the Pondson-Callows' had been wearing jewels that held a value equivalent to many months, possibly years, of his pay; he could have had any one of them. Lady Anna Renwick had sent him seven invitations in the past six weeks, and she was single. Lady Lydia Chatfield should have been easier to forget. Yet when she smiled, one side of her lips turning up before the other, he found she was harder to fool. Harder to forget. It was dangerous. Potentially messy. He ought to cut it here. But hadn't he tried? He hadn't contacted her for six weeks; he'd fully expected to forget all about her in that time. He had not. He had thought of her thin fingers – her red nails and loose rings – grabbing on to the edge of the desk, on to his shirt. He had failed to forget the exact shade of the oyster silk suspender belt against her pale thighs or the dark triangle of hair between her legs. And every time he had thought of her, the muscles in his stomach flexed instinctively. It wasn't just the sex he remembered and craved. He thought of her running through the snow, inappropriately and hurriedly dressed. Keen, then awkward with sincerity, despite her habitual good manners and well-practised sophistication. She was not easy to forget.

They drained their teacups. He glanced at his timepiece, which was strapped to his wrist. Such a thing had been worn by those engaged in aerial combat; now everyone loved the idea. It was just after five. They could go home now.

Or not.

'What shall we do?' he asked. She shrugged. Her skinny shoulders rose up high, like a puppet's, and met the ends of her glossy blunt-cut hair. Her eyes were clear and desperate. Women often looked at him in that way. He knew he could propose anything and she'd agree. As other women had. Women he'd taken in dark alleyways or cheap guest houses that cost just shillings and their reputations. He'd had them in the back of borrowed cars or in their lodgings while their roommates feigned sleep. He'd fucked hard, hoping with each thrust to shove away the dead bodies, the twisted limbs and the black staring eyes that could no longer see. He put his fingers up women and attempted not to think of the three occasions when he'd tried, and failed, to shove the spilt bellies and innards back inside a dying man. He told himself that death and sex were separate. But they weren't. He'd been used. Tricked. The bastards had used sex to get them all to go and kill.

He shut his eyes and clenched his fists, but the images stayed tattooed on to the insides of his eyelids; the violence clung to his fingertips. He was so often alone and angry. More alone and more angry when he fucked. There was brutality in his thrusts, even though he tried to control it. The women saw it, if they looked for it. He didn't want it to be that way. Not with her.

'Let's walk.' He flung down enough coins on the table to pay for the tea and generously tip the waitress, then they stood up and left.

Outside, she shivered and pulled her coat tightly around her; the weak spring sunshine was no match for the long shadows thrown by the imposing multiple-storeyed buildings. They found their way back to the Cromwell Road and walked until it dissolved into Brompton Road. They kept going past Harrods, where no doubt she spent too much time and too much money. They pushed on past Knightsbridge tube station and Hyde Park Corner. He had a vague idea that they were heading to Green Park; they could walk along the Mall to St James's Park. He had no idea where they would go after that.

As they put one foot in front of the other, they both thought of their previous trudge together, through the luscious, pure surface of fresh snow. Away from other people they became freer. Free from the inequalities that wealth, and lack of it, laid down; free from the constraints of being someone else's wife; free from the guilt and grief of war. They were simply a couple, walking. They slowly shook off the awkward unfamiliarity and were doused in genial relief as they rediscovered their connection. At one point he put his hand on the small of her back as he guided her across a road; she then linked her arm through his. Their steps fell together; he thought it was as though they had been drilled, she thought it was as though they had been together for ever. They both liked it.

As they walked, he told her about himself. He was the eldest of four. His parents owned a corner shop in Middlesbrough, a town in the north of England that she had never heard of. He found it was possible, essential, to painstakingly tell her some flimsy, long-forgotten details from his boyhood. He wanted her to know him. To see him stripped of his recent acquisitions – medals, uniform, a disarming ability to say just the right thing in an aristocratic lady's parlour. She listened with assiduous attention. He liked it. He felt fascinating.

'Didn't you ever consider going back there after the war?'

'The north makes me too pensive. After I got back to England, I knew it would be impossible to live in a place where everyone was the same as my mam and dad – everyone that is except perhaps for me. I feel less dislocated in London, where hardly anyone is the same as anyone, and everyone is lonely. This is where I belong, with the other lonely people. For now.'

'For now?'

He told her about his dreams of travelling; he'd like to see Africa, America, even Australia. She gasped, looked panicked, and he joked, 'Wouldn't you like me to live a long way away? I'm nothing but a nuisance.'

'No,' she replied simply. 'Stay close.' She looked afraid, anxious. She wanted him, badly. She was too willing to please him. But then he wanted to please her too. Or at least impress her. Something. It was hard to name exactly what it was he wanted in relation to her. Something different. He was mesmerised by her red rosebud lips, glistening and apart. He watched them when she talked and when she listened. Everything around her seemed less distinct. The crowds and the streets blurred to one homogenous mess. She alone stood out, gleaming.

He told her about how it was for him before the fighting. He'd been so young then. Not just seven years younger; aeons younger. He'd often been carefree and careless, but not with any hint of anarchy; back then his freedom came from a lack of knowledge. He had not known what mankind was. What it could be. Could do. He'd served behind the counter in his father's shop. 'A comfortable living. Pleasant.' His father was popular, because he was generous with his tick and he gave the skinny, poverty-stricken, lice-ridden kids free sweets if they stayed out of trouble, out of the way. But

Edgar had grown too large for the space behind the counter, squeezed between his parents, with his younger siblings elbowing in too. He'd yearned for something bigger and more physical, so when he turned fourteen, he'd got a job in the shipyard.

'Hard work,' his mother had warned. Worried, she'd folded her arms under her big bosoms. He'd got his physical size from her side of the family. She saw the shipyard as a step down. She'd scrambled to reach her lower-middle-class position and she didn't like the idea of her son flinging himself back down the greasy pole into a working-class job.

'Man's work.' His father, a neat and honest man, who had always envied the bulk, if not the poverty, of the shipbuilders who visited his shop, had seemed proud.

Edgar had felt ropes roughen his palms and heavy loads broaden his shoulders. He'd tasted the salt in the air, and after some months, he'd begun to smell of it himself. The North Sea air, air that had travelled a long way to arrive up the River Tees, sat in his hair and skin. 'I used to wonder how far that air had come. At least from France, maybe further, from the Baltic. I was breathing air that Scandinavians or even Russians might have breathed. It seemed a marvellous thing.' He beamed at her and she smiled back, dazzled. What a world it had been then. Before. When the world was connected by sea breezes, not grief.

It was a time of simple pleasures. Easy laughter with the men he worked and drank with. Cold beer. Hot girls. A regular although decidedly modest salary, to put into his mother's hand at the end of the week. At the weekends a gang of them sometimes got on their bikes and pedalled over to one of the villages, Guisborough or Great Ayton, eating apples and cheese from brown paper bags on the North York Moors. It was a time when he still thought of the soil as a good thing: fertile and giving. He barely remembered that lad now. The smell of the sea made him think of the crossing to France. Soil was intrinsically linked with death, rotting corpses, blood, rats and shit. Except when he was with her. Then breezes smelt good again.

'You've been a soldier for seven years?'

'Yes. I'm not sure how to stop being one. I went early. There were Hun raids on Hartlepool, Scarborough and Whitby as early as December nineteen fourteen. The war came to us quite quickly.'

'You volunteered?'

'There and then. For God's sake, Lid, please don't be impressed.'

Edgar realised that he couldn't banish the bounce in his step as he walked by her side. Something that he usually reserved just for the few short hours of elation following a sexual conquest. He hadn't touched her that way for weeks, and yet he still bounced.

He found it astoundingly easy to tell her the most extraordinary and macabre things about himself. He was amazed that she was equally seduced by both. She accepted his breathtaking successes as a foregone conclusion; did not blanch at his compromises or his ambition. He told her more about his family. One of his sisters had just married, at Christmas time. 'She's picked a lazy oaf but she seems happy enough, at least for now. There's no accounting for taste.' He wondered if she could understand his world full of necessary economies, self-motivation, self-improvement. She seemed to. But how could she? Really? Had she ever spent an afternoon watching flies die a slow death on the sticky ribbon of paper that hung from the ceiling? Had she ridden a bike? She had never earned a penny in her life. Yet did it have a bearing?

She seemed to summon every fibre of her body and to direct it towards him; focused and alert, she drank him in. Up. She'd squealed, delighted, when he mentioned that he had three younger siblings. 'I'm one of four too.' She was plainly thrilled that they had this in common, as there was obviously precious little else. Ironically, her jubilation highlighted the amount of history and experience they did *not* share. 'We're four girls,' she gushed. Edgar imagined clouds of powder and perfume lingering in the air. Swirling skirts and blushing cheeks. Silks, satins, ribbons, jewels. His life had always been more of a cocktail of the slightly toxic smells of Lysol disinfectant, Boraxo soap and Brasso; his mother had scrubbed and cleaned her way out of poverty.

'You're not the oldest, though,' he stated, rather than asked.

'No, I'm the youngest.'

'Ah, so you are the baby, the one that's ridiculously spoilt and indulged?'

'Not really.' She looked startled at the idea. 'We were all brought up in a seen-but-not-heard environment. We didn't bond especially. We shared a nursery and then lessons, but we existed in separate, private stratospheres. If anything, we were rather competitive with one another.' He liked the way she'd pricked his ballooning fantasy about swirling skirts and sisterly secrets. He liked the reality of her.

'Are your sisters all married?'

'Yes. Lillian, the eldest, married a doctor. Papa wasn't especially impressed. Anna did better, she got herself a baron, but he lives in Scotland. So far away from anything.'

'Well, not far away from Eilean Donan, Edinburgh Castle or the Wallace Monument,' he pointed out, laughing.

'She misses society! And he's quite a bit older than she is.'

'How much older?'

'Fourteen years. Mildred married a lawyer, but he's a lot shorter than she is.'

'In that case, you're the victor?'

Lydia looked embarrassed; she didn't seem to know how to answer. No doubt she was wondering how he could talk of her marriage as a triumph. How he could talk of her marriage at all. 'They all have children. Bundles of them,' she muttered.

'Did all your brother-in-laws serve?'

'The doctor was excused – essential work; the baron was too old to be drafted, but Mildred's husband served.'

'Did he survive?' Edgar was used to asking this question brusquely and without excessive sentiment. Lydia looked startled.

'Yes, thank you,' she replied, as though someone had just offered her a chocolate. 'Injured out. He spent months in a sanatorium in Wales but he's fit and well now.'

'That's good to hear.'

She paused and flexed her leg behind her. He wondered whether she had cramp. She most likely had blisters at least; he'd forgotten that she was in heels.

'We should have a drink.'

31

ALL SIGNS OF the bright spring day had now disappeared. The air had cooled and showers tapped on pavements. The street lamps were lit. They gave off a halo of light, blurred by the drizzle. She liked it that he guided her through the streets. That he knew where they were going, that she did not. She gave herself up to him entirely, but for all that she was relieved that he took her to a dance hall rather than a pub. After the war they'd all become mad for dancing; pent up, wound up, they needed to spin and twirl in the opposite direction. Lydia was very used to frequenting smart nightclubs such as the Embassy Club in Bond Street, where Edwina and Dickie Mountbatten sometimes dropped by. Ava had taken her to some daring, less respectable hangouts. The Grafton Galleries boasted a band of black fellows playing jazz but closed at two in the morning, early as far as Ava was concerned. It had once been fun to spot celebrities, film stars and boxers; now Lydia knew she'd be bored by such places. Edgar led her along Tottenham Court Road and abruptly turned right and led her down some stairs. They passed through an enormous wooden door and stumbled into a vast underground cellar. As she tottered after him, she couldn't help but notice that the walls were wet, even on the inside; the place smelt of drains and sweat. That said, it looked and felt considerably more beautiful than Lydia had anticipated. Festive rather than sophisticated. Paper streamers decorated the mirrors and lights, and balloons littered the floors. There must have been three hundred people dancing cheek to cheek, or at least with some body part or other connecting. The dancers were disordered, undisciplined and suggestive.

'I like it here. Drinks are sold until four providing food is ordered at the same time. We could eat some eggs? Do you fancy eggs?'

She didn't want to eat, not really. In fact she doubted she would be able to, around him, but she nodded eagerly all the same. The important thing was to be near him; to feel the heat of his body through his jacket, through her own. She wished she'd been able to change into something more glamorous. She had so many beautiful evening dresses, and whilst she'd given an enormous amount of thought to her day dress (and had alighted on the most perfect frock for a visit to a museum), the pretty cotton and lace looked almost virginal and distinctly out of place in the smoky good-time club. She nervously fingered the ribbon around the dropped waistband. He noticed, grabbed her hand and – palm upwards, fingers still curled – dropped a kiss on her fingertips. She quivered.

'You look beautiful,' he told her. It wasn't said as a compliment, more of a fact. She'd heard it before, but she'd never believed it in the way she did now. 'Champagne?'

The hard-faced barmaid informed them that champagne cost 22s. and 6d; £2 after legal hours.

'As much as that?' gasped Lydia. She didn't usually have to care what drinks cost, but she knew they were being substantially over-charged. She felt uncomfortable letting him pay, but it would be unforgivable to offer to pick up the tab. Edgar glanced at her in a manner that assured her he would manage. She turned away from the bar and started to look for a seat. She picked a table tucked in the corner. Secluded. She should not try to impose anything on him, not even fiscal caution. She didn't want to. She was attracted to his unruliness, his masculinity, his confidence, his spontaneity, his impulses. He was a living, breathing party; all her Christmases and birthdays rolled into one. Why would she try and change a thing?

They drank the bottle, then ordered another. The air in the bar felt muggy and used, as the place became raucous and crammed.

Groggy, gin-fuelled men lurched, slurring their words and thoughts. They leered at the women, who were smoking, dancing, and shrilly swapping stories about their day or their lives. As the temperature rose, the women's noses and foreheads began to glisten; barely breaking their conversations, they reached for their compacts and dabbed on flattering powder. Lydia found she enjoyed the rough nature of the pleasure everyone was wallowing in.

So far Lydia and Edgar's relationship had been staccato: abrupt, disconnected sounds, then terse silences. Now, the applause came. Thunderous and continuous. Finally, they found one another. Relaxed, they found one another. They talked and talked; thoughts, memories and jokes tumbled out and splashed in amongst the puddles of champagne and the cigarette butts. They shouted over the crowds when the bar was rammed and they hoarsely whispered to one another when the crowds finally thinned and the night nudged into the next day. He was interested in her. He asked question after question. Rat-tat-tat, like a machine gun. He wanted to know about her childhood, her weekend, her friends, her maids. He had full lips that naturally seemed to want to grin and kiss. She made him laugh. Out loud. Big, hale and hearty. He flattered her. His laugh made her heart split. And although it wasn't the first time she'd heard 'You fascinate me. You're exquisite. You're incredible,' it had never sounded better.

Lydia was keyed up, animated. She oozed desire and desirability. She caught a glimpse of herself in one of the mottled Victorian mirrors that hung above the wooden panelling where they sat. It struck her that she'd never looked so glamorous and sparkly. Her eye make-up had smudged, but she didn't care, because she remembered he liked it that way. Her eyes seemed deeper, her brows sharper, just the correct and fashionable weight and arch. Her arms seemed toned, her neck longer. And him? He was delicious. Everything about him was mesmerising. The power of his thighs crammed under the round table, the whisper of whiskers emerging in a blue-black shadow over his strong chin, the shape of his lips: plump, pink and eager. He was breathtaking. Heart-stealing. Life-changing.

'Shall we dance, darling?' she suggested breathily.

He smiled, amused; her endearment was almost too obvious and yet perfect. 'Would you like that?'

'I've thought about it from the moment I saw you.' She grinned playfully. They stood up together: the northern hero, the southern debutante. Nothing in common. In every way alike. She had so much attitude. Suddenly she was bright and enthusiastic in a way that she'd never before been. In a way she had always been. She knew it; she'd just never known who else she might let in on the secret. The truth was, she was wild and thoughtful, sexy and unsure; a mass of contradictions. She was all of it and nothing at all. But it was hers to play for, to sway for. Liquor and a flame burning inside her gut. She didn't place her hands in his, or on his shoulders or his waist. She put her hands on his head and ran her fingers through his hair. She nodded her head and swayed her hips. Her breasts were hard and upright, her stomach flat and lean and her bum pert and high; it was all on display, visible – in reach – but not in contact. She was teasing. Promising.

The notes drummed through their bodies. Relentless. Throbbing. Carefully they danced around one another. He kept his hands wide but the air slipped between them, heavy with possibility.

The atmosphere clotted with smoke and yearning. They returned to their seats but began to fidget and wriggle on their chairs. She repeatedly crossed and uncrossed her legs; he tapped his fingers on the table, on his glass, on the back of her seat. His fingers, her crossing legs, they were linked somehow.

'Shall we have another bottle?' It would be their third.

'I think I shall be sick.'

'Then what?'

'Let's go to a hotel.' She whispered her suggestion. Electrified with excitement and certainty.

'That your husband will pay for?' Edgar shook his head. Despite talking about her friends, relatives, acquaintances and associates all evening, Lawrence, as a topic of conversation, had been noticeably absent.

Lydia was irritated by this nicety. This unnecessary show of male peacocking, misplaced pride. It made no sense that he'd comfortably take Lord Chatfield's wife without any show of a twinging conscience, but would not take his money. A small amount of money that Lawrence probably wouldn't notice anyhow. Did Edgar value money so? More than he valued her? Perhaps that was why he couldn't believe she imbued it with next to no importance. Her head began to swim; she felt flushed. She didn't know what else to offer. She just wanted him. 'It's only money. It doesn't mean anything,' she pleaded.

'Those with money never respect it in the way those without it do. As they should,' he replied quietly. It seemed a very sober thing for such a drunk man to say.

She felt chastised. Childish. The air had become taut and tetchy. All she wanted was a suitable place to beat out their longing. Somewhere close by. If he offered, she'd be taken here on the small polished table, in amongst the discarded, congealed scrambled eggs and empty champagne bottles. Convenience had begun to overwhelm any thoughts of caution or care. This was to be expected from him but was distinctly perilous for her. 'Don't you want me?' she asked with the sulky patheticness that all drunks can muster.

'Very much.'

'Well then.'

'We could go to my place. It isn't what you are used to, but—'

'Yes. Yes. Now.'

They caught the tube and got off at Aldgate. They walked down thin, wet passageways. They carefully stepped around men begging on the streets and others tumbling out of pubs, locked in brawls or embraces. The East End was the ripe underbelly of London that Lydia was not aware of. Trembling, tipsy on her heels, she leaned into him, clung tightly to his arm. They'd drunk far too much; she didn't want to fall over and embarrass them both. She was relieved when he stopped, even if it was at the door of a terraced house with chipped blue paintwork. He pulled out a key, then put his finger to his lips. 'Shush, I don't want to wake my landlady. I'm not supposed to have women upstairs in my rooms.'

Lydia followed his instructions because she didn't want anything to spoil her moment of fulfilment, which was evidently at hand, but she could not imagine a grown man taking orders from a woman in curlers and an apron, which was how she imagined his landlady, all landladies. Specifically, she could not imagine *this* man doing so. She was so used to being the one who gave instructions that she assumed everyone had the same luxury.

They sneaked in and up. She giggled when the wooden stairs groaned, a telltale on their intended debauchery. He smiled indulgently but put his finger to her lips. Instinctively she slipped out her pointed red tongue, licked him. Two spots of cerise colour appeared on his cheekbones. A feminine, surprising hue. The mark of excitement, not embarrassment. He picked up his pace as he leapt up the steps.

Like Lydia's servants, he lived in the eaves of the house. His room spread across the entire floor. Its air was too tidy to be described as bohemian, but the contents were too shabby to be described as respectable. It was more than Lydia had hoped for but still far less than anything she'd ever been entertained in before. The kitchen area flowed into the living area, that poured into a space where the bed dominated. She could not see another door that suggested there was a bathroom; she supposed he shared with other lodgers on the floor below. There was at least electric light, a tap over the sink, and a coal fire which Edgar attended to immediately. Then he turned out the metal overhead light that blasted the room with a blue-white shock, and lit four candles. The candles didn't give much illumination or heat; just a gentle orange glow, but she preferred it. There were clean pots draining next to the deep stone sink: a plain green plate, saucer and cup, one knife, one fork. Two splintered wooden chairs stood next to the small table, but one was piled high with a stack of dusty, yellowing newspapers; she thought she was probably his first and only visitor. Neither the Duchess of Feversham nor Lady Renwick nor any similar woman could have been invited; she was sure of it.

He picked up the papers and held them whilst he glanced around the room, looking for somewhere to put them down again; his expression suggested that he was noticing the unappealing poverty for the first time. He dropped the papers on a dusty, overstuffed sofa, disturbing a skinny tabby cat that was lying in the crook of the arm. Facing towards the fire was a battered leather chair with a tartan rug hung over the back; there was also a wardrobe, a set of drawers and not much else by way of furniture. Nothing by way of ornament. She felt comforted by his books, lined up along the walls and in towers in the middle of the floor, but there was a lingering smell of decomposing vegetables and not quite clean clothes, even though the skylight was open. She didn't sit down.

He petted the cat. 'Do you like cats?'

'We have dogs. Three of them.' And then, to ingratiate, 'There is a kitchen cat. A mouser.'

'What's her name?'

'I'm not sure.'

'I like cats. They don't expect too much. People talk of a dog's loyalty, but I find them needy.'

She wondered if he found her needy, if he would ever need her. He offered her milk or beer to drink. She said she'd have beer, although she thought she should probably stop drinking. He handed her the bottle.

'No glasses, I'm afraid. I've never thought to buy that sort of thing. You know.' He shrugged and glanced around the utilitarian space, then waved his hand, almost an apology. 'Crockery sets, rugs, vases and such. We managed with so little in the trenches, I got used to it. Besides, I don't spend much time here.' Although she didn't say anything, he added, 'I'll buy some for next time.'

They stared at one another hopefully, unable, unwilling to say anything more, sensing that something delicate but vital was being established, something that words might ruin. Lydia wasn't sure who moved first, but they were upon one another in an instant. Greedy for each other. They kissed hard. Tasting one another's lips, stained with champagne and cigarettes. Their tongues, cautious at first, became brave; animated, fleshy, wet, intertwined. A promise. A memory. A foreshadowing. They stumbled, backing up against the kitchen table, causing the teapot and condiments to rattle. He pulled and plucked at her clothes and she at his, but waistband, braces, pearl buttons and tight tailoring all seemed to work together to confound and frustrate. Neither was prepared to stop kissing, so they continued to blindly and ineffectively tug. She bit his lip, not quite gently. He grabbed her head and kissed her harder so she couldn't tease. Then he kissed her neck, her ears, her throat. She groaned. He pushed his face to her breasts. She wanted his tongue and lips and hands to find her smooth breasts, her hard nipples.

She yanked at her dress and it fell to the floor. Many women, even the modern ones, still wore girdles and even bandeau bras; not to create nipped waists and heaving bosoms, but the opposite. They wanted to be desexed, masculine if possible. Lydia, naturally flat-chested and slim, didn't need to worry; her underwear was delicate, a mass of laces, silks and chiffons. She looked like a gift, wrapped in floral patterns and ribbons. He stood back, took a moment, drank her up.

Next, slowly, he finished what she had inexpertly started: he unbuttoned his shirt and let it fall to the floor. He was magnificent. Strong and defined. Toned. There was not an ounce of unnecessary about him; he bulged with power and vigour. Keeping his eyes fixed on her, he took off his socks and shoes; he let his trousers and underwear drop too. He stood naked and glorious, his hard penis showing what he wanted. She started to wrench at the ribbons on her camisole, but he stopped her. He picked her up. Not the way a groom picks up a bride and carries her over a threshold, but by putting his hands under her arms and carrying her as one might carry a muddy child from the garden to the bathroom. Teasingly he kept her from his naked body. She went limp in his arms. Weightless. He laid her on the bed, gently removed her heels and finally, finally climbed on top of her. The heaviness of him stopped her breath.

It was unbearable.

It was everything she'd ever wanted.

She sighed, the sound of release, and acceptance and longing. She felt him along the length of her; at last her body and mind opened.

They forgot everything other than each other. They drifted beyond their pasts and did not need futures. They had all they required there on the thin mattress, on the iron bed, in the spartan bedsit. Neither lover was aware of anything beyond an annihilating consciousness and impression of the other, rousing and amplifying. There was no music to hide in. The only sound was the sound of bare skin slithering over fabric, as their arms, legs, bodies skated across one another in an impatient, intense grappling; that and the sound of the wetness of their lips and tongues as they landed, kissing and licking. Imperceptibly he inched her out of her clinging, silky underwear. She lay proud and pink. Exposed and exhibiting. His eyes fell from her face to her breasts, to her waist, to her bush of pubic hair. He reached out and placed a finger in there. Cold and smooth on her hot excitement. She thought of the marble statues in the museum and the snow they'd trudged through. He moved his finger leisurely, bit by bit, until pleasure swelled into a fat throbbing, so powerful it was almost painful. She shuddered and flinched; snatching at his body, she pulled him back on top of her, digging her fingers into the flesh on his back, his buttocks. At last she took hold of him. She had never had occasion to name the part before, even in her head, but now she took his beautiful penis, first in her hands and then in her mouth. She'd never imagined this was something she might do, and was surprised that, with her lack of experience, she instinctively knew how to please him, and that she was clear about her own desires.

Selfless, they both worshipped. Raining kisses and caresses on each other until their lips and throats became dry, they explored and pleasured one another. She luxuriated in him. Forensically she investigated the different tones of his skin; from the smooth and tanned to the bristled red. She came to know how his freckles and moles were scattered, where his veins flowed like tributaries of a river and which hairs were smooth and glossy, which were coiled and unruly. She studied him as though he was the only and first man. She nuzzled his groin and armpits, inhaling the bitter strains of his sweat as though he was perfumed. She smelt his breath, his hair. He roamed over her with similar frank pleasure.

He kissed her neck, breasts, shoulders, thighs, feet. Her body arched towards him, ached for him.

The moment finally came when he was inside her. It was different from the time in the study. This time there was no distance; he held her tightly, he repeatedly kissed her face. Her lips, her cheek-bones, her eyelids, her nose. Deeper. Closer. Backwards and forwards. In and out. Not too far out. Rolling, growing, plunging. It was impossible to know where she stopped feeling, where he began. Awed, she understood the concept of being as one. She understood life, death and loss whilst he came inside of her. Whilst she came out of herself.

32

Afterwards they lay side by side, breathing deeply. Exhausted. Sweat glistened on his forehead; his face was blotchy and bright with the attractive sort of colour that is raised through exertion. She wanted to lick the sweat, taste his saltiness again, but her body was spent; she couldn't even summon the energy to roll on her side. She did not modestly pull the cover over herself but lay, magnificent, available. Complete.

He fetched a mug of water for them to share, then got back into bed and lay beside her. He lit a cigarette, which they smoked in silence. Somewhat revived, she rolled on to her side and stubbed it out in the ashtray that was on the floor, then she pulled his arm around her for warmth and a sense of protection.

'Where does he think you are tonight?' There was no need to elaborate on who Edgar was referring to.

'He's in the country, at his parents' place.'

'That's very convenient for you.'

'And you,' she reminded him. She closed her eyes. Sleep and rest were needed. Her body was being dragged into that comfortable moment just before a loss of consciousness when the world seems fluid, pliable and unthreatening in any way; he roused her.

'Come on, you have to get dressed.' He kissed her ear and then climbed out of bed.

'What?' She was bleary, drugged with loving and couldn't understand his meaning.

'You can't stay,' he said abruptly. He pulled on his underwear and stooped again to pick up his trousers. On the kitchen table the candles were still burning; just inch stubs remained. That and the fact that the sky, visible through the skylight, was still a deep blue-black suggested it was probably about four in the morning. She groped for the bedside clock and confirmed her guess.

'I'm sorry?'

'You'll have to go.'

'No, there's no need. I told you, Lawrence is away. The servants will assume I stayed with Ava. Come back to bed.'

He ignored her request, sat on the edge of the bed. His broad bare back was blue like a silhouette in the moonlight. He started to put on his socks. 'I never let anyone stay,' he muttered. There had been so many? There were so many still? The thought slashed her. 'You must get a cab.'

'Don't be ridiculous, I can't get a cab at this time, how would I explain it? Why must I leave?' She felt tears scratch her throat; she wondered if he could hear them in her voice. Fear and insecurity flooded through her body; she was going to drown in a sudden feeling of lacking. Was she a disposable conquest? Someone he'd had and finished with? Someone he could dismiss like a hire-by-the-hour whore? Was he an unscrupulous cad, an animal, after all? 'Why must I leave?' she demanded again. 'How could you say such a thing to me?'

Edgar's shoulders were rounded. He did not look like a man who wanted to hurt. For the first time the shadow of defeat seemed to fall over him.

'I'll shout out, Lid. I'll cry.' She didn't understand. 'That's why I took these rooms, high up away from other paying guests.' He turned to her. 'I get visions. Memories. When I sleep. I don't know how to stop them.' She realised for the first time what an enormous effort must be involved in being Edgar Trent, the hero. She now knew that every move he made hovered between arrogant swagger and a desperate vulnerability. He must try so hard, all the time, to maintain the stance, because it was striven for, not given up naturally. He was wounded and suffering even though there were no bullet holes.

'I don't mind.'

'I do.'

'But you mustn't. Not with me. It's fine, with me.' Gently she placed her hand on his back. He was icy but she carried her warmth out from under the covers. 'Sleep with me,' she urged.

He sighed and slowly crawled back into the bed. Suddenly he looked like a boy, not a man. Wary, reluctant, trapped. She knew he'd be vowing to himself not to fall asleep. He wouldn't let her in yet, but he had not made her leave. She turned on her side and he cuddled in tight. Cupping her breast.

Lydia woke in the night. Her bladder was full and she knew that sleep was impossible until it was dealt with. The chamber pot smelt ripe. There was no one to remove it and she was beginning to doubt whether there was any indoor plumbing. More likely there was a water closet outside in the yard. After what they had done together there ought not to be any shame between them, but she knew she could not urinate in front of him. She turned to him.

'What are you looking for?' he asked. 'The piss pot?' As she'd suspected, he had stayed awake. He'd propped himself up on a pillow and was now sitting bolt upright, like a guard keeping watch. She nodded tightly. Her body small and rigid again, quite unlike it had been when they made love.

'Is there a lavatory?' she asked hopelessly.

'It's outside,' he confirmed. Rain battered against the window.

'I might be seen, and it's bitterly cold.' She wasn't sure which bothered her more. 'I'll be fine. I'll wait.'

'Until the morning?'

'If I have to.'

He climbed out of bed. The room was so cold now that she could see his breath on the air: a blue cloud in a dark room lit by a grey moon. He shimmered, and despite her embarrassment, her only thought was how beautiful he was. He reached under the bed for the chamber pot. She listened carefully, getting used to the sounds of the house, and followed his footsteps down the creaky wooden stairs. The latch on the back door eased up and clattered down. The door swung wide. Urine splashed down a drain. Footsteps inside the house again. Water running in the stone sink. Lydia thought how thin the walls and floors were. The sheets, the curtains, covers. How thin poor people's lives were, in comparison to her own. He washed the pot and brought it back to the room, setting it down on the rug in front of the chimneypiece. He poked the fire. Placed another log on it. Jabbed it again. Competent.

'I'm going outside for a smoke,' he told her.

As she squatted by the flames, relieving herself – feet grey with the cold, bottom scorched from the heat of the fire – she giggled and thought of the gifts Lawrence had presented to her. The fine shawls he'd draped around her shoulders, the valuable necklaces he'd placed around her neck and, once, an exquisite tiara, presented in a navy blue velvet case, that he'd set on her head. She thought of the clean piss pot and knew she'd never felt so loved.

SUMMER

33

THE HEAT YAWNED through the house, blasting the usually impervious marble floors and walls, the gravel driveways and the green lawns, breaking down even their cool indifference. It hung in the air. No one could find a comfortable way to sit or stand. The thing to do was lie down whenever an opportunity allowed itself, although it wasn't possible now. The black garments seemed to grab at the heat, fastening it close to the exhausted bodies; it clung to thighs, brows and backs of necks. The Earl of Clarendale was dead. He'd rather unconventionally chosen a summer month to die, not a season for grieving.

His wife would miss him. Theirs had been a union that was the very epitome of the standards of their day. They had respected one another, quietly but firmly supported one another and, when necessary, they had drawn a veil. But the countess was a woman who had lost two sons and therefore could not feel violent objection towards this loss. Lawrence, her only surviving child, and secretly – to her shame and relief – the one who had always been her favourite, had assured her that as dowager she would always have a home at Clarendale Hall, and her daughter-in-law, Lydia, was the compliant sort. Many dowagers were turned out of their homes on their husband's death. They had to make do with a smaller house on the estate and a staff of three. At least that wasn't to be her fate. She would have to hand over the jewels and tiaras; they weren't hers, they belonged to the Countess of Clarendale. Yes, she'd have to give up her name too, but women were used to that; the moment the earl had closed his eyes she had started to refer to herself as the dowager, it didn't do to linger. She could continue to play croquet on the lawn, to have bridge evenings, and no doubt Lydia would allow her to instruct the servants. She imagined she would be content enough, going forward, and contentment was all she desired. The dowager rather despised the younger generation's obsession with chasing happiness and meaning. One read so much about it in the papers nowadays. She thought it was vulgar and unnecessary. Quite unchristian and demanding. Futile.

True enough, the young people had been through so much; yet hadn't everyone? She couldn't understand why what they had witnessed and endured had led them to believe they had a right to happiness; for her it was quite the reverse. She believed one ought to nurture a hope for contentment, but that no one had any *rights* at all.

The dowager was satisfied with how the private funeral had passed off. The service had been swift and serious; the time at the graveside had been kept to a dignified minimum. There was just the wake to endure — tea and an afternoon sherry for the men — then her close friends and neighbours would leave her to get on. The sandwiches were beginning to curl, a sure sign that it was time for everyone to go home and resume their normal business. The private funeral was always the hardest part. As she'd dreaded, the servants had become upset; they had a tendency to do so. Some undoubtedly would miss the old earl. He had been a fair master, a good man; their grief was genuine. Others cried because a funeral brought back difficult memories of their own losses. Poor souls. It underlined the fact that they'd never had the benefit of a service or a coffin for their men. She understood. Her middle boy had never come home. At least with her eldest they'd been able to give him the proper send-off; he and his father now lay next to one another, next to grandfathers and great-grandfathers. It was as it should be. No body to bury was hard. There was so much loss for everyone to deal with. It was tiring. The dowager was exhausted. Everyone was. The old women were ashamed that they'd been a generation of mothers who couldn't look after their sons, couldn't save them, and now, as some sort of punishment, they had to watch the bloom in the young women's cheeks fade and wither.

She had read recently that three million people in the United Kingdom were grieving for a close relative: a son, husband, father, brother. Besides her son, this household had lost two gardeners, three maids had lost beaus, the cook had lost her son and the chauffeur came home with only one arm. They kept him on, naturally; it was the patriotic thing to do, though he couldn't actually drive them anywhere. He made himself useful fixing things around the estate and house. He managed very well. The dowager admired him. He fought his exhaustion, he was tireless; she saw him out on the estate at all hours, at the crack of dawn and as the sun set. She got the sense that he liked to be alone.

There would be a formal memorial service in London for the earl; it was absolutely necessary so that the great and the good could pay their respects. She wanted the memorial to be notable, dignified and written up in all the broadsheets. She gazed out of the window at the flower gardens; there were carnations, roses, sweet peas. The roses were overblown and drooping. All the flowers looked drowsy and fed up. During the war they'd grown potatoes, onions and carrots in those beds and on every other spare inch of land. Practical foods that kept them going. In fact there had been more than enough; she'd had the excess produce sent into the village, sold to those who could afford it, given to those who couldn't. The lawns had been turned over to producing hay for the horses. It was lovely to see flowers in the beds again and to know that peaches and grapes were growing in the greenhouses. The dowager's peaches were a weapon in her hospitality arsenal; she always did terrifically well at the county fair. She would have to be careful to manage it so that things continued as they were in the gardens. She doubted that Lydia had any ideas of her own. Lydia could be managed, tactfully. Embraced, guided, supervised. Technically she would be the mistress of the house, but the dowager thought it was only a technicality.

The vicar's wife had been quite stupendously tactless this

morning. By way of making conversation she'd commented, 'So, what changes shall we see, I wonder? Do you think there will be a great many more parties? The young like to party, don't they?'

'I don't anticipate anything too wild. Lydia is such a sensible girl,' the dowager had replied in a tone she felt ought to have signalled the end of that line of conversation.

'Children's voices, it's all the house needs,' whispered the vicar's wife. The dowager thought this a ludicrous and irritating comment; if there were to be babies, wouldn't they be here already? Her daughter-in-law was barren. A terrible pity, but there you had it. Her husband's nephew would inherit, ultimately. She cast a glance at him, hovering over the decanter, looking every inch the smug man a step closer to his goal. He'd always been a pasty, ghastly, sneaky child, and by the look of him he'd never grown out of it. And there was Lydia; she looked wan, peaky.

Lydia noticed her mother-in-law smiling at her and she smiled back. It was a hesitant smile, because she wasn't sure of the appropriateness of smiling too broadly at her father-in-law's funeral. People were watching her, she knew it. She was a countess now, she supposed. Somehow that made her more interesting to others. It was a nuisance; the last thing she needed, or wanted, was more scrutiny. She didn't feel as though she was in the same room as the mourners; it was as though she was watching them, like one might view a picture hung in a gallery. She found it hard to engage, hard to concentrate at all. The intense heat was making her sloppy; Edgar was making her crazy. Often, nowadays, she found that she wasn't in full control of herself, wasn't quite conscious of herself. She spent her days remembering their last contact, anticipating their next. The sweltering sun, battering against the drawn curtains, seeped into every pore. The strange gloom of mourning lay like smog, and the scent of the fat white lilies was so sweet it was almost burdensome, but none of these things was to blame for her comatose state.

It was only possible to stay in the moment when she was with him. Then she was alert, vibrant and lucid. She saw, heard, felt and thought things deeper and sharper than she ever had before. Just *being* had an almost painful clarity, like attempting to look straight at the sun: impossibly bright. It was as though she had lived her life looking through a telescope and he had suddenly come along and adjusted the focus. Ahh! Now she could see the horizon, now she could see it all! The meaning of life; the chance of happiness. But when she was not with him, everything became blurred and confused again. The normality that she had previously found adequate, even entertaining and fun, for all the years before she met him, now seemed dreary and pointless. When she was not near him she felt as though she was struggling under the weight of a relentless hangover. Groggy and dizzy, she stumbled through her days and conversations.

They had not managed to see one another for eleven days. It was becoming harder and harder to function. She thought only of him. The weight of him on top of her. His smile breaking through. The scar on his rib where a bullet had grazed. His big, misshapen feet. There was no chance of sending and receiving telegrams because privacy, let alone secrecy, couldn't be guaranteed when she was at Clarendale. She had telephoned him, twice; both times she had spoken to his intractable landlady, rather than Edgar himself. It was torture. Depressingly, the landlady had been surly and insolent; Lydia had not dared leave her name.

'Who should I say telephoned, madam?' Lydia had heard the disapproval and prudery in her voice. Why hadn't she called her miss? How could she have known Lydia was married?

'Oh, don't bother. It's not important.' She'd quickly slammed down the handset.

Then her fog had darkened. She became paranoid, weepy and despairing. Would he know it was her that had telephoned? He must. This – all that she felt and thought – couldn't be one-way. Could it? Madam, rather than miss. What did that mean? Did Edgar have a pattern? Had there been other married women? Were there other married women now? The thought made her breathless, careless. Lydia knew of such things, of course. A single girl had her reputation to lose and a man looking for sex wouldn't bother there. Too complicated. Single girls were only noticed if a man wanted to marry. Married women *couldn't* marry. Married women were the ones to pursue for uncomplicated sex. This argument found its way into Lydia's head and ran round and round, many, many times a day, like a bird trapped inside a room, flinging itself against walls and windows in confusion. She hated what she knew of the world, and what she thought of the world, when she was not with him. She was ashamed of her doubts and fears. They seemed like a betrayal. When she was with him she was so sure. So positive. It was everything. They were invincible. They could not get enough of each other. He consumed her. She fed him.

They had been lovers for three months now. They met up two or three times a week. He accepted more and more invitations to the parties that she attended, because although they could not spend the entire evening together as they would like, without arousing suspicion, they could at least see one another. Feast their eyes. They did find ways to be alone. They met in the daytime. He'd spend the morning at the office in the army HQ and she'd spend the morning dressing, waiting; they'd meet just after lunch. She'd have the chauffeur drop her off at a gallery or museum. They sometimes made a show of looking at the exhibit, even taking tea; other times they would simply run to the underground and take a train to his flat. His landlady charred in the afternoon for families who lived in Islington; he could sneak Lydia in and out any time between two and five. They had these slivers of heaven, alone in his bed with its skinny mattress and a patchwork blanket that his sister had made for him.

She was changed. She talked quickly, as though she had more words to get out, which indeed she did. More ideas, more thoughts, more point. She roared with laughter when she was with him, something she'd never done previously; she'd always confined herself to polite laughter, giggles and guffaws. She explained loudly. Ate hungrily. Made love enthusiastically. She didn't apologise if she missed her step and tripped on the stairs. She simply got up and rushed on. There was no time to waste with apologies, regrets or remorse.

But eleven days was such a long time. Eleven days was for ever. She'd had no choice but to come to the country. The earl had

asked for her. She'd sat with him for three days; he'd been unconscious for much of it. She hoped he knew she was there, but she
couldn't be sure. She'd tried to think of a reason to go to town
between the death and the funeral, but there wasn't a viable one.
She was stuck here in the depths of the West Sussex countryside.
For how much longer? she wondered. It took an immense amount
of will and attentiveness to hold on to her certainty and for that
reason she appeared dazed and confused to others. They muttered
among themselves how very badly she was taking the earl's death.

The dowager leaned towards Lydia and commented, 'Darling, I
think it's very wonderful of your friends to join us today. Lawrence
said Mrs Gordon in particular has been an enormous help to him
over these past few months.'

'Sarah is so very practical and together.'

'And generous with her time.'

'Yes.'

'Her sister, too.'

'Bea likes to be useful.'

'Quite right.' The dowager paused; she eyed the long net curtains
that fell into folds like a gown on the floor. Her gaze drifted
around the room half-heartedly; Lydia's followed. The panelled
walls looked gloomy; the grandfather clock had been stopped. 'So
does your other friend, come to that. The modern one.'

'Ava.'

'Yes, that's it, Ava Pondson-Callow. A double barrel with barely
a title, how interesting.'

'Her father is a knight.'

'Inherited title?'

'No.'

'Hmmm. She is a busy young woman, I hear.'

'Ava is on a number of committees,' Lydia confirmed carefully.
She wasn't sure if the dowager was simply making conversation
or whether she had a point she wanted to raise. Lydia felt uncomfortable talking about Ava; she'd used her as an alibi on countless
occasions recently and lived in constant nervousness that she would
be rumbled.

'I saw her dash off just after the service.'

'Yes.' Lydia had been relieved that Ava couldn't stay and chat with Lawrence.

'Where is she going today?'

'She had to go back to London. She has a trustee meeting for the National Council for the Unmarried Mother and Her Child, first thing tomorrow.'

'Oh. How very progressive.' The dowager tried not to look as though she had just eaten something that was slightly past its best.

'Yes.'

'Still, it's good of her to make the time.'

Lydia smiled, understanding that her mother-in-law was being as conciliatory as possible. It was unlikely that the dowager actually wanted unmarried mothers to be mentioned in the drawing room. Lawrence coughed; no doubt he thought that the conversation should be moved on, but Lydia knew he wouldn't risk saying anything specific. She would not tolerate any criticism of Ava, outright or implied, and he was aware of as much.

In the past, Lydia might have agreed with her husband and mother-in-law, acquiesced that illegitimacy shouldn't be discussed in mixed public, but her relationship with Edgar had changed things. Running to and from his lodgings she had seen women, deserted and desperate, wearing rags, starving so that an unrecognised child could eat. She'd seen a lot of shocking poverty in the East End. It was hot now, but there had been snow in March, and as she'd walked holding Edgar's hand, even love couldn't block out the desolation of the dire and abounding poverty. She'd seen people sleeping outside, likely to freeze to death overnight. In the mornings, when dawn forced her from his flat, she'd passed a line of men snaked outside the gates to a factory; obviously they hoped to get a day's casual work. Their backs, once broad enough to fight a war, seemed vulnerable, their necks looked too thin to hold their heads as they'd hunched over their hands, pathetically trying to blow warmth into them.

The light in the over-hot drawing room bounced from the strings of pearls hanging around the women's necks and danced on the silver tea urn next to the plates weighted with untouched cakes. Lydia seemed to be living in two different worlds. Irritation fuelled her mischievous side, and although it was her father-in-law's wake, she couldn't stop herself from prolonging the conversation that was making her husband uncomfortable. 'Ava's work is so vitally important.'

'Well, quite.' Lawrence's ears turned pink.

'These women and children shouldn't suffer so. You've seen them, Lawrence. You must have. Lining the streets and huddling under bridges and viaducts. Grubby hands stretched out. I don't doubt that some of the men at your club are responsible for one or two of them.'

'Not the gentlemen, not the *right* sort of gentlemen, but there are bounders who have no sense of responsibility,' he admitted.

'These women could starve.'

'The children are innocent, we can all agree on that,' commented the dowager in a placatory tone; she was far more used to managing tricky conversations than either her son or daughter-in-law might imagine.

'Evidently they need help, but is it ladylike?' This contribution came from one of Lawrence's old school friends.

Lydia knew that Lawrence would have liked to have asked as much, but he limited himself to musing, 'I just question whether this sort of work has to be done by single women. Is that necessary?'

'Women your wife is intimate with, you mean?' asked Lydia.

Lawrence did not answer her question; he simply added, 'However, considering the demands on her time we must be grateful that she came to support you at the service and to pay her respects to my father.'

'Quite,' they all chorused. They were much more used to politely mollifying, rather than saying anything they really thought or meant.

After a moment or two of silence, only interrupted by the sound of uselessly fluttering fans, beating the air like bird wings, Lydia said, 'Actually, I think I need to go back to London for a day or so.'

'But the house is shut up.' Lawrence had closed it, expecting to spend a longer than usual summer in the countryside. There was a lot to be done. Having said goodbye to his father, he now had his mother to comfort and an estate to run. Lydia had been too horrified by the suggestion of leaving London for three months to form a coherent argument against doing so.

'I could stay with Ava.'

'Why do you need to visit London?'

'I need to go and buy some more clothes.'

'Didn't you shop just last month?'

'For London clothes. Now we are going to be spending so long in the country, I need some suitable things for here.'

'But don't you do the same things in London as you do in the country: lunch, chatter, dinner, dance? Is there any real need for more gadding about? More extravagance?' He sighed wearily.

Lydia doubted this was a financial issue. They had plenty of money. Too much, probably. She bit her lip. She had to remember he was a grieving man, a man about to inherit a great deal of responsibility; he was bound to be tetchy. He wanted her at his side. It wasn't his fault that he irritated her, thwarted her; it was her own. But what was she supposed to do? A woman like her? What was there for her to do? Besides, since when had Lawrence baulked at the traditional set-up in their lives? Lydia had never heard him hint that he might find her life of indulgence and privilege a little lacking in true purpose, although it was a thought she'd had herself, with increasing frequency, since she'd met Edgar.

Edgar.

His name licked her soul and bit her conscience. She wasn't planning on shopping at all. It was impossible to resent Lawrence's implication that she was idle or giddy when he'd been given that very idea because she needed an excuse to visit London to have a secret meeting with her lover. Lydia hated herself and yet at the same time loved the woman who had attracted Edgar. That woman couldn't be wrong; it was impossible. She chose to smile broadly, although her smile was as tight and tense and insincere as a circus clown's.

'You are right, but even so, the two styles are not interchange-able. You must know that by now, Lawrence.'

The dowager stepped in. 'I won't accept that you are such a fashion heathen, Lawrence, despite what you'd like to pretend. How can you imagine satins and silks are the same as brogues and tweeds? You're being ridiculous, my dear.'

Lawrence wasn't soothed by his mother's intervention, as she'd hoped. Instead, feeling bullied, he became increasingly fractious and glowered. Lydia decided to put an end to the debate.

'I need more black clothes. It's as simple as that.' She was being deceitful, but she now realised that wasn't a new thing in their marriage. Before Edgar, she'd deceived Lawrence – *and* herself – on a perpetual basis. She'd pretended they were happy. Now, her deceit sickened her because she recognised it as a charade; before, she'd thought it was simply all there was.

Lawrence infuriated her, disappointed her, disgusted her, and yet her infuriation and disappointment with herself was equal.

She was not disgusted with herself, however. She could not bring herself to regret a moment with Edgar. He'd taught her so much. How to live and how to feel. She transformed under his touch, and as if to underline this fact, he'd taught her words for her body that she'd never thought she could use. Her breasts changed from day to day. When he was tender they were breasts; when he took her with more passion, she thought of them as tits. Her tits. A crude and hard word. A true and real word. The hair between her legs, which she had never been able to name, had never had need to name, he called her bush. He stroked her there; his fingers were swallowed up. He told her he loved her vagina. She didn't know if she would die of embarrassment or hysteria. At times yearning for Edgar made her weak. She longed to touch him, even though she knew it was like putting her finger in a flame. She would not feel the pain instantly, but the moment she withdrew she'd be blistered and in agony. Her sex and her heart beat for him as though there had been no other man. No husband. She trembled. The familiar faces that filled the room merged into one dull, indistinct blot. She was left alone in a searing, painful lucidity. All she wanted was Edgar.

Lydia longed to be outside; to feel the sun, uncomfortably hot, scorch her skin. She welcomed it like a lover's playful pinch. It was suffocating to stay in the stuffy, shaded room. 'I need some air,' she blurted suddenly.

She stood up and left the wake, heading for the gardens, pretending not to notice the murmurs and concerned glances.

'She's taken the earl's death quite excessively badly.'

'I hadn't realised she was so fond of him.'

'No. Nor had I.'

34

OUTSIDE, THE AIR was so still that sound carried endlessly. Lydia could hear the clink of a teaspoon against a saucer, the sound of the servants' footsteps pit-pattering through the house. She thought she ought to whisper. Or scream. She ran to the east front, past the yew hedges and the borders of gladioli. Past the terracotta statues that depicted the seven virtues. She knew them well and automatically named them in her head as she sped by: temperance, charity, diligence, patience, kindness, humility and chastity. She'd never before thought they were in any sort of chronological order, but now, she wondered. She sat, heavily, with the over-hot daisies, on a grassy slope. The sun had baked the ground and she was wearing black, so there was no danger that her dress would be ruined; still, she should probably have sat in a chair or at least on the steps of the lower terrace. If anyone spotted her here, they would think she was behaving oddly. She was. Did she want them to notice? Sheep baaed, from far off, where they were scattered in a field in the opposite valley. It sounded like a child crying. Lydia wanted to cry herself.

'The view is magnificent.'

Lydia was startled by Sarah's voice; she hadn't realised she'd been followed. She didn't turn; she feared her friend would see too much in her face. Instead she agreed with fake enthusiasm, 'Isn't it?'

The view of the Downs was picturesque to the point of unreality. People often commented that not only did they want to drink it in, they wanted to bottle it and take it home with them.

'Can I sit with you?'

'Of course.'

The two women listened to the birds and longed for a breeze to lift the brim of their hats or the edge of their skirts. The grass smelt dry, starved; Lydia felt the same.

'So, all of this is yours now,' commented Sarah.

'Well, Lawrence's.'

'It's the same thing.'

'I suppose.'

'You are lucky to have it. So many people are having to give up the big houses.'

'Indeed, it's a marvellous time to be an hotelier or someone looking for a big home to house the old or weak-minded.'

'Inheritance tax is enough to send one quite mad,' Sarah sighed.

'Yes.'

'But Lawrence has enough?'

'I think it's all fine.' Truthfully, Lydia hadn't given the question any thought at all. Over the last couple of years she had seen friends crippled by taxes and forced to abandon houses that had been in their families for generations. The ones who suffered the worst were those who'd lost a father and then a son in the war. Two deaths meant two sets of taxes. 'He's never mentioned any monetary issues,' she murmured.

'Lucky you.'

'Lucky me,' Lydia replied, trying hard not to cry.

'Are you quite all right, dear?'

'Lawrence and I . . . Things aren't as they should be.'

'He's just lost his father.'

'I know.'

'Is it because of the baby issue?'

'Not just that.'

'You'll have to give him up now.'

'Who?' Lydia could no more imagine Sarah, of all people, knowing her secret than she could imagine a man landing on the moon. For this reason – rather than any consideration as to whether she ought to dissemble or not – she didn't admit to him.

'Edgar Trent,' Sarah clarified calmly.

'Oh.' Lydia felt an explosion in her gut. To hear his name said aloud, here in Clarendale, was at once a profound liberation and a shock. 'How did you know?'

Sarah didn't want to have to say that she'd seen them together in Sir Peter's study. The image of the sergeant major's peachy white buttocks moving backwards and forwards, his powerful thighs, dark, hirsute and broad, had not left her consciousness, but she was too shy to admit as much to Lydia. She felt as though she'd done something wrong by discovering them, and her feelings of shame annoyed her. It was the adulterous couple who were the wrong-doers; they were the ones who ought to feel smeared and stained by guilt. She sidestepped. 'I've seen how you are together, ever since Ava's house party. At Lady Cooper's lunches and the Duchess of Feversham's spring ball, for instance.' She kept her eyes determinedly in front of her, fixed on the view. She knew this conversation would be easier that way.

'But we rarely talk to one another when we are in public.'

'You often share that look.'

'Which look?' Lydia seemed genuinely curious.

'The one that mixes deep and eloquent consciousness with, well, frankly, lasciviousness. It's a look that's only possible between lovers who are at once muted and yet invigorated by the presence of others.' It was true they had shared this look many, many times. Sarah had watched how they came together at dances and soirées. Together and yet apart. They did not flirt excessively, the way those contemplating embarking on an affair sometimes did. They did not acknowledge each other openly by pawing and grappling in dark corners, the way those in established liaisons did. They circled one another. Stayed close by. Sarah thought that the tension between them sparkled on the air, zinged when they spoke to one another, flashed if they didn't. They did not touch in public. After that time in the study she had never seen them so much as shake hands. They did not dance together. She saw the effort it took for them to stay apart. It was as though they both knew they would not be able to control themselves; if they were to hold one another, they would have to have one another.

249

'Oh.' Lydia seemed stunned. 'Do you think anyone else has noticed?'

'Probably.' Sarah had looked for all this and therefore had seen it. The incident in the study had directed her view; it directed everything. To her, they were obvious, somehow inevitable. Had other people seen as much? Would they? Sarah knew that gossip was grubby, yet essential to the circles they mixed in. She felt a shiver of panic and fear climb up her spine. It was a good thing that Lydia thought people might notice them; that for all their attempts at discretion they were obvious. The way she looked at him was revealing; the way she ignored him was telling. Thinking that she'd given herself away to Sarah might instil a note of caution. Lydia was behaving recklessly. Pointlessly. She wasn't trying hard enough to hide her infidelity. To stop it. What if Lawrence noticed? 'If not yet, then they will soon. You will be discovered, Lydia. These things always are. What will you do then?'

They sat for a long time. Lydia didn't answer the question. She watched as the sheep were herded into a ribbon and then trotted down the valley, their baaing intensifying. She was startled by a huge crow flying closely overhead, wings flapping like washing snapping on a line. She listened to the sound of a carriage on the gravel, the thrum of engines, the neigh of horses. The mourners must be leaving; grief for an old man could be nothing other than efficient.

At last she said what she knew to be true. 'I can't give him up, Sarah.'

'Of course you can. You mean you won't.'

'Can't, won't. It's semantics. I mean it's impossible.'

Sarah turned to her friend and for the first time in the conversation she tried to make eye contact; Lydia refused and continued to stare ahead. 'You have to give him up. Lawrence is a good man. He doesn't deserve this.'

'Lawrence isn't a bad man, I admit that. But Edgar. Edgar is a great man.' It was only when she sang his praises that Lydia was prepared to face her friend. Sarah was shocked by the intensity and passion that oozed from every pore; she could see it in the thin, faint lines around Lydia's lips, she could see it in the gleam of her huge eyes.

'You mean his war effort?' Lydia nodded tightly. Sarah's exasperation overflowed into barely contained anger. 'Arthur is dead. Samuel is disabled beyond anything a man should endure. Avoiding the Front was a blessing, not a blight. Lawrence didn't do anything wrong.'

'Didn't he? I think he should have been there. With everyone else.' Lydia looked panicked but certain. 'I wish I could think of it differently, but I can't.'

'If he'd gone, he might not have come back.'

Lydia tried not to move her face, not a fraction of an inch. She did not want her features to betray her, expose her. It was accepted that a man not coming back was an utter tragedy. Who wanted more death? One more death was one too many. Her own husband's was unthinkable.

Yet she did think about it. If he had gone and not returned, she would have loved him more.

'Oh, Lydia.' Sarah reached for Lydia's hand and tenderly squeezed it. She wanted to be patient. 'No good comes from looking back. We ought to go forward.'

'I agree with you. Edgar is all about the future.'

'You are deliberately misunderstanding me. You constantly judge Lawrence's past actions.'

'What else am I to do with them?'

Sarah roughly dropped Lydia's hand, almost threw it away. Her friend was being such a bloody-minded fool. The heat and the conversation produced tiny beads of sweat on her upper lip and lines of concern etched across her forehead. She wanted to shake Lydia, slap her. Anything to stop her messing it all up, throwing it all away. When she did speak, her breathing was hard and fast. 'I've felt such unmitigated jealousy of you. For years. Your man is safe and well. He didn't drown in mud, mashed into pieces fighting a war that had no purpose. You have no idea how easy things are for you. The money you have, the status you enjoy. You're welcome at every home. Gifts and perks are lavished on you; the rest of us grub around for less, so much less. But it's not enough for you, is it? Tell me, Lydia, what would be enough?'

Lydia had never heard Sarah speak so angrily, not even in the very early months of grieving for her husband. She had always remained patriotically, stoically, properly quiet. If she thumped her pillow or shredded and smashed possessions, memories or ideas, she did so privately.

Lydia didn't think she could do anything other than meet honesty with honesty. She whispered, 'I don't love Lawrence, so rather than having it all, I have absolutely nothing.'

Sarah gasped as though someone had thrown a bucket of icy water over her. 'You fool, you total fool, Lydia. Where have you been the last seven years?'

'Right here, exactly where you have, and I know what they fought for. A home.'

'You have the most marvellous home.' Sarah gestured around her unnecessarily.

'No, I have the most marvellous house.'

'Lawrence is a good husband. He doesn't deserve this.'

'I'm sorry for that.'

'I bet you are. This would be infinitely easier for you if he womanised, or drank, or gambled, I suppose,' snapped Sarah sarcastically.

'He never would.'

'No.'

'Too extreme for him. He didn't even fight. The defining moment of his generation and he was behind a desk.'

'Safe.'

'Yes.'

'You make it sound like a bad thing.' Lydia forced herself to meet her friend's eyes, and it was all there. 'I see,' said Sarah. A very bad thing.

35

AVA WAS GLAD to close the door of her apartment behind her. The drive back from West Sussex had been hot and bumpy, her skeleton had rattled and she felt the beginnings of a headache. She dismissed the thought; there was too much to do in London to waste time being frail. Ava's will was more than a match for motion sickness. Her veil had failed to keep the most minute flies from her face and a quick glance in the mirror confirmed what she feared: dead insects were splayed like a rash. She removed her hat and used a handkerchief to brush off the tiny carcasses, and started to imagine the pleasure of slipping into a cool, refreshing bath. The maid, hearing her mistress in the hallway, appeared from the kitchen. Ava noted that she didn't demonstrate any sense of urgency, more a touch of insolence; her weight was all on one hip, as though standing straight was too much effort. No doubt she'd been enjoying a glass of fresh lemonade with the housekeeper and considered the arrival of her mistress an inconvenience. The thought, 'One can't get the staff nowadays' drifted across Ava's mind, but she was so bored with hearing it she refused to articulate it.

She believed herself to be somehow different from those who did fling out this lament with regularity and bitterness. Perhaps the long hours she'd spent as a girl in her father's factories had adjusted her perception of working people in some intangible way. She looked the very epitome of aristocracy and yet she was not. It wasn't the American thing, or the new money thing; Ava knew she had beauty and spirit enough to overcome either variance. She wondered whether the crashing of the machinery in her father's factories, that had been the lullaby of her childhood, had somehow altered the rhythm of her thinking in many a profound way. It was as much of a mystery to her as it was to everyone else: why the most beautiful and successful debutante of her year, perhaps of the decade, had no interest whatsoever in marrying. But she did not. She saw opportunity and possibility in singledom; she saw only drudgery and confinement in matrimony.

'Good evening, Jane. Will you draw me a bath, please. I need to get these bugs off instantly.'

'Lord Harrington is here to see you, miss. I put him in the drawing room.'

Inwardly Ava fumed. What was Charlie doing here? She hadn't invited him; she didn't want to see him. However, she could not allow the maid to see her frustration.

'Thank you, Jane.' She glanced at the wall clock; she'd give him fifteen minutes. 'Do you remember how to mix martinis?'

'Gin and dry vermouth?' Jane sounded unsure.

'Yes, into a mixing glass with ice cubes, stir, strain into chilled cocktail glasses, and garnish with a green olive or a twist of lemon peel. Got it?'

'Yes.'

'Mix some and bring it to us, will you. Be sure there is plenty.' And then, under her breath, 'I'm going to need it.'

Charlie was splayed out on the chaise longue. His masculine body looked out of place in Ava's fashionable but distinctly feminine room. He somehow seemed staid and utilitarian compared to her turquoise silk throws and gleaming mirrored furniture. She'd had fun with Charlie last autumn; he'd been a rather attentive lover and had showed surprising stamina. He'd amused her, possibly even charmed her for a fleeting period of time, but her relationship with him had dragged on far too long. She'd begun to grow weary of him perhaps as far back as Christmas; she'd taken a new lover since and yet the man still hung around rather like a stale odour.

'Charlie, what an unpleasant surprise.'

He laughed, assuming, incorrectly, that she was joking. He jumped up and pulled her in to a tight hug, landing repeated kisses on her face. They were sloppy and inexpert; there was a tinge of desperation about them.

'I'm hot.' She pulled away.

'I know,' he laughed.

Ava flopped into a high-backed chair which gave her space; Lord Harrington had no alternative but to step away from her. He turned to the gramophone and lowered the needle on to a thick wax record.

'Must we? My head aches.'

'We must. We always must.' He turned up the volume and started to jig, alone, oblivious to her mood. He always was. It was one of the most useful and annoying things about him. Useful because he had no chance of getting under her skin; annoying because if he'd had the slightest understanding of her, he might have left her alone tonight.

'I've just got back from a funeral, Charlie. Be reasonable.'

'The Earl of Clarendale?'

'Yes.'

'Knew him, did you? Were you particular friends?' Charlie seemed to bite the word 'particular' and Ava couldn't be sure if he was asking whether she had slept with the old earl; an incredible thought, but Charlie did have a rather vicious jealous streak running through him that flared up at the most inopportune and extraordinary times. He suspected almost everyone she spoke to.

'His daughter-in-law is a great friend of mine,' she said coolly.

'Oh, yes.' Lord Harrington sounded both relieved and a little bit ashamed of himself. 'Lady Chatfield. Or rather should I say the Countess of Clarendale?'

'Yes.'

'So how was the send-off?'

'As one would expect. Dignified. Lots of lilies, hymns, some decent readings.'

'Let me guess. Did they sing "Jerusalem"?'

'Yes.'

'And they read the one hundred and twenty-first Psalm?'

'They did indeed.'

'How very expected.'

'He'd have loved it. I was always rather fond of the earl. I like rich men, nearly all of them, but I really liked Lydia's father-in-law because he didn't give a damn about anyone else.'

'Ava, you shouldn't talk ill of the dead.'

'I'm not. I'm just saying he had a magnificent pair of jowls that amalgamated with his neck. He always looked like he was thinking about himself and that he was more than content with what he was considering.'

'My, you are a wonderful girl. So original.'

Ava didn't acknowledge the compliment; instead she reached for a cigarette. She was grateful when Jane brought in the cocktails; she needed something that would take off the edge of irritation. She couldn't trust Charlie to behave in front of the staff; he'd been brought up to ignore their existence and therefore was dangerously indiscreet. He seemed strangely excitable and unruly this evening, and she didn't want a scene to be witnessed, so she dismissed the maid and poured two generous martinis herself. They swiftly knocked them back. He poured them both another, which were drunk with equal haste and lack of counsel. Then Ava asked, 'So, why the unexpected visit?'

'I have left Lady Harrington.' His shoulders straightened a fraction, but his eyes betrayed wariness; despite his innate confidence, he wasn't one hundred per cent sure about his actions in this case. Deserting a wife wasn't the thing his sort did easily.

'Your wife?'

'Exactly so. For you,' he clarified.

Ava shuddered. 'But I told you not to. I've often told you not to.' She put down her empty cocktail glass on the polished table and then thought better of it; she walked to the pitcher of martini and poured herself a third. 'I don't want this.'

Charlie moved quickly towards her and wrapped his arms tightly around her. 'Darling, *you* can't be afraid of a scandal. You're not the sort to care what other people will say. We'll keep your name out of the courts and papers. That goes without saying, I promise.

I'll have to provide evidence of adultery, naturally. I can't expect Dorothy to take the fall. We'll do it the usual way. Pay someone to come to Brighton with me, have a detective follow us, pay a maid to bring in a breakfast tray and say she saw me at it. All that sort of thing.'

The mechanics as to how, exactly, one secured a divorce in 1921 were something Ava was familiar with. She thought the process was repugnant; not because it was sleazy, although it was that, but because it was hypocritical. The real offenders were rarely named in court. Prostitutes were hired to provide evidence.

'Even so, Charlie, I think you ought to go back to your wife.'

Lord Harrington did not let his grip on Ava loosen. He held her awkwardly; she couldn't move her arms. It was all too, too embarrassing. 'Darling, I don't think you quite understand. I've told her about us.'

'I'm sure she knew before. She'll take you back.'

'But there was a terrible scene. I did it all for you. Don't you want me?' The question sounded pathetic coming from a man who had fought on the Somme. Ava was embarrassed for him. Charlie's weakness quickly transformed into mistrustful anger. 'Is there somebody else? There is, isn't there?'

'Not particularly.'

'I heard that you danced all night with Victor Renold at the Duke of Marlborough's party.'

'Who?' Ava genuinely couldn't recall. She danced with lots of men and boys; she didn't always catch their names.

'Is it Bertie Hetton? I heard you partnered him for the scavenger hunt that ended in Margate.'

Ava smiled brightly, hoping that she could still ease her way out of this ghastly embarrassment. 'That was the most enormous fun. I sat in the flapper bracket on his motorcycle. We won thirty pounds, you know.'

'You bitch.' She felt the blow in her ear and jaw as his huge hand swiped at the side of her face, then, almost instantly, she felt pain in her knee as she banged it against a side table; he had literally knocked her off her feet. She found herself staggering on her high heels, sucking deep breaths of air but not finding any oxygen. Straightening, she brought her hand up to the side of her face and glowered at Charlie. He was tall, big and broad. He seemed bigger than she'd ever thought of him before. She considered slapping him or throwing something at him but she was horrified to find she was frozen, afraid. He looked crazed with fury. Mad and large, he could do some terrible damage. Her hands were shaking; she wished they weren't. She told herself it was adrenalin, not fear, but she wasn't sure, and either way she appeared weak.

'Go home now, Charlie.' Ava didn't recognise the quiver in her own voice.

He picked up his glass, and for a moment she thought he was going to top it up; instead he threw it into the fireplace. It was too hot for a fire to be burning, but the shards of glass flew up the chimney and across the rug; the martini splashed over the hearth. Ava was mesmerised by the mess. She couldn't understand how such a thing was happening in her drawing room. Then, like a lion, he pounced and grabbed the back of her head, crushing his lips down on to hers. She became aware that he must have cut her when he struck her, because she could taste the iron of her own blood on his lips. She struggled away from the kiss, wriggling and ineffectually kicking his shins.

'Don't make a fool of me!' he yelled. He seized her hair and brought her face crashing down on to a mirrored console. The pain of the impact was excruciating. Ava thought of accidentally belly-flopping into a lake as a child; hurt and shock invaded her body. Then he shoved her backwards with such violence that her feet lifted up off the ground and she went flying through the air. She could not control her limbs; she crumpled and fell to the floor. Frenzied, he kicked her, two, three times before she scrambled behind a chair. He chased her, but his aim was less true, and the furniture and skirting took some of the blows, causing him to roar in frustration. She covered her head and stomach, a tight protective ball, but she felt his heavy shoe on her ribs and spine. For a moment she believed she was outside her body, looking down on this ghastly, uncivilised scene of terror and fury, but with each fresh heavy kick or strike she entered back into her body with the outrage of searing pain. She became conscious of every individual cell and blood vessel bruising or bursting, each nerve ending anticipating, then taking, a blow. She could hear and feel her heart thumping thunderously in her ears but she couldn't hear her own voice. Was she crying out? Why wasn't anyone coming to help her? No, she had not shouted for help. She *had* to find her voice. Her eyes were squeezed shut, but she forced them open; with tunnelled vision she glared at him.

'Stop it, Charlie! Stop it!' she shouted.

He crouched down, trying to get closer to her. It wasn't clear if he wanted to hold her or continue to beat her. His face broke apart; the vicious anger vanished and self-pity invaded. 'I'm sorry, I'm sorry.' Then, 'Why? Why don't you want me?'

Ava hurt too much to reply. She squashed herself as far as possible against the wall and away from him. Her blood was on the William Morris wallpaper. She could smell dust in the carpet. She swallowed down her vomit.

36

H E HAD NOT expected her visit, and yet he found himself
hoping for it. Normally they telephoned one another or sent
a telegram to confirm an arrangement first. This afternoon he'd
heard his landlady close the door behind herself at two forty-five
precisely, as was her habit; just five minutes later, there was an
impatient rapping on the door. He'd been lying naked on his bed,
still and calm, wanting to nap but finding he was too hot to sleep.
He thought of ignoring it – it was probably kids playing knock
and run, and by the time he dressed and got downstairs they'd
have scarpered – but the knocking continued; it was almost frenzied.

As he opened the door to her, she fell upon him, lavishing kisses
on his face: lips, cheeks, eyelids. She stood on tiptoes to do so. Girlish.
Enchanting. He could smell sunshine in her hair and taste her lipstick.

He pulled her in off the street; someone would see them and
there would be gossip. Sometimes her picture turned up in the
society pages of newspapers; some of the women about the doors
made a hobby of cutting out the pictures of pretty aristocrats and
sticking them into a scrapbook as though they were family; she
might be recognised. The door closed behind them and the cool
tiled passageway seemed to be a sanctuary from the noise and the
heat of the street. She was a balm. Her sweet-smelling body, her
petticoats and smile. He'd missed her; more, he needed her.

It was snatched and sudden and thrilling. He kissed her repeatedly;
her mouth, her neck and lips. Soon they were tangled in one another.
He could feel her narrow ribs pressing into his chest; she was getting

too thin. Her breasts were hard and small. He loved them. Actually loved them. Ached to touch them, to fasten his lips on her sweet pink nipples. His hands slipped down her hips, tilting her pelvis into his own hardness; his mouth found the fleshy petal of her earlobe. Then he held her hands above her head and used his own to pin her to the wall. He was not trying to restrain her – although he had; she was rooted – he was trying to resist tearing at her, taking her. He wanted to slow it down. Get upstairs at least. He couldn't have her here in the passageway. Could he? She opened her eyes and stared at him; for one disconcerting minute he thought she was reading his mind. Her eyes said yes. Yes, he could have her here, or on the stairs, or over the banister. He could have her anyhow or any way. She was his. He kissed her again, stronger, harder.

Over the past couple of months he'd found, to his astonishment, that there were times when he could forget. There were times when death didn't linger and pollute. When he was inside her, engulfed, there were moments where he felt alive. And glad to be so.

No longer able to resist, he ran his hands down her silk-clad body. Every curve tantalised and comforted in equal measure. There were no words. He didn't tell her he'd missed her. He didn't ask what she was doing here. He didn't want to know how long she could stay. All words disappeared; they were superfluous. They were left in a nude, raw silence. Stripped to desire. The only sounds he could hear were the tick of the hallway clock, kids playing in the street outside, laughing and hollering, and the sound of their tongues exploring one another. The heat oozed under the door and bit his bare ankles; upstairs, he'd pushed his feet into shoes but hadn't had time to put on socks. He was wearing loose, baggy trousers held up with braces; his shirt was only half fastened. She kissed his collarbone, leaning into him; she grabbed at his hair, stroked his chest, felt the solid abdomen, then started to scrabble with his flies, inexpertly unbuttoning them. Her hand swiftly found his hardness. The excitement was staggering; the relief immense. He had to concentrate very intently on not allowing it to be all over in that instant. Blistering with anticipation, his lips meshed with hers; he kissed her so completely it became difficult for him to know where he ended, where she began. He pulled up her dress and she wiggled out of her knickers, then he sank into her. Home. He stared into her eyes and she stared back, never losing one another. Not for a second. It scalded, it was implausible, it was exactly right. He felt the climb, the summit, the freefall. It was over in a matter of minutes. As he sagged against the wall, breathing deep and fast, he caught the smell of her skin: slightly damp with sweat, but still with notes of lavender and lime. He thought it might never be over.

They ran up the stairs. Hand in hand, her knickers in her handbag. Giggling, they fell through the door of his room. He bounced, delighted to find himself happy; willing to accept the mood, however temporary it might turn out to be. Many women resented his moods. They wanted him to forget and move on. He understood, he wanted that too, but it wasn't something one could control. Lydia did not resent his moods; she said she admired them. She seemed to understand that his experience had made it impossible for him to be blithely pleasant all the time. If he was feeling low, she always knew when she should try to cajole him into better spirits; when she should sit silently close by. But today, after taking her in the dingy hallway, up against the floral wallpaper, he was buoyant. Like a drunk he spun round the room, arms wide, waiting for her to notice.

Her eyes danced about and she spotted it immediately. 'You've bought a gramophone,' she commented, laughing. She quickly went to inspect it. Crouched down by it and ran her fingers along the varnished wood. 'Do you have any records?'

'Three. So far. We can buy more.'

Lydia picked through the discs and selected 'Sweet Lady' by Frank Crumit. She smiled as the disc rotated; it rose and fell seductively, like a woman dancing with veils. He'd kept his promise. Slowly, he'd started to amass items of comfort.

'Tea?' He held up one of two tiny yellow and gold cups and saucers. They looked ridiculous in his big hands; he'd bought them for her, not him, and he never used them when he was alone, preferring his mug. She looked at them thoughtfully, then beamed. She dug into her bag and retrieved a small blue box, wrapped in Selfridges ribbon; it housed a delicate, engraved silver teaspoon. She nearly always arrived with a small gift. A vase, a cushion, a pair of wine glasses; items carefully selected to be neither excessive nor intrusive. They were building something together. When she wasn't there herself, he liked to see the things she'd brought around the place; he assumed she was motivated by the same train of thought. She wanted to leave a physical trail, so he wouldn't forget her. She didn't know it wasn't necessary.

'Tea would be perfect.'

He had not been sure when exactly she would come to him, but he had known that she would and had prepared. He reached up to a shelf above the kitchen sink and pulled down a tin of shortbread biscuits; she'd once mentioned that shortbread was the only thing that made shooting in Scotland in August bearable. Carefully – with no hint of self-consciousness that he, a man, was serving a woman – he set a tray. The plate for the biscuits was a different but equally lovely pattern to the cups and saucers, and different again to the milk jug and the sugar bowl. Lydia seemed to like to buy piecemeal, lavishing attention and distinction on each purchase. A matching set would have seemed ostentatious and care-less. The eclectic china was somehow more wonderful and impactful.

They sat and sipped their tea. Lydia was beneath a shaft of bright sunlight that splashed through the rooftop windows; like a cat she soaked up the golden warmth. Her hair was ruffled and her dress askew. Edgar sat in the cooler shadow and watched her.

'Are you surprised to see me?' she asked.

'Yes.'

'Good surprised or bad?' She was fishing.

'Most definitely good.'

She grinned. 'I couldn't telephone from the country. It was too . . .' She paused, wondering how to phrase it. 'Hectic.' He could imagine. Wealth bought everything except privacy in one's own home.

'Is the old man dead?'

'And buried.'

'When?'

'Yesterday.'

'And you got away to London today?'

'I had to be here. With you.'

She said that sort of thing. She didn't hold back or exercise any caution. He was cautious enough for both of them. She ate the biscuits hungrily, laughing and chattering as she did so, and then, when they had finished their tea, they went to bed.

They could not get enough of one another. In the trenches, some men had slept with their girls' silk stockings pulled over their heads. Edgar hadn't got it at the time, but now he did. He wanted to be inside her all the time. He wanted to be permanently joined. They made love until they were sore, almost sick, but they could not stop. Over and over again their bodies found one another. Lips, breasts, legs and fingers.

The afternoon nudged into evening, but they were reluctant to leave the sanctuary of the stuffy, sultry attic and so dined on shortbread and tinned pears before the room was captured by the cooler blue of a summer's night.

'I've missed you. I've missed you,' she murmured, as he withdrew and rolled off her, finally satiated.

He lay on his side and gazed at her, running his hands the length of her body, feeling both her softness and her firmness under his caress. He'd missed her too, but he could not say so. Instead he said, 'Where does your husband think you are tonight? In Eaton Square?'

She yawned. He knew that she pretended to be bored when she was infuriated. She didn't like him acknowledging her husband, but how could he not?

'No. The house is closed up for the summer because of his father and what have you.' She stretched out her arm and felt around blindly on the bedside rug, hoping to locate a packet of cigarettes; the sight of her slim, pearly arm caused his stomach to contract with desire.

'Then where?'

'With Ava.'

Edgar sighed and checked the clock. It was after three. 'I suppose you had better get back to Ava's, then.'

'I want to stay here tonight.' She stared at him; her expression was one of both challenge and vulnerability, swirled together like a potent cocktail. He couldn't say what he wanted exactly, but her staying wasn't practical or sensible.

He kissed her shoulder, gently. 'What if Lawrence telephones Ava?'

'He hasn't done so before.'

'But there's always a first time.'

'No, he won't telephone.' There was something about the firmness and clarity in her voice that made him pity her and hate Lawrence. It was illogical, because most lovers wanted to hear of the strife and discontent, or at least indifference, between their mistress and her husband, but Edgar felt slighted on her behalf.

'Doesn't he care?' He couldn't understand this cool and distant man she was married to. If Lydia had been his wife, he might go mad with lust, he might never let her out of his sight; he would at least want to telephone her regularly if she was away. 'What's wrong with him?'

She gently put her finger on his lips. 'Don't talk of Lawrence. He's not like you. You don't know him.'

Hurt, he asked, 'Why are you loyal to him?'

'I'm not.' She looked surprised. 'I'm ashamed that I'm not, but I'm not. I just don't want him here with us. This is our place.' She kissed him slowly. 'Don't let Lawrence in.' After a moment or so she added, 'I thought I might stay with you all week. I've brought a bag with me. I have everything I need. A whole week. Wouldn't that be glorious? What do you think?' She'd stayed over in the past, but only for a night at a time. She'd always had to sneak out before dawn.

'How will we avoid the landlady and a scandal?' He smiled as he asked the question, ready to be won over to her way of thinking.

'Darling, I know you've seen off worse.' She put out her cigarette, closed her eyes and was asleep in moments. He envied her her tranquillity. He didn't question her lack of conscience; he knew too many people who had had to give up the nicety of conscience.

He climbed out of bed, stretched and then walked around the room. He pulled out a stool and climbed up on it so that he could poke his head out of the rooftop window to breathe the London air. It wasn't refreshing or reviving. It smelt scorched and polluted. He got down and strode to the basin. He threw cold water on his face. Nothing helped.

'Just come to bed. Sleep,' she implored. She sat up, eyes barely open, her voice soupy with fatigue.

In their three months together, he had never once fallen asleep next to her. He'd learned in the trenches how to ignore exhaustion. The reliving of the earth-shaking roar of the guns prevented sleep; he preferred staying awake to being a witness to what he'd done, so he'd learned how to push past exhaustion like a ruthless Roman marching along a road towards a village he must conquer. But they had made love several times, and the heat was soporific; he needed to rest. For once he was being lulled to sleep, rather than falling into it like a pit of gloom. He wondered whether he could resist. 'I don't care if you shout out,' she murmured. 'I won't think any the less of you if you do. There's nothing you could do that would make me think less of you.'

He knew she was wrong about this. It was the sort of thing people said if they hadn't seen the bleak filth of life. Yet he climbed back into bed and lay down next to her.

He didn't scream out that night, or the next. By the third night they'd both forgotten that he'd ever feared he would. They went about their business like a contented and legitimate couple. He had to visit the office in the morning, so she called on friends or shopped. In the afternoons they went for slow walks in the public parks and visited tea shops. He held her hand. He was tall and the sun was bright; his long shadow marked a way in front of them. The evenings were the best. They did all manner of things. One evening they went to the cinema, where the doorman was dressed as a vampire. He held out his warm hand for Lydia to shake; she practically jumped out of her skin. They giggled and squirmed their way through the picture, crunching on peanuts and sucking on oranges. That night they ate omelettes and peach melbas at the Savoy; another time they had soup with oyster crackers at a milk bar. Every night they danced in clubs before returning home to his lodgings to make love. They didn't talk about his screaming, but they both wondered whether she'd fixed him.

37

O N THE FOURTH night they decided to have a quiet supper at a little restaurant in Islington and then skip the club and return to his bedsit before nine o'clock. It was a risky manoeuvre, but Edgar managed to distract his landlady in the back room while Lydia crept upstairs, sneaking like a child locating a midnight snack. They made love again. She laughingly complained that it was almost becoming too much. Climaxing practically hurt her, she was so exhausted, whereas he went longer and longer each time, his body getting used to hers.

The screaming, when it came, was savage and relentless. The men were burning; they'd lost half their bodies but they could still scream. Their agony pouring, spewing over everything. He could smell their searing flesh and their blood. That of his men and the enemy. Both the same. He shot first, watching them splay their arms, reminding him of Punch and Judy puppets expressing surprise. *Whooosh*. Something wet splattered on his face. Another man's chest, or brains or ear. Over they go. Over the top. Wasn't worth thinking about. Couldn't think anyway, the guns were too loud. He ran on, his boots sinking in the soft mud and swollen, bloated bodies. He scrambled over dead men and not quite dead men. They stared at him, shocked and horrified, although they must have known; after all these months, they all knew how they would end. He could still pick them off, *bang*, splayed arms, puppet, strings cut, *bang*. This wasn't the worst. Too close to shoot now, no more bullets anyway. Slug the Hun. Bash in his fucking face with the end of your gun. If you're lucky, he goes down after two or three heavy blows. If not, you have to do the worst. Shove it in. Stab him. Stupid fucking short blades. Couldn't skin a rabbit. Over and over again. Stab, stab, stab. Fuck. Fuck. Fuck. Don't look at his face. Don't think of it as a face. Don't think of him at all. He'd do the same to you. Was trying to. Don't be sorry. Scream at him. Scream at them fucking all.

'It's all right, it's all right. Baby, it's me. I'm here.'

The sheets were damp with his sweat, but not the sweat of sweet loving; the sweat of terror. Of horror. He shook and whimpered. He could smell piss. She didn't notice, or pretended not to.

She held him tightly even though he threw her off two, three times. She linked her arms around him again; not so much of an embrace as a padlock. She spoke in a low, calm tone, murmuring endearments over and over again. 'Darling, darling. My love. My love. It's OK, it's OK,' she soothed. He began to realise it was her kissing his ear, not rats trying to gorge themselves on his flesh, assuming he was an already dead man. Her skin was soft, nothing like the rough fabric of a uniform. She poured him a glass of milk, like a mother does for her child. He drank it obediently. He was shaking. She prised his fingers off the empty glass and took it from him. She changed the sheets and scrubbed the mattress as best she could. He couldn't look at her. She took his hand and led him to the reading chair. He thought that if she put a blanket around his shoulders, they were finished. I can't have her think of me that way. Damaged. An invalid. I will not think of myself that way. I can't. If he did, it was over for him. If he sank into despair or depression, he'd never be able to pull himself up, it was too much effort. He'd given it everything. Everything and more. He had nothing left. He needed her to admire him, believe in him and in the war, because if she questioned, he'd disintegrate. He'd often thought that the war was a tragedy and a vast idiocy, a squandering of youth and of time, but he couldn't have *her* articulate those same thoughts.

But she didn't nurse him. She crawled on to his knee, her nakedness on his lap; he could feel the dark moistness of her sex.

She was erotic and honest at the same time. He could see the fine hairs on her slender arms as she pulled his heavy, strong ones around her small body. 'Tell me,' she whispered. 'What was it like?'

'They told us not to tell you.'

'I know, but we're breaking so many rules, one more can't matter.'

'People say that all we need is work and then everything will be fine, everything will go back to how it was before, but it's a lie. They hand out soup and pamphlets; if you are lucky they might show you how to walk on your new sticks, but no one teaches the men what they really need to know.'

'Which is?'

'How to forget, or at least, how to lie. Lie to oneself.'

'I don't want you to lie to me.'

'I know.' He said nothing for a long time, and then, finally, he admitted, 'It's a hideous thing to live with.'

'Everything you witnessed?'

'Not that alone. Also the things I did.' He glanced at her, nervous that he'd find condemnation in her expression but determined to face it if he must. She looked calm, interested. He fell silent for many minutes. She didn't prompt him. At last he said, 'We were not all in it together, like they told us. At least we weren't for long. Not once we started to fight, because some made it through and others didn't. That's an insurmountable difference. It was lonely. They talk of comradeship, and it was there, alongside desperation and death, but we couldn't make each other feel better; we could only watch each other die.'

He told her that junior officers had a life expectancy of six weeks at the Front. He admitted that when they first promoted him from private, to lance corporal, to corporal, to sergeant, he hadn't wanted it. None of it. Dead man's shoes. But he had no choice. There was never a choice. War took that away. He watched as men were slaughtered brutally, and their pathetic, disfigured bodies piled high. He told her that he'd helped pick up parts of his friends no bigger than a cat or a dog, put them together in grisly indiscriminate graves. He'd ignored the likelihood that the wrong arm was going in with the wrong torso. Made do. Did their best. Didn't admit that their best was nothing. Nowhere near good enough. 'A chance bullet takes out the man next to you. The one behind you, in front of you. It makes no sense. Whistled past my ear so many times. Took me down twice. Down but not out. Those injuries probably saved my life: eight months and then four months in the san.'

A bullet through the shoulder and then another buried deep in the thigh was seen as a bit of luck. A year less risk. He told her he'd been terrified and despairing at times. Lots of times. By talking, he was breaking the gentlemen's code that the War Office had asked the men to live by. Best not to mull, they'd insisted. Best to forget, but he remembered it all. Perhaps it wasn't courageous or right, but he told her everything anyway. He couldn't not.

She listened carefully. It was clear from her face that she was shocked, horrified. Disgusted. But not at him; at the whole bloody mess. He'd had to do those things. He was under orders. There was a war going on. War, just another word for filth. Hell didn't cover it. He'd been lucky and he'd been vicious, ruthless. That was how he'd survived. He had quick reactions; he ducked faster. He wanted to live. They all said the same – they had wives, sweethearts and mothers to go home to – but he'd always believed he wanted it more. He'd seen them give up. The light in their eyes went out. They wanted it to be over more than they wanted to survive. Then they were done for. He'd done anything he'd had to, to survive. When he was shot for the second time, he'd burrowed down deep into the dead bodies and let the battle rage around him. He didn't try to get the attention of the stretcher-bearers because, despite agreements made by grey men who didn't go into battle, there was always a danger that men could be picked off as they were being loaded up. He'd waited for hours, until the ceasefire, when the corpses were collected. He'd felt the bodies turn stiff above him and the lice crawl off the dead soldiers and nestle into him. Lice were transparent when hungry and turned black like raisins when they'd had their fill. As they swelled up with his blood he'd thought, thank fuck, at least I'm not dead yet, I'm not in hell. Although he was.

He had been told he was brave; over and over again they said it, and they gave him pips and medals. But brave was dangerous, brave was a step away from reckless. People said it was a miracle he'd survived, and they were right. He was always first over the top – as an officer it was his duty, he didn't have any choice – but he kept low and the bullets flew to his left, to his right. He tried to keep some standards. Didn't give a shit whether the men cleaned their boots; not that sort of standard. He tried to keep some humanity. He didn't read his men's letters. He let them self-censor, although it was his job to score out the words that might be truthful enough to upset those back home. He didn't report the queers, and once, when his senior officer accused a man in his platoon of being a deserter, a coward – Edgar knew the lad had been talking about shooting off his own foot – he argued that it was a case of neurasthenia. The officer had been so surprised that a chap from Middlesbrough even knew the word, let alone the rights it carried with it, that he'd hesitated. The truth was, they all had chronic mental and physical weakness and fatigue; he could have got them all out on that technicality. He saved one life. A coward's life. But a life all the same. It was something. Edgar's men liked him.

The misery was beyond articulation, and yet here he was pouring it all out. Loneliness and terror were the henchmen of silence. 'By the end, I hated everyone. I hated the other men who survived around me and had seen what I had done; I hated them because they had done the same. I hated the senior officers and politicians who insisted we push on, over and over again. I hated the enemy for not just bloody giving up and going home. And I hated the rats,' he confessed. 'I'm not afraid of them; I just hate them. The ones in the trenches became as large as Labrador puppies as they stuffed themselves on rotting dead men's flesh. The rats developed a reaction to dead man. Ironic, hey? Eating flesh made their faces bloat and turn chalky. They became like lanterns in the darkness of the trenches. I often woke with a start as a rat's tail whipped my cheekbone, searching out another meal.' Lydia quivered, but he did not stop. The violence and terror poured from his mouth, an unbrookable stream. 'My stomach turns when I pass the abattoir on Canton Street. The death reek is unforgettable. Have you ever seen a dead body, Lid?'

'Yes, my aunt and then Lawrence's father.'

'Laid out, were they? Peaceful?'

'I suppose. They didn't look quite themselves.'

'I've seen dead men that I've killed and they weren't laid out and peaceful. They were crying for their mothers and sweethearts. They smelt of piss and fear. I've pushed men off my bayonet and known that the only thing I could do for them was plunge it in again. Can you imagine?'

'No.'

'No, and you shouldn't have to. I shouldn't ask you to. We fought with knives and even our bare hands.'

Eventually his words slowed. His eyes stung and his throat ached with grief and stories. 'You can tell me more another day,' she whispered.

'Yes, I can, can't I.'

They let sleep take them. Knotted together – a tangle of limbs and thoughts, disappointment and hope – they slept on the wooden reading chair.

38

SHE WOKE NEXT morning back in the bed. He must have carried her there at some point. The sun was flooding in through the rooftop windows, like a bar of gold bullion stretching down from heaven into the bedsit. He was whistling and she could smell bacon frying. The place was already too hot. She'd soon discovered that his lodgings were eternally too hot or too cold; even when it was bright outside, they'd shivered in here. The place was heated by a largely ineffective penny-in-the-slot gas stove, so it was nearly always necessary to light the fire in the grate. The fire was a hungry, dirty monster which greedily consumed a sackful of coal in just a few hours and emitted volumes of smoke that covered Lydia and Edgar and all his possessions in a film of black soot. Edgar had to regularly trudge down two flights of stairs, out to the coal shed in the yard, to get another sack. This chore invariably led to irritating encounters with his unyielding landlady en route; she would question the wisdom of him burning coal in spring and insist he pay for it there and then, not trusting any of her tenants to settle at the end of the week. Edgar did not waste his charm on his landlady, but he was fair and polite and never baulked at paying over the odds for the coal. He even paid for all the chimneys to be swept. His rooms were, by Lydia's usual standards, grubby and inconvenient. Yet she was mostly comfortable and happy here. Happier than she was anywhere else.

Lydia was scared and amazed by her happiness. It filled her being and her head. She had never imagined it could be so. She had always thought happiness was synonymous with conforming to strict social standards and amassing enormous wealth. She thought beautiful clothes had an awful lot to do with it too. She'd spent a lot of time with him, alone. Talking. Making love. Just being. Every moment was irresistible, essential; and yet secretly, in a strange, unfathomable, contradictory part of her brain, she always hoped to find fault, to tire of him. She'd quietly hoped that her deep longing was lust, not love. That her fascination with him would wane. It had not.

And now, now that he had opened up to her, laid himself bare, she was bound: heart, body and soul. She was his. As inconvenient as it was.

'Are you hungry?'

'I'm starving.'

He beamed at her. His good looks were such that she was surprised afresh every time she set eyes on him. 'Boy, you are good-looking,' she would often murmur, without embarrassment or device. Just a fact.

He made a meal for her: strong tea, fried eggs and bacon, with big chunks of bread that weren't quite fresh. She watched as he threw it all together. He managed the pan and spatula, plates and cutlery with his right hand. He used his left to take his cigarette in and out of his mouth. He had rolled up his sleeves. His white shirt hung loosely around his neat waist as it flowed from his broad shoulders. His trousers were kept up with braces. She loved him completely and hopelessly.

'Why don't I stay here with you?' she offered.

'Oh, that wouldn't work.' He didn't look up from the pan.

'Why not?' She kept her eyes trained on him.

'You wouldn't like it.'

'I think I would.'

'You'd get sick of me.'

'Never. I never would.'

39

L AWRENCE HAD STUDIED the books and consulted with his lawyers and accountants. He thought there was a way to make it work, but only just, and it would demand sacrifices. He thought it was ironic that by inheriting a fortune, there was a very real danger that he might actually be worse off, unless he exercised great caution. Luckily, the late earl had not been a spendthrift. He'd been a careful and wise man, alert to the charge of squander. He had never allowed his wife to throw parties for two and a half thousand guests, the way the Marchioness of Londonderry did; he had not kept a staff of forty, he had only one motor car and he'd thought holidaying abroad was something only youngsters did. Even so, death duties were so extreme that to keep Clarendale running and in the family Lawrence would have to sell off a substantial amount of farmland, perhaps the odd painting and, unfortunately, Dartford Hall. It was the loss of Dartford Hall that irked. Yes, it was a draughty pile, in need of renovation, but he had a sentimental attachment to the place because it was his and Lydia's first home. They'd been very happy there, all things considered, the war and whatnot. But it had to go.

Lawrence straightened his back, tapped out his pipe and told himself that this was an opportunity; detaching himself from agriculture could, if handled properly, be progress. He would release more cash than he needed to pay off the tax and then he'd invest in government bonds. Here in Britain, for sure, it was the patriotic thing to do, but in America and the colonies too. Spread the risk.

If he could generate an income, drawn from dividends and independent of the land, he'd be secure. He would be able to pass the Clarendale estate on.

To whom was a different concern.

He turned in response to a knock at the drawing room door; Sarah popped her head around and smiled warily.

'I'm sorry to disturb, Lawrence.'

'Not at all.'

Her smile nudged a fraction from apologetic to relief, and then settled upon being nervously ingratiating. 'I thought you might like a cold drink. It's so hot again.' She pushed through the door, revealing the fact that she was carrying a rather cumbersome tray, laden with a jug of lemonade, two glasses and a plate of biscuits, freshly baked by the smell of them. He rushed to assist. Having taken the tray from her, he looked about helplessly: where to set it? Sarah smiled at his obvious lack of experience in serving himself. Carefully she cleared some papers and a novel from a side table so Lawrence had somewhere to place the tray.

'Are you joining me?' he asked.

'If you don't mind.'

'I'd be happy to have the company and a break from all of this.' Lawrence waved at the piles of paperwork. Sarah's eyes followed attentively.

'Shall I open the patio windows?'

'It is stifling in here.' He was suddenly aware that the room smelt fusty and male. He'd been bent over the papers for days; the air had been breathed in and then out too often.

'Everyone always benefits from fresh air,' Sarah said tactfully. Lawrence noted that before she opened the window she looked around and located two or three paperweights, then carefully placed them on the piles of documents. As the sweet summer breeze whooshed through the room, the papers fluttered but were not disturbed. She was a thoughtful, careful woman. They sat on chairs, facing partially towards one another and partially towards the view of the wide lawn, which was framed by heavy elms and sycamores that drooped down into a stream.

'Shall I pour?' asked Sarah. Lawrence smiled and nodded; it would be peculiar to have it any other way. 'Have you heard from Lydia?' she asked conversationally.

'Not since Thursday, when she sent a telegram to say she'd arrived safely.'

Lawrence noted that Sarah's face did not move a fraction when he gave this information. If she thought his wife neglectful in her correspondence, as he himself did, then she did not say so. 'Have *you* heard from her?'

'No.' She smiled reassuringly. 'Why would I? If she had time to send a telegram to anyone, then it would be you.'

'I suppose she must be very busy.'

'London is hectic.'

'I ought to ring her at Ava's.' He knew he didn't sound enthusiastic; he wasn't.

'I could do that for you,' Sarah said quickly. 'I've been meaning to telephone Ava; we hardly managed a word at your father's funeral, and Beatrice is going to stay with her again soon. Let me telephone.'

'Well, send Lydia my . . .' He hesitated. He meant love – *Send Lydia my love* – but it wasn't something he could say to another woman, even a dear friend like Sarah; he rarely said the word to Lydia herself. He settled for, 'Send her my best wishes. Tell her not to spend all my money on new shoes.'

Sarah laughed appropriately at his small joke. 'She must be tempted, though. If I were her, I'd buy all the pretty things in Bond Street, Selfridges and Liberty combined.'

Lawrence grinned. 'Ah, and here's me thinking you were the perfect wife. I now see your flaw. You are a wastrel.' He wagged his finger playfully.

'No, I am not,' Sarah spluttered with mock indignation. 'I said if I were *her*. Lydia looks wonderful in everything she puts on. I can't imagine how she ever holds back.'

Lawrence didn't know how to respond. He knew Sarah well enough to understand that she was not fishing for compliments. She didn't want or expect him to insist that she would look just as beautiful as Lydia in all those fashionable clothes women liked so much. For a start, it wasn't true. Very few women looked as beautiful as Lydia, and he would not insult Sarah's intelligence by throwing out a platitude. Secondly, it would be unseemly, almost flirtatious, for him to make such a comment, even to a steadfast family friend like Sarah. In the final analysis she was a woman and they were alone. Yet he did want to say something. He wanted to tell her that she was lovely. Lovely in an enduring, magnificent way. Her beauty was rather like an old stately home, not quite fashionable any more but solid, undeniable, valuable. Since Arthur's death, who was there to tell her such things? Lawrence searched around for a means to express himself but, as so often was the case for him, he couldn't think of an elegant way to say what he wanted. He chose instead to ignore the comment, letting the chattering birds in the trees fill the gap.

Presently he asked, 'Do you think I made the right decision letting her go to London?'

'I really don't think you had much say in the matter. She's a grown woman.'

'She's gone alone. Wouldn't hear of taking Dickenson with her.'

'She probably didn't want to overburden Ava by taking her maid along too.'

'I wonder what people must think, her off shopping and partying and what have you, so soon after my father's death.'

'Oh, I don't think anyone of any value will think about it at all,' commented Sarah breezily. She turned to Lawrence and smiled at him reassuringly. 'All the people we care about are far too busy to waste time gossiping about what other people are doing, aren't they?'

Lawrence thought this was sensible and agreeable, if not entirely accurate. He really wished Lydia had not headed off so swiftly. He understood that she cared about how she looked and that she would want the most flattering and beguiling black clothes, but he'd rather she'd stayed here and not bothered with mourning rituals; no one really expected anyone to wear black for longer than a week nowadays. He'd have liked to have her around. He wanted to discuss some of the decisions about the property sales; he wanted her to start to instruct the servants here, otherwise his mother might never give up the habit. Last night he'd been thinking about when he was a boy and used to go fishing with his father and his older brothers. They'd spend hours up to their thighs in the stream, sunlight and salmon dancing on the glittering surface; tadpoles slipping carelessly in and out of the frilly grasses near the water's edge. It was a lovely memory and he'd have liked to share it with someone; but none of them were here now. Brothers and father dead. Lydia gallivanting. He couldn't risk sharing it with his mother – it might upset her – and he had no intention of saying any of it to Sarah, so they fell silent again. It was a companionable silence, though, not awkward or toxic. He could hear the fountain flowing; although it was out of view, he could imagine it clearly. He knew every inch of Clarendale. The dogs were barking at something or other. Playful chaps.

'Thank you, Sarah.'

'What for?' She looked genuinely startled.

'Well, being here, with Mother. With me. It's kind of you to agree to stay on.' It had been Lydia's suggestion. She'd mentioned it the day before the funeral, saying to Lawrence how wonderful it would be for Sarah's children to stay at Clarendale Hall for a spell. 'They never get a holiday,' she'd pointed out. 'It will do Sarah a power of good too. She needs a break from all the gloom at Seaton Manor.' He'd thought that Lydia wanted to spend time with her godchildren, and had agreed instantly, but then Lydia had made her plans to rush off to London, leaving Sarah and the children to their own devices.

'The children are having a marvellous stay.'

'Finding things to amuse themselves, are they?'

'Too true.' Lawrence had seen them on the croquet lawn in the mornings and heard the rhythm of the racquet and the ball when they played on the tennis court just after lunch. 'They've spent a great deal of their time fishing in the stream,' said Sarah.

'Have they really?'

'Yes. They end the day smelling revolting, carrying something worse, but sun-kissed and happy.'

'I'm very pleased.' Lawrence resisted intruding on Sarah's

contentment by adding his own stories about fishing. He realised that it was enough that the stream was being enjoyed in that way again; he didn't need to talk about his childhood now that others' childhoods were blooming at Clarendale.

Sarah let out a contented sigh and sat back in her chair. She closed her eyes for a moment. Lawrence thought perhaps she might even nod off; he wouldn't mind. The woman was a hive of activity, always playing the piano or doing something with knitting needles, or crochet needles, or darning needles – some sort of needles anyway – or running about looking after the children, or her brother, or neighbours; it was rather a treat to see her peaceful and at ease. He watched her lips part, just a fraction. The creases round her mouth and eyes softened. Her breathing became deeper. Then she seemed to sense him staring; she opened her eyes and grinned at him. 'How rude of me.'

'Not at all,' he reassured her.

'It's so tranquil here. I've always loved Clarendale, from the very first moment I saw it.'

'When was that?'

'Your engagement party.'

'Quite so.'

'What a night that was.'

'Indeed.'

'You had a full-size orchestra, one hundred musicians playing from a marquee on the lawn.'

'That's right.'

'I remember the smell of jasmine and candle wax lingering in the air. There were literally thousands of paper lanterns. It was so romantic.'

'Yes.'

'Arthur and I made love in the herbaceous border.'

Lawrence choked on his lemonade. It was such an audacious comment, and so out of character, that he thought he must have misheard. Sarah turned to him and grinned, revealing a rarely exposed mischievous side. 'There's a very real chance that John was conceived here.'

'Well.' He was without words.

'I only have good memories of Clarendale,' she added.

'I'm glad.' Lawrence tried to recover some of his composure. He had never made love outside a bedroom, not with Lydia or with either of the two women he had had love affairs with before he married. Both of those women had been rather loose and adventurous, but even so, neither of them had suggested or hinted that al fresco might be an option. He hadn't realised that proper couples, married people, his friends, did such things. He was disconcerted by a feeling of both inadequacy and envy. Then he remembered that Arthur was dead, and he simply felt grateful that the man had known his wife outdoors. 'It's so important to hold on to the good memories, if we can,' he said.

'Yes, if we can.' The truth was that the war had taken away the pleasure of pottering about the past, or bravely plunging into the future, come to that. It required enough courage to stay in the present.

'Sarah . . .' He paused. Her comment about making love in his garden had chiselled away at the usual formality that existed between them, but the question he wanted to raise was deeply personal to them both.

'What?'

'Do you think . . . Are you angry that . . .' How to begin? 'What I'm trying to say is . . .' He could not say it. He could not ask if she resented men like him, ones who had had desk jobs. He didn't want to hear her answer, not really. What he wanted was for her to politely excuse him; he wanted a salve. She'd give it, he was almost certain, but it was selfish to demand it of her. For months now Lydia and Lawrence had been locked in a grim stalemate. This absurd notion that she had, that they were being punished. What rot. Who could believe in a just world after what their generation had endured? God was not balancing the scales, adding and taking away weights at will, like some sort of grocer measuring out flour and currants. Save a son here, inflict infertility there. It didn't make sense.

None of it did.

That was the only thing they could be sure of: none of it made sense.

Besides, it was some time ago. They ought to move onwards and upwards. It wasn't polite to linger and poke the embers. Sarah had the right idea: the only thing to recall was the bright times. Why relive the atrocities? Nothing could be undone. It was clear Lydia was humiliated by his actions, resented him. On occasion she behaved in a way that made him think she almost despised him. He would not ask Sarah for a salve, it wasn't fair. He could do without, because he hadn't done anything wrong and he had to believe that. Questioning his position, well, that way madness lay. Instead all he said was, 'I'm glad you find peace here.'

It was clear that Sarah understood the deeper level of his comment when she replied, 'I lived with years of gnawing anxiety when he was at the Front. There was so much time to fill. Endless. I tried to punctuate my days, make sense of them.'

'Keep to a routine.'

'Yes, that's what we were advised, wasn't it?' That sort of advice came from the Home Office, although not Lawrence's department; he hoped it had helped. 'In the mornings I'd visit the children in the nursery room. Then I'd sew or darn. In the afternoons, I'd garden.'

'Very useful.'

'Well, I was able to grow vegetables. Then the afternoon would creep into the evening, another day gone, no telegram. That was all that mattered. Get by without the postboy stopping at your gate. Thank God when he stopped at your neighbour's. Ask God to forgive you for that thought. I would have been better becoming a VAD or something, exhausting myself physically so that there was no room for mental examination. It might have been some relief to be too busy to long for the next letter to arrive, to dread the next telegram.'

'But you had the children.'

'Yes, indeed, it would have been impossible for me.' Sarah sighed wearily. 'It is just one of my many fantasies about the war. One of the lesser ones.'

'You must miss him very much.'

Sarah pulled her face into something that was supposed to approximate a cheery or at least a brave smile; in fact she looked savage. Lawrence regretted the platitude. He had meant it sincerely, but it had fallen short of its mark.

'One recovers from the shock, eventually, just as I don't doubt one gradually gets used to the fact one can't walk and is dependent on a chair, but one never gets over the loss and one will never be the same.' She paused. 'I wouldn't wish it on another soul.' Her attitude was in stark contrast to Lydia's. Neither woman really accepted things as they were, but Sarah endured, whereas Lydia railed. There was something about Sarah's sad but quiet dignity that made her appear absolutely stupendous. 'Every man who came home was a miracle.' She looked directly at Lawrence and held his gaze. 'Every man who stayed home was a blessing.'

Emotion welled up in his throat, choking him; it blocked his airways and stung his eyes. He coughed. She turned away from him and looked out at the garden. Lawrence leaned towards her and placed his hand on hers in absolute gratitude. She continued to look out on to the green lushness and didn't acknowledge his contact.

'I'm waffling, sorry. I don't know what's come over me. I only wanted to say that here is one of the only places where anxiety slips from me. I appreciate the invitation. I like being here, and so do the children.'

Lawrence nodded, knowing that the moment of understanding, which he'd relished, must dissolve. He withdrew his hand and settled back in his chair. 'Look, here they are now.'

'Talk of the devil and he shall appear.' Sarah laughed. Lawrence knew she was joking: her entire demeanour lit up when the children were in her sight. In fact she twinkled so brightly that it caused Lawrence to understand that the rest of the time she wasn't very happy at all.

Both adults watched as the children made laborious progress up the bankside and stumbled towards the open patio doors. They'd been spotted. Molly waved enthusiastically; John was lugging a steel pail that evidently was full of water and who knows what else, so he did not expend any unnecessary energy by throwing a greeting their way.

'Hello, you two. Had a good day?'

'Excellent, thank you,' replied John. Molly ran to her mother and tried to climb on her lap.

'Oh, sweet one, you are filthy. You'll get me dirty too.' But Sarah's objections were half-hearted; she couldn't resist the weight of her younger child on her knee.

Lawrence turned to the boy. 'Caught anything?'

'Two frogs.'

'Good show.'

'May I have a biscuit?'

'You should wait until you are offered,' said Sarah quietly but firmly. She was a stickler for manners; she didn't want it said that she'd brought up the sort of children who were spoilt or unruly. It was bad enough that they did not have a father; much harder if everyone expected the worst of them because of the fact.

'Oh.' John hung his head, embarrassment and disappointment blistering out from his demeanour.

Lawrence allowed a heartbeat and then said, 'Would you children like a biscuit?' Smiling, they reached out; their day's adventure was smeared on their hands.

'You ought to go and run your hands under a tap,' said Sarah; it was now her turn to look embarrassed and disappointed.

'Oh, a bit of mud never hurt anyone,' offered Lawrence. He glanced at Sarah to check that he hadn't offended her by contra-dicting her in front of the children. He didn't want to undermine her, just put her at her ease. He was pleased to see that she looked relieved and not in the slightest irritated.

'It's lovely here,' murmured Molly, as she rested her head back on her mother's chest.

'Isn't it? However, we'll have to leave tomorrow.'

'Really? So soon?' Lawrence found the idea of Sarah's departure disquieting.

'No!' the children chorused; they clearly found it upsetting too.

'You're welcome to stay as long as you like.'

'Thank you, you are very generous, but I got a telegram from Bea today. I think Cecily would like me to return. You know, to help with Sammy.'

'I see. Absolutely. Selfish of me to delay you.'

'I don't want to go home, Mummy,' groaned Molly. 'Not yet.'

'But the stable master said he'd take us riding tomorrow,' said John. 'We never go riding at home. There's no one to take us.' Lawrence knew that the staff at Seaton Manor were overburdened with the care of Samuel and there was no time for anyone to indulge children with horse-riding lessons in the holidays.

'And we'd planned to go fruit-picking,' mumbled Molly. She put three fingers in her mouth, a habit Lawrence had noticed she employed to stop her crying.

'Uncle Earl Lawrence said he'd teach me to shoot,' added John, with ill-disguised petulance. He kicked the gravel hopelessly; small stones splattered about and pinged against the pail. Lawrence looked sheepish. It was true, he had offered to take the boy to the target range; there had been talk of clay pigeon shooting by the end of the summer, perhaps even grouse in August. Lawrence had been making plans. He hadn't thought about when the children would have to leave; it was careless of him. Truthfully, he'd been as excited by the idea of the shoot as the boy was, but now he felt dreadful; he hadn't wanted to put Sarah in a tricky position. She looked hot and flustered.

'That's not how you ought to address the Earl of Clarendale, John.'

'Oh, that doesn't matter one bit. I think it's rather a fun name,' said Lawrence.

'I'm not going home.'

'You certainly are, young man.'

'But I like it here.'

'May I make a suggestion?' Lawrence could see that both Sarah and the children were becoming increasingly irate, and locking horns never did anyone any good. 'Perhaps you could go home and help Cecily but the children could stay on here. If you don't mind and don't think they'll be too homesick.'

Before the words were completely out of his mouth, John and Molly started to plead and yell.

'Can we, Mummy?'

'What a super idea. I won't be homesick, not one bit. I promise. Can we stay?'

Sarah laughed. 'Oh, I see. I'm totally dispensable, am I?' Lawrence could tell she was torn. She didn't like to be separated from the children and she wouldn't want to exploit his hospitality, but on the other hand, she couldn't fail to see how excited and delighted they were at the prospect. He waded in.

'Well, I know I'd love that, and Mother would too. She's adored having the children about. You could come back again at the weekends, if you want and if Cecily and Bea think they can manage.'

'Well, I—'

'Please say yes, Mummy. Everyone wants you to.'

Sarah gave in with a graceful smile. She wasn't one for disappointing people. 'Well, if *everyone* wants me to, how can I do anything other?'

'Good, that's settled,' said Lawrence firmly. He leaned back in his seat and closed his eyes for a moment. The heat from the sun rested on his lids in a pleasant, almost soothing way. It was the first decision he'd felt totally content with in several days. Sarah had such a charming smile. It was a joy to see her use it.

40

'THERE YOU ARE, darling. I've been quite mad with worry. No one at all knew where you'd disappeared to.' Ava kissed Lydia on both cheeks, but despite her words she did not look agitated or overly concerned.

'What happened to your face?' Lydia gasped, shocked. Ava had become used to her beaten appearance and forgot that it was startling. Shocking. Initially she'd been macabrely drawn to every looking glass in the house; she couldn't stop examining the violence, couldn't stop thinking about it. But she was pretty sure that the cut on her lip was healing reasonably well, and she was able to open her mouth again properly. For a day or so eating had been difficult; her jaw ached, and if she chewed vigorously, she opened the cut where her top lip met her bottom one. Her temple was still tender, and she suspected that injury might leave a scar; she'd had another headache this morning. She'd watched as the bruises lost their angry red hue and rushed through a kaleidoscope of colours; at first they had darkened to a bluish purple which, despite the fact that Ava was far from the romantic sort and rarely subject to silly notions, she could not help but compare to the colour of forget-me-nots. Then they'd turned a sludgy green, the colour of the English Channel in the autumn, and now they were saffron, suggesting that the bruising was almost healed. Another day or so and she would be able to go out and about again without any comment at all.

'Oh, nothing.' She waved her hand dismissively. 'A horse. I got thrown from a horse. A huge ignorant brute. One moment he was placidly plodding along and the next this terrible flash of temper.'

'How awful.'

'Yes.'

'Will you sell him? You're cut rather badly.'

'I'm certainly trading him in, but I'll mend. More importantly, and stop ducking, where have you been?'

'What do you mean?'

'Lawrence has sent two telegrams and Sarah called here looking for you. Everyone seems to be under the impression that you're staying with me.'

'What did you say?'

'I fudged it, darling. I said you were at Bond Street. I've been praying ever since we wouldn't find you in the bins at the back of the Ritz, cut up into tiny pieces. I had terrible visions of having to explain myself to Scotland Yard. You have put me in the most awkward position.'

'Thank you.'

'So, I take it you have been with the sergeant major.'

Lydia gasped. 'How did you know? Did Sarah tell you?'

'Does Sarah know? How interesting. No, Beatrice told me.'

'Beatrice knows?'

'Yes, and you ought to know she's furious about the whole thing. She wanted to blow the whistle on the fact that you are not staying with me.'

'But how does she know I'm not?'

'Because she is. She's in the parlour.'

'Oh, I see.' Lydia turned pale.

'Yes, which is why it's been rather awkward that you used me as your alibi, without even having the manners or sense to tell me.'

'I'm sorry.' Lydia looked momentarily chastised.

'Did you take a hotel? Did anyone see you?'

'We stayed at his lodgings, in the East End.'

'Oh, darling, how frightful.'

'How long have you known about him?' It was clear to Ava that Lydia couldn't wait to start talking about her lover.

'Beatrice mentioned that she saw you at the V and A with him. I put two and two together and came up with fornication.'

'But that was March. You've known all along?'

'I've been wondering when you'd come to me. Shall we have tea, or something a little stronger?'

41

BEATRICE COULD HEAR whispering in the hallway. She recognised Lydia's voice and her first thought was relief. She almost jumped up and ran to greet her, but then she remembered how furious and disgusted she was with her friend so she sat stock still. She wasn't sure whether she was exhausted by the heat in the drawing room or the heat of her friend's passion. Beatrice felt hollow, ground down, worn away. She was leaden, large and loveless. Certainly, the sun beat against the windows so ferociously it was almost impossible to breathe. The cloying air clambered up her nose and into her mouth, the sweet sickliness of it overwhelming; it caused sweat to prickle on the back of her neck and her thighs.

When Ava had first suggested that Lydia was having an affair, Beatrice had refused to contemplate the idea. It wasn't possible. Ava pointed out that of course it was *possible*. 'Then it isn't probable,' Bea had countered. Lydia was beautiful and married to a decent and wealthy chap; that was the recipe for – and pinnacle of – success and happiness. Surely. Why would she have an affair?

Beatrice had carefully watched Lydia over the past three months. She'd noted that Lydia often seemed skittish, distracted, even anxious on occasions, which, she had to admit, were not necessarily states of mind that one associated with success and happiness; at other times though she had seemed exhilarated, joyful to the point of rapturous, so Bea had never once had reason to believe that Ava's salacious suggestions were fact. Ava had been generous, even kind, to Bea of late, but there was no denying that she had a vulgar mind; experience had made her weary and she thought the worst of people as a matter of course. In her own mind Bea had staunchly defended Lydia. She would not believe it of her.

But where had Lydia been this last week?

A whole week. Lawrence thought she was with Ava, which she blatantly wasn't. Sarah had telephoned here too; Beatrice had suggested they telephone the police, as something ghastly might have happened. Sarah had replied firmly, 'There's no reason to panic, to alert anyone or to escalate this situation,' which suggested she knew that Lydia was safe, if not well. Bea had been forced to accept the unsavoury evidence.

Now Lydia floated into the room. She looked utterly beautiful, even more exquisite than her glorious norm. She had an iridescent glow; her skin was luminous rather than its usual creamy perfection, her smile brighter and broader. She actually looked taller. Beatrice felt hate slither into her heart. She did not hate Lydia just because Lydia was betraying her husband; she hated her because she had it all and more. She oozed excess. Beatrice imagined she could smell it on her: the surplus, the sex and the warmth.

Bea was determined that she would not give Lydia any satisfaction in terms of acknowledging her unexplained absence. No doubt she was desperate to talk about her passionate love affair; well Bea didn't want to know. She didn't need details. Couldn't bear them. She had big news of her own, which she had just been about to impart to Ava when Lydia had interrupted. She actually resented the thought that Lydia's reappearance might overshadow it.

Recently, Ava had started to listen to Beatrice in a way that no one else did, generally. It was flattering. Ava clearly looked on Bea as a project, but Bea didn't mind. She felt someone ought to take her in hand; she hadn't been managing her life particularly well so far. Now that Lydia had arrived, Ava's attention might falter. Bea decided to plough on and not make a single reference to Lydia's prolonged absence. She stood up to greet Lydia, because not to do so would be notably peculiar, but she let the kiss linger in the air. She did not dare make contact; it was impossible not to think about where Lydia had been, what she'd done.

'Bea, how lovely to see you.' Lydia smiled that bewitching smile of hers, which Bea had always loved yet now mistrusted.

'Thank you. You look wonderful. Are you wearing a new dress?'

Lydia glanced down at her turquoise silk georgette dress, with an air that suggested she was surprised to see she was wearing anything at all. She shrugged. 'No, I think you've seen this before.' Her entire demeanour was carelessly casual. Bea wondered could she be oblivious to the concern she'd aroused of late.

'I can't imagine what it is then. Maybe you have a tan.' Beatrice turned away and quickly sat down.

'It is so very hot.' Lydia slunk into a chair and flung her hat aside. She shook out her hair. It was unkempt and unstyled, yet she looked glorious. Free. Lascivious.

'Do you want tea, or should I call for cocktails?' asked Ava.

'Tea,' replied Bea at the exact moment that Lydia requested cocktails.

Beatrice stared at her hands as though they had the answers to all life's great questions written upon them. Usually so willing to comply and conform, she was in the habit of adjusting her desires to fall into line with others, but this afternoon she did not grasp the alternative but resolutely stuck to her choice.

'I don't mind,' smiled Lydia. 'It's that awkward hour, a little late for tea, a little early for cocktails. Whatever.' She pulled out a packet of cigarettes from her bag and offered them around. Ava took one, Bea shook her head. 'You can have one, you know, there's no one watching you. No one will tell,' Lydia teased.

'Who would there be to tell?' snapped Bea. '*I* don't have to answer to anyone.' She placed a heavy emphasis on 'I'; Lydia would have to be utterly self-absorbed not to notice, but just in case, Bea drummed the point home. '*I* don't have a husband, and it's been a long time since they stopped insisting I needed a maid to follow me everywhere.'

'Isn't it a blessed relief?' commented Lydia, seemingly unperturbed by Bea's hints about accountability. She dragged on her cigarette and then tapped her ash into a huge glass ashtray that sat on a gilded occasional table. The smoke seemed to be painted on the air; it was so stifling it didn't drift. 'Part of the reason I married was because I was sick of being chaperoned. So restrictive.'

Ava laughed but couldn't understand; she'd never been chaperoned in the traditional sense. Her mother tried, but somehow Ava had put herself beyond that sort of control. No one was ever quite sure of her whereabouts and no one ever had a clue as to what she was thinking.

'Well, I suppose,' muttered Bea. 'I've never thought of it that way. It was simply the case that we had to give up the spare maids because money was getting tight, but during the war everyone made sacrifices, so there was no embarrassment; no one guessed we were strapped.'

'No one minded anything much during the war,' Ava agreed. She'd begun to understand Bea's financial constraint, something she'd never considered until Bea came to stay with her.

'Then after, well, I was no longer the sort of girl who needed chaperoning. In fact, I was no sort of girl at all.' Bea paused, barely allowing the pity of her words to settle in the room before she added, 'Sir Henry Vestry has asked me if I'll take his daughter, Georgina, out into society. I'm sure you remember, her mother died of the flu and her father married a divorcée, so there isn't anyone suitable to launch her.'

'How very flattering. They must trust you a great deal,' said Lydia. Her smile and eyes were unnaturally wide.

'I'm old. I'm over,' Bea stated simply. 'That's what it means. Nothing else.'

'Don't be silly, it will be jolly.' Lydia sounded strained and unconvincing.

Ava patted Bea on the shoulder and said, 'I am going to ask the maid to bring champagne.'

'Ava, that's very kind, but I don't really feel like celebrating.'

'No, darling, absolutely not, but you can drown your humiliation,' said Ava, and she rang for the maid.

The women stayed silent until the maid had poured the champagne and left the room. They all drank up quickly.

Beatrice would borrow diamonds, Georgina would wear pearls.

Pearls were for girls. Diamonds were to compensate for the loss of natural bloom. They probably were a genuine compensation if they had been given to you by a doting husband to celebrate the birth of a bouncing baby or years of matrimony, but they were cold comfort if they were on loan from a wealthier pal. Bea could see that Lydia was scrabbling around her brain for something compensatory and cheering to say on the topic. Ava, brutally honest, didn't bother. She'd accepted the information for what it was. Society's view of Beatrice Polwarth was that she was past it. Twenty-six, an old maid.

'I don't quite see myself joining the church parade just yet, sitting in rows on green chairs in the park,' commented Bea.

'No one is saying you have to.'

'I've been invited to chaperone, Lydia. That's exactly what they are saying. Finished. Before it even started. Done. Gone.' Bea thought she might cry.

'Will they pay you?' Ava asked.

'Yes, rather generous expenses and, of course, lodgings for the season.'

'Well, that's something marvellous. You have a job. You're the first one of us to secure paid employment since the war.' Ava refilled their glasses. 'Congratulations!' Bea knew that Ava's rare enthusiasm was genuine, but she couldn't share it.

'It will be fun,' added Lydia tentatively. 'They have a house in Belgravia, don't they?'

'Yes. Very smart. Four floors,' admitted Bea.

'And a pile in Oxfordshire. Didn't the King visit there last year?' No doubt Lydia remembered that back in January, at Ava's party, Beatrice had been thrilled with the idea of rubbing shoulders with aristocracy, and was trying to rouse and tempt. Bea resented the implication that she was a child who could be offered a shiny ribbon or an ice. She might have held that view just a few short months ago, but it felt like a distant epoch. She had believed then that there was still a chance for her to find love, or at least companionship; her biggest concern had been whether she could afford the season. Now she would be funded, but her season was past.

294

She was one of a large crop of apples that, rather than be picked, would fall from the tree and rot into mulch among the browning foliage. Lydia left her chair and perched on the footstool next to Bea. She placed her hand on Bea's arm. Bea withdrew, tucking her arms close to her body, out of reach; no doubt Lydia thought it was something to do with the chaperoning. 'You'll get to go to dazzling parties.'

'And sit on the sidelines.'

'There will be fathers in attendance, older brothers.' Lydia smiled gently. Beatrice wished she wasn't so beguiling. She did a very good impression of someone who really cared. It was confusing. Bea wanted to hate Lydia. Lydia was a woman who had everything Beatrice herself longed for and more. The fact that she seemed not to value her treasures and privileges in the least was the most galling part. Bea was almost sure she did hate her. Yet she seemed so much like the friend she'd always loved, especially when she added, 'You'll have spare time, too. You can continue with your sketching.'

'I'm not sure.'

'Will you go to Nottingham to choose her lace? We all went there, didn't we?' Lydia's gentle nudge down the avenue of their shared past was alluring. Almost irresistible.

'Do people still do that?' Ava asked with a yawn.

'Absolutely.' Bea was surprised to find she had a view on where the lace for the veil and dress should be purchased. 'It's traditional and patriotic.'

'Silver-trimmed?' probed Lydia.

'Gold,' replied Bea emphatically. She hadn't really given the issue much thought, much less discussed it with Georgina, but that was her instinct. 'I mean, Sir Henry can afford the best, so why wouldn't we?' She missed Ava winking at Lydia at the mention of the word *we*.

'A train?'

'Well, I suppose eighteen inches. The maximum.' Beatrice began to feel the effects of the champagne and her friends' curiosity. She had never basked in the limelight, even during her own season; she might do very well with reflected glory. She might make do.

'Won't that look rather odd with the short skirts that are in fashion?' asked Lydia.

'I shan't allow her to wear a short skirt,' replied Bea, scandalised at the idea.

'But she must, if she wants a man. She can't be dull,' commented Ava.

'Gosh, this is going to need some thought.' Bea was suddenly determined that Georgina Vestry would have a good season. A triumphant one. She would make a match. She would not be condemned to spinsterhood; her arms would not ache to hold babies. Bea would see to it. 'The new fashions are a worry at court. The three small ostrich feathers and the wisps of tulle look simply silly in shingled or bobbed hair.'

'What's a girl to do?'

'What indeed.'

'So you'll take the job?' Ava asked.

Bea considered. Chaperoning was a position of both independence and responsibility. Her opinions would be elicited, considered and valued. She'd be needed. She'd have company. 'I think I'll telephone them right now, or maybe I should deliver the news in person.'

'I'm sure they'd love that.'

Bea stood up, straightened her spine, threw back her shoulders. She would not take the underground; she would take a cab. She could afford it. She was a working woman. A woman of independent means.

42

A S BEATRICE BUSTLED out of the room, Lydia felt the air tighten. They had avoided an emotional breakdown; they had manipulated and manoeuvred the facts so that Beatrice found the silver lining in the dark, dank cloud. It was something. Not everything, but that was what they were all supposed to settle for now.

Lydia would not. She was here to tell Ava as much. She would not settle or conform. She'd tasted it all. Smelt it, licked it, held it. She wouldn't give it up. Couldn't.

Ava rang for her maid. 'Bring more champagne and make sure it's chilled,' she snapped, showing an uncharacteristic lack of composure. 'It's so hot,' she groaned, by way of explanation for her short temper. She turned to Lydia. 'Well?' It was all-encompassing.

'I love him.'

'Don't be an idiot.'

Lydia smiled brightly, her eyes ablaze with certainty, a protest against the sharpness of Ava's rebuke. She did not know how to explain her love; all she could do was definitively assert it.

'You love having sex with him. It's not the same thing at all.'

It was true that the sex mattered. His presence in a room made the hairs on her arms stand up; every fibre in her body ached as it leaned towards him in some secret, unfeasible way. When he slipped his tongue in her mouth she felt volts shoot through her being, her soul. He was a funny, unconventional, self-possessed, imprudent indulgence. She did not have to discuss with him the difficulty of finding a reliable housemaid, or whether a badger cull was necessary. They did not wonder whether they ought to invite Lord So-and-So for dinner because he had so much influence at the Home Office. They'd never bicker about how appropriate it was for Lydia to spend so much time with the increasingly scandalous Ava Pondson-Callow. They would not have a conversation about her need to produce a baby. Lydia was happy to live in the moment, shunning her past and refusing to contemplate the future. Their moment was glossy and gleaming. So dreamy. But then there was the other side. The deep and dark, depressed side he had shown her. The frightening realities. He'd blown the lid off her privileged and cosseted existence. She loved that just as much.

Ava sighed and shook her head. 'Sex makes such fools of us all.'

'It's not just about sex.'

'It's always just about sex.'

'There's honesty between us.'

'A sexual honesty?'

'Yes, that and an emotional one too. What we feel for one another is rare and fragile. It can't be articulated or labelled.'

'What you feel for one another is depressingly commonplace, and it is known as adultery.' Ava sighed and reached for her cigarettes. 'It's becoming horribly messy, Lydia. You must give him up.'

Lydia felt irritated and patronised. She'd come to Ava because she'd thought she was the most likely to understand; Ava was the least conventional of all her friends, the most willing to kick at traditions and laugh at rituals. She'd expected indulgence; an excited exchange about the deep mysteries of sensational physical satisfaction and complete emotional and intellectual fascination. She had not imagined she'd encounter resistance or disapproval. 'Why do you care, suddenly? You've never been what one might describe as virtue incarnate.'

'That is very true.'

'Well?'

'I care because it's you and you're going to get terribly hurt.'

'You're wrong.'

Ava pulled heavily on her cigarette holder, held the smoke in her lungs and then blew it out in a series of neat and impressive concentric rings. Even when she was in the middle of something so serious, she could not help but be stylish and impactful. She turned to the gramophone and selected a Sophie Tucker record; one hand busy with her cigarette, she used the other to place the record carefully on the turntable and lower the needle into the fat grooves. The piano notes and the rich, gravelly, come-to-mama voice exploded into the room. Lydia let the words wash over her. Something about living alone and liking it. Ava stood in the middle of the room; like an actress on stage in the spotlight, she swayed, alone, almost aloof.

'What do you do together? Besides the sex, I mean?'

'We walk.'

'Walk?'

'Yes.'

'Where?'

'Anywhere. Everywhere. It doesn't matter.'

'It will, though, soon. You know that, don't you? It will matter very much where you are going.' Ava twirled. 'It's time to let him go, Lydia.'

'He anchors me,' Lydia whispered.

'Does he? Where?'

'In reality.'

'Tell me about his reality.'

Lydia described the secret, stolen times that she'd shared with Edgar in his lodgings. She gave the sort of detail that made it quite clear that she was well beyond decorum. Ava had never been so consumed with a man that she'd consider being indiscreet in public or emotionally naked in private. She wondered whether she envied Lydia or pitied her.

'Don't confuse reality and poverty,' she warned. Lydia forced out a bright smile, refusing to allow Ava's words to cast a shadow.

'I won't give him up.'

'You made a huge mistake, spending so much time with him. It allowed you to fall in love with him.'

'No, it wasn't like that. I was in love with him from the first instant. Ever since, I've looked to find something I might not love.

299

Not like, even, but there's nothing.' Lydia beamed. 'He's quite perfect.'

Ava scowled. 'Why do you think he chooses to live in the East End? I just can't imagine you among those skinny, litter-strewn streets. All those dreadful, ugly houses, plummeting into squalid rot.' She shivered dramatically.

'Money, I suppose. Lack of it.'

'But he's an officer. He must be paid reasonably. He could afford Earls Court or Hammersmith. It sounds rather mean, the place he lives. I wonder what he does with his money.'

'Well, he doesn't gamble or drink excessively, if that's what you think.'

'I don't know what to think.'

In fact, a sound that Lydia often associated with Edgar was the sound of ice clinking as he downed a whisky, or bottle knocking against glass as something was poured, but she was not prepared to admit as much to Ava, since Ava was being so unexpectedly contradictory. 'Anyway, just about everyone who came home drinks too much,' Lydia added defensively.

'Is he one of those that likes to make a virtue out of poverty?'

Lydia recalled the luxurious gramophone, the gold teacups, and the beautiful brass art deco reading lamp. 'No, I don't think so.'

'Odd.'

'He probably sends his wages home to his family.'

'How very touching. I've seen those places in the East End: simply ghastly. It's a depressing, drab, grimy wasteland, I can't think how you've spent a week there.'

'You've been to the East End?'

'And how is that more shocking than the fact that you have? I do a lot of my charity work there.' Ava thought of the persistent stench of rotting organic matter, sulphur, tobacco and sweaty bodies; the brew of poverty. 'How do you tolerate the smells?'

Lydia thought of their attic room. Warm and fragrant; perfumed by the melting sweetness of roses opening, growing fat and then falling away in a loose sensual movement, like her throwing off her clothes for her lover. She thought of the dense, musky smell of their lovemaking.

'It's authentic, Ava. Sincere.'

'Our reality is true too,' replied Ava sharply.

'It's not. There's nothing real about the endless parties. The masked balls, fancy-dress balls, themed balls. Frankly, it's total balls.' Ava's eyebrows shot up to her hairline, revealing surprise at her friend's use of the colloquialism. She guessed that the sergeant major had taught Lydia this vulgarity and, no doubt, so much more. 'If our world has anything to do with reality, it is only that it exists as its opposite. It's escapism at best, which is why you go to the rallies for women's rights and talk to those terribly poor women about contraception, and why you refuse to marry the rich men who fall at your feet. You want to be in the thick of it too, Ava. You and I never were. Not even during the war.'

'You mean because we didn't lose a lover or a brother?'

'In part. We were protected. We still are. It's not right. You know it isn't.'

Lydia was struggling. She wanted to articulate what she felt with a fiery ferocity, but only recently had she acquired the knack of serious, thoughtful speech and she still needed practice. Now that she'd fallen in love with Edgar, nothing could be the same again. She'd jumped to a higher and more sincere plain; it was not possible for her to feign an interest in what she had previously valued and possessed. All the wealth and history that had been so vital, now somehow – inexplicably – seemed frail and tenuous. Land, art, money, furniture were ephemeral and transient. Love, experience and concepts about humanity and being seemed to be the only authentic truths. It was the opposite of everything she'd ever been taught but she knew it was so. What she felt for Edgar was somehow intrinsically linked with how she felt about justice and injustice, heroism and cowardliness, splendour and ignominy. Love and cruelty.

Ava sighed. 'Darling, I can see perfectly well how a working man might seem exotic and wonderful. We've been brought up with such constraints and controls. He's a novelty. He must be utterly intriguing.'

Lydia did not feel or recognise class distinction when she was with him. It wasn't that. At least not that alone. Perhaps his sensual bulk was largely a result of his manual labour, perhaps his quick mind was a product of necessity, but she did not romanticise his origins. She admired his social mobility. She was relieved that largely he remembered when and when not to pronounce his aitches, that he was confident about the distinctive use of 'them' and 'those' and that he did not allow himself to slip into lazy colloquialism. The fact that he looked marvellous in black tie, white tie and uniform was as important to her as the fact that he knew which to wear when. Besides, his taste in art, music and books, though uneducated, was direct and true. So much more real than many of the opinions she heard inherited and passed around until they wore thin.

What they had was beyond class peculiarities. It seemed right and of the time. 'Indeed, we were raised to value condescension and to be ignorant of people outside our accepted class, but—'

Ava interrupted. 'Well, you've certainly put paid to that. I gather you know him very well now.'

Lydia was exasperated. 'I'm not simply trying to be original. I'm not making a point.'

'What if Lawrence finds out?'

Lydia could not hide her thoughts. One glance told Ava everything.

'Oh, my God, you can't *want* that. I'm not sure he's the sort of man who, through sheer good manners and the force of society, would tactfully ignore an infidelity. He'd be wild.'

'I don't think I'd want him to ignore it.'

'You're going to hurt him.'

'That's not my plan.'

'Maybe not, but you're going to hurt him all the same.'

Lydia was beginning to wonder whether Ava could understand this at all. She was all about theatre: she used emphatic gestures and flourishes when she told stories; she oozed entertainment. Despite her endless love affairs, she had never been in love. Would she know what was real? 'Edgar is not some sort of social experiment.'

Ava raised her eyebrows, communicating her scepticism. 'His

sort of people have a rough deal,' she conceded. 'I always say we should do everything we can, but that doesn't include steadily working one's way through the Kama Sutra with them.'

'I hadn't realised that there were such rigid limits to your philanthropy.' Lydia was pleased to see Ava respond with a smirk. She needed to alter the atmosphere. She needed Ava on side. She couldn't do this entirely alone. She couldn't say what she'd come to say if her friend failed to understand her. She tried another angle. 'You looked heartbroken that Beatrice has accepted the job as a chaperone.'

Ava perched on the arm of a high-backed chair and looked out of the window on to the hazy London street. 'You could tell? I thought I hid it rather well.'

'I doubt Bea noticed but I know that you think it's a shame. I know you don't care if she marries or not; you're sad because if she makes a career out of being a chaperone, she's going to have to attend these endless parties ad infinitum, until she shuffles off to a retirement home.'

'I do agree the endless parties are a bore. I'm not sure when I came to that conclusion. It was so much simpler when one thought it was all about brilliantly shimmering fabrics and sensuous fringed shawls embroidered with Chinese motifs.' Ava smiled weakly. 'I do think Bea could have done more than become a chaperone, although she could have done less too, so it's not a *great* shame. I am actually rather proud of her for finding a solution. Her options are limited.' Ava was more than used to chasing disadvantaged women, imploring them to listen to her and to act on her advice – although normally she did so in dingy and dirty kitchens or draughty and dusty town halls. She recognised a compromise; chalked it up as a triumph. She'd also learned powers of persuasion and tenacity. 'But you, Lydia, you are a countess now. There are no limits for you. Your reality is splendid and wide open.'

'The sumptuousness of it offends me.'

'So now you don't want to be wealthy, is that what you're saying? That's ridiculous.'

For a moment Lydia didn't know what to do. She let the music and the smoke bathe her and then she mumbled, 'The truth is, Ava, I can't go back to it.'

Ava gasped. 'But you have to go back.'

'I want to divorce Lawrence.'

'No. No, Lydia. It's unthinkable.'

'It's all I think of.' Lydia could feel the blood pumping around her body. It was the first time she had articulated this thought. She'd half expected the world to implode when she did so.

'Has he asked you to go away with him?'

Lydia paled, and then shook her head. He'd never asked her to leave Lawrence. It was excruciating and dishonourable to consider that he didn't want her in that complete and utter way, but it was all she could assume. The pity of it was she did not care. Even if he was irreparably damaged and unable to love her the way she loved him – unconditionally, unreservedly – she would still leave Lawrence for him. She'd take whatever Edgar was capable of offering. She glanced shyly at Ava and could see that Ava looked relieved. No doubt she was reassured that this man was perhaps better than she'd feared. She would be thinking that he at least had recognised the impossibility of their situation, even if Lydia refused to acknowledge it. Ava would think that Edgar not asking Lydia to leave was enough to stop Lydia leaving. She was wrong.

'It's unnecessary. You could use your wealth and position to influence. To change things. There's no possibility of you doing the same if you are shacked up with the sergeant major. You know the code. It's rigid. At all costs a scandal must be averted. Within our circle we can, quite frankly, do whatever we like, as long as no one actually talks about it.'

Lydia sighed heavily. She would not budge. She could not. 'But whose code is it? And whose circle? Ava, you are American and your father's title is new. You can't believe this nonsense.'

'And you are from a family who inherited a title during the Civil War, and have married into one that goes as far back as Queen Elizabeth's court. You *must* believe it. What can you be thinking about? You will be cut. You won't have friends or society.'

'Maybe not this society, but there will be people who will want to know us.'

'Dreadful, low people; you'll hate them.'

'I don't think so. Besides, I'll still have you, Ava. You won't feel the need to bend to society's rules, will you?'

'Oh, Lydia.' Lydia felt cold with dread, because for the first time in her life she saw uncertainty in her friend's face. She wondered how strong Ava really was. She was relieved when Ava sighed. 'Certainly, if it comes to that, but I hope it doesn't. Imagine it, Lydia. Be sensible. There will be no racing, no hunting, no more skiing trips to St Moritz. I know you'll miss the warmth of the sun on your back that you get when you sit on a chair in the Riviera.'

'Maybe, but I will have to learn to live without those things.'

'Edgar Trent is the thing you ought to learn to live without.'

'I can't.'

'You're talking nonsense. Think, Lydia,' Ava implored. 'Your relationship as it stands has a thrilling, imprecise glamour. If you live with him, you'll be nothing more than a common or garden mistress. Such dull proximity will kill whatever you have. I can see that it must be seductive, but can it really be enduring?'

'I think it can. I don't understand, Ava, I thought you'd be with me. You've always been so free.'

'I have, yes. But it's not for you.'

'Don't patronise me.'

'Being independent costs, Lydia. You can't afford it.'

'Why must you always reduce everything to money?'

'I'm not talking about money. Not at all. It costs you your reputation and your family. Your safety. You're not the sort of girl who is prepared to pay that price.'

Both women fell silent, exhausted by their exchange. Lydia noticed that the record had finished. She listened to the swooshing and cracking as it continued to turn endlessly and the needle scratched circles.

'It wasn't a horse,' admitted Ava.

'Sorry?'

'It was Lord Harrington.'

'Charlie?'

'Yes.'

'He hurt you?'

'Beat me. Yes.'

'Why?' Lydia was aghast. 'Charlie Harrington has always been so devoted. So besotted.'

'Quite. He got the most ludicrous idea into his head. He wanted to marry me.'

'He has a strange way of showing it.'

Ava shrugged. 'I suppose, you know, he had a very terrible time over in France. He was injured out. Spent months in a san in Wales after being shot in some battle or other; there were so many, it's hard to keep track. They saw such a lot of violence. I think it's become difficult for them to tell right from wrong.'

'And so you are saying this is acceptable? That a man can beat a woman whenever he wants to, because he was a soldier?' Lydia's astonishment manifested itself into fury.

Ava looked steadily at her friend. The bruising somehow seemed more glaring, more ugly to Lydia, now she knew where it had really come from. 'No. I'm not saying that at all. It's totally unacceptable. I'm just trying to warn you how complicated these men are. Having been through what they have. How dangerous.'

Lydia recognised the enormity of Ava's confession. She wasn't one to make a fuss and she hated looking vulnerable. Lydia wanted to run to her and hold her but Ava had closed her eyes. The pain and the shame were private.

'Ava, you're not the sort that one doles out advice to – you're rather more the sort that does the doling – but I do think you should report Charlie.'

'No good would come of it.'

'It would stop him. He'd be punished. That's good enough. You work with these poor women who are hungry and beaten, physically or morally, and you try to change things. You don't want to accept it has to be that way for them, so why would you think it has to be that way for you? Tell your father. Tell Charlie's father. Tell Charlie's wife. Kick up a stink.'

Eventually Ava opened her eyes and stared at Lydia. 'He's unhinged you.'

'Yes, you are right. I'm quite mad about him.' The two women were ostensibly agreeing, yet they were in reality totally opposed. One celebrated the insanity; the other despaired of it.

'You are joining an army of women who have had a dalliance with heartbreak and humiliation.'

'Maybe.'

'Why would you do that?'

'Because I can do no other.'

'You have always had a hungry heart. I suspected as much. I wish you were more sensible.'

'I do too. On some level. I see this will ruin me, but life without him is nothing at all. Better that I am ruined than dead.'

'Don't be dramatic. You wouldn't die without him.'

'Wouldn't I?'

'Goodness, what a shame for you.'

'I don't think it's a shame.' The words were small but determined. Lydia beamed, refusing to dim. Her beam was stronger, broader and braver than ever, as though she was letting it all out. 'Ava, I'm having Edgar's baby.'

43

SARAH HAD EXPECTED Ava's telephone call. She alone had been absolutely certain of Lydia's whereabouts and realised that a catastrophe was imminent, but she had not anticipated the scale. She had not thought that Lydia would be so very awkward about returning to Clarendale, or that she would start to talk of a divorce. She had *never* envisaged a baby. The friends were all agreed that they could not let Lydia have her way in this. She had to be saved from herself. She had spent a week in her lover's lodgings. From Ava's description, Sarah could only assume he lived in a hovel; how could Lydia want to stay there? She'd been stupendously lucky not to have been spotted in all that time, but it was impossible to imagine her luck would continue. As the eldest of the women and the only other one with any experience of being married, Sarah was seen as the best person to try to talk some sense into Lydia.

Lydia was being intractable. She repeatedly stated that she wanted to leave Lawrence and that she wanted to do so immediately. This was nonsense and Sarah refused to contemplate such a thing. She had initially thought that they could ask Lawrence to open up the London house and Lydia could possibly be persuaded to live there if she were allowed to continue to see her lover. Sarah knew of a number of very respectable couples who lived out their entire married lives in this way, quite separately. If the means were available to do so, it was by far the most elegant and acceptable solution, but Sarah soon realised it would not do in this case. There was a baby on the way. Lawrence would have to be made to think it was his, and if this was absolutely impossible – as Lydia insisted – then at the very least the world would have to think it was his. Lydia must return to Clarendale. There was no alternative.

Ava had allowed Lydia to stay with her for another forty-eight hours. She had used that time to summon Dickenson from the country. Friend and loyal maid bundled Lydia into a car and had her driven back to Clarendale. If Ava's account was to be trusted – and Sarah found that she did trust her; it was a rare moment, but they found themselves in agreement – Lydia sat stony and silent for the entire journey. She refused to utter one word until she got out of the car at Clarendale, then she turned to Ava and muttered, 'This is not over, and don't make the mistake of thinking it is.'

Lydia's friends saw the importance of not inflaming the situation. No one wanted hysteria. Although it was paramount to physically remove Lydia from the sergeant major's home, it would be explosive if she was forced to be cooped up with Lawrence with no other company or distraction. They had considered and rejected the idea of her hosting a party. There was the issue of mourning for the old earl; it would be unseemly and, besides, Lydia could not be counted on to behave as expected. She might try to invite Edgar Trent. He might accept. She might drink too much. There would be a scene. Everyone was relieved when Lydia offered to bring the children home to Seaton Manor. Sarah naturally invited her to stay for a few days and Lydia immediately accepted. Lawrence remained blissfully unaware of both his wife's infidelity and her pregnancy.

The summer continued to sweat. Sarah instructed the servants to set out four deckchairs and a large parasol on the patio. Bea had already departed for Oxfordshire to start her work with Georgina Vestry, but Sarah had hopes that Cecily and Samuel might join her and Lydia in the garden. There was a picnic rug and cushions for the children. Sandwiches and Scotch eggs were offered up, along with the promise of jelly and ice cream. Sarah and Cecily and Samuel's children gambolled about the garden trailing sunhats, butterfly nets, hoops, bats and balls, their faces turning pink with exertion, their limbs turning brown with the sun. Sarah wondered whether she ought to insist that the girls, at least, cover up – no one had approved of freckles when she was a child – but she found that she really wasn't vain enough to interrupt their merriment. Despite the lure of home-made lemonade and sunshine, Cecily and Samuel remained indoors, Sarah considered whether she had the energy to go inside and fish them out. An enormous amount of cajoling would be required. She decided against it. If Lydia ever settled for more than a moment, Sarah would like to speak with her, and privacy was necessary for that.

She watched as Lydia flitted about with the children. They were playing catch and Lydia seemed to be eternally 'it'. She chased the elder children with vigour but they still outran her; with the little ones she faked an ineptitude that elicited giggles and whoops of delight. Lydia had always been a beauty, but Sarah now identified something more. She was radiant, joyful and free. Her movements seemed fluid yet powerful. Assured. Her lips were plump and promising, frequently wide apart framing a heartfelt laugh. Her glossy hair sparkled in the sunlight like a halo, which was ironic when one considered her behaviour. It irritated Sarah; she didn't want to be confronted with physical evidence that Lydia's transgression was anything other than ruinous.

The children's nanny finally appeared from the house; no doubt she'd been skulking in the cool kitchen with Cook and the maid, taking advantage of the fact that Lydia was prepared to entertain the children. Her conscience must have got the better of her, or perhaps Cook had asked for some help in preparing supper, which had effectively expelled the indolent nanny; either way, her appearance meant that the children were peeled away from Lydia's care and Lydia had no alternative other than to join Sarah.

'Come and have some lemonade,' Sarah offered.

Lydia paused and looked about her. Sarah knew she'd been avoiding a one-to-one conversation from the moment she arrived; she'd played with the children, sat with Samuel and twice disappeared off to the village in the past twenty-four hours. Lydia looked helpless; she was without options. She flopped into the canvas deckchair and put on her sunhat, pulling it down over her eyes. It was unclear whether she was trying to avoid the sun's glare or Sarah's. Sarah continued to crochet. It wasn't that the table doily was of paramount importance; it was just that she too had a need to try to keep busy, and the constant darting and stabbing of the crochet hook was absorbing. Lydia stared at the growing dangle of lace with something that looked a lot like resentment. Sarah stayed mute. She knew how to bide her time. To wait. It was something they'd all learned during the war. Some called it patience; others called it the art of killing time. Sarah thought it was a horror that they had to kill time, since, after all, that was the most precious thing, but she had become as proficient at doing so as anyone. She'd spent months waiting for Arthur's leave, waiting for letters, waiting for news. Back then, she'd thought waiting was the worst thing, but it wasn't. Enduring was worse. Enduring was waiting's bigger, more ferocious brother. Once Arthur had been killed and Samuel was sent home mutilated, there was nothing for her to do but endure.

They sat silently for ten minutes, with only the click of the needles to distract. Sarah was impressed and frustrated by Lydia's refusal to open the conversation, when the issue so clearly needed discussing. But she had known Lydia since she was born. She did not feel a preamble was necessary.

'You mustn't leave Lawrence.'

Lydia sighed. 'I know what you think.'

Sarah's heart was swollen with envy for everything Lydia had, and her head ached with anger that she might consider chucking it all away.

'Do you honestly think you can divorce Lawrence and then marry this man?'

'Yes.'

'You are insane.' She stated it plainly, as though it was an unequivocal truth. Lydia didn't bother to argue. 'You have everything a girl might dream of. Wealth, status, a husband, security.'

'I know.' Lydia bent her head so that her chin rested on her chest, and Sarah got a sense that she did at least understand what she was threatening to sacrifice.

'A baby on the way,' Sarah added tentatively.

'It's not Lawrence's baby.'

'You can't be sure.'

'I am sure.'

'But Lawrence doesn't have to know.'

Lydia shot Sarah a look that was a complicated mix of shock and pity. 'I don't want to deceive him.'

'He'd have an heir. Your baby would be an earl.'

'My baby might be a girl. Besides, either way, I want him, or her, to grow up with Edgar.'

'And what does the sergeant major have to say on the subject of impending fatherhood?'

'I haven't told him yet,' Lydia admitted.

'You're sure of him?'

'Yes, and I'm sure of myself.'

'But, Lydia, what can Edgar Trent offer?'

Lydia didn't reply. She leaned towards the table and reached for the lemonade glass, beaded with condensation. She gulped down the drink in an unladylike manner. Sarah thought Lydia had become earthier, somehow, since this affair business. She didn't like it.

'What will you do, Lydia? Your father will disinherit you.'

'I'll get a job.'

'What sort of job?'

'I could teach.'

'Don't be silly. Married women are practically barred from most gainful employment. I can't begin to imagine how a divorcée's application might be received. Don't you read the papers? Men, and at a push single women, have the first shout. A land for heroes, not loose women.'

'I don't imagine there are many ex-soldiers rushing to teach dancing or deportment.'

'The baby. How will you work when you have a baby?'

Lydia put her hand on her stomach; it was still flat, no sign of the tiny miracle she was harbouring. A smile played on her lips. Her baby. She shrugged. 'All right, I won't work. I'll stay at home, keep house. I'll nurse the baby. Edgar has employment.'

'I imagine his annual salary is less than you spend on shoes in a season. Do you know how close a bedfellow poverty is to doubt?'

'We're not talking about a reckless hand-to-mouth existence. We'll buy a house in the suburbs.'

'Oh, yes, I can just see you in suburbia. Its streets are beautifully monotonous; every front garden is a replica of its neighbours,' snapped Sarah.

'When did you develop such a condescending attitude?'

'When did you develop such a laissez-faire one?' The women stared at one another; frustration and disappointment stained the air. 'Romantic irresponsibility is intensely attractive, but the reality will be quite different.'

'I love him, Sarah.'

'But you loved Lawrence once.'

'No, not really. Not enough. I don't think so.' Lydia looked regretful.

This wasn't the way Sarah had envisaged the conversation flowing. She didn't understand her own bile and mounting frustration. Why couldn't Lydia see what she had? Why would she dream of throwing it all away? There had been enough destruction. Too much. When would this war stop claiming victims? When would enough be enough? 'Soon he will irk you.'

'How?'

'I don't know precisely. Perhaps his poverty, or his experience. The very things you love about him now.'

'I don't love his poverty; I'm not some deluded heroine. I do wish he was wealthier, but it isn't enough to turn me off.'

Sarah sighed and tried another tack. 'Do you remember your wedding?'

'Of course I do.'

'It was such a celebration.'

'Please don't.' Lydia shifted uncomfortably on her seat.

'You should. You should remember,' Sarah urged. 'You should

think carefully about what you are throwing away. I admired, so heartily, your huge trousseau. The slips and knickers all trimmed with lace, each set fitted into perfumed pads and embroidered with L and L intertwined.'

'Well, Dickenson has a gift with embroidery.'

'Talking of gifts . . . the things you received! A sapphire pendant, a tiara, rings, bracelets, pins, clocks, candlesticks, cufflinks, wine coolers.'

'But does any of it mean anything?'

'First-edition books, ink stands, art.'

'I don't need any of it.'

'Don't you?'

Lydia shook her head. Sarah was beginning to feel desperate. She considered how else she might make her friend understand the gravity of her situation.

'You think he's marvellous because he fought in the war.'

'Yes, yes, I do.'

'He's marvellous because he *survived* the war. That's all. Lawrence survived too. There isn't a real difference.'

'How can you say that? You of all people. After what you lost.'

'I'm trying to save you, Lydia. I have to be honest. Believe me, I don't want to think so much. I know that deviating from the inherited wisdom, in any way, might hurt me. I need the disciplines of faith and valour, otherwise vicious bitterness will run unbridled. Questioning why and what for is a luxury I can ill afford, but for you, my friend, I'll run that risk. There's so much at stake.'

Sarah knew they'd fed her lies. She tried to pretend she didn't know, because it was too much to have lost him and to have been lied to as well, but she did know. They'd returned Arthur's uniform. It was horrifying. It was torn, back and front, where the bullet had entered and left. The khaki colour had all but disappeared; the uniform they returned to her was grey and brown, caked with mud and stiff with blood. It smelt not of him but of earth and death. It was worn and damp. Sarah had itched just having it in her parlour. There was blood on the trousers too, and they were torn at the leg. Cut away by the look of it. She didn't understand that. She'd been told the bullet in the chest was clean and quick, but the uniform suggested three wounds: chest, leg and hip, all on his right-hand side. The torn trousers suggested an examination, maybe attempts at repair, which meant it had taken longer than they'd said for him to die. Sarah didn't understand why they'd sent these garments of horror home. So shabby and vulnerable; that wasn't how they'd been taught to think of their men. And then, a day or two later, a worse thought had struck her. If she had his uniform, what had they buried him in? Was there an immaculate spare? Oh God, she hoped so. But she'd never been able to ask anyone.

The carnage had damned Sarah to live the rest of her life in a world devoid of assurance or sanctuary; a world in which everything and everyone she loved existed under a heavy and dreadful cloak of fearfulness. What if there was another war and her son, John, had to fight? What if Molly died in childbirth, or they were both lost in an automobile accident? Love was continually besmirched by the threat of death. Joy and pleasure were without duration. She longed for a sense of security. Since losing Arthur, she'd only ever had the briefest of hints that it existed anywhere, and that was when she was at Clarendale, in Lawrence's safe, steady and practical company. How could Lydia even consider giving that up?

'Do you remember the day I received the telegram?' Both women received telegrams on a regular basis. News of births, party invitations and train delays were all communicated this way; however, they knew exactly which telegram Sarah referred to. Some things were enormous.

'Yes, I do.'

'I was on my way out of the house. Delivering jam to a neighbour or some such.'

'Right.'

'I was wearing my blue taffeta. The one I'd bought on our trip together to Paris, before, when one could buy pretty frocks.'

'I know the dress you mean. I've always admired it.'

'Do you know what I thought, after the postboy brought the news?' Sarah met her friend's gaze; Lydia moved her head an infinitesimal amount from left to right. 'I thought, if only I'd left the house an hour earlier. Or ten minutes earlier. If I hadn't been there to receive him.'

'He'd have left the telegram. The news would have been there when you got home.'

'Yes, but I'd have been a wife, with a husband, for a day longer; the children would have had a father a day longer. We'd have had an extra day even if he hadn't. Do you see?'

Once he was dead, she'd had nothing to do. Even though the war had continued to rage, for her it was all over. The worst had happened. It was, at least, the end of trepidation, although it was the beginning of profound and unrelenting grief. An unfathomable, abolishing void. She was swallowed by a sense of walking in a dense fog, which hid all there was to see and stifled all there was to hear. Her grief was aloof and rigid.

'I'd do anything to buy another day, another hour, ten more minutes. I'd give up every possession I own; I'd sell my soul. I'd certainly get over a ridiculous notion that my man had somehow dodged it.'

Lydia looked saddened and sorry. 'It's not Lawrence I want to buy time with. You say you'd give up every possession.'

'Yes.'

'But you think it's strange that I'm prepared to do so.'

'I'm saying I'd give it all up for Arthur. Arthur was my husband.'

'Arthur was the man you loved.'

Sarah pulled her eyebrows together, causing her forehead to fold like a fan as she expressed her displeasure. 'It won't do.'

'But it is.'

'Is what?'

'It is what it is. And it's impossible to be anything else.'

Sarah tutted, vexed. 'You must hate yourself.'

'Sometimes, but never when I'm with him.'

44

A VA HAD HAD a long day. She'd spent it at Marie Stopes's mothers'
clinic in Holloway. The family planning clinic had opened
(with much hullabaloo) in March, and Ava worked there in a
voluntary capacity, as a secretary, two or three days a month. She
told herself that the voluntary position allowed her an advantageous
degree of flexibility so she could pursue other interests; truthfully
she'd have liked a more permanent role. Not that she needed an
income, but she enjoyed being at the forefront of this social change;
it was so unquestionably useful. However, as she wasn't a qualified
doctor or nurse, there wasn't a suitable post for her, especially as,
unlike practically every other establishment in Britain, the family
planning clinic preferred to hire married women. If they employed
single women to officially advise on contraception, they ran the
risk of attracting more adverse publicity. The secretaries were seen
by many as powdered hussies and were often described as 'no
better than they ought to be'. Ava would have confronted any
controversy – some thought she courted it – but Dr Stopes and
her husband felt differently and would not make her a permanent
offer. Besides, the clinic had not been the roaring success Dr Stopes
had anticipated. The numbers that attended were modest. Since
March, just ninety women had sought advice on contraception
and fourteen more had wanted advice on how to become pregnant.
With an average of just one or two clients a day, the time spent
at the clinic could drag. Ava always managed to read *The Times*
from cover to cover.

It had been impossible, considering the environment, for Ava not to ponder on Lydia's situation. She was only a few weeks pregnant; she'd missed just one of her monthlies. Ava's first thought on hearing this was that perhaps Lydia wasn't pregnant at all; she was hardly eating at the moment and rather excitable; that sort of thing could affect a woman's cycle. But Lydia had excitedly told her about morning sickness and tender breasts. It did seem as though she might have caught. Ava knew of enough pregnancies that didn't make term. She wondered whether Lydia's would. Whether it was for the best or not. Edgar's son, Lawrence's heir. It was an age-old problem and not an insurmountable one, providing Lydia could be persuaded to be sensible about the whole question.

After work, the private detective she'd hired dropped by to debrief her on his early findings. Ava wasn't sure what she was looking for exactly, but she'd know it when she found it. A deterrent. A tangible, irrefutable reason for Lydia to walk away. This business between Lydia and the sergeant major could never work, because all they had to keep them together was love, and in Ava's experience love was the epitome of ephemeral. The sooner it was closed off the better. Disappointingly, the detective – a short, clever, far too worldly-wise sort of man – didn't reveal an awful lot that she didn't already know. Lydia had told her that Edgar Trent hailed from Middlesbrough, the son of a shopkeeper; he had opted to work in the shipyards and had enlisted the day he turned eighteen, just three months after it had all begun. His war history was familiar to her and rumours of his heroics were verified by army records, as was his rank and his salary. He paid his rent a month in advance; he was never late. He had no recorded debts or loans. He did have a bank account, and after making a discreet call to a very dear friend of hers who was on the board at Lloyds, Ava discovered that it was a very modest savings account into which he paid a meagre amount every month. The difference between what he earned and his obvious outgoings was considerable. Ava considered whether this man was, after all, truly a saint and sent a sizeable sum home to his parents each month. She really couldn't find anything disappointing about him.

'Did you follow him?' She felt grubby asking the question.

'Yes, it's all logged here.' The private detective slid a brown leather notebook across the table. He kept his chubby fingers on it for a moment longer than necessary, leaving sweaty prints. Ava waited until they'd vanished before she picked up the book. No doubt the detective had formed theories as to why she might be interested in the sergeant major; he probably assumed she was compromised. Ava didn't care. She was entirely focused on stopping Lydia spinning into a catastrophe.

The log was strangely exciting. Although there were no lurid details – simply a record of Trent's comings and goings – Ava felt a wave of intimacy as she read that he left his lodgings at half past seven in the morning, walked to his office for eight, bought a paper from a street vendor on the way. Knowing that the man had eaten fried fillet of lemon sole at Maison Lyons, Marble Arch, at lunchtime was somehow oddly personal. She couldn't help but imagine his strong jaw and mouth masticating. No wonder Lydia was helpless.

'What do you mean by this, "Some animosity with waitress"? Was it to do with the bill?'

'No, miss. I don't think so. I was sat at a discreet distance, so unfortunately I could not hear the details of the conversation, but the disagreement happened before the bill was presented.'

'Was it to do with the food quality, then?'

'No. I'm pretty certain the gentleman was happy enough with his food. Didn't leave a scrap on the plate. I got the feeling the aggravation was altogether to do with a different source. It looked personal to me.' The detective lingered over the word *personal* in a distinctly unsavoury way.

'Did it now? Did you talk to the waitress and ask her what it was about?'

He licked his lips. 'She wouldn't talk to me, said she was too busy, but I got her name. Ellie Edwards.'

There was nothing else of note in the forty-eight-hour account of Sergeant Major Trent's activity. Ava wrote out a cheque and gave the man cash for expenses. She instructed him to continue his surveillance and had the maid show him out. He left behind him a slight whiff of indecency that made her want to throw open the windows and let in fresh air.

The next day Ava caught a cab to Lyons on Marble Arch. The maître d' insisted on showing her to a table himself. He picked one in the centre of the vast room so as to show her off to as many of the other customers as possible; this frequently happened to Ava and she barely noticed. Today she was all grace and charm; she smiled profusely and then asked if she could speak to Ellie Edwards.

'Is there a problem, miss?'

'Not at all.' The maître d' waited for further explanation, Ava beamed at him but refused to elaborate.

He flushed and then muttered, 'She's serving that table over there. I'll send her to you the moment she's finished.'

'Would you? You are too, too good.'

Ellie Edwards was a chubby, confident-looking girl with fashionably bobbed hair. Ava noticed, and appreciated, her carefully tweezered brows and scarlet lipstick; she wore her short uniform with aplomb.

'Mr Walsh said you asked after me, miss.' Some girls of Ellie Edwards's social class were intimidated by women of Ava's sort, and most women, of whatever class, were intimidated by Ava in particular. However, Ellie did not show any sign of excessive courtesy or dissolve into desperate kowtowing; she stood with her back straight and her chin jutting out. Her stance was assertive, almost combative. Ava recognised a woman who could hold her own.

'Yes, do sit down.' She gestured to the other seat at her table.

'I'm working, miss. We're not allowed to sit with the customers.'

'Perhaps you can make an exception.'

The waitress seemed torn. She was reluctant to acquiesce to the wealthy woman's suggestion, and Ava guessed that she didn't want to appear too obliging. There were a number of discontented workers with this sort of attitude, even in the service industry – especially in the service industry – and Ava was used to encountering it. On the other hand, the girl clearly relished the opportunity to flout her boss's rules by sitting with a customer. In the end she sat down but refused to pull her chair right up to the table.

'What do you want me for?' she asked. 'You're not a customer of mine. I always remember my customers.'

Ava smiled brightly, although she felt a distinct lack of warmth for the chippy young woman. 'I'm sure you do. I imagine you are an excellent waitress. I'm not here to complain about anything.'

'You're not?'

'No.'

'What then?'

The lie slipped effortlessly off Ava's tongue. She never had any misgivings about ruthlessly obliterating the truth if expedient. 'My brother served under Sergeant Major Trent of the Fifth Battalion Yorkshire Regiment. I'm trying to track him down. I have something I want to give him. I was told you might know him.'

This sort of request was commonplace and had been for many years. Women were always tracking down men who had fought with their men. Sometimes there were gifts to give; other times answers were sought. How? Where? Did he suffer? There was an unwritten rule that one ought to cooperate as much as possible, in order to help people find peace and some sort of comfort.

'I don't think I know a Sergeant Major Trent.'

'Oh?' Ava paused.

'This thing you have to give him. Is it valuable?' The waitress couldn't hide the avaricious glint in her eye.

'Yes,' Ava said, calmly luring her in. 'Very. Do you know him now?'

'I should say I do.' Ellie Edwards showed no qualms about completely contradicting herself. She drew her chair up to the table and leaned close to Ava. Ava felt the girl's warm breath on her face and smelt her perfume, which was sickly-sweet and cheap. 'You can give whatever it is to me and I'll see he gets it.'

'No, I can't do that. I need to speak to him, deliver it into his hands.'

'You can trust me.'

'Without a doubt.' Not a bit.

'He's my husband.'

'Your wh— I'm sorry. Did you say husband?'

Ellie nodded. 'I don't wear a ring at work because the boss is one of the old sorts. He doesn't like married women working. Thinks we should all be at home. That's not for me. I'd be bored out my skull, I would. You won't go saying anything, will you, miss? You don't want to get me into trouble.'

'No, I'm not going to cause you any trouble. You are quite sure we're talking about the same fellow?'

'Edgar, Edgar Trent? Tall, dark, from Middlesbrough?'

'Yes.'

'He's my husband all right. I'm Ellie Trent, I am. So if you have anything to pass on to him, I'm good for it. I'm your girl.' She giggled, showing a youthful excitement that had been lacking thus far in the conversation. 'Or should I say, I'm *his* girl. Give me what you have for him and I'll pass it along.'

'No. That won't do. Give me your address and I'll bring it to him myself.'

'Well, I'm on Hoxton Lane, number one hundred and nineteen B, off the Marylebone Road, but he doesn't spend every night with me. There's another girl who shares and sometimes he stays at the officers' club.'

'Will he be with you tonight?'

'Maybe. For sure tomorrow.'

'I see.'

'Are you all right, miss? You look very pale.' The young woman was being solicitous now that she believed there was something about this encounter that she'd benefit from. It wasn't a character flaw so much as a consequence of a poverty-stricken upbringing.

'I'm fine, absolutely fine.'

'Sometimes these things can be a bit draining, can't they? Sort of shocking. People say be careful what you wish for nowadays.'

Ava stared at the girl. For a moment she didn't understand how she knew so much, but then she realised that Ellie was referring to Ava's fictional hunt for her brother's friend.

'Yes, yes, they do. Very careful indeed.'

45

'I'M SORRY, CECILY, I didn't mean to disturb you. I'm looking for Sarah.' Actually, Lydia was not looking for Sarah; she'd been hoping to find empty the small room that the Polwarths rather euphemistically called the library. She imagined Sarah was in the drawing room or the garden, and she was avoiding her. Lydia needed to be alone. She wanted to sit quietly among the two cases that held shelves of dusty but familiar books and think. She was sick of hearing Sarah's arguments against divorce, she was sick of being at the receiving end of concerned and anxious glances and sighs. It was unnerving. She was resolute that her firm love for Edgar could brave the onslaught of disapproval, but she didn't enjoy wading through the disgust.

She was in love with Edgar. That was her beginning and end. Nothing else was important or relevant. No one seemed to disagree with that point; the wrangling and conflicts were about what that meant. To Lydia it meant she could no longer live with Lawrence. That she had to give up her life of extreme wealth and privilege and go to Edgar as soon as possible. She could not imagine how else she would continue to exist.

Being with Lawrence was torture now. His voice, his touch, his breath repelled her. It wasn't his fault, it was hers, but still it was a fact. Despite the constant disapproval and dissuasion Lydia endured here with Sarah, she knew it was preferable to returning home. Simply being alone with him was unthinkable; even though at Clarendale there were more rooms than she'd ever managed to count, she knew she would still feel trapped. A prisoner. When she looked at Lawrence, she was plagued by guilt and shame and disappointment. Guilt and shame were the usual accessories of an adulteress, she imagined. Women like her were expected to bear that much. It was the disappointment that overwhelmed her. Disappointment that she hadn't managed to stay in love with him. Disappointment that he didn't deserve her to. She could not imagine eating with him or sitting with him, let alone sleeping with him. The thought of his naked body, which she'd been familiar with for eight years, seemed alien and nauseating.

And Edgar? What she felt for him was the absolute opposite. She was consumed by him. She felt comforted and yet simultaneously excited by him. He was the source of all her eroticism and gave meaning to her womanliness. He charged her up and yet he was her peace and heart's ease. She had to go to him.

'I'll go and see if Sarah is in the garden,' lied Lydia. 'I don't want to disturb you.'

'It's not a problem. Come in. I'll send for some tea,' said Cecily.

'Oh, no, I couldn't possibly. I shouldn't . . .' Lydia wasn't confident that she was in the frame of mind that would allow her to make polite small talk, and whilst, technically, Seaton Manor was Samuel and Cecily's home now, Lydia never thought of Cecily as its hostess. Lydia had been visiting this house since she was a child, to play in the nursery with Sarah and Beatrice. Cecily was perfectly lovely; indeed, before Sammy was injured, she'd been bright and buoyant, a welcome addition to their group, but now she was often depressed and difficult. Small talk was impossible because no one knew what to say to her any more.

'Do,' Cecily urged.

Lydia noticed that Cecily had something on her lap that she had clearly been involved with before she was interrupted. It was the huge leather family photo album. Lydia abruptly remembered that her problems were not the only ones in the world. During the war, compassion had been rationed; the individuality of loss was buried beneath the obscenely large numbers, and they'd all but forgotten the habit of sympathising. Lydia felt enormous pity for Cecily. A lost half-soul, with a lost half-life and a lost half-husband.

'Tea would be lovely. If I'm really not disturbing you.'

'Not at all.'

Lydia carefully closed the door behind her and then chose to sit on the sofa next to Cecily.

'You're looking at old photos?'

'I do, from time to time. In here, on my own. Not too often. I don't allow myself that.'

'Let me see.' Lydia carefully took the heavy album from Cecily and laid it on her lap. She turned the stiff card pages and the wisps of tracing paper flapped in between, wafting like a bride's veil in the breeze. First there were photographs of Sarah, Samuel and Beatrice as children. There were formal ones that had been taken in a studio; the girls were dressed in white embroidered frocks and enormous ribbons almost the size of their heads, and Samuel wore a sailor suit. In the more informal shots, taken on holidays in the Mumbles in Wales and then later on the beaches in the South of France, the long-ago children wore woollen swimsuits and were building sandcastles. There were photos of Sarah as a debutante, serene and joyful, and Beatrice as a debutante, awkward and lumpy. Then Lydia turned a page and discovered Sarah and Arthur's wedding photo. A copy of this photo was on the chimneypiece in the drawing room, and Lydia, who had been a bridesmaid, had one of her own, so was familiar with it. It was a group shot of the entire bridal party: a mass of white lace, enormous hats, crêpe georgette and roses. The men wore moustaches, serious expressions and dark suits that seemed a fraction too large even though they were often made to measure. On the next page was Samuel and Cecily's wedding photo.

'You looked beautiful.' Lydia had attended the wedding and had thought she remembered it well, but she gasped now, faced with the evidence of Cecily and Samuel's youth and vibrancy. It was the fashion and accepted as the correct thing to do, to look at the camera for these momentous shots. Unusually, this bride and groom were staring at one another. Devoted, delighted, expectant, exhilarated. It was 1911; no one had ever heard of the Archduke Franz Ferdinand of Austria, and most would have struggled to pinpoint the Balkans on a map.

Lydia forced herself to keep turning, but part of her wished she'd never picked up the album. She knew what it was inevitably marching towards. Death and disfigurement. There were so many similar family albums all over the country, all over the world. It was sickening and desperate.

There were photos of John as a chubby baby, bouncing on Sarah's knee, Arthur proudly standing behind. Then another of Molly on Sarah's knee and toddler John holding his father's hand; this time Arthur was in uniform. It was the last photo of Arthur in the album. There were similarly composed shots of Cecily and Samuel too. Cecily, round and proud on a chair, a bouncing baby on her lap, her husband standing tall by her side. First the boy's christening, then the girl's. The third child, Jimmy, was conceived while Samuel was on leave. There was no photograph of that child's christening, because by the time the ceremony took place, Samuel had been blown in two and what was left of him lay recuperating in a hospital. Cecily hadn't the energy or inclination to arrange a photographer to shoot just her and her children. Perhaps she hadn't wanted the event to be committed to paper. Maybe she couldn't stand the thought of the film and image being dipped and treated in a series of chemical baths, the fixer making the image permanent and light-resistant, undeniable evidence of how her life was.

The first year of the baby's life had been so terribly hard. Cecily rarely had the chance to push the perambulator; she had to leave that to the nanny, as her hands were full pushing Samuel's chair.

Lydia flipped back to a photo of Arthur and Samuel standing in the village, near the bandstand. She knew the village well enough to place the informal shot accurately; it had been taken from the doorway of the post office. Both men were smoking and laughing. They looked relaxed; their uniforms were pristine, unused. Their shoes shone. Unlike their prospects. They were well fed and rosy. Gosh, yes, those public schoolboys had rushed at it.

At least, most of them. So desperate to validate their pampered existences. What an invigorating impression of reason and purpose they must have felt, at least until the very moment their heads or limbs were blown off.

Lydia had been there the day the photo was taken; it was one of the recruitment drive days. As officers, Arthur and Samuel had encouraged the village men and boys to sign up for the King's sovereign. Lydia remembered the strapping men and their sons, who scribbled their names or marked a cross. They wore English apples in their cheeks and carried farm boys' stockiness. English milk, wheat and meat had fed these boys, made their shoulders wide, and the English sun and wind had tanned their arms. The English generals sent them to their deaths. They laughed and joked, not taking anything too seriously, certainly not themselves, certainly not the war. There had been a brass band and bunting. Clever, ambitious young men stood side by side with the sly and the ninnies. All sorts of men. They accepted their situation with equal poise and equal dedication.

'We lined the streets and waved flags as they went to their deaths,' muttered Lydia.

'What were we supposed to do? Let them go without a cheer?' Cecily sighed.

'But we acted as though it was a party.'

'We didn't know. We can't blame ourselves for what we didn't know.'

Lydia patted Cecily's hand. 'You are very brave.'

'No, I'm neither brave nor cowardly. I'm resigned, which is something much more horrible.'

'It must be very difficult.' Lydia hated herself for uttering such an understatement, but she had to say something.

Cecily sighed so forlornly that Lydia thought she might expunge every breath in her body. 'Sometimes,' she whispered, 'I wish it was over.'

'For him?'

'Or me.' Cecily trembled under the weight of her enormous, brutal confession. 'You see, it's impossible for anything to be as it was before. He can't enjoy anything and so I can't either. He's in so much pain. Did you hear the thunderstorm last night?'

'Yes.'

'We needed it. The rain has washed the fields, and this morning I noticed how sweet and fertile everything smells. For a moment I stared at the sky, blue and firm, a broad and strong backdrop for the puffy clouds to bounce upon, and I felt glad to be alive. Joyful. I wanted to slip outside and run on the wet grass, race so fast that the air would explode in my lungs, but then I thought of Sammy and I hated myself. It's a betrayal to be glad, for even a moment.'

'No it isn't,' said Lydia gently.

Cecily turned to her looking dissatisfied, as though she was saddened by her friend's lack of empathy or acknowledgement. It must have cost her to admit something so pitiful.

'I know about your officer.'

'Did Sarah tell you?'

'I heard her and Beatrice talking a week or so ago.'

'I suppose you condemn me, like everyone else.'

Cecily didn't answer the question; instead she asked, 'What's he like?'

'How do you mean?'

'I mean, what's he really like? Why him? I've known you for years now, Lydia, and it's not like you to be inappropriate or reckless. Why now? Why him?'

'From the moment I met him, everything changed. I didn't even want it to particularly, but it did. I realised he was everything. Everything that was important. Now, when I'm not with him, even for an hour, let alone a day or a week, there's a feeling of emptiness where his exciting and thought-provoking presence has been.' Cecily nodded slowly. 'You talk of how I used to be, but I feel completely altered. I have no way of accessing the woman I was before him, because she wasn't really there anyhow. She was, *I* was, half formed. And now, now I don't know how to go back to the old world. I don't even want to. It's all pretend occupation and random and wretched chatter.'

Cecily reached out and took hold of Lydia's hand. 'Is it deep, and hard? Almost painful but breathtaking at the same time? When he's with you? When he's in you?' she asked breathlessly.

'Yes,' Lydia whispered, relieved to give the words life at last.

'And you have to have him. All the time. Is that how it feels?'

'It is.'

'Oh, how wonderful. I remember that.' Cecily's eyes sparkled with the threat of tears. 'I understand.'

Lydia closed her eyes for a moment and breathed in a sense of release. Her friends had fought her so ferociously on this; telling her that he was unreliable and untouchable. Insisting that a lifestyle was to be valued over life itself. Finally, someone understood her.

'Like you, I've changed beyond recognition, beyond my own memory. I can't remember her.' Cecily picked up the solid album and pointed to her wedding photo. 'I can't remember that bride who existed in a blur of soft edges and misty romance. For her there was only music, dancing, laced undergarments and Sammy. Sammy in his masculine glory. She was so curious, so vital. So alive. He was all that too! I was just discovering him. My thighs ached with the exploration. Now it's my back that aches, pulling him off chairs and out of bed, lowering him down in the water closet and into that damned chair. My back aches and my heart. You've sat with him, Lydia. You know how it is. Does he look or sound like a hero to you?' Lydia made an effort to stay absolutely still. She could not risk uttering a comment. Sammy looked nothing like a hero, or even any sort of a man. He was a half. 'Don't accept what they've left you with, Lydia. You don't have to. If you want your sergeant major, go and get him. Take everything you can, while you can. Do it for those of us who are resigned to our destinies. Be greedy. Be alive.'

46

JANICE DICKENSON WAS sick with fear. Her hands shook and she could feel a small line of sweat trickle down her back. Her maid's uniform was often uncomfortably airless, designed for modesty and propriety rather than comfort, so she had suffered in the long sleeves and dark colour this scorching summer, but the heat she felt now was less to do with the temperature and more to do with an overwhelming sense of anguish and panic. Her mistress was going to ruin them both.

Miss Lydia (because that was how Janice referred to her mistress in her head, having never got used to Lady Chatfield, let alone the Countess of Clarendale) had returned home from Mrs Sarah Gordon's place in a hurry. Janice had thought this was a good sign. She thought the friends had done their duty by persuading her mistress to remember her responsibilities. She thought this silly gadding about had come to an end. Then Miss Lydia had asked her to send a telegram to Sergeant Major Trent, as a matter of extreme urgency.

Can't live without you Stop I'll meet you at yours Stop 2 o'clock Thursday Stop

This was bad. Wrong. Janice wasn't a fool; months ago she had begun to suspect Miss Lydia was having an affair. On countless occasions she had fastened her mistress's brassiere and dropped a silk camisole over her breasts; she had carefully drawn silk stockings over her mistress's feet and smoothed them up her legs. She'd listened to her conversations, drawn her baths, sent her telegrams and letters. She knew every inch of her. She'd been disappointed, but not surprised. Miss Lydia had always been a bit too pretty and pouty – rarely did any good come from that – and the sergeant major was glorious! Irresistible. Janice had seen him for herself, and he was undoubtedly the sort of man who took your breath away. Could steal your heart away. Besides, for the upper crust, affairs and grand passions seemed to be par for the course. Janice knew as much. They were all at it. Her own sort didn't go in for that type of thing so much. Admittedly, there would always be fellas who drank too much and got what they could on the side, but her own mother, sisters and friends would never think of it. They were all too exhausted – with work and childbearing – to scrub up enough to try it on with some other bloke. The rich were idle. That was the problem. They had too much time on their hands, and love affairs seemed to be their greatest distraction. Indeed, Janice thought just about everything else they did was simply a prelude to their affairs, or a way of facilitating them. The parties, the riding, the hunting; it was all about sex in the end. Janice believed there would be a damned sight fewer disruptive goings-on among the upper classes if they only had to scrub their own back steps or wash their own sheets, come to that.

She had sent the telegram. She'd had no choice. Miss Lydia had asked for a receipt and, besides, even if she hadn't sent it, her mistress would have found some other way of getting word to this man. If she had sent the message with another maid then there would be sure to be trouble. The others weren't as careful as Janice was herself. Gossips. No loyalty. No understanding of which side of the bread the butter was on. Besides, she'd thought the telegram referred to just another rendezvous. One of a number. Illicit, but not a catastrophe. Now she understood it was so much more.

Lydia had spent the day rushing around her room, collecting up clothes and shoes, books and jewels. She'd barked unclear, constantly changing instructions at Janice as to what should be packed.

'How long will we be in London, my lady? A week?'

'Maybe more.' Lydia was vague, flustered. She paused from rooting through her tray of make-up and turned to her maid. 'Do you know what, Dickenson? I don't think you need come. Not at first.'

'At first, my lady?' Janice was confused. The travelling was the arduous aspect of going to London. There was interaction with the chauffeur, train conductor and ticket inspector at this end. It was always bothersome, sometimes fearful. Then when they arrived in London, the transfer of luggage had to be handled, taxis had to be hailed. Those were Janice's jobs.

'I shall send for you,' added Lydia.

'Send for me?'

'Yes, in a week or two. In fact, I'll send for all of this.' Her mistress gestured around the room; she looked fraught for an instant and then uninterested. 'Just pack the essentials.'

'Essentials?'

'Day clothes, underwear, shoes. Flat ones.'

'Won't you need any evening wear, my lady? Nothing glamorous?' Janice was shocked.

'Well, maybe one or two, but try to keep it light. I really can't carry it all alone.' Then, almost to herself, as she started to root through her bedside cabinet, she added, 'Besides, where would it go? What use will it be?'

Janice thought of the vast wardrobes in the London house on Eaton Square and couldn't imagine there might ever be an issue of storage. Then it dawned on her: her mistress wasn't going to Eaton Square.

Lydia continued to rush around the room. Despite her affirmations that she wouldn't need to dress glamorously, she pulled out her turquoise satin dress, the one that had what Janice had once heard Miss Ava Pondson-Callow describe as an 'almost vulgar amount' of diamanté beading, and threw it in the suitcase. She then selected a champagne-coloured two-piece. The lace chemise bodice was lined with silk and fell to a ruched dropped waistband. The skirt was a mass of accordion pleats in silver and gold bands, hemmed with georgette. She chose blue shoes with a heel. By the time she was fully dressed, she looked perhaps more stunning than Janice had ever seen her before. It was the smile.

'I need you to be an angel, Dickenson. See that the earl gets this envelope, this evening. It's probably best you take it to him after he's had supper but before he has his port. Don't forget, will you?' Janice would have taken offence – had she ever, in all her years of service, forgotten to deliver a message or complete a task to the best of her ability, politely, efficiently and discreetly? No, she had not – but then Miss Lydia pulled her into a tight and unprecedented hug. 'You'll be fine, Janice,' she whispered. 'Don't worry about a thing. I've managed all that for you. I promise.'

The physical intimacy was surprising enough. The words were horrifying.

From a window on the second floor, Janice watched the countess scurry to the waiting Rolls-Royce. From her viewpoint she could see the brilliant green lawns where she had often witnessed guests sprinkled in indolence enjoying the hospitality of the old earl. Some would sit under the shade of the trees; others would take a stroll or play croquet. In her mind she could hear their laughter and the knock of the croquet mallets. She'd often watched other people having fun, while enviously living a fine life by proxy and longing for the day when Lydia would become countess and Janice herself would be one step closer to this magical, glorious world. How could Miss Lydia take it all for granted? Stop seeing the charm and advantage?

With trembling fingers Janice opened the letter.

47

LYDIA HAD ONE stop to make before she relinquished all her influence and power in the society she had grown up in. She had telephoned ahead and arranged to meet Sir Peter Pondson-Callow at Claridge's. She did momentarily wonder what people might think if she was spotted at a hotel with Sir Peter, an infamous, although ageing, philanderer, and then she remembered it hardly mattered; it was only a question of days until her reputation would be beyond redemption. There would not be a charge of sluttish behaviour that was too low or too outlandish to be tossed her way. People who had done worse and believed in nothing would hoist and fly flags of morality and outrage. She knew it would be like that. It was her choice and she was content. Funny, but universal condemnation felt a lot like freedom.

Although Lydia was prompt, Sir Peter was already waiting for her when she arrived. He was impeccable in a tailor-made suit and ludicrously expensive shoes, yet he looked anxious, and a little bit smaller and wider than Lydia remembered him to be. His almost frightening good looks had long since mellowed into an air of distinction, but today, as a result of Lydia calling and saying she needed to talk about Ava as a matter of urgency, he appeared somewhat careworn and less suavely debonair than usual. Lydia was pleased; she needed him to care. He had to.

His hospitality was, as usual, generous to the point where it was bordering on the oppressive. As their meeting was at eleven forty-five, Sir Peter was unsure what they should eat or drink, and yet he felt responsible for the young woman's sustenance. He offered croissants, fruit salad and salmon and eggs; when Lydia demurred and said it was too late for breakfast, he suggested they pick something from the à la carte menu. Lydia politely declined, protesting that it was too early for a formal meal.

'A drink, at least.'

'Yes, that would be lovely.'

'Coffee? Sherry? A cocktail?'

'I'll take an elderflower cordial, please.'

He seemed relieved that she'd finally accepted something and swiftly gave instructions to the waiter who had been hovering, desperate to offer service, as Sir Peter was known for rewarding with big tips.

In a display of manners triumphing over desire, Sir Peter also ordered an elderflower cordial, but when it arrived he caught Lydia's expression and asked, 'Am I likely to need something stronger?'

'Perhaps,' she replied, her voice hinting at an apology.

'Bring me a whisky,' he instructed the waiter curtly. 'Single malt, nothing before the turn of the century.'

They were seated in a quiet corner of the hotel lobby, away from the through traffic that trailed up and down the grand staircase and to and from the bar and restaurant. Lydia and Ava had often partied in the ballroom; Lydia imagined she could hear echoes of Gershwin and jazz, the tap of heels stepping out the foxtrot, the Charleston. It had been a bold move calling Sir Peter, but Lydia was certain that she was doing the right thing. She had at last found her voice.

'So, Lady Clarendale, to what do I owe the pleasure of this invitation?' Pondson-Callow was a man who liked to get to the point. His time was valuable; he made sure people knew as much, but he knew it above everyone else.

'Lydia, please.' Lydia sipped her cordial and wondered how best to phrase it. She knew enough about men to realise that Sir Peter was the sort she had to captivate; not in a sexual sense – being such a close friend of his daughter's immunised her against his attentions – but he demanded entertainment from everyone he spoke to. He expected women to be decorative and purposeful;

that was the reason Ava was such a hit. He'd always had high expectations. 'I'm here because I want to ask you: what do you think of your daughter?'

'That's a bizarre question.'

'Impertinent, too. I realise as much.'

Sir Peter drew back his shoulders. 'I think she is an especially impressive young woman,' he announced with pride and confidence.

'Agreed. I'm quite sure you love her,' added Lydia. She wanted to ingratiate herself, win him over; at the moment he looked solid and defensive. It was unlikely he'd ever had to negotiate such a strange and unwieldy conversation before. He reminded her of an ancient medieval king. The sort who had kicked, clawed and scrambled into power, then ruled sternly yet wisely; the sort who had never forgotten what he came from and was always prepared to jump back into action and go into battle, if necessary.

'Is my daughter in some sort of trouble?' asked Sir Peter, with an apprehensive sigh.

'Yes.'

He swirled the amber-coloured whisky around the glass and avoided Lydia's eye. Then he lowered his voice and coughed. 'Is there a child?'

Lydia was startled. For a moment she thought Sir Peter was talking about her own baby, and nearly blurted out the wonderful truth before she understood his meaning.

'No.'

'Thank God for that.' His relief was palpable; it was a difficult, indelicate conversation. Lydia could only imagine how her own father was going to receive the news she would have to deliver soon; she didn't dare think of that right now, and shoved the thought aside. It was important to stay on track. 'Not that I'm suggesting that it's even a possibility,' Sir Peter blustered, recovering. The Pondson-Callows weren't the sort to leave themselves exposed for a moment longer than necessary.

Lydia needed to be frank, so instead of accepting the posturing cover-up Sir Peter was offering, she pursued the truth of the issue, the truth of Ava.

'Ava is always extremely careful about that sort of thing. She doesn't take risks.'

Colour flooded into Sir Peter's face. Whether it was a blush of embarrassment or the stain of rage, Lydia couldn't be sure. However, it was clear that he was prepared to be frank when he muttered, 'Quite. Quite,' and took a large gulp of whisky, practically draining the glass.

'You say she's especially impressive.'

'Yes.'

'I'd say she's a brilliant woman.' Sir Peter nodded. 'What are your plans for her?'

'My plans for her?' He laughed, seemingly amused by the suggestion. 'Lydia dear, you're her best friend. You know her better than anyone; what makes you think I have any ability – or right, come to that – to plan for her?'

'But someone must.'

'I've never thought so.'

Lydia put her glass down on the silver coaster on the gleaming polished table. Looking directly at him she said, 'You may have heard rumours that she was close to Lord Harrington.' She knew that he'd understand the word 'close'. Sir Peter had heard whispers, though no one had dared to explicitly mention the intrigue to his face. He was a formidable and inestimably wealthy man; his sort rarely heard bad news directly, so few had the guts to deliver it.

'Are they still close?'

'No, she tired of him.'

'I wonder when she will be attracted to a single man. When she will settle down.'

'That's just it, I don't think she will.'

'Are you trying to tell me . . .' Sir Peter seemed at once astonished and horrified. His cheeks puffed in and out in panic; he looked like a fish that had inadvertently jumped out of its bowl and was gasping for air and life. For a moment he considered the possibility that Lydia was trying to tell him that she and his daughter were *close*; as open-minded as he'd always been, he would not be able to view that as anything other than unnatural. Lydia understood his concern and smiled to herself.

'No, not that. It's just the thing with Lord Harrington ended rather badly.'

'How do you mean?'

'He beat her.' Lydia wished there was another way to deliver this news. So bleak and wrong. The father's face rushed through a variety of emotions: shock, disbelief, outrage, impotence. He leapt out of his chair. Lydia placed a restraining hand upon his arm and wordlessly signalled for him to sit back down, remain calm, not create a scene. Sir Peter fell back into the chair, his body rigid with anger.

'When? When did this happen?'

'Two weeks ago.'

'That's why we haven't seen her.' He shook his head from side to side as though juggling the inconceivable thought.

'I only found out a week after it happened. She wasn't going to tell me. You know how private she is.'

'How is she, exactly?'

'Mending, but I think it was quite vicious. There's bruising and cuts. She gets headaches.'

'I shall kill him. The bastard. Tear him limb from limb.' Sir Peter's face was scarlet with outrage. 'I'm sorry,' he spluttered. It was clear to Lydia that he was apologising for his language but not the sentiment.

'Quite. I understand. Although obviously that can't happen,' she said smoothly.

'It bloody well can and it will.' His hands trembled with rage.

'No.'

'Then we must go to the police.'

'Ava won't hear of it.'

'Sod the scandal. He has to be held accountable.'

Lydia felt an intense warmth and admiration for this man; a father who was careless about the gossip and disgrace, but crazy about his daughter and concerned that justice was sought. 'Really, there is nothing to be done that way. Ava won't have it.'

'Well I'm sorry, young lady, but I don't agree. I thought Ava was interested in the women's movement. I thought she wanted to help those who suffer domestic violence and abuse from brutes.'

'She does, absolutely.'

'By pretending that it hasn't happened to her? Impossible. Ridiculous.' His anger spluttered out in all directions, like a faulty firework; he jumped and sizzled and blistered.

Lydia was beginning to think that she had, after all, made a mistake in coming to Sir Peter. She had not accounted for his unpredictability or his determination and urgency to do the right thing. He reminded her of Ava. She ought to have known he would be a wild and strong beast, his own man and difficult to handle. She took a deep breath and tried to regain some control. 'Her love affairs are her own business. I think you have to accept that. She's twenty-eight.'

'But why does she get involved with such men? Such monsters?'

'I think she is bored. Directionless. So many of us are.' Lydia had only just understood this much about herself and now she was looking around her with fresh eyes and recognising that she wasn't alone. There were armies of women, different but the same; single, married and widowed women, adolescent and elderly women stumbling around looking for purpose and reason. They were trying to understand the world they lived in. A world run and brutalised by men.

'But she has her charities and her causes. They keep her busy.'

'Her contributions are unstructured and therefore unsatisfactory.'

Sir Peter seemed startled. Was he even listening to her? Or had she lost him to plots of revenge and retribution? Lydia clambered to bring him back.

'I just came here to ask you one question, Sir Peter.'

'What was that?'

'If Ava had been a boy, what would she be doing now?'

'Assuming she'd survived the fighting? I'd have her by my side in my factories and boardrooms. I'd be planning an early retirement, happy knowing that the companies were safe in such hands. Like you said, she has a brilliant brain and she's ruthless. She'd make an astounding businessman.'

Lydia smiled, relieved, and sat back in her seat.

'Wouldn't she, Sir Peter? Wouldn't she just?'

48

LAWRENCE WAS FINDING it difficult to concentrate on exactly what the groundsman had to say about fencing the borders. He hoped he didn't appear rude. There was nothing as churlish as disinterest and he should know. His mind kept running back to Lydia and the conversation they'd had this morning. It was satisfactory. He hoped, perhaps, that things were on the mend.

Lawrence had been pleasantly surprised when she'd arrived back from Sarah's two days before he'd expected. He thought he'd take the opportunity to involve her in his plans for the estate. He'd practically had to demand her presence; it was almost as though she was avoiding him. Last night she'd requested a tray in her room and refused to come down to dinner; she'd said the heat made her queasy. Whilst he couldn't very well call her a liar, he did doubt her. He'd all but had to march her into his office this morning. He'd sat her down and explained what had to be sold off in an effort to pay the death duties, and what they might be able to retain. He'd been disappointed when she hadn't made much of an effort to even pretend to be concerned. Instead she'd smiled, vacantly, politely, and repeatedly said, 'Do as you think best, Lawrence. I'm certain you know more about it than I do.'

He did, naturally, but still her unresponsiveness frustrated him. For months now she had been like quicksilver: fast, shiny and flowing. He couldn't get near her. She seemed somehow threatening, even dangerous, and he couldn't exactly explain why he thought this; it was more of an unquantifiable feeling. Lawrence didn't generally get muddled up with hunches and such. He liked the direction of his life to be ordered via information, analysis and logical determined study. He resented her for dragging him into the quagmire of irrational thought.

He knew that the only sensible way forward was to clear the air. There had been so much toing and froing of late. They were losing sight of one another. It was becoming messy. The way he saw it, there was only one way to reinstate order. He must address the issue that he knew was troubling her. So he took the bull by the horns.

'I know what you think, Lydia.'

'Do you?' Lydia was sitting on the leather chesterfield sofa in his office. She was wearing pink, which struck him as peculiar, since she'd made such a fuss about buying appropriate mourning clothes. Perhaps she'd decided that she didn't appear as fetching in black after all; she certainly was a picture in pink. She looked like a flower: silken, dewy. As he looked at her — staring resolutely out of the window, or at the bookshelves, anywhere other than at him and his towering pile of papers — he felt livid that whilst she was his wife, and by the word of God and the law of the land she belonged to him, he had a feeling that she did not. Not at all.

'Yes, I do,' he stated confidently. 'I admit that working as a civil servant during the Great War meant that I escaped the worst of the physical adversity.'

'Hah.' The sound erupted, spiteful and honest. Finally she turned to him; he almost wished she hadn't. Wondrous disbelief dissolved into dry contempt; it was obvious she thought that what he'd said was a gross understatement. Lawrence did not allow her glare to put him off his stride.

'But I still suffered. I lost my brother, friends and contemporaries.'

'Yes, I know you did.' She softened. Encouraged, he pushed on. 'And now it appears that I may lose you.' Lydia had gasped. A short, nervous intake of breath. He didn't want to appear dramatic. It wasn't an appropriate way for a gentleman to conduct himself, so he clarified what he meant exactly. 'Or at least the respect you owe me.'

'I wasn't aware I was in your debt.'

'I am due certain things, Lydia, as your husband. Respect is most definitely one of them.'

She'd shot him a look that he wished he did not understand. It was horribly clear. She pitied him. Her expression made him smart. He knew this was much worse than when she had been disappointed in him, or even ashamed of him. She sighed. This disagreement was making them both so weary.

'Do you know, Lawrence, after all I've heard of the war recently, I'm glad you weren't there. I really am. Your parents were right to keep you out.'

'I'm still not comfortable with your suggestion that I was *out* of the war, Lydia. I served.'

'No, you didn't, but that's fine.'

Lawrence had begun to wonder whether it was sensible to pursue the matter any further. What did she know about the war after all? He took a deep breath. This business was tedious. He chose to close off the matter. He didn't quite understand how or why, but it seemed as though she'd had some sort of change of heart. He was grateful for the first hint that she was reconciled to their situation, after so many months of resisting it. Now they could move on again. They were going to be all right. That was what she was saying.

Lawrence turned to the groundsman and gave him one hundred per cent of his attention, just as he deserved. Onwards and upwards. Order was the name of the game. It must be reinstated. The fields were scorched, but this was England. The seasons would change, the rain would fall, and it would once again become a green and pleasant land. Lawrence felt a sense of clarity and security flow through his body. Sticking to the correct path was paramount. Rules were rules. Method was vital.

It never crossed his mind that Lydia was absolutely not saying that they were going to be all right. Lydia was leaving. She was simply glad that she was leaving Lawrence. Glad that he hadn't died. It was as charitable as she could be.

49

LYDIA TOOK A cab from Claridge's directly to Edgar's lodgings. She instructed the cabbie to drive right up to the door. She had never been so bold before. Her fingers rattled with nervous excitement. On the rare occasions she had taken a cab to his place, she'd taken the precaution of being dropped off around the corner and then sneaking up to the house, only knocking when she was sure the landlady was out. Today, in her excitement, she could barely wait for the cab to slow to a stop before she opened the door. She remembered a similar moment, when Lawrence's chauffeur had dropped her off outside the V&A museum all those months ago, and she'd scrambled up the steps desperate and terrified about meeting Edgar. Now, there was no fear. Now, she was free. She had made a decision; bold and unpopular, but inevitable. She was no longer Lawrence's. She would divorce him and become Mrs Trent. She was carrying Edgar's baby and they'd be a family. She would not skulk or hide herself for a moment longer.

She knocked firmly on the door; she noticed a flake of peeling paint fall softly to the pavement. She paused and then knocked again, louder this time. Children with dirty faces and bare chests clustered around; some were intrigued by the taxi, fascinated by her clothes, others looked bored and apathetic. The same look that their fathers wore when they clustered jobless on street corners. The heat had not let up this summer and shone down ferociously on her stockinged legs. Beads of sweat the size of pinheads were appearing on her forehead.

Lydia listened carefully. She detected movement as the landlady approached the door and, finally, opened it. Lydia had seen parts of the landlady in the past: her backside waddling towards the kitchen as Lydia nipped upstairs; her head decorated with a headscarf through the balustrade as Lydia sneaked downstairs; an arm, a leg. Despite only having these disembodied snatches, she had mentally drawn quite a detailed picture of how she imagined the woman to look. She was gratified to see how accurate a conjecture she'd made. The landlady was fat and dressed in a blue checked nylon housecoat; she had the sort of face that told the world she was difficult to impress or please, and held no truck whatsoever with trying to impress or please others.

'Yes.'

'Good afternoon, I'm here to see Sergeant Major Trent.'

'Are you now?' The woman folded her arms under her vast bosoms. Lydia thought of maids plumping the cushions in the drawing room.

'Yes.' Lydia was too well brought up to barge past the woman; a lifetime of strict social etiquette did not allow her to charge up the stairs to his attic room as she would have liked, even though she had just left her husband to be with him. She breathed shallowly, impatient with herself. With the world.

'He's not in.'

'Then I shall wait for him.'

'That'll be a long wait.'

'When are you expecting him?' Lydia tried to summon her best smile, but she was finding negotiating with a woman in a housecoat, whilst standing on the street, embarrassing. The children's slack-jawed gazes were disconcerting.

'I'm not expecting him.'

Lydia checked her watch. He would be here soon, no doubt. He'd never made her wait, and in the telegram she'd said she'd be here by two. He'd probably popped out to buy some flowers or cake. 'Perhaps I could wait in the front room.'

The landlady suddenly appeared sly and amused. She held the door open and said, 'If you like.'

344

Lydia perched on the edge of the sludge-green synthetically covered armchair. The room was a tight, unsuccessful space that had aimed at smug respectability and landed somewhere near undesirable pretension. The furniture was solid, but unfashionably wooden and austere. There was too much of it for the small room. There was an enormous sideboard that housed a vast collection of small, ugly ceramic ornaments in the shapes of various wild animals; Lydia could not imagine anyone loving them. There were two armchairs and a wooden table in between. The table was too high for comfort; it was scattered with home-made crocheted mats and dominated by a poorly embroidered runner. A second table doubled up as a cocktail cabinet. None of the bottles were decanted. Lydia noticed that the labels on both the gin and the whisky wore ink marks to indicate how much remained, a mean-spirited attempt to deter guests from helping themselves. Everything was covered in a thin coat of dust and appeared a little sticky. There were no pictures on the walls or chimneypiece. The whole place smelt of mothballs. The landlady did not offer a cup of tea or even a drink of water.

Lydia wondered whether Edgar often sat in this room. She couldn't imagine it. He was so much more than a man to Lydia. He was a mass, a presence. A geography. A class. Although she had never seen him in his home environment, he was inextricably linked to the mysterious north. When she thought of him, she was reminded of a childhood holiday to the Pennine mountains, the range that formed the backbone of England. At the time Lydia had been somewhat afraid of the bleak, narrow, unknown, chilly, hilly land that was trapped between one churning grey sea and another – the sort of land that Edgar came from – but she'd also been excited by it. Edgar somehow encompassed and exuded the region's wild, battling spirit of adventure, drama and desire. Maybe it was because he'd been prepared to fight for the land that he seemed to be intrinsically linked to it. He was earthy, virile. In her mind Lawrence was not attached to the land; even though he held the deeds to large chunks of the south, being rich and prosperous and self-serving did not entitle. Whilst the accepted definition of power and prestige lay with Lawrence, and Edgar was considered harsh, uncouth and even dangerous, she could only think of him as he was: uncompromising and brave.

Lydia's breasts felt heavy; she almost put her hand on her stomach, but she felt the landlady's eyes trail her and she worried that the woman might understand the gesture. She wished she could take a nap.

She focused on the clock on the mantelpiece. Not long now.

50

SARAH HAD NOT known what to make of the telephone call. When Dickenson had rung, she'd assumed it was to relay a message from Lydia about some or other social arrangement, but there was something about the maid's tone that alerted her to a problem.

'Ma'am, would it be too much to ask for you to come over here?' Dickenson had asked warily.

'Is Lydia unwell?'

'No.'

'But she's asked for me?'

'No, ma'am.' A pause. 'She's gone.'

'Gone out?'

It sounded as though the girl was near to tears. 'Please don't have me sacked. I know I shouldn't have read it, but I had a feeling.'

Hiding her impatience, generated by mounting concern, Sarah said, 'I'm terribly sorry, I have no idea what you are talking about. Do stay calm.'

'She's left the earl, ma'am, and she's given me a note to tell him so.'

The maid would not read the letter out to her over the phone – Sarah supposed she could understand that, and her sensibility and decorum was appreciated; loyalty and discretion were needed now more than ever – so a journey to ascertain the facts was necessary. Sarah immediately telephoned for a taxi; even waiting for Dickenson to send Lawrence's chauffeur seemed too slow. She gave no thought to the expense; she simply had to be there.

Sarah had qualms about reading the letter, too. Correspondence between husband and wife ought to be sacrosanct. But then Lydia had detonated the concept that there were things between husband and wife that ought to be revered. The envelope was a thick, creamy parchment; the feminine penmanship was neat and tidy. Sarah slid open the envelope. The words were careful, concerned. Lydia had retained enough humility to resist resorting to clichés or trying to explain how she felt about Edgar. She'd constrained herself, stuck to the bald facts. The determined and sparse note was perhaps all the more horrifying for it. She was pregnant with another man's child. The marriage must end. She hoped he could forgive her.

Sarah gasped. Poor Lawrence. How was she to deliver this note? She would not. It should not exist. In temper and panic she ripped the letter in half, then in quarters. Like a child she wanted the evidence out of the way, as though that somehow might obliterate the facts too. She thought of Molly hiding toffee wrappers in her pillowcase. She strode to the chimneypiece, but it was too hot for a fire. She looked about and found a heavy onyx cigarette lighter. She set alight the offending letter and envelope. She held it over the grate and watched the expensive creamy paper turn black and curl, then flake away to nothing. The heat of the secret scorched her fingertips and her hands were left sooty. She was just rubbing them together when Lawrence walked into the drawing room.

'Sarah, how wonderful to see you.'

'Thank you.'

'Are you cold?' He clearly thought she'd been attempting to light a fire. Naturally he looked surprised; it was still seventy-five degrees Fahrenheit outside, even though it was nearly seven in the evening.

'Not at all.' She didn't offer an explanation as to why she was poking around in the embers. She thought that in situations like these it was best not to elaborate.

'Did you come here hoping to find Lydia?'

'Yes.'

'Dickenson tells me she's gone to London.'

'Yes.'

'I'm not absolutely sure when she's expected back.' He looked apologetic.

'No.' Sarah didn't know what to say. She'd burned the letter, but that wouldn't be enough; it wouldn't get Lydia to return. She needed to speak to Ava, who would know what to do; she'd bring Lydia back, because back she must come. Sarah suddenly felt nauseous. She didn't like secrets. It had been enough having to live with the knowledge that Lydia was having an affair all these months, but this latest development had an urgency and desperation that Sarah couldn't contain. This would blow up in their faces.

Her eyes skimmed the room. She was looking for a way in to some small talk, but she found she couldn't motivate her tongue because her mind was busy trying to conquer her internal disbelief. It was all as she'd expected. She knew the antique tapestries that hung on the walls, the books that lined countless shelves; she was familiar with the embroidered cushions and spreads, the panelled walls and grandfather clock. She glanced at Lawrence. Why would Lydia leave all of this?

Lawrence was looking at the carpet. His hair was receding and the skin on his skull was a little pink; he'd been outside inspecting the fences most of the day. She thought he ought to always wear a hat. Suddenly she had an urge to caress the bald patch. Silly of her. The evening sunshine slid in through the window, past the nets, and splashed across the Asian rugs. The air was still, calm.

'Would you like to stay for supper, since you've come all this way?' He didn't look hopeful.

Sarah nodded eagerly and Lawrence beamed, relieved. 'Gosh, that's marvellous.'

'I haven't brought an appropriate dress.'

'You look fine. Quite lovely.'

Sarah didn't understand it. Here she was in the middle of a distinctly horrible situation. A crisis. And yet. A small bubble of delight had popped in her stomach.

He thought she looked fine, quite lovely.

51

A CHURCH BELL struck eleven just as Lydia disembarked from the train at Clarendale. She looked around the lonely station and wondered how she'd got there. The air was still, almost steamy; the warmth of the day rose from the concrete.

'Are you all right, miss?' The stationmaster called down the platform, his voice crackling through the blue-black air, disturbing a bird in the hedgerow; it was obvious he didn't really want to rouse himself from his room.

'Quite, thank you,' she called, and then kept her head down. She didn't want to be recognised; if he realised that she was the Countess of Clarendale he would probably want to telephone the house and have the chauffeur pick her up; at the very least he'd insist on telephoning for a cab. Lydia wanted to walk the three miles. Or to be accurate, it was the least offensive option out of the scant choices available to her. She certainly didn't want to pass pleasantries with a driver and she shrivelled from the idea of having her return announced at the house. She put one foot in front of another.

It made sense to walk. It was a warm night, the streets were safe, her bag wasn't too heavy; her heart was breaking. With each step she told herself she was not returning to Lawrence, about that she was adamant. It perhaps might seem that way to an onlooker, but in fact she was checking whether Edgar was waiting for her at the house. There had been some mix-up. Had to have been. He'd be there. She was sure of it. There was a possibility that

Dickenson had made a mistake when she'd sent the telegram. Instead of writing, *I'll meet you at yours*, she might have wired, *I'll meet you at mine*. Lydia would not allow herself to consider that they had never, ever made such an arrangement and if Edgar had received such a telegram he would have wired asking for clarity. Instead she told herself that the unfeasible, unlikely explanation was the answer. She was not returning to Lawrence. She was just walking. One step, and then the next.

She walked alongside the dense, overgrown hedgerows, next to dapples of daisies and clumps of cowslip closed up tight against the night. She did not notice when long nettles reached out and whipped her ankles; she just tried not to slip into the roadside ditches. Her feet were blistered, the result of being squeezed into narrow heels all day and tramping aimlessly, pointlessly around the dusty London streets; her hand was sore where she'd sweatily clasped her suitcase, and her back ached. It was an indescribable throb that she couldn't accurately attribute to anything other than her depressed state.

She had not known what to do with herself when she left his lodgings. She'd thought perhaps he might be waiting in one of their usual meeting places, the V&A or the Savoy. She'd visited both and made enquiries at several more bars, but she had not found him.

Now, she trudged through the village, dodging the tipsy men who had been kicked out of the pub and were stumbling about the streets; one moment all jovial and good-natured, the next at each other's throats. They were all about the age that suggested they would have been sent to war. What were their experiences? she wondered. What had made them so wildly inconsistent?

She had sat in the landlady's front parlour for an hour and a half. Then the heat had begun to overpower her, and her eyelids – ton weights – had fallen shut; she had jerked awake with the motion of her head tumbling forward on to her chest. The desire to lie down was tremendous. It was the pregnancy. Since the baby's conception she had been floored with vast waves of the most profound fatigue; she couldn't fight it. She thought of Edgar's cool bed, upstairs in the attic room. She wanted to lie on the sheets that rarely smelt clean but always smelt of them, and inhale his scent; wait for him there. It was ridiculous that she, his lover, the mother-to-be of his child, was being pinned to a chair in a fusty lower-middle-class parlour. No longer prepared to accept it, she had wandered into the corridor, the one where just a couple of weeks ago she had made love to Edgar against the wall.

'I'm going to wait for the sergeant major in his rooms,' she called. She made her intention an unequivocal declaration rather than a request, deciding that asking permission was beneath her and, besides, unlikely to offer up the result she needed.

'He hasn't got any rooms.' The landlady emerged from the gloom of the shadowy kitchen. Waddling, so as to keep her sweaty thighs from rubbing against one another.

'I'll wait upstairs.' Lydia already had her foot on the third stair; she was holding the banister. The air was too hot and close for this wordplay. He didn't have rooms as such. He had one room. Did the old witch of a landlady want her to say 'bedroom'? Was that the point she was making? Would she gain some vicarious erotic charge by hearing Lydia admit as much? She was clearly enjoying Lydia's discomfort.

'He's cleared off.'

Lydia had paused, mid step, her foot waving helplessly and awkwardly in the air, missing the tread. She didn't know whether to place it on the next step up, or the next step down.

'I'm sorry. I don't understand.' She heard the quiver in her own voice and hated herself for it. Her tone suggested she understood all too well.

'Left yesterday. Although he was paid up to the end of the month. Fair and square about his money, I'll say that for him. Although that's all I can say.'

The insinuation was far too clear, far too much. Lydia shot up the stairs, not believing the stupid, evil woman. She'd flung open his door, expecting to find him in all his glory. White shirt open and flowing, dark trousers held up with braces, bare feet and a big smile. Eyes that never took no for an answer. 'Hello, Lid.'

The attic room was deserted. Abandoned, empty. The landlady

might have given every impression of being lazy, but she, or at least someone – perhaps Edgar himself – had worked efficiently to obliterate all traces of his existence. There was still a chair near the chimneypiece, but there was no tartan rug hung over the back of it. A clean green plate, saucer and cup, a knife and fork were piled neatly next to the deep stone sink, but there was no sign of the delicate yellow and gold cups and saucers, or the tiny silver spoons, the candlesticks or the gramophone. There were no books. The two splintered wooden chairs and the small table remained, but the dusty, yellowing newspapers had been removed. The bed had been stripped and the mattress lay, grubby and exposed; no signs of the love it had absorbed, the passion it had hosted. Lydia inadvertently shivered a little to think how they'd used it; it wasn't clear to the nosy, lingering landlady whether her tremor was disgust at the meanness of it all, or desire. Lydia could smell rotting vegetables again, because there were no bunches of roses to mask the stench; there was no scent of heady, sweet loving.

She could not misunderstand the barren wasteland.

The cat appeared from nowhere and rubbed up against Lydia's stockinged legs. He nuzzled his head into her calf with force. Lydia, desperate, was prepared to interpret his actions as affection rather than hunger. She bent down and petted obligingly, then scooped the cat up. She held it close. 'You too? He left you too?' she whispered.

'Left in quite a hurry, did the officer. He said he'd come into a bit of unexpected money.'

'May I have his forwarding address, please?' Lydia tried to remain efficient and detached, but it was agony.

'Didn't leave none.'

Lydia had begun to sway. She held the cat tightly to her, too tightly; it miaowed and struggled to be set down. She didn't notice until it scratched her arm and then leapt from her, a mass of protest and anguish that she'd tried to domesticate it, if only for a few minutes. Her stomach churned; she felt a slackening in her jaw and anus. Everything seemed loose and detached.

'Are you all right? You've gone a bit peculiar-looking.' Lydia was certain that the landlady wasn't genuinely concerned. She was enjoying the drama and was particularly happy that the victim was a well-to-do sort whom she'd no doubt judged as no better than she ought to be.

'I need some water.' Lydia staggered to the stone sink and turned the dripping tap. The water gushed into the green cup and on to her fingers; it splashed on her dress. *No glasses, I'm afraid.* His words came back to her, so vivid, so real that she turned with a jolt, expecting to see him. *We managed with so little in the trenches, I got used to it. Besides, I don't spend much time here.* She stumbled to the bed and sat down on the browning mattress. She put her hand on it. Their sweat, their stickiness. And others', too? Who? How many must there have been?

'He can't have gone.' She coughed, trying to encourage her voice to have some conviction. She looked up at the landlady with defiance.

'Well, this empty room says differently.' The landlady remained at the open door. She clearly wanted Lydia to leave. Lydia could not. Instead she lay down and inhaled the thin mattress. Nothing. He wasn't there. It smelt of dust. She let out a howl. The sound came from deep within her gut and her history. She pulled herself into a tight ball, fists clenched, knees tucked into her belly, head pulled into her chest. Like a foetus. Vulnerable. The howl reverberated around the frail walls of the house, out through the open windows and into the street. She wondered how far it would travel: at least to France; maybe further, maybe to the Baltic.

With each step that Lydia took towards the great house of Clarendale, she remembered something Edgar had said to her; something inconsequential, like the fact that John Charles Robinson became curator of the V&A in 1853, or something enormous, like the fact that rats gorged themselves on human flesh until they lit up like lanterns. Worse than remembering what he'd said, she felt something he had done to her. The arousing scratch of his whiskers, the gentle touch of his fingertips, the important feeling of him inside her. That could not stop. It must not. Where was he? He'd crept so close, and then run away.

Unwillingly she remembered that after lovemaking, when there was nothing and no one to dilute them – just the essence of them – he'd often closed his eyes. Avoided her, tried to shut her out. She'd always thought that, with time, she'd get him to give up that habit.

Lydia hadn't eaten all day, and she felt sick, woozy and disorientated. She didn't know if it was shock and disappointment, or the baby. Oh, her baby. She put a defensive hand on her belly. How was she to protect this baby now? There had been a shift in her thoughts and focus regarding becoming a mother. Before Edgar, she'd believed that having a child was her duty. She'd longed for it in the way one might long for one's horse to win on Derby Day. She had not felt a deep, unrestrained longing. She had needed a baby to alleviate the menacing, unsound but genuine fear that without one she was nothing. She had not anticipated any extreme intimacy with a child; she simply hadn't wanted to be blamed for dashing Lawrence's dreams and birthright. She looked back at the woman who had harboured these detached and clinical thoughts and didn't recognise her; was almost repulsed by her.

This baby was vitally important. More important than anything, certainly than herself. What she felt for it was tender, grand and enormous. This baby was everything. It was Edgar's child.

Where had he gone? Why would he go? It was madness. It was hell.

She couldn't face knocking at the grand entrance of Clarendale Hall. She knew she must look a fright. Her dress was streaked with perspiration and the day's grime; her face was awash with mascara tears. She decided it would be simpler and more discreet if she simply sneaked around the back of the house. A patio door or a window was likely to be open. She knew how it would be. Net curtains, in folds like a gown, fluttering in the night breeze. An orange light flooding from the drawing room. Picture perfect; the jaws of hell. She would slip in and go to bed without being noticed. She could face Lawrence and the consequences of her note tomorrow.

Her own distress was so virulent and raw that it didn't cross her mind that Lawrence might be up late, perhaps agonising over her letter, the one that stated her intention of leaving him, starting a new life. Or perhaps he'd be drinking more whisky than was good for him, maybe sitting head in hands in the drawing room, lit only by candles. She certainly didn't expect to see his shadowy figure move quickly from one side of the room to the other, darting towards Sarah, arms outstretched, to cradle her face in his hands and then draw her towards him in a passionate kiss. A kiss that went on and on.

52

SARAH COULD NOT sleep. Lawrence's kiss, strong, engulfing and welcome, had left an imprint that robbed her of the ability or even the need to rest. The kiss, his kiss, had been quite unlike the disappointment on the dance floor with the stranger. Lawrence was not Arthur – no one ever could be – but his kiss did not seem like a compromise or a letdown. His firm and fine lips had fitted; they had not clumsily clashed teeth. His fingers framed her face tenderly and yet with a manly assurance that had thrilled. Sarah was awash with glee and excitement for moments at a time, until she remembered that Lawrence was a married man. He was married to her friend.

Part of her was astonished to find that she immediately comforted herself with the fact that her friend had a lover and was expecting a child with that other man. It seemed so selfish to be thinking this way, but she couldn't help herself. She wished she'd kept the letter. Yet she took some pleasure in the fact that Lawrence had kissed her not knowing his wife was abandoning him. He had kissed her because he wanted *her*.

Lawrence was a gentleman. He'd pulled apart. Eventually, not too suddenly. Obviously reluctantly. And he'd apologised. Sarah knew he was apologising for the impossible position he'd placed her in, but she got the feeling that he wasn't absolutely sorry about the kiss. The kiss had not tasted of regret. There was no re-enactment of the scene that Sarah had witnessed in Sir Peter Pondson-Callow's study between Lydia and Edgar Trent. Lawrence had not tugged at her undergarments, or clasped his mouth on her nipples. Although she wanted him to.

She did.

She knew she shouldn't. But she did. The confusing mix of contradictory emotions was almost enough to make her want to stay hidden in this room for ever. She could not face what she had done; she could not decide what to do next. And yet the morning sun illuminated the pretty floral curtains in a way that made her want to fling them open, throw the window wide, inhale the sweet fragrance of the freshly mowed lawns and hear the birds singing. She wanted to run downstairs and eat her breakfast with relish. She thought perhaps she'd taste the food again. For so long now she hadn't much cared what she ate – eggs were all the same as porridge or kippers – but now she thought she fancied grapefruit and toast. She anticipated the citrus sharpness that would contrast with the sweet preserve.

She wondered what to wear. She hadn't anticipated staying and hadn't packed an overnight bag. When Lawrence had suggested she stay, the maids had found her a nightdress and toiletries but all she had to wear was yesterday's dress. She wished she had something a little prettier. An audacious and unreasonable thought crossed her mind: she could sneak into Lydia's room and borrow one of her innumerable dresses. No one would notice, not if she picked something Lydia hadn't worn for a while. That wouldn't be difficult; Lydia had so many frocks, she was able to rotate her garments at leisure. It wasn't exactly wrong, Sarah tried to tell herself. If Lydia were here, she would certainly allow her to borrow a dress; she'd often done so before. Although, admittedly, in the past Sarah had never been motivated by a desire to look lovely so she could seduce Lydia's husband. It was probably erroneous, yet a delicious and rare sense of mischief flooded through Sarah's body. Lydia had left her clothes and left her husband; she didn't want them any more. It would be silly to waste them. She swung her legs out of bed and, still barefooted, sneaked out of the room and along the corridor. For the first time in many years, Sarah felt glad to be alive.

53

L YDIA WOKE FROM her groggy, interrupted sleep to the noise of
the birds singing in the garden. They sounded like screeching
sirens. She'd slept badly. The skin underneath her eyes stung. She'd
cried quietly most of the night. Her stomach felt hollow and she
knew she ought to go and find something to eat. If she didn't,
she'd probably have another awful bout of morning sickness. Yet
she could not get out of bed. The very thought was too much for
her.

She was at last in tune with her generation. Despair crept through
every vessel in her body. Grief-stricken and struggling, she wondered
what it was all about. It was a world where people no longer were
forced to rise to the challenge of patriotism or faith, nor indeed
did they have to fall for it. Theirs was a life that lurched from wild
jazz parties and exciting love affairs to mass unemployment and
abandoned women, a land where no one rose for anything at all,
not even breakfast. Lydia felt uninspired and futile.

She could hear the dogs barking and scampering around the
house, unaware of the human pain, their claws clicking on the
flagstones, eyes and noses wet. She missed his cat's peaceful indolence. The household waited. Each wrapped in the labyrinth of
their own drama.

When the door to her room squeaked open, she wanted to hide
under the covers. She expected Dickenson, which would have been
bad enough; it was Sarah, which was significantly worse.

Sarah stumbled. 'Lydia, what are you doing here?'

'I live here.' As Lydia said it, she felt like a fraud. She did not live here; well, at least she almost hadn't. Did she mean to come back?

'I thought you'd left.'

'I see.' Lawrence had clearly told her everything; Lydia could imagine the scene. Intense and charged. Culminating in an illicit kiss. She wondered when and how she would tell her friend that she'd seen her kissing her husband. Perhaps she'd leave it to Sarah to broach the subject. She wondered how much she cared.

'Did you change your mind?' Sarah came into the room and sat on Lydia's bed. She'd done as much so many times before since their girlhoods that it didn't seem peculiar.

'No.'

'Then what?'

'He did. Oh God, Sarah, he's left me.' Lydia gave in to another burst of tears; even though part of her had sworn that she'd never turn to Sarah for succor again, she was not able to resist. She had scant options and was in dire need of some comfort. Sarah crawled closer to her friend and took her in her arms. She held Lydia as Lydia quaked and gulped. 'What am I to do?' she sobbed.

Sarah sighed wearily. Once again she felt the colour drain out of her life; fleeting opportunities collapsed and she was forced to pack away her own needs. She'd only allowed herself to hope momentarily. She could stem the flow. She was obliged to. She thought of Lawrence's dark, thoughtful eyes, which never lost their kind expression of involved interest, and she knew she had to turn away from them. She was surprised to realise that because she'd suffered much, additional pain was at once unbearable and frothy. 'You must stay here with Lawrence,' she said.

Lydia, who was so much more used to saying what she actually thought nowadays, cried, 'But I don't want to.' A thought occurred to her. 'And he won't want me to.'

'He hasn't seen the letter. He doesn't know anything. I kept it from him.'

Lydia didn't understand. She'd seen them kiss. She'd assumed it was a consequence of Lawrence's emotional state after reading the letter that said she was leaving him, pregnant with another man's child, in love with another man. She'd thought the kiss must have been motivated by revenge, or anger, or jealousy. If not that, then what? She wanted to ask Sarah but could not bring herself to.

She thought back to the advice Sarah had given her when she'd first stated her intention of leaving Lawrence. Sarah had suggested that Lydia could continue to see Edgar; she'd pointed out that people carried on illicit affairs all the time. She had been unequivocal that the important thing was to protect the family name, to avoid a scandal. Was it possible that Sarah and Lawrence were having an affair? Had been having one for some time now? Lydia was so distraught she couldn't think straight. It was possible, but for all that, it didn't seem probable. If they were having an affair, why would Sarah encourage her to stay? She wasn't married. She stood to gain so much if Lydia left.

Perhaps the kiss hadn't been anything significant; a drunken mistake. Heat of the moment. Yet Lydia had seen it. It had looked significant. The kiss had made her ache with jealousy. Not that she was jealous about Lawrence's affections, but it had reminded her of stolen kisses she'd enjoyed with Edgar.

'The baby,' she muttered.

'Exactly, you have your baby to consider.' Sarah pulled away from Lydia and swung her legs off the bed so that her back was turned. 'You need a home. The baby needs a father. You must stay.'

'But it wouldn't be fair on Lawrence bringing up another man's child.' Over the past two weeks Lydia had staunchly argued as much, on a number of occasions, to her friends; this time she sounded less adamant. Sarah heard the hesitancy in her voice and knew that Lydia was reconsidering her position. She closed her eyes, trying to trap in the tears.

'Not fair, no, but the best of a bad job,' she replied. 'He'll be a good father. I've seen him with my children while they stayed here this summer. Besides, he might *be* the father.'

'I'm certain he's not,' said Lydia meekly. She hadn't made love with her husband for months.

'Nothing is certain. Not marriage or parenthood. The good

won't be rewarded and the bad won't be punished. You can lament the fact or you can use it, but it is what it is,' said Sarah sharply. 'You have to stay, because there is nowhere else for you to go. Edgar Trent doesn't want you.'

Sarah stood up but still wouldn't turn to her friend. Lydia guessed she must be embarrassed or ashamed about kissing Lawrence. There was no need. A silly mistake, no doubt. Certainly nothing significant, because if it was, Sarah would not be arguing so staunchly for Lydia to stay. Lydia decided the decent thing was to forget all about the silly kiss; it was better never to mention it to either Sarah or Lawrence. There was enough confusion.

The two women sighed in unison.

'You should get up, Lydia. Have something to eat and get on with being the Countess of Clarendale.'

AUTUMN

54

A VA LOVED AUTUMN. The summer had been too long, hot and disruptive. She didn't just mean the temperature and the strikes that had made the headlines; she meant all the disorder and upset her friends had endured. But now the crisp, sharp days had finally usurped the troublesome, indolent ones. Ava enjoyed the sense of productivity that accompanied autumn. Somehow – because the towns were fogged and the countryside misty, mornings were dim and dusk arrived quickly, then lingered for a long time – people were conscious that a lot had to be achieved in the few hours they had. There was a sense that people hurried to wherever it was they were going. Scarves protected as boots stamped out the paths of workers scuttling to and from factories, hospitals, schools and offices. Ava was among them. Ava had an office to go to every day of the week.

Her father had made a surprise offer for her to take control of a number of his smaller concerns. He'd made it quite clear that depending on her progress, she ought to expect speedy promotion. One day, if she proved able and willing, she would be in charge of his entire empire. Ava did not doubt she was both. It was what she had been waiting for. She'd secretly anticipated as much for ever, but since both her twenty-first birthday and her twenty-fifth had come and gone without an offer of regular employment, she certainly hadn't dared to ever count on it. Having direction and focus was a relief.

Her mother was outraged. She'd said that all chances of

matrimony were ruined if Ava took up full-time employment, but Sir Peter Pondson-Callow had been unwavering. Ava would work. She'd put her phenomenal brain to use. 'No doubt she'll make us all very rich,' he'd said, then offered his daughter a cigar.

Ava's first thoughts were about diversification. She wondered whether they could get into electronics; it was a booming industry. But first she needed to set their house in order. She had long since studied examples of model employers such as Bournville and Cadbury, and now set about introducing social reforms into her father's factories; she believed they would improve productivity and worker loyalty. She wanted to increase the women's wages by twenty-six per cent to bring them in line with the men's. When Sir Peter spluttered his outrage at parting with such substantial amounts of cash, Ava suggested a compromise. 'How about a ten per cent increase in wages and then we offer bonuses instead.'

'What sort of bonuses?' he asked warily.

'Boots.'

'Boots?'

'For their families. We make boots but a number of our employees' children go to school barefoot. We should give them shoes and boots.'

'The little buggers constantly grow.'

'Then they can return the shoes when they grow out of them. We can pass them down to the younger children. I think we should give them eggs and milk too.'

'Eggs? Milk?'

'Do you know how many days you lost to sickness and strikes last year?'

'Too many.'

'Exactly. Milk is threepence a pint and eggs a shilling a dozen at retail. You could buy in bulk for a fraction, then distribute on a Friday. A treat for the weekend. They need the nutrition. It's desperate. The properly poor wait until the market stalls close down and then they forage. It isn't dignified. It isn't right.'

'How do you know how much eggs cost?' Sir Peter asked, surprised but impressed.

'I know a great many things, Father. For example, I know that only one third of the working-class volunteers were considered fit enough to fight the damned war, they were so malnourished.'

'Lucky them.'

'Well, at least until conscription started.'

'Desperation, you mean,' sighed Sir Peter. He had never seen the glory in war, although he'd made more than a bob or two from it.

'Since they did all fight, I think we ought to do more to change things.'

'So single-handedly you're going to make it the land fit for heroes they were promised, are you?'

'I'm going to try,' said Ava grimly, ignoring the amused scepticism in her father's tone. She did not tell her father about plans to distribute condoms to the workers, male and female alike. But she did mention the introduction of a Christmas savings scheme, and she allowed the workers to understand that she'd hire an open-topped charabanc in the summer, so they could have a day trip to Brighton. All expenses paid. Productivity went up by nineteen per cent in the first month of her employment.

Ava often wondered what had prompted her father's change of mind on the subject of her employment. Whoever or whatever it was, she was extremely grateful. She had never felt so alive and useful as she did when she sat in front of the clock-in cards, ledgers and order books.

It was almost with reluctance that she left the office, even though it was past eight and she needed to go home and change. She only relinquished her position at the desk because she'd promised the girls that they'd meet up for cocktails at nine. Beatrice wanted to update them on Georgina Vestry's progress as a debutante, and both Sarah and Lydia were in dire need of a jolly night out.

Lydia had not thrived since the summer. She had resigned herself to her fate as Countess of Clarendale, but she did not give the impression she appreciated it, let alone relished it. She was lacklustre, rather like a garment that had been left out in the sun for too long and been bleached; she'd lost all her colour and vitality. She did not giggle or dance; she spoke calmly in measured tones, rarely bothering to pass an opinion on anything or even indulge in gossip. It became difficult to discern what pleased her and what didn't. If indeed anything pleased her. She'd get used to things, Ava told herself. She'd done the right thing. It was clear Lydia missed the sergeant major, but that would pass, in time. Indeed, Ava had rather expected the desire to wane by now.

Still, at least Lydia's morbid dowdiness was understandable, but Sarah was no better and her gloomy attitude really did perplex Ava. Sarah had always been the sort to keep her chin up. There was no doubt that she'd silently endured much. Then, during the summer, Ava had thought she was showing signs of finally casting off her perpetual grief: she'd started to take an interest in clothes and her appearance, she'd started to read newspapers again, and had twice suggested excursions for their entire gang. It had all come to an abrupt and inexplicable stop; it was frustrating to see her dim again.

Ava believed that when people were down in the dumps, the only answer was to fly high in the sky, so they met in the Silver Cat, a new nightclub that was being widely reviewed and generally raved about. Whilst she had become a professional working woman, Ava certainly didn't want to be dull, and she felt it was almost her duty to investigate the new hot spot. She wished she'd picked more effervescent chums to accompany her, though. Freddie or Doug would have offered to dance, paid for the drinks and, most importantly, smiled.

Ava never thought she'd find herself in a position where Beatrice seemed the most jolly and interesting among her group. Bea seemed to be oblivious to the moody silences and waxed lyrical about Georgina's dress for the Queen Charlotte's debutante ball, the Vestry girl's coming-out date.

'So she's picked white chiffon, over a gold slip which in due course will be turned into another dress.'

'Very practical,' commented Sarah.

Whilst this was indeed true, Ava thought they were all perhaps missing the point of a debut ballgown. Surely the important thing was whether it shimmered, flowed, enhanced and captivated.

'I've had a rather dreary day practising the walk and curtsey for when she is presented at court.' Bea professed a sense of tedium that Ava doubted. It was clear that Bea enjoyed her new role enormously and was gaining considerable vicarious pleasure from preparing Miss Vestry for court. She looked alert and tested. It clearly suited her being around youth and vitality; there hadn't been enough of that in Bea's life, and it seemed that it was to some degree catching. Bea detailed Georgina's other plans. She spoke with authority. 'Sir Henry Vestry has taken a box at Covent Garden. Did I mention that? Well, it's essential that debs see a little life, and the opera and ballet set the tone. Don't you agree? It's so important to give them the sort of occasion that is correctly dazzling and luxurious.'

'They'll all be starry-eyed,' commented Sarah.

'Exactly.' It seemed that Beatrice had gained the respect of the young woman; Ava didn't doubt that it wouldn't be long before Georgina Vestry turned to Bea for romantic advice. Oh, the irony.

'Did you use a tablecloth as a veil for the practice?' Ava asked.

'Yes.'

'I remember doing that!' Ava had walked around her drawing room with Lydia, both trailing tablecloths from their heads. Walk. Stop. Curtsey. Rise. How they'd giggled. 'Do you remember, Lydia? We thought the whole aspect was such a riot.'

Lydia smiled wanly but didn't enter into the conversation beyond commenting, 'It seems a very long time ago.'

Ava sighed. She didn't subscribe to wallowing and was beginning to find Lydia's broken heart a bore. Bea picked up the mantle, showing a newly developed maturity and tact, or simply perhaps she wanted the conversation to come back round to her again. 'Georgina is a charming girl, and very pretty. I am sure she'll make a good season, but graceful she isn't. All she has to do is curtsey without getting entangled and then move off.'

'Yes, the tricky bit is not getting entangled,' commented Ava. She reached for a cigarette and cast a pertinent look at Lydia, but Lydia was oblivious.

Her stomach was beginning to swell now; she was about five

months' pregnant. Lawrence talked about an imminent arrival. Ava couldn't believe that he hadn't realised the baby wasn't his. Perhaps he had. Maybe he'd decided to accept the child. Ava didn't know whether that was because he wanted Lydia to stay, or because he desperately wanted an heir, or because he simply wanted to avoid the humiliation and outrage that would ensue if they separated. She wasn't even sure if the matter had been discussed between the couple. If it had, Lydia had not related the conversation to her friends. In fact she never mentioned the child's parentage, or the issue of how she would explain the baby being born approximately four months after Lawrence was anticipating. Perhaps she was in denial. Publically, at least, Lawrence appeared suitably delighted by the news that he was going to be a father, although like many men of their generation and class he clearly did not feel he had to become too caught up in the business of the actual pregnancy. He would reserve his enthusiasm for when the child was actually born.

Ava was relieved that Sergeant Major Edgar Trent's name had not fallen from Lydia's lips. Lydia restricted herself to conversations about the decoration for the nursery, and names. At the moment she was refusing to interview nannies; she insisted she wanted to take care of the child herself. Nonsense. That was not the type of thing their sort did, but no one had pointed out as much just yet; not even Sarah, who was normally the oracle on all things maternal. Ava wondered whether Lydia recognised the generous chivalry of Lawrence's silence, or whether she felt hideously obliged. Trapped.

55

LYDIA WAS BEGINNING to know silences as well as she knew speech. With Lawrence there were silences because they had nothing truthful to say to one another any more. Small talk had sufficed for so long but now it was exposed as dreary and dishonest. How had she ever appreciated his small talk? Now she despised his inability to say anything worthwhile. Their marriage was currently no more than an arrangement where two wary strangers shared a drawing room, a dining room and a name. They did not share a bed, and Lydia was determined they never would again. Since they did not talk to one another, she had no idea what Lawrence thought about their cold and pragmatic arrangement, or – and this was especially distressing in so many ways – whether he had even noticed it. They both pretended that the combination of the stiflingly hot summer and her pregnancy had necessitated separate bedrooms. Neither commented that now, when the leaves were falling fast and a dusky mist extinguished the autumn hues into a bland greyness, she was probably cold, alone at night.

Her friends were silent because they withheld, they tiptoed around her, rather than blurt their condemnation, fear or disgust. She watched them now talking about Beatrice's vivacious charge. A young woman who was just starting out. Lydia envied her and pitied her. The joys. The heartbreak.

Her friends seemed animated, interested. She couldn't join in. She wished she had it in her to humour Bea and at least pretend an interest in the young woman she was presenting at court, but

371

she didn't. She could not summon the required energy. It took every iota of self-control to remain perched on the bar stool, sipping her Virgin Mary; really she wanted to run. Out of the nightclub and along the London streets. She could imagine her feet pounding the pavement but she couldn't imagine what direction they'd go in. Where could she go?

Her own silence was the silence of utter seclusion and horror. Even if she tried to articulate her heartbreak, she knew she would fail. There were no words big or deep or epic enough; nor were there any that were discreet and careful enough either.

When he first disappeared, she had succumbed to bouts of uncontrolled crying, exhaustion, headaches and a loss of appetite. Sarah had commented that they were the very same symptoms she'd suffered when Arthur had died. Sarah had held her hand while she lay in bed or sat naked in the bath, weeping. It was good of her. Lydia had appreciated her physical presence combined with her mute acceptance that Lydia must grieve. However, after two weeks Sarah had told her she had to pull herself together.

'How can you say that?'

'It's what they said to me.'

Lydia appreciated Sarah's empathy. She generously equated her own phenomenal loss – her husband's death – with Lydia's lover's desertion. Lydia recognised that Sarah was being as sympathetic as humanly possible, and even if her extreme indulgence was a result of feeling guilty about kissing Lawrence that night, Lydia felt grateful and indebted. She wished she could tell Sarah not to worry, that she was welcome to Lawrence, but it would shame Sarah. Humiliate everyone involved. Another silence had to lay siege to reality. Lydia saw that there were some similarities between their losses, but there was one terrible difference too.

Arthur hadn't wanted to go. Edgar had.

Lydia didn't know if it would be better if he were dead. She had briefly entertained the thought that he might be. Loathing the idea, and yet in a terrible dark part of her almost wanting it at the same time. But she knew he was not dead. She felt his presence in the world. She'd feel his death. Besides, not many ghosts packed up all their possessions and left their lodgings spick and span.

Months had passed and she still couldn't rouse herself. She knew she was boring her friends. 'You're behaving foolishly,' Ava snapped one day. 'This excessive emotion is terribly common, darling. You must move on.' Lydia did try to keep alert in company. Exercise was vital; she had the baby to think about, but depression seeped into every pore and fibre of her body. She was not sure whether what she felt for Edgar was hilarious, or feeble or phenomenal; she only wished she was still able to feel it about anything.

The Silver Cat was a very smart nightclub. Possibly the most lavish and elegant that Lydia had visited. Everything shone as people abandoned themselves to a few hours of intense pleasure. She wished that she and Edgar could have danced on the waxed wooden floor, underneath the vast mirrored ceiling. Then she considered the notion that he might very well be here. Dancing. Why not? He had to be somewhere. He loved jazz and was thrilled with the players who flocked to England from America's Deep South. 'Music and this sort of dancing transcends all class barriers,' he'd told her. Music was equally theirs.

She scanned the room, carefully examining every man who was swinging back and forth, elbows bent, arms facing forward as if they were going to clap another set of hands. It was futile. Few were as tall as Edgar, or as broad; none was as compelling. He was not here. She remembered dancing the Lindy Hop with him. He'd swung her high up off the ground. She'd thought he might drop her. And now he had. She believed he was a long way away. Long gone. The joyful, lusty dancing couples haunted her. She tried hard to concentrate on her friends' conversations and caught snippets.

'Nightclubs are opening up in rows and rows.'

'The dressmakers are dizzy with work.'

'I went for a ride in Freddie's new motor car. It's a dream.'

Lydia thought of the conversations she'd had with Edgar. They'd been bigger. He'd told her how surreal it was that there were shops, comfortable beds, clean clothes in the towns just half an hour's walk from the front line, and yet the men were up to their waists in mud. Living like animals. Becoming animals. 'At first I was outraged that this was the case, then amused. Well, hysterical, I suppose,' he'd confided. Then he'd become angry and challenging with her. 'It's the same now, isn't it. You live in your palatial home; other people live under bridges and in cardboard boxes.'

'It's not the same.'

'Isn't it? What's the difference?'

She hadn't been able to think of one.

Could it have been the differences that made him leave? she wondered. In the end, were they insurmountable? For him, at least?

She'd once asked him if he felt guilty for surviving. He'd replied, 'Yes. All the time. Every day. Every minute. Except . . .'

'Except when?'

'Except now. When I'm with you.'

It made no sense. How could that have just stopped?

'Do you know, gals, I think I might have to call it a night.' Lydia tried to smile, but the concerned expressions from Sarah and Bea and the frustrated one from Ava suggested she had failed.

'It's not yet ten o'clock, Lydia. Really?'

'The baby. I'm so frightfully tired. Such inexpressible weariness . . .' Lydia trailed off. She'd used the excuse of her pregnancy frequently to avoid lunches and soirées, to avoid sport and to go home early; she didn't have to be too specific.

Ava rolled her eyes, no doubt thanking God for condoms. She thought that the inconvenience the pregnancy had brought to Lydia was astounding. Lydia thought it was the only thing that was keeping her going. She kissed her friends good night, but as she leaned into Ava, Ava pulled away.

'I'm sorry, Lydia darling. I know this is ghastly to hear, but this nonsense really has to stop.'

Lydia glanced towards Bea and Sarah, hoping for some support; they looked at their shoes, unprepared to give her any more. She felt drained and picked upon. No doubt she was hormonal, too. They would use all these excuses and explanations when later the three friends discussed and considered her reaction. Lydia thought there was only one reason for her inability to stay calm and not just passively nod, as she had done so far, to the suggestion that she shut up and put up.

She loved Edgar Trent.

He was everything to her. Her world was ripped wide. The core of her exposed and raw. She didn't understand how or why she felt as she did, but she was resolute. 'I don't know what you mean by nonsense,' she snapped.

'He's not coming back, Lydia. And you have to get used to the idea.' Ava didn't add that many millions of women had done so before her, in more tragic and senseless circumstances; it was implicit.

Lydia muttered the thought that she nursed and cherished, the one that made her weak and ridiculous, the thought that every abandoned lover secretly nurtured. 'He might.'

'He's married, Lydia.' Ava let the words be absorbed.

'What?'

'I had a detective follow him. I discovered he was married.'

'I don't believe you.'

'Well it's true.' Ava kept her tone flat. The loud jazz beat in Lydia's head and she couldn't make sense of what she was being told.

'But I asked him. At the beginning.'

'And what did he say?'

'He said not.'

'He lied.'

Lydia shook her head violently. 'You've made a mistake.' She looked up at Ava with defiance.

'I've met her. She's real. He left with her.'

'How do you know he left with her?' Lydia was becoming increasingly high-pitched as shock and hysteria hijacked her sense of decorum.

Ava took a deep drag on her cigarette, blew the smoke away from her friends, sighed and then replied, 'Because I spoke to him. I made it possible. The only reason they weren't together was lack of money. So I gave him some.'

'You gave him money to leave me?' Lydia gasped, choking on the words and the betrayal.

'You make it sound so vulgar.'

'You paid him off?' Sarah and Bea reached for Lydia as she stumbled. They thought for a moment that she might collapse. She glared at them, and they shrank from her raw pain.

Ava looked as calm and assured as she always did. She had not intended to tell Lydia that Trent was married, but Lydia simply wouldn't let him go. She was messing everything up for herself. Drastic measures were necessary. 'What if I did? He took it, didn't he? Then he disappeared.'

Lydia was quivering like a beggar in the snow. She groped around for her bag, unsettling her drink. It crashed to the floor. Tomato-juice blood and shards of glistening glass tears.

'He's not coming back, Lydia. Face it, old girl.'

Lydia put her hands over her ears and shook her head. She wanted to be deaf to this cruelty. Ava felt she had to push on. Once and for all close this thing.

'Oh, Lydia, he should have been a bit of fun; why did you have to take it so seriously? Darling, I do have to wonder – and I've wondered this for a very long time, since I first saw him mess up the snow at my father's house – is he just one of those who likes to spoil perfection? I think we have to agree. Quite simply, the sergeant major is a bounder.'

56

LAWRENCE HAD COME to London with his wife. He preferred the
countryside, but he'd had to meet with his lawyers, and besides,
he didn't like Lydia gallivanting around on her own in her condition. It wouldn't do. Both Sarah and Ava had been adamant that
Lydia needed a break in town, needed to have a girls' night out,
as they called it. She certainly needed something. She was definitely
blue; what was that term people were using nowadays? Grummy.
Yes, that was it. She was grummy. He didn't understand why. They'd
longed for this baby. He'd thought it would make everything all
right, but she wasn't blooming the way a woman should. He had
never been close to a woman who was about to give birth – he
was the youngest in his family so he hadn't seen his mother pregnant, and there were no sisters or sisters-in-law – but he did think
that she was perhaps a bit on the small side. He'd thought she was
worrying about that. So he had consulted the best doctors in the
country. Two different ones. After examining her, they'd both said
the same thing: that she was perfectly well and that the pregnancy
was progressing just as it ought. They said she was the correct
weight for her stage. He'd been surprised but relieved. He assumed
other women ate for two, let themselves become undisciplined
and greedy. That wasn't Lydia's style. He thought she'd buck up
once the doctors had reassured her that all was well, but she hadn't.
He didn't understand it. Surely a baby ought to put paid to all
this nonsense she was harbouring about them being punished
because he hadn't been on the front line.

Lawrence was pleasantly surprised when he heard Lydia arrive home at ten thirty. He'd thought that Ava might have her out till all hours. He stood up and waited for her to come into the drawing room; perhaps they could have a cup of Horlicks together. She didn't come in; he heard her footsteps bound upstairs. The under butler knocked and said he thought perhaps the countess was unwell.

Lawrence knew he had to go and investigate. What would the servants say if he didn't respond to his wife when she was in a delicate condition? Yet he dreaded it. Talking about all this baby business was woman's work; he wondered whether he ought to send Dickenson up instead. He might have, except he heard banging and crashing coming from Lydia's bedroom, and he was pretty certain that whatever was happening in there wasn't something he wanted a maid to witness.

He pushed open the bedroom door and found her pulling out drawers and rummaging through them with great haste and little care. She flung open the bedside cabinet and rattled around in that, and then turned to the wardrobe. She hurriedly flicked through garments and then, seemingly not finding what she was looking for, began to pull them off their silk hangers and throw them on the floor. He heard two of the dresses rip.

'Lydia, what are you doing? Stop it at once.'

He thought perhaps she was packing, but she didn't seem to be attempting to retrieve any particular item and there was no sign of suitcases. She cried, 'There's nothing. Nothing. I can't find a thing.'

'What are you looking for?'

'Proof. Proof that he was.' He thought she had broken off her sentence without finishing it, but it appeared that that was all she wanted to say. *Proof that he was.*

'Who? What are you talking about?'

Lydia continued to frantically rummage, but did not answer his question.

'A cinema or bus ticket. A telegram. Something! Why didn't I keep a thing?'

'Stop this at once, Lydia.' Lawrence was beginning to feel

distinctly unnerved. She was making no sense at all and he loathed hysteria. He caught her by the shoulders and forced her to turn to him. She squirmed out from under his grip and dropped to her hands and knees to look under the bed. He bent down, caught hold of her wrists and with a little force pulled her up on to the bed. 'Sit there and tell me what is going on.'

Lydia's face was streaked with tears and pain. She seemed to hesitate for a second, and then seemed too exhausted to resist.

'I had an affair,' she sighed.

The words flapped around the room. Lawrence was so totally and utterly surprised by them that his initial reaction was a sort of spluttering cough of amusement, disbelief and then outrage. 'What? Who?'

'Sergeant Major Edgar Trent.'

Lawrence could not fail to hear the pride and excitement in his wife's voice as she announced her lover's name. He knew exactly who Sergeant Major Edgar Trent was. The non-commissioned officer who had blasted on to the scene this year. The man was known for his bravery and was an asset on a hunt. He often had dirt under his fingernails, but no one ever commented because somehow – and of course this was impossible after three years – people thought the dirt was probably from France. Ridiculous. It couldn't possibly have lingered there, but in some way it might have. The sergeant major was popular in the smoking room; always had a story and a considered opinion if one asked him to contribute. Lawrence had thought he was a good sort – not quite one of them, obviously, but a decent enough chap. Now he despised him and thought he was a low and brutal cad.

'Do you love him?'

'Yes, I do.'

Lawrence fell back on to the stool in front of the dressing table. It was a flimsy, puny stool and the sad weight of him nearly toppled it. He maintained his balance but his dignity was shot through. He slouched rather than holding himself rigid as he had done all his life. He had always remained upright. Much good it had done him. He raced through a jagged cacophony of emotions. He was incredulous. It could not be. Not Lydia. No, not his dear and sincere Lydia. But it was so! She had just confessed it. It was an absolute and filthy diabolical certainty. It was an outrage. Soiled, disgusting, wrong. Damn you. Just wrong. Then the outrage left him. He was crumpled like a sheet of writing paper, screwed up and tossed into the waste-paper basket.

Lydia said, 'Please don't cry.' She could not stand to have reduced him to such a defenceless wreck.

'I am not going to cry!' His heart was angry at the idea but his voice did sound as though he might sob. He clamped his mouth closed. Stiffened his lip.

'If it makes things any better, he does not love me. He does not want me,' she added.

'It doesn't make anything better.'

They sat silently with their own thoughts. What to do? What to do next? wondered Lawrence. He was all out of ideas.

'You know the baby isn't yours.'

'I know no such thing.'

'I'm five months' pregnant, Lawrence. Six at the most. We haven't . . . Not for . . .'.

'I'm your husband, Lydia. If that baby is born while you are married to me, it's my baby. It's as simple as that. That's the law.' Lawrence rather thought marriage ought to mean something. It ought to mean that a chap and a girl loved one another, and that they kept on loving one another, but if that couldn't be the case, then it had to mean other things instead. Social standing, respectability, continuity. 'You will of course be married to me when this child is born.'

'No. Thank you, Lawrence,' Lydia replied gently, but with certainty. 'I thought I could be. I thought it was for the best, but it won't do.' Tears were still falling down her face. Fat, splashy, silent sobs. Lawrence followed the progress of a single tear. Down her creamy cheek, to her pointy chin, and then it curved, keeping tight to her smooth, pearly neck. The neckline of her dress was wet with tears. She must have been crying for a long time.

'You said he doesn't want you.'

'He doesn't, but I know now how being wanted feels.'

Lawrence registered the criticism at once. There was a fire in the centre of her eyes that he didn't understand. He saw it but knew it was beyond his reach, beyond his initiation. He was not the man she wanted. He would always be lacking in her eyes. He didn't like being looked at in that way. He did not have to be. He was sick of the constant implied disapproval. He ought to be admired. Respected. Even loved. Was that too much for a man to hope for? He thought of Sarah. Sweet, sweet, gentle Sarah. He'd known her as long as he'd known Lydia. He might well have picked her in the first place, except she'd already been engaged when they met. He remembered thinking Arthur was a lucky chap. She was such a bright, bonny wife. So devoted. Of course, Arthur's luck had run out. Lawrence had spent a great deal of time with Sarah and her children this summer. She was a warm woman who doused him in a sense of approval. They had shared just one kiss. An impetus moment. Wonderful.

'What will you do?' he asked.

'I shall bring the baby up on my own.' She squeezed his hand until the white knuckles and blue veins on hers bulged. Lawrence thought her skin was too thin; she couldn't hold on to any weight, despite the pregnancy. She was losing her looks. They all would. They would all get old in the end.

From the moment it began, Lydia had been undecided as to whether discovery would be a relief or a disaster. She now found it was a relief. She didn't want to be alone, but she had no choice. The incessant lack would be easier to bear without Lawrence's best intentions. She thought of the nights that she and Edgar had fallen asleep together. He'd spoon into her, and even if they had just made love, he seemed to be perpetually hot and hard. As they lay on their sides, he'd place his penis between her legs, cup her breast and she'd feel the heat of his chest all along her back. So tight and safe. Her favourite times were when he'd finally trusted her enough to fall asleep by her side. She'd felt his hardness yield, relent.

He'd once promised her that she'd become straightforward and confident; she felt she owed it to him and to herself to finally do so. She thought of how he'd described going into battle, and she now truly understood.

'You put your hands on the ladder and went over. That was what you had to do. Time after time. Bile in mouth, shit running down your leg; it didn't matter: one foot in front of the other. Onwards and upwards. And in part it was a relief after all the waiting.'

57

H E LOOKED UP at the heavy wooden sign overhanging the shop
front and inspected the font to see what his money had
bought. *Mrs Trent's Tea Rooms.* The gold lettering was flowery and
Edwardian. He would not have chosen it himself; he'd have preferred
a bold modern art deco design, but he had not been consulted.
As he pushed open the door of the tea room, a bell rang announcing
his presence; eight of the ten tables were occupied, but no one so
much as glanced his way. He slid into a wooden seat at a small
table for two, and self-consciously fingered the edge of the white
embroidered tablecloth, aware of its overwhelming femininity. He
didn't fit in this place. His bulk, his dark suit, his experience were
all wrong. This place was for women. Women with bags of shopping and gossip. Women who wanted to chatter and giggle, indulge
with a cream scone or a frosted-top lemon cake.

He recognised the sense of dislocation, which had reappeared
with increasing frequency in the past few months. It threatened
to overwhelm him. He could not allow that. That was why he'd
had to do something about it.

He'd had the same perpetual feeling of isolation when he'd first
arrived back from the Front. Camaraderie had collapsed on the
boat home. Men were left with nothing but a sense of shame and
futility; the memories of the crimes they'd been forced to commit
and witness. They'd had a horror of catching one another's eye;
they'd all seen enough to last a lifetime. When he'd got home to
Ellie, he'd thought things might improve. He'd hoped that somehow

she'd be able to plug the abyss of loneliness and seclusion. That was what a wife did, wasn't it? But he'd found that Ellie was a stranger to him, just like everyone else. He should have known she would be, since they'd only met twice before he went to the Front.

He used to think she was one of those girls who'd got caught up in the romance of the men going to fight for their country. She wasn't; her thinking was clearer than that. He'd met her in a pub on Clapham Common. He'd gone there with a bunch of lads from home. They were all heading the same way. Down to the training camp, then across the water. Only one of them had ever been to London before and he had an aunt who ran a pub in Clapham. That was how they'd ended up there that particular night. The war made Edgar understand that that was what life amounted to. A series of arbitrary, almost whimsical decisions that added up to what people wanted to believe was destiny.

He'd bought her drinks all night and then they'd had sex in a back alley, up against a coal shed. There were a lot of women who thought they were doing their bit by dropping their knickers and, in a way, they were. It did make him feel better; stronger, more manly. He wasn't wet behind the ears like many of the boys. Even though he'd only just turned eighteen, there'd been a couple of girls who had been more impressed than they ought to have been by his height and stature. Ellie was buxom and easy. He didn't mean that in a derogatory way. She was easy in the sense that she didn't make hard work of sex. He'd admired her refreshingly frank attitude. The women he'd known up until then had used sex as a blunt negotiating tool or an exquisite bribe. The night before they were off to training camp – where the biggest treat he could anticipate was bread and dripping – Ellie had mattered to him. He hadn't taken advantage of her. She'd wanted it as much as he had. He thought perhaps they were all terrified of death and they needed to bite at life.

He'd written to her saying that the lads in camp thought it was funny that he'd got a splinter in his arse from the rough wood of the shed. She'd written back and told him she'd fared much worse. She'd got a bun in the oven.

He'd been happy. Overjoyed, in fact. He'd thought that if he died, now it would be all right because he'd go on. In a way. He was awarded special permission to leave the camp and get a train back to London so he could make an honest woman of her. Hasty marriages were popping up like mushrooms in warm, wet dung; people understood. The registrars were accommodating.

Ellie had looked pretty. She'd worn a blue dress and carried marigolds, picked from a neighbour's garden. She'd borrowed the dress from her friend, who had cried throughout the short ceremony because she'd bought it to wear when her fiancé came home on leave, but he was already dead. Ellie had said that the dress shouldn't have to go to waste. Edgar remembered thinking that she'd make a good soldier, this woman who was about to become his wife.

Her mother came; a big woman who didn't express much delight or disapproval over the rash union. The dad was long gone. None of his family could get down to London for the wedding. His father wrote and said they hadn't been given proper notice and couldn't make arrangements to leave the shop. One of his sisters wrote to say that the truth was his mam was livid that he'd been stupid enough to be trapped by a saucy southerner. He'd thought it was funny at the time. The expression, *saucy southerner.* It wasn't so funny any more; he now believed his mam had had a point. The wedding was witnessed by Ellie's mother, her weeping, grieving friend and a bloke he'd met in the pub that morning. Private Harry Wilson from the 9th Battalion York and Lancaster Regiment. They'd bonded when they heard one another's northern accents drowning in a sea of longer vowels. Harry was on leave; his train home wasn't until five o'clock, so he'd been willing enough to stand as Edgar's best man. At Wandsworth registry office Edgar found out that his new wife's middle name was Margaret and that she was three years his senior. Afterwards they ate corned beef and potatoes, followed by jam roly-poly, in a small restaurant. Ellie had liked it because there was a single red carnation in a vase on every table; she said the place had class. He'd paid for everyone's meal but there hadn't been time to be alone. He'd sighed with the frustration of an eighteen year old; Ellie had laughed and said there wasn't any need, not since she was already in the family way. He'd thought that *need* wasn't the same as *want*, and that his own mother and sisters would never use an expression like 'in the family way'.

He didn't die, but the baby did. It didn't even make it to a proper baby. He'd been on the Front for two weeks when he received the news. By then he was glad the baby was dead, because what man wanted to bring a baby into the sort of world he was part of? Ellie had been very pragmatic about the whole business too. She'd said it was nature's way and pointed out that it wasn't as though either of them had ever really wanted a baby. When he wrote to tell his mother the news, she replied expressing doubt at the veracity of the pregnancy in the first place. She'd heard of other girls who'd got a big, daft, honourable man that way. Edgar had been furious at his mother's suggestion that he was gullible and susceptible to a pretty face. He was already feeling weary and distant. He wasn't the lad who'd gone to war. She had no right to belittle his decisions. He also resented the fact that she'd artic-ulated something he was trying not to think himself.

The next time he returned to England on leave, he and Ellie missed one another because she'd been invited on a holiday to Ireland and she said it was too good an opportunity to miss, since she never travelled anywhere. She was definitely the sort of woman who liked to seize an opportunity if it came along. It was about this time that he began to understand that his wife wasn't much of a letter-writer. The second time he got leave they went to Brighton and stayed in a bed and breakfast. He'd been depressed. It was winter 1916. He'd already seen and done too much in France. The continual chaos, uproar and desolation had ground him down. Day by day the bombardments grew in intensity. One side or the other had to pummel their foe out of being. He'd begun to understand that the talk of honour was dishonest. Ellie told him he was a bore and that he ought to buck up. 'You're ruining my holiday,' she'd said. 'Don't you know how hard I work, six days a week? On my feet ten hours in a row.' He wished he'd used his leave to visit Middlesbrough.

Mrs Trent's Tea Shop was a fancy place. Ellie had known her

mind, been certain about every detail and gone for it. Her ambitious plan had been flawless. Ruthless.

'What do you think, duck?' She appeared by his table. She wasn't wearing the black and white uniform that the two waitresses were wearing. She was dressed in peach; she looked every inch the proud proprietor.

'You seem busy.'

'Rushed off our feet.' Ellie never wore an expression or demeanour that suggested she was hurrying, but she often talked about her fatigue. Before the war she had been in service; she'd taken the job because her mother had insisted it was a step up. It hadn't suited her. She had aspirations and lacked the ability to subjugate her will, or even pretend to be doing so. He didn't blame her. He rather admired her for not settling. He remembered when she first told him that she wanted to own a tea shop. He'd thought it was a fine goal for a woman like Ellie to have. After the war, when she still talked about it, he'd felt himself shrink from the moderate, parochial ambition and the vulgar, grasping woman. It wasn't her, it was him. He'd come home a different man.

He pulled the papers out of his briefcase.

'Oh,' she said, as she leaned forward and fingered the leather, greedily assessing the quality. Edgar sighed. It wasn't his case. The lawyer had lent it to him so that the papers could remain pristine during transit. He couldn't afford such a thing. She'd cleaned him out. He didn't resent it. He didn't want a penny of the money. It made him sick thinking of it.

Yet he could not forget the hot, sticky afternoon.

Ava Pondson–Callow had arrived at his office. She'd calmly explained that Lydia had discovered he was married and, naturally, did not want anything more to do with him.

'Just like that?' he'd stuttered.

'What did you expect?' she'd asked. She hadn't looked at all hot or bothered. He was sweating, shaking.

'I have an envelope. Inside is a substantial amount of cash.'

Edgar didn't understand at first. Then he did. 'I don't want her money.'

'The correct thing to do is accept it and leave town immediately. It's a generous amount. It ought to be enough to ensure there's no scandal.'

'I'd like to speak to her.' He'd remained calm. It was paramount to be the officer, not the shipbuilder. He'd always thought Lid accepted both men; Ava Pondson-Callow would only respond to the officer.

'That's out of the question.'

'Has she sent me a letter?' For reply, Miss Pondson-Callow had raised her eyebrow in a pastiche of pity.

'She's requested you never contact her again. No letters, no telephone calls, no telegrams. If there is the unfortunate situation where you see one another in the street, she wishes for you to walk by. You are dead to her, Sergeant Major Trent. You have broken her heart and humiliated her completely. She cannot and will not forgive you. The only decent thing to do now is disappear.' Ava had paused, and then her beautiful lips had spat out the words with total contempt. 'With your wife.'

Lid had once said that there was nothing he could do that would make her think less of him. As the words had tipped into their history he'd felt an incredible sense of doom. He knew she was wrong. He'd wrecked everything before they'd even met; it was only a matter of time before she discovered as much.

A quick fumble with a blowsy chambermaid had ruined his life.

He had not been able to tell Lid about the boyhood marriage. There had never been the right moment, at least not after the initial lie in that village pub. He had not admitted to his marriage when she first asked him because he'd had no idea what she would come to mean to him. Besides, he never thought of himself as married. Those three days in Brighton were the longest he and Ellie ever spent together. He'd come home from France too numb to think of anything, but when he did start to reason, his first thought had been that he must divorce Ellie Edwards. She would not hear of it. She was careful not to give him grounds and she refused to acknowledge it when he repeatedly gave her them. Without her cooperation the process was set to take seven or so years. He'd come home a hero, and although it was quite clear that his intensity daunted and bored Ellie, she thought she would do better as a married woman than a single one in a world where men were better paid and hard to come by. He'd given her half his salary every month; she found that very convenient. He should perhaps have made her situation less so, but it seemed a step beyond dishonourable. He paid the money and cut the woman. He did not anticipate ever becoming involved with another and so decided to let the matter of a divorce slide. What did it matter to him if in the eyes of God and the law of the land he was married? His belief in both had been smashed in the carnage.

Three or four times in the summer he'd tried to start to explain his situation to Lid. He knew he had to. After all, he'd told her all about the war and she'd understood that perfectly, better than he did himself. She'd been a balm and a solace. Out there he'd become a barbarian, a feral and ferocious man; rigid, reduced, realistic. He'd forgotten what a woman felt like, what soap smelt like. He was marooned far from the uninitiated. Then there was her. Silly, crazy party-fiend Lid, and she, somehow, made a connection. Built a bridge across the isolation.

But he had not been able to bring himself to make this final confession. She thought he was pure and heroic. Strong and invincible. He couldn't stand being dashed in her eyes. He feared she'd have condemned him. Thought less of him. And he couldn't have borne that, because Lid was everything. She was the reason he'd grown from boy to man. The reason he'd fought, murdered, survived and saved in France. The reason he slept again in England.

He was deeply and utterly ashamed of the thoughtless, undignified marriage. Ashamed that he'd once been a man who had found Ellie Edwards an attractive enough prospect; that seemed ludicrous now. How could he explain it? The truth was, the war had caused a particular type of panic. Everyone had become greedy and grasping. People latched on to second best because the best might not come along, or it might have been and gone, and time was short. Time was definitely short. Maybe if he'd been married to Lady Anna Renwick or similar, he might have confessed. Lid was married herself, after all. But he hadn't trusted her enough to see past his youthful mistake. He thought she'd be disgusted by the root of him.

And he'd been right.

When she'd found out the truth, she'd slashed him down.

Edgar shook his head. There was no point in dwelling. He wasn't that man. He needed just two things now. He needed Ellie to sign the divorce papers so he could return them to his lawyer and then he needed to get on the train that would take him to Plymouth; from there he'd set sail for Australia. A new life.

'Would you like a cuppa? We might as well make it civil like.'

'No, thank you. I have a train to catch.'

'As you say.'

Ellie slowly, carefully read the papers. She wasn't a fool and had no intention of signing anything if she hadn't read and digested it completely. Edgar fought down a mounting sense of frustration. Ellie had seen a number of drafts; there were no surprises in the agreement. He had paid her a lump sum of £800 so she would sign. She would have no further claim on his income or future prospects; £800 was the entire amount Ava Pondson-Callow had handed over in the envelope.

He had not known what to do with Lid's money. Giving it back was not an option, since she had banned him from ever contacting her again. If he involved a lawyer, her husband was sure to find out, and that would ruin her. He'd thought he might give it away to charity. He could have used it to buy himself a relatively prestigious foreign commission and in that way fulfil her request for him to leave town, but when it came down to it, he found he could not spend her money on himself. It made him feel dirty.

For weeks he'd forced himself into the accepted pleasure palaces, the nightclubs he'd haunted with Lid and some of the new ones too. He felt he had to be there because he could be and so many men couldn't, but even when he was there he was absent, apart. He missed her. He found it difficult to stay in conversations, to remember the name of the fella he was playing cards with, the girl who was spreading her legs for him. In the end he'd decided to use the cash to sever his ties with Ellie. Then he used his private savings to buy a passage to Australia. He didn't have a commission, but he was still a soldier of the British Empire and he could continue to work his way up as he'd done in the war. He had prospects. He would not accept the limits others tried to impose on him.

'Do you have a pen?' Ellie asked finally. He did; it was a fountain pen that Lid had bought him. He couldn't stand the idea of Ellie touching it.

'No, sorry.'

She borrowed one from the waitress. He blotted the papers. The relief. Freedom. At last. He quickly stood up. Ellie slowly surveyed his impressive physique. 'I suppose one last tumble for old times' sake is out of the question.' She grinned lasciviously.

'Goodbye, Ellie. Good luck.'

Offended, she snapped, 'I don't need your luck. I have plenty of my own. Ta very much.'

It was too true to refute. Sergeant Major Trent tipped his hat and left the tea house that bore his name. He didn't look over his shoulder.

58

THE TRAIN CLANGED and juddered to a halt. Edgar swiftly disembarked. He'd been standing holding his suitcase for twenty minutes; it had been a long journey and he wasn't one for sitting still. There wasn't any real need to hurry – he had four hours before he had to board *Themistocles* – but he was restless. The chilly air slapped his cheeks and slithered down the back of his neck. He turned up his coat collar and put on his gloves. The gloves that had once warmed her tiny white hands.

It was possible to catch a horse tramcar from the station to the dock, or even a motor bus, but Edgar chose to walk along the narrow and overcrowded streets, despite the icy temperature. He always preferred to be in charge of his own motion. All around there was evidence of slum clearance. The government were finally cleaning things up, as they'd promised. It had been life and death, survival or extinction, personal and national for too long. Now, all society wanted was indoor lavatories and gas cookers. People were unsettled; they wanted what was due. It didn't seem much to ask. So whilst it was a time of disruption and commotion, the trouble was sweetened with the sense that it would give birth to progress. The air was blue and sharp but tinged with vitality.

He dodged lumbering trucks laden with cargo, and dashing passengers, clasping tickets, who oozed a sense of excitement and anticipation. He was disappointed to discover that he couldn't share their exhilaration. He'd longed to travel for years, but now that the moment had arrived, he did not feel eager. He felt resigned.

He had to go, and go he would, but it was harder than he'd imagined leaving this green and proud land. Leaving her completely.

When he reached the dock and spotted the hulking monster of a ship, he did at least feel a sense of steady relief. *Themistocles* was a reliable old girl. She'd made many trips to and from Australia before the war. During, she worked as a troopship and a hospital ship, resuming service to Cape Town, Sydney and Brisbane on 2nd July this year. He felt he could relate to her. Couldn't every soldier whose pleasure had been interrupted by enforced duty? She'd be his friend. He breathed in the salty, damp sea air and listened to the gulls screech as though they were anguished. He'd always felt they were greedy, needy birds. Still, they reminded him of Middlesbrough and simpler times when he was a boy, working at the shipyard. He caught a whiff of hot battered fish and chips, laced with vinegar; his mouth watered and he wondered whether there was time for a bite. One last taste of England.

It was not unusual for him to imagine he'd seen her in a crowd. He'd spot her and then, on the double-take, he'd be disappointed. He'd almost trained himself not to raise his hopes. She was up in front of him by about ten feet, leaning over the railings that separated the passengers getting on the ship from the people who had come to wave them off. If he joined the queue to board, he'd file past her. Up close, of course, he'd see it wasn't her, but just a ghost of her, a less crucial woman, and once again he'd have to manage that jagged spike of disappointment. He glanced away and then back again. Expecting and waiting to note that this woman's hair was not quite as glossy, that she was a little too tall or that her profile was not as chiselled. He looked once more; she stayed resolute. She remained his Lid. Perhaps more anxious than he'd ever seen her before, and maybe a little bulkier in her enormous fur coat, but it was Lid.

He pushed through the crowds that suddenly seemed to be surging in a way that forced him further from her. 'Lid, Lid.' He knew what she'd asked him to do – if they were ever to find themselves on the same street he must ignore her – but this was no coincidence. Couldn't be. She was looking for him. 'Lid!' he yelled above the noise of the crowds and the relentless crashing of cargo being loaded.

She bristled. Her head turned a fraction. Like a doe in a forest, hearing someone's tread snap a twig. He staggered through the throng, unchivalrously shoving people out of his way, and a moment later he was by her side, his hand almost touching hers. He could smell her. The familiar, wonderful scent of her. Sensuous possibility. A muffled, musky perfume that grasped his heart and squeezed. She did not smell of violets or roses or any other manufactured toilet water; she smelt of something that suggested shadows and depth. Passion. Its darkness was at odds with her beautiful delicate features. He became intensely aware of her body beneath her bulky coat. The cold had settled on his skin in a way that made it impossible to reach out to touch her. He was frozen. He longed to be back in the attic, under the worn sheets and the crocheted patchwork blanket his sister had made and Lid found so quaint. He longed to turn back time. He did not know where to begin.

'I had to come,' she said. Her confession slipped out as though she was ashamed of it. He nodded eagerly, but then stopped. Why was she here? To forgive him? That was impossible. To yell at him? To take this final opportunity to tell him he was a low cad and he'd ruined her, if not socially then most certainly her peace of mind? He almost didn't care which it was. He would take a tongue-whipping. He'd bear all her fury. It would be worth it. Here she was! He could rest his eyes on her again. Her glance alone filled his world. It was enough. It was everything.

She looked about her, seemingly nervous, dazed. 'Have you got time for a cup of tea, perhaps? Or a cocktail? I understand you don't sail until—'

'Yes.'

They sat in a shabby hotel bar, two overpriced glasses of gin and a tricky history between them. She refused to take off her coat, which unnerved him. It was as though any moment she might bolt for the door, which he didn't want. No, not at all. A silence engulfed them. He stared at her but she kept her eyes trained on the threadbare ruby-red carpet. An elderly, slightly pernickety man held court with the landlady across the polished wooden bar; his pipe smoke and dogmatic opinions drifted towards them. It reminded Edgar of the long nights in the trenches; when the air was still, the enemy could just about be heard. Before they'd all drowned in weariness and before the eternal monotony of slaughter calcified them, there had been card games and sometimes chatter or even jokes from both lines. Sometimes one side would cease their chatter and listen to the other. Traditionally it was believed that at those moments men searched their souls and realised that differences were minuscule, politics surmountable, but Edgar had always felt otherwise. It was at those moments that he felt most drained and desperate. He found the similarities were more painful than the discrepancies.

At length Lid muttered, 'You're married.' The words burned the air; they were branded into their story.

'Yes.' Edgar sat up straight. He was accountable.

'Is she here?' Lid glanced around the bar as though she expected his wife to jump out from behind a potted palm.

'No. I'm divorcing her.' Lid let out a breath that clouded the air and yet cleared his vision. She did not hate him. She was relieved there was no wife. He rushed his explanation and bungled it. 'I'm going to Brisbane.'

Lid nodded; she looked baffled and exposed. 'Why did you lie to me?'

'I knew you'd never forgive me.' His reply was naked and pitiful. He clasped closed his plump lips. Holding life in. He wanted to shut his eyes too. A way of avoiding the tender, crude, undiluted sense of her.

'You know nothing,' she snapped. She reached for her drink and took a large gulp.

'But I was right. Once you found out, you despised me. You gave me cash to be silent and disappear like a redundant gigolo.'

Her expression was the most human he'd ever seen. He'd fought in a war for four years. He'd seen hate and terror, abhorrence and mistrust. Her expression caught all of that and yet it was made still more vivid because there was something else. He was almost sure there was love too. 'It wasn't my money. I didn't—' She broke off. 'Oh, what the hell. I thought I could fix this but I can't. I can't.' Her eyes blazed with outraged indignation. She stood up and started to walk quickly towards the lobby. Away from him. He pursued her, his eyes trained on the rhythmic sway of her bottom under her fur coat. He was sure he could hear the hint of silk; her dress or her underwear? He thought of her thighs gently touching and parting as she strode. He felt such lust, and a need to hold her. Her coat slipped open and he saw her ripe, swollen belly.

'Lid!' She was already out on the street. He threw some coins on the table and gave chase. He caught her just a few yards up the road; the street was wet and oily with rainfall and she couldn't hurry, she couldn't risk missing her step. He caught hold of her hand and pulled her round so she had to face him. 'Is it mine?' he demanded.

'Of course.'

She was carrying his baby. Growing their child. His future nestled just there, inside her womb.

'Weren't you going to tell me?'

'How exactly could I have done that? You disappeared.' Her anger splintered out into the street. Like shards of glass from a window vandalised by a brick.

'I'm sorry.'

She nodded. 'So am I.' There was something about her tone that seemed final. It was, after all, goodbye.

'So the earl will have his heir,' Edgar commented. He tried not to let the bitterness shatter his voice. He understood. At last, he understood it all. She was not his. She never had been. How could he ever have imagined she was? He had always shared her, although he had never wanted to. He'd tried to stay away. Tried not to go to her. After that first time in Sir Peter Pondson-Callow's study, he'd realised she was somehow different to the other women he knew, married or single. He hadn't called for six weeks. He'd resisted because sharing a woman he cared for was beneath him. However, her pull had been too strong. He'd caved in and sent word. He'd never asked her to leave her husband and his millions. It didn't make sense. What could he offer? Once, she'd joked that she'd like to stay with him. He'd told her it wouldn't work, but maybe, just maybe it might have. He'd seen crazier things. It seemed to be the final insult to lose her to a man who hadn't even fought. But then maybe that was how it had to be. Lawrence was unsullied. Besides, she'd made her own decision in the end. She'd sent the money.

'You reduced us to a financial transaction.' He spat out the words. 'You were buying me off. You're just here to see I get on the boat and go across the world, where I can never cause any trouble for you and the earl.'

Fury engulfed him. She should not have come to the dock. He was just learning how to do without her. He'd at least had the memories. His version of what he thought was true. He'd thought she loved him, at least briefly. Not constantly, not above everything, but in some way. But now it seemed he'd been wrong. He knew he loved her. Constantly and above everything else. If the war had taught him anything, it was that it was only worth being angry with those you loved. Being angry with those you hated was a waste. So he became vicious. 'I've read about women like you.'

'Like me?'

'Rich society women who want some fun with a common man. Want to know if we do it differently. Want to see if we are dirtier.'

She looked shocked. 'How can you think that of me?'

'There was a case in the paper just recently: Lady Henning and her dance teacher. Friend of yours, is she?'

'We're acquainted,' she admitted.

'So tell me, is it the fashion? I don't mind at all. It's all the same to me,' he snapped sarcastically. 'Worked out rather well for you and the earl, didn't it? The pregnancy was a bonus.'

'Shut up. Shut up. You brute. Don't you understand anything at all?'

He understood all too well. He felt he'd been here before. Used. Knee deep in mud and blood. A sense of hopelessness swept over him. He ploughed into his instinct to survive. He turned and walked towards the dock. He had a ship to catch.

59

BEATRICE HAD FOUND the drama of the day all too thrilling. They had driven since before dawn to get to the dock in time. It had been Ava's idea. For reasons that she didn't quite make clear, she had apparently continued to have Edgar Trent followed. The private detective had discovered that the sergeant major had bought a passage to Australia and was due to set sail today. Ava was the one who had persuaded Lydia that she must travel to Plymouth and at least tell him about the baby, tell him she'd left Lawrence. She maintained that she'd insisted on this line of action because she was fed up to the back teeth with Lydia's dreadfully long face. 'We simply can't leave her to rot in that awful semi in suburbia.' Bea suspected it was because she finally recognised that Lydia was deeply, irrevocably, although most certainly inconveniently, in love with Edgar Trent. Ava had admitted, 'Perhaps one ought to stay out of other people's love affairs, but . . .' She hadn't finished the sentence. Bea had finished it for her.

'But you thought you were doing the right thing.'

'I did, darling. I really did. Now it appears I was wrong.'

All the friends had been surprised at the intensity of Lydia's feelings for the sergeant major and at her commitment to him, even long after he had gone. She'd left Lawrence two months ago; since then, Sarah had become his companion with what could only be described as indecent haste. Lydia had not shown a moment's resentment, but talked of how lovely it would be if John eventually inherited the estate and the title. Needless to say, this would only be possible if Lawrence could formally adopt Sarah's children. A swift divorce was in everyone's interests. Lydia remained dignified. Alone. Beatrice couldn't help but admire her. Her initial disgust and horror at Lydia's affair dissolved into something softer; if not understanding then certainly compassion.

Bea had fully expected that the mad dash along the winding English roads would culminate in a passionate reunion. Ava had also been quite certain that this would be the outcome. She'd bought two first-class tickets for the passage and gifted them to Lydia. 'Darling, I draw the line at you travelling third. Even in the name of love.'

Beatrice was becoming practised at enjoying love vicariously. Georgina Vestry had made a marvellous season and had in fact received two proposals. The girl was sensible beyond her years and did not seem in a desperate hurry to accept either one, even though she was terribly fond of the lawyer and no doubt would agree to him in time. Bea thought that the importance and effect of the white kid gloves and brocade shoes that she herself had picked out was not to be underestimated. Other ambitious parents agreed. Behind fans, mothers whispered their belief that Beatrice Polwarth had a surprising knack for chaperoning and, when Georgina did marry, there would be two or three new offers of employment.

Beatrice had fully anticipated a very emotional but satisfactory day. Ava had already suggested that she could drive home once they saw off the ship. 'Me, drive? Really?'

'Absolutely.'

'What super fun.'

They were becoming quite tight; an unlikely friendship, but one that Bea believed would endure all the more for its slow start. Beatrice had not expected to see Lydia again. They'd said their goodbyes before she ran off into the crowd this morning. Her trunks of luggage were now on board; she didn't own any furniture or art any more; packing had been relatively simple. So the weeping and near-hysterical woman stumbling towards them was a shock.

'What happened?' Bea demanded.

'Couldn't you find him?' asked Ava.

'I found him. He doesn't want me.' Lydia opened the car door and flung herself in the back. Her sobbing was thick and fast. Beatrice was concerned that the baby would be disturbed.

Ava, who was a great friend and an overwhelming enemy, sighed. She had the ear of prime ministers, princes, dukes, industrialists, newspapermen, writers and artists. If there was one thing she knew, it was men, so Lydia had to listen when she said, 'I seriously doubt that. Did you tell him about the baby?'

'Yes.'

'That it's his?'

'Yes.'

'Is it the wife?'

'No. He's divorcing her.'

'Did you tell him you had left Lawrence? That you love him?'

'No, no. I didn't tell him either of those things. I've never said it and nor has he.' Lydia looked exhausted. It had been a strain, this entire business. 'I've given everything up for him. Twice. And each time I go to him, he vanishes or ducks. I can't give any more. I can't humiliate myself further.'

'Oh, Lydia.' Ava looked as though she could cheerfully wring her friend's neck.

They all sat in silence, staring out at the melancholy sea. The only sounds were the shrill, sad squawks of the gulls and Lydia sniffing into her handkerchief. Minutes ticked by.

The air in the car was stale with disappointment. It reminded Bea of her old room at her brother's house. Fetid and frigid. Beatrice's room in Georgina's house was considerably brighter. She made a point of always having a vase of fresh flowers on her dressing table; she could afford such indulgences now and she believed she deserved them. There was also a room at Ava's that they both referred to as Bea's room; that smelt divine. Ava thought nothing of liberally spraying sent around. Musky, sexy scent.

Lydia had been renting a house in Hounslow. It was thoroughly modern, with every convenience that an enlightened housewife could dream of. Except a husband. It smelt of polish and bleach. As expected, practically no one visited. Ava said it was because the house was nowhere near anywhere but they all knew the real reason. Even Beatrice had to keep her continued association with Lydia under her hat; Sir Henry wouldn't like his daughter's chaperone visiting a house so drenched in scandal. Ava had had to put considerable effort into persuading Doug and Freddie to visit. They'd done so once. It hadn't been a very cheerful evening. There was no dancing or drinking; it was awkward.

What depressed Beatrice the most was that Lydia hadn't seemed to care about the smell, the location or even the loneliness. She hadn't cared about anything until yesterday, when Ava told her to pack her bags, for a short time life had been blown back into her. She'd twitched, then fluttered. But now she was very still once again.

Would she go back to that forlorn house and simply wait for the baby to arrive? The neighbours wouldn't like it. An unmarried mother was not welcome in suburbia. She wasn't welcome anywhere. The poor child. Poor Lydia. How had it come to this? Bea pitying Lydia? The world was indeed topsy-turvy. Why couldn't things simply have been better? For them all.

Bea felt a sudden surge of outrage slam through her body. This wasn't how it was supposed to end, not after all the glamour and promise and beauty. Certainly not after all the death and loss and waste.

Eventually, Beatrice cleared her throat and said, 'Naturally I'm not the expert on matters such as these. Far from it. And I am quite certain that the whole business has been horribly wearing, as you say. Totally exhausting and yes, sometimes humiliating. I can't begin to imagine . . .' She paused, almost losing her nerve. A glance at Lydia, pregnant yet hopeless, spurred her on. 'But I do know one thing.'

'What's that?' asked Ava dutifully, but without much optimism in her voice; she didn't expect to be enlightened.

Bea kept her eyes trained on Lydia and answered as though she had asked the question although she hadn't given any indication that Bea had her attention. 'If I ever met a man who lit me up in the way that Edgar Trent has illuminated you this past year, I would stop at nothing. *Nothing*. Do you hear me?' Her voice almost tore with the effort of being so exposed. 'We deserve it all. We do. Every one of us. Lydia, you deserve your man.'

Lydia looked shyly at her friend from under her lashes. She was listening.

'He's brave and marvellous, but damaged and out of his depth. It's my opinion that *you* need to save *him* this time, Lydia. Isn't there an expression? Once more unto the breach, dear friend?'

'You think I should go to him, again?' Lydia sounded incredulous. Beatrice nodded, she didn't have any more words, she'd given her all. Her chins and bosoms wobbled. It was regretful that even at moments of great sincerity such as this, she could not be anything other than lumpy. 'What do you think, Ava?' Of course it was natural that Lydia would turn to the oracle on such matters.

Ava shrugged. Beatrice understood. This level of intensity was beyond even Ava's experience; it was beyond almost everyone's. A huge seagull fell out of the sky, flapping and squawking; it landed on the bonnet of the car. Ava wound down the window and yelled, 'Shoo, shoo. Ghastly thing.'

The three women stared at the ugly bird. No one moved.

60

IT WAS ALL fucking pointless, he told himself as he stormed up the gangplank. War, love, death, life. They all brought nothing other than heartbreak. How had he ever thought it might work between them? After all, what did she know about his way of life? A life with budgets and restrictions, a life that teetered on poverty. Real budgeting had nothing to do with 'Shall I buy three dresses today or be a good stick and just buy two?' Real budgeting was having to decide between food or heating. Your food or the baby's.

The baby. There was a baby.

A fleeting hint of wishful thinking, something that could be mistaken for hope, fluttered over his consciousness. He roughly pushed it aside. But no. He would manage. He'd go to Brisbane. Alone. And he'd never, ever mix himself up with a woman again. Even as he made the vow, part of his brain acknowledged that he couldn't if he wanted to. There wasn't another woman like Lid. Not for him.

He imagined her sitting in one of the many enormous drawing rooms in Clarendale. He'd never visited the place but he didn't doubt for a moment that it was an undeniably impressive old pile. In his head he could see it clearly. She was bedecked in jewels and wearing the most elegant and fashionable clothes. His baby was in a crib beside her. There was a doting nanny on hand and an endless line of helpful staff preparing food, warming beds, shuttling coal. Then he tried to imagine her expression; it would be one of serenity. He could not. The fantasy was overpowered by a memory.

All he could visualise was her impish and gleeful smile, her long neck, her small pert breasts and her magenta nipples. She was sitting up on his bed, watching him make breakfast. *'Why don't I stay here with you?'* she offered.

'Oh, that wouldn't work.'

'Why not?'

'You wouldn't like it.'

'I think I would.'

'You'd get sick of me.'

'Never. I never would.'

The memory punched him in the gut. Left him breathless as every memory did.

The gangplank was heaving; people jostled against one another, clinging to their families and their belongings. Boots slammed down on the steel; shoulder to shoulder they marched forward. There was a palpable sense of apprehension all around. Some were excited, others anxious. Everybody just wanted to get on board and set sail. Everyone wanted to move on. 'Oh, God!' Edgar yelled out the words not as a curse but as they were said in the old days; as a prayer. The crowds, surging and insistent, the noise, blaring and clattering. Boots. Up and down. Thud, thud, thud. Relentless. Suddenly they were all upon him again. The men who'd died, who'd stabbed and shot and bled. The ones he'd massacred. The ones who'd wanted to kill him. They were clambering and clinging. He couldn't see hopeful emigrants marching towards a new future, he was swamped by the bloody and the dead. They're not real. Not real, he told himself. But what were these visions doing visiting him in day time? These horrors could usually be contained to the night. He could not breathe. There was mud in his mouth, up his nostrils. He was going to drown. He needed air and space. He needed Lydia.

Only Lydia could help him. Only she would soothe and restore.

He understood what he needed. What he wanted. If he made her his wife, he might be able to justify it all. Or understand it. Or at least accept it. She, and no other woman, could do that. He turned around again and started to violently push his way through the crowds that were trying to board, heading back to the shore. Terrified, in a way that he'd never been before, he understood at last what was at risk. He took deep breaths and forced his brain to accept these were not dead and dying soldiers, they were just passengers. Ordinary people. Living people. He had to get through them. He scanned the dockside. He had to find her.

'Lydia! Lydia!'

He thought of that day in Pondson-Callow's grounds when the snow had settled. He'd gone off alone. Grumpy. Defiant. 'Edgar! Edgar!' He remembered turning, and there she'd been, tramping through the snow towards him. Searching him out. Ill-advised, hardly dressed for the occasion, but glorious and free-spirited. 'Edgar! Edgar!' He did not remember her calling to him then.

But he could hear her now. Lydia was coming.

He could see her pushing through the throng, coming up the gangplank towards him, following his footsteps once again. He knew it was her for certain, even at a distance. This wasn't one of his visions fuelled by wishful thinking. He felt her gaze, heavy but not a weight; she was an anchor. A huge sense of elation and peace washed over him. He'd never experienced anything with such certainty before. There would be no more doubts or dissuasion. He'd pull her aboard and they'd set sail. Here she was. The ending of dearth. The beginning of overabundance. His hero.

He held out his hand through the throng and she clasped it tightly. He drew her close to him as stewards, intent on doing their jobs, ushered them back up towards the boat.

'You came back,' he whispered into her hair.

'Absolutely. Even though you were terribly rude and never asked me to.'

'You were waiting for me to ask?'

'I was, but Beatrice convinced me I was being passive.'

'Beatrice did?' He raised the corner of his mouth and his eyebrows in amusement and gratitude.

Then he kissed her. Kissed her again. Kissed her until his lips were sore, until his throat was dry and the skin on her chin was raw. He remembered his room, and the times when they'd been outside in the open air too. She had quaked, shivered, called out, swallowed him whole, but they never became tired of one another and they never would. He anticipated their cabin, their eventual home. More was needed. She burned for him. He for her.

'There's no going back.'

'I don't want to go back.'

'Not now, no. But one day you might, and—'

'Never. I won't. No more looking back. We're going forward, my darling,' she said with absolute clarity and certainty.

They were enough for each other, but they could not get enough. It couldn't end. There was too much more to be had. The sun glinted on the water, sparkling. They held one another tightly. They held their futures.

BIBLIOGRAPHY

Brittain, Vera, *Testament of Youth*, Virago, London, 1978

Horn, Pamela, *Women in the 1920s*, Amberley Publishing, London, 1995

McDonald, Fiona *Britain in the 1920s*, Pen and Sword Books, South Yorkshire, 2012

Nicholson, Virginia, *Singled Out*, Penguin, London, 2007

Nicolson, Juliet, *The Great Silence: 1918-1920 Living in the Shadow of the Great War*, John Murray, London, 2009

Pugh, Martin, *We Danced All Night: A Social History of Britain Between the Wars*, Vintage, London, 2009

Shepherd, Janet and John, *1920s Britain*, Shire Living Histories, Oxford, 2010

ACKNOWLEDGEMENTS

Thank you to my wonderful, supportive and brilliant editor, Jane Morpeth, and to the entire team at Headline. I've said it before, but I'll say it again, they are a lovely lot. Georgina Moore, Vicky Palmer, Barbara Ronan and Kate Byrne deserve particular acknowledgements; they work ferociously on my behalf and are a formidable, incredible team. I also owe a huge thank you to the marvellous Jamie Hodder-Williams.

Thank you, Jonny Geller. I will never forget your reaction on first reading *Spare Brides*; the memory is one of the highlights of my career. I possibly shouldn't care quite so much about impressing you – but I do. Thanks to all at Curtis Brown for your continued support of my work, home and abroad.

Thank you to my family and friends, my fellow authors, book sellers, book festival organisers, reviewers, magazine editors, TV producers and presenters, The Reading Agency and librarians who continue to generously champion my work. Once again I'd like to thank my readers; I hope you love reading this one as much as I loved writing it.

As ever, thank you, Jimmy and Conrad, for providing inspiration, meaning, encouragement and love. It's all about the two of you. Always.

Enormous thanks to Sarah Gordon for her wonderfully generous support of the Helen Feather Memorial Trust. The aims of the Trust are to support people with cancer and raise money for carefully selected Cancer Research Projects.

To learn more about the Helen Feather Memorial Trust visit www.helenfeathertrust.co.uk